Dorothy Hewett

was born in Perth, Australia in 1923, the daughter of a wheat farmer. She was educated by correspondence, at Perth College and at the University of Western Australia. She has worked as a journalist, mill-worker, advertising copywriter and political organiser and for nine years she was a senior tutor at the Western Australian University.

In 1945 Dorothy Hewett joined the Australian Communist Party, but resigned from it in 1968, after the invasion of Czechoslavakia. In 1949, she left her first husband and travelled to Sydney with her lover, a boilermaker. They lived together for nine years and had three sons. During this period Dorothy Hewett wrote *Bobbin Up* (1959), her only novel, in response to a writing competition. It is based on her own experiences of working in a large Sydney spinning mill, her membership of the Australian Communist Party and life in the working-class suburbs of Sydney. *Bobbin Up* has been translated into Russian, Hungarian, Bulgarian and German, and Dorothy Hewett is currently writing a musical and a film script based on the book.

Dorothy Hewett began writing poetry and short stories as a child. A well-known Australian playwright, she is the author of fifteen plays (including two for children), several of which have been performed at the Sydney Opera House Drama Theatre. In 1974 she received a three-year grant from the Literature Board of Australia Council and in 1984 was awarded a one-year fellowship by the Literature Board for autobiography. Dorothy Hewett was Writer-In-Residence at Wollongong University during the same period. The author of three poetry collections and editor of *Sandgropers* (1973), an anthology of Western Australian writing, she continues to write plays and poetry and is working on her autobiography which will be published by Virago.

Dorothy Hewett has five children and now lives with her second husband in the inner-city, Sydney.

BOBBIN UP

DOROTHY HEWETT

With a New Introduction by the author

PENGUIN BOOKS – VIRAGO PRESS

PENGUIN BOOKS
Viking Penguin Inc., 40 West 23rd Street,
New York, New York 10010, U.S.A.
Penguin Books Ltd, 27 Wrights Lane, London W8 5TZ
(Publishing & Editorial) and Harmondsworth,
Middlesex, England (Distribution & Warehouse)
Penguin Books Australia Ltd, Ringwood,
Victoria, Australia
Penguin Books Canada Limited, 2801 John Street,
Markham, Ontario, Canada L3R 1B4
Penguin Books (N.Z.) Ltd, 182–190 Wairau Road,
Auckland 10, New Zealand

First published in Australia by the
Australasian Book Society 1959
This edition first published in Great Britain by
Virago Press Limited 1985
Published in Penguin Books 1987

(CIP data available)

Printed in the United States of America by
R. R. Donnelley & Sons Company, Harrisonburg, Virginia
Set in Baskerville

TO LES

Who taught me to love and understand the tenderness, courage and struggle of the Sydney workers, and without whom this book would never have been written.

ACKNOWLEDGMENTS

I wish to acknowledge my debt to the many people who helped in the creation of this book . . . the girls of the Sydney Spinning Mills, particularly Al, the Sydney Realist Writers and Vera Deacon.

Words and music of "OVERTIME STAGGERS ROCK" by LES FLOOD.

Introduction

☆

Bobbin Up was written in 1958 during eight weeks of the coldest Sydney winter on record.

I wrote it on the end of the laminex kitchen table, working into the early hours of the morning after the children were in bed, warming my hands over the electric stove, because we had run out of money and coal.

I had taken my holiday pay after two years of working as an advertising copywriter for a mail order firm, writing soul destroying ads for a catalogue that dispatched its shoddy goods over the length and breadth of Australia. The promise of a job on the miners' paper, *Common Cause*, had fallen through because "they didn't believe in employing married women". The irony was that I wasn't even married, and had been working for two years as sole support for my three sons and their father.

For eight years I had scarcely written anything, except the odd piece of left-wing journalism. Silenced by political activism, the deep-seated anti-culturalism and socialist realist dogmas of the Australian Communist Party, plus the terrible struggle to survive, I found myself for the first time for years facing a typewriter with time to spare in between putting the catalogue to bed. The boss didn't really care what we did in the interim as long as we "looked busy", so I started writing again; short stories, the odd attempt at a poem.

I joined the *Realist Writers*, a left-wing writing group, led by the Australian novelist Frank Hardy, and tentatively recommenced the promising writing career that had been interrupted by politics.

It was Frank Hardy who started me writing. "This is what you do best," he told me. "Use your talent to further the working class struggle." He was the first person for years who made me believe in myself, and to get me started he suggested that we both write a novel for the Mary Gilmore Literary Competition, closing date eight weeks hence.

I had written a novel when I was eighteen and destroyed it at the age of twenty-two because it didn't have the right political sentiments. This time I took the short story I had recently completed, which became Chapter 15 in *Bobbin Up*, and worked backwards from there. My experience as a short-story writer helped to dictate the style: a set of loosely connected chapters around a central theme... the metaphor of that dark satanic mill, the Jumbuck in the novel.

But there were other and deeper stylistic reasons. My novel was not to have a hero figure. It set out deliberately to tell the brief history of a group of women millworkers in Sydney, whose lives interconnected at the mill and then separated off as they walked out the gates when the whistle blew.

I had arrived in Sydney from Western Australia in 1949 with my boilermaker lover, and had immediately gone to Marx House, the impressive Communist Party headquarters with the hammer and sickle prominent over the Sydney streets. No wonder, gazing at it in astonishment, I believed implicitly that the revolution couldn't be far off now. Anyway hadn't we been told at a Communist Party school in Perth only a few months before that there would be "revolution in three years"?

I told the District Organizer I wanted a job "in the worst factory in Sydney". It was the kind of vague Utopian gesture that middle-class girls, trying to expiate their guilt, indulged in to "proletarianize" themselves, rather like George Orwell's descent into the abyss of the Paris and London poor. The District Organizer couldn't believe his luck. Here was somebody who actually *wanted* to suffer.

He sent me to the Alexandria Spinning Mills, a woollen mill in the inner city suburbs that no sensible working-class girl would have been seen dead in, if she could avoid it.

There was only one place further down the working scale, and that was "the Jammy" (the Jam Factory).

I started work on the Monday and on the Tuesday the Coal Strike began. Factories all over Sydney shut down, the workers were locked out and a grim two months began. We were thrown out of our tiny room, seven stories up with no lift in a substandard King's Cross residential, because we could no longer pay the rent, and slept in a single bed in the front room of my *de facto* mother-in-law's cottage. A respectable working-class woman she took us in but frowned at our relationship.

We ate in a soup kitchen organized by the Communist Party in the industrial suburb of Redfern. I typed up the strike stencils and wrote the propaganda leaflets extolling the miners' cause and calling for the solidarity of the working class. The Coal Strike was bitterly unpopular, the Chifley Labour Government called out the troops, and the miners went back to the pits having gained nothing but debts and misery. There had never been even the faintest chance of a victory.

I got my job back at the mill. It was an extraordinary experience for a girl from a rich, middle-class family with one year of Arts at the University, and a couple of part time jobs during the war as reporter on the daily paper and salesgirl in a Perth bookshop. Completely unskilled of course I worked on the rovers and overheads, heavy work in a hell of heat, steam and grinding noise. After a year of this and eight months pregnant I was asked to leave, "in case you fall into the machines and bugger'em up love," said the prototype of Jessie.

During my year at the mill, full of revolutionary ardour, I took on the job of union delegate that nobody else wanted. I went to the Textile Workers' Union meeting (there was only one a year), and was immediately branded a redragger for calling, with a sublime ignorance of reality, for equal pay for women textile workers. Even to appear at the union meeting meant risking the sack, because the right wing Textile Union officials reported back to the boss anyone foolhardy enough to be seen there. But by some miracle I survived to report back to the women, collect their union dues, and try to mediate occasionally between them and the union rep., who appeared in the mill infrequently, all smiles, jokes and dapperness.

The women treated my attempts to politicize them with blank incomprehension, good natured chiaking or grim smiles. "Get down off your soapbox Skin" they laughed in the lunchbreak.

Because of my Western Australian private school accent they all thought at first that I was a Pommy anyway. I learnt to roughen my accent, and to be slower and more laborious in filling in my sick pay form. "You're very handy with the pen there love" they said suspiciously.

I learnt to talk about the practical things that really interested them: the problems of kids and husbands and boyfriends, unwanted pregnancies, what they did in the weekends, and to complain about the machines speeding up and the men perving on us in the washroom.

There was never any talk of strike when I worked at the mill. The period of strikes in the Textile Industry was over, and the Communist Party was a dirty word. Hadn't the Party sold them out and told them to go back to work for the war effort when they struck for higher wages during wartime? Hadn't the Communist Party masterminded the Coal Strike and forced them to lose two months pay?

It was nine years later that I sat down to write *Bobbin Up*, taking a notebook and walking through those inner-city streets of Sydney that had so shocked me by their poverty and sub-standard housing when I arrived, still wet behind the ears, from my comfortable middle-class existence in Perth.

We had squatted in a house in Redfern, an inner-city area, where the damp was so bad a green mould grew in weird patterns on the walls in winter time, and I washed up in a lean-to scullery in my raincoat. There were no mod. cons., no sink, no hot water, no proper plumbing, and power points were at a minimum. We had so many electric leads running off the central kitchen light we were always blowing the fuses. "Christ mate, what's this, Bunnerong?" said the good-humoured Electricity Department repairmen everytime we had another blackout. Bunnerong was the central Electricity Powerhouse for the city of Sydney.

For the first time in my life I mixed exclusively with the working class. The south Sydney section of the Communist Party met in our front room. The area was known then as the Red Belt of Sydney. When the Referendum to Ban the Communist Party looked as if it would be won hands down all the comrades disappeared suddenly underground, and we were left with a back room full of illegal pamphlets. We spent the day burning the most damning of them in the back yard, the smoke and ashes drifting over the little semis and nearby factories.

But miraculously the vote was a close NO, and we celebrated that night in the Pensioners' Hall, dancing the tango and the foxtrot and the modern waltz, while the defective plumbing sent the pensioners' piss dripping down from the toilets upstairs.

Next door on Saturday nights the neighbours had the street jumping with monumental booze parties that always ended up in fisticuffs, heads and fists thumping against the wall. *The Old Piano Roll Blues*, played with panache on the old piano, was always the signal for the start of "a blue".

Across the street the double for Hazel came staggering down the hall with the light behind her: "You're not goin' ter use my body."

The Redfern branch of the Communist Party was a bit of a thorn in the side of Marx House, or the Centre as it was called. Inclined to anarchism and not taking kindly to directives from up top, they tended to go their own way and explain later, if at all. They believed they knew best how to deal with the area many of them had grown up in. They believed the Centre was out of touch with the realities of life in the Red Belt, and they were probably right. Punchdrunk ex-prizefighters, old activists from the Depression days when the unemployed built their bag and tin humpies along the banks of the Cooks River, a few who'd "done time", workers from Malleys and the Glassworks and the iron foundries in the district, some with long hair and strange ways, "the lunatic fringe" of any radical movement, political or religious, they didn't fit in with the stereotype of the honest, respectable worker who stayed in the same job all his life, building up a political and work reputation for stability and tactics.

When *Bobbin Up* was criticized at special Communist Party meetings to discuss its strengths and weaknesses one of the principal criticisms was that it presented the Australian working class as "lumpen proletariat" and "anarchistic". What the critics failed to realize was that the working class I was writing about were exactly like that, unorganized, close to illiteracy, the "lower depths".

Until I shifted further out to Rockdale in 1963 I never really met the respectable working class, idealized by the Communist Party. He was the family man next door, a skilled worker, in a white singlet mowing the lawn in the weekend, while a guard dog went mad on a chain behind him. He didn't exist in Redfern, and the Alexandria spinning Mills had never met such a paragon.

Redfern was always the bottom of the heap. Foregathered there were the old, the halt, the maimed, the drunks, the mad, the unemployables, the substandard, the failures of society. The odd seemingly "respectable" families were few and far between. An acute housing shortage in Sydney after the war meant that the slum landlords never repaired their properties, but rents were comparatively low, and in many condemned, half-ruined houses pensioners, drunks and whole families shacked up, using the floorboards to fuel the Victorian iron grates in the cold winters, and gaining access to the upper floors by climbing up a rope once the staircase was gone.

There were streets of urban Aborigines, and once, in the name of the Redfern Tenants' Protection Society, I was responsible for moving three Aboriginal girls and their crowd of bare-arsed kids out of a horrific slum ruin to a Housing Commission settlement in the outer suburbs, thus taking away their only means of livelihood as part-time prostitutes, and no doubt earning their undying hatred as an interfering, do-gooder, "whitey".

You learnt to live and let live in Redfern, and the generosity of neighbours was often surprising. Girls trying to rise in the world never gave their address as Redfern, but had the current boyfriend drop them off in other suburbs, and then stealthily walked home. Yet there was a weird species of civic pride, a sense of community. You never dared refer to Redfern as a slum, and some houseproud wives blackened the front steps and polished the brass door knockers until they shone.

A blind eye was turned towards various peccadilloes, and standards of bourgeois honesty were elastic. In the Council election some members of the Communist Party who'd lived in Redfern all their lives, voted many times for the candidate they favoured, using "bodgie" names, or the names of the dead, and were proud of it.

When we shifted to a liver brick house in Rosebery with a garden with two peach trees rotten with fruit fly, it was widely considered that we had "sold out". That house, opposite a wire factory that worked night shift, was the model for the house of "Bonus-Happy Mais" in *Bobbin Up* ... the next step up the ladder of respectability. Redfern, Waterloo and Alexandria formed the nucleus of South Sydney, and they never really made it into "fashionable" inner-city suburbs, like Paddington and Woollahra, and even Surrey Hills, and parts of Darlinghurst.

In Surrey Hills then Kate Leigh, the big, tough madam of an infamous brothel and criminal network, reigned supreme. She was a leftwinger who secretly donated money to the Communist Party funds, while the Centre, if they ever knew, turned a blind eye. Kate Leigh's rival was Tilly Devine, Catholic madam of Darlinghurst's gangland. Tilly was a conservative politically. She once travelled to London in her own private stateroom on board the Queen Mary, and, it was rumoured, was "presented", magnificently overdressed, at a Buckingham Palace Garden Party.

In the fifties Paddington and inner Woollahra were working-class suburbs; rows of semi-detached two-storied Victorian villas with rooms to let. In the late sixties they became fashionable and trendy, the semis with their rising damp refurbished with face lifts of plastic paint and the iron lace balconies repaired. Before we shifted to Redfern we lived like Beth and Stan in *Bobbin Up* in a room in Moncur Street, Woollahra, and I caught the bus, running down Oxford Street on dark winter mornings. If I missed the 6.30 a.m. I was five minutes late bundying on for the 7 a.m. start at the mill, and automatically lost a quarter of an hour's pay, a blow when wages were only £8 a week, with four hours per week compulsory overtime.

I walked home after work with Al and Beryl (or characters like them) past the little park that still exists, where the old men played draughts in the sunlight; home to the house in Moncur Street where Aime and Alf and Polly Tickner lived, and Beat ran a book on Saturdays. As far as I know "Al" was the only one of the girls at the mill who ever read *Bobbin Up*. "She made me flat-chested," she said, with a grin, "I'm not *that* flat-chested am I?"

When I wrote *Bobbin Up* eight years later I split myself and my boilermaker lover into Beth and Lenny, and Nell and Stan Mooney. Beth and Lenny are the rough likenesses of ourselves as we were in those first golden days of our love affair when Sydney was still a glorious adventure for the provincial girl from Western Australia. Eight years later after three kids, the Hungarian Revolution and Kruschev's revelations on Stalinism to the Twentieth Congress in Moscow, we were closer in attitudes to Nell and Stan, our original political idealism and belief in ourselves and each other corroded by time, and bitter experience.

We had read Kruschev's speech in horror and disbelief. Could it possibly be true or was it all another C.I.A. plot, but the evidence was too damning. When we rose at the party meeting to ask the inevitable questions we were told that "mistakes had been made", but negativism must be combatted. The task now was to build the Party, rocked to its foundations by members voting with their feet, and that the new political campaign was "the fight against monopoly".

The portrait of Nell merely touches on these doubts and questions, the disgust at the betrayals, that finally led me out of the Communist Party in 1968. In 1958 I was still half afraid to even voice my own growing uneasiness and *Bobbin Up* still mirrors a naive political idealism that had little to do with reality. "Sincere Dishonesty" Ray Matthew called it then in a review in the Australian paper, *The Nation*, and he was right. Looking back on the 36-year-old Communist who wrote *Bobbin Up* I am embarrassed at her proselytizng, stubborn blindness, this Antipodean Alice in Wonderland who had a protracted love affair with an idealized working class.

And yet... and yet... there is a weird truth working within that "sincere dishonesty" (and it was sincere). The portraits of the mill girls are "real". They are living, breathing Australian working-class women who speak with a living tongue, and the mill itself as a metaphor for their lives grows larger than life and realer than real throughout the pages. Up to this time, and maybe ever since, there was little working-class literature in Australia. The lives of such women remained a mystery. They could not write themselves, and they had no spokesperson to translate them into literature.

And the city of Sydney itself comes alive in *Bobbin Up*, something of my own fascination with the first big city I had ever lived in, its beauty, squalor and turbulence, its living quality has come through.

As I wrote on that kitchen table far into the night Sputnik had appeared in the southern skies and people did crane their necks excitedly to see it pass over. The songs that I used in the text were top of the pops on the radio. All these details do help to give the book a strange verisimilitude, but they also perhaps tend to limit it to reportage.

I find now the most embarrassing scene in the book is the scene in Tom Maguire's backyard as Tom and Peg watch Sputnik overhead, accompanied by, fortissimo, "a song pouring like a ladle of boiling steel from the throats of the world's toilers". Afterwards we listen in to Tom Maguire's soliloquy on why he, a militant wharf labourer, never actually joined the Communist Party. It is because of his "individuality", his rebellious spirit, his anarchism, and now because of Sputnik, apparently, he has changed his mind. Sputnik has recruited him. It is one of the places in the book where the author as commentator takes over, and rams her naive politics down our throats.

Nell Mooney was described in a book review at the time as "poor blind Nell" and, of course, in many ways, she is just that. But oddly enough I doubt if I could have written Nell with such truth at a later time of political disillusionment with the Communist Party. Nell is a type of "believer" and she is the prototype of many Communists of her time and place in history. I write about Nell as she is because I believe *with* her . . . her starry-eyed sentimentality and Utopianism were mine, and her limited self-knowledge was mine also.

As for the Communist Party meeting and the roneoing of the leaflet *Bobbin Up*, Communist Party meetings in Australia then were just like that, the members talked that way and the leaflet with its heading that causes so much argument: *There is a name for a man who lives off women* was produced, and the idea for the article did come from the alter-ego of Stan Mooney.

Sometimes sentimental, sometimes didactic, sometimes clumsy and overwritten *Bobbin Up* was the work of a still young writer struggling to find her own style and voice. Its form, which was criticized at the time as too loose and episodic, seems to me to suit the subject perfectly, and the ending which was criticized as "unrealistic" by the Communist Party critics of the time, seems to me to work on a level beyond banal naturalism.

Not many years later there were sit-in strikes by workers in Australia, and some of them were women, but apart from that the sit-in strike in the silent mill works on a symbolic level, a level beyond the reality of the times. It helps to elevate the naturalistic detail of the women's lives, not in any programmed socialist realist way, but in an action that grows organically out of the style of the novel. It is a redirection of the normal movement from chapter to chapter when the girls file out of the mill to go home to their separate lives. Now they stay inside the mill, part of its huge and overpowering darkness. Its sinister silence becomes an extension of their bodies and their lives.

The incantation at the end, when, like a camera eye, we move out from the inside of the mill across the rooftops and factory chimneys, the rivers and streets and neon signs of Sydney through the medium of

Patty singing, is, I think, finally kept in check with the last ironic comment of Lil, spreading a bag on a butterbox for the pregnant Beth:

"Rest your legs luv. It's likely to be a long wait."

Rejected by the first panel of readers in the Mary Gilmore Novel Competition, the manuscript of *Bobbin Up* was discovered lying in a cupboard by one of the final judges, and subsequently given second prize. The novel was published in 1959 by the Australasian Book Society, a left-wing publishing company now defunct, originally masterminded by a group of Melbourne radical writers. The publishers "cleaned up" the text by substituting "sh-ouse" for "shithouse" and "fugging" for "fucking", but some readers still objected to "the language".

At a Communist Party branch discussion I attended the members asserted that the "working class didn't talk like that". Australian Communists seemed to be extraordinarily tone deaf to the lively nuances of the Australian idiom. A seaman said I must be a nymphomaniac, and a male Communist maintained "her husband must have written it for her, because no woman could possibly know all that".

Prudery, bigotry and male chauvinism, reflecting the working class mores of the time, were commonplaces in the Australian left-wing movement in those days.

But there were enough enthusiastic readers for that first edition (3000 copies)of *Bobbin Up* to sell out in eight weeks. It has never been reprinted in Australia. There were a number of foreign editions: Russian, Hungarian, Bulgarian, German, and an English language edition published by *Seven Seas Books* in East Berlin. Then the book faded out of existence. Only now I find it returning like a doppelganger. There are plans for an Australian film and a stage musical, based on the novel. Old copies are sought for teaching purposes in Womens' Studies and some social history classes in Australian Universities and Colleges of Advanced Education.

What are the reasons for this? Has time made *Bobbin Up* "historical" or "exotic", does it still tap some nerve of recognition in a period of mass unemployment and recession, is it the reflection of the new interest in novels by and about women, or have they risen up with some odd, compulsive life of their own, that silent majority I worked beside thirty-five years ago?

Dorothy Hewett
Sydney, NSW, Australia 1984

Chapter One

☆

SHIRL was nineteen years old, four months gone and just starting to show, bumping through Newtown on the back of a second-hand Norton.

Through neon signs, traffic signals, lighted shop fronts, they slid on a long blurred streamer of speed down King Street. The summer wind, full of the smoke of bushfires from the Blue Mountains, whipped her skirt high above her knees. She was plastered against a leather jacketed back with "NEWTOWN ROCKETS" exploded across it in crude white letters. A group of bodgies, holding up the front of a milk bar, bright as parakeets, whistled her shrilly down the wind.

"Lairizers!" Jack muttered.

Shirl snuggled against the worn, sweaty leather, thrilled at the concern and protection in his voice. No one had ever wanted to protect her before.

The bodgies' whistle was lost in the grind of a tram braking behind them. The Norton skidded on the tramlines, swerved from under the nose of the tram and darted up a side lane on the short cut to Alexandria. Shirl had a glimpse of the trammie, swinging on the footboard, rows of empty faces, heads nodding like stalkless blue flowers in the light from the neon sign. . . .

NOW ON
HOT FISH
CHIPS
SPRING ROLLS
SAVS
PEPSI COLA

The sign clicked on and off, the faces were gone, whirled away on the streamer of speed, bumped into oblivion through the close, smelly darkness of the little semis, pressed suffocatingly onto the footpath.

"He's got the whole world in his ha-a-nds," blared a child's persuasive Cockney, through a half-open doorway.

Shirl closed her eyes. She didn't want to see. She wanted to whirl deliciously away into space with the wind in her hair. What was there to hear and see and smell in the lane but people, her kind of people? She understood them but she didn't want to be part of them. If she opened her eyes she knew exactly what she would see . . . men in shirtsleeves smoking on the step, kids climbing over their knees, the bulk of a woman going backwards and forwards against the naked light bulb, drying up.

A baby wailed from the corner, drowned in the roar of the Norton, drowned in the clang of a tram, drowned in a big empty semi-trailer, revving and rattling up the hill, drowned in a train whistle mournfully shrieking from Redfern Station.

Shirl touched her belly gently, exploringly, with her finger-tips. A half-conscious smile curved her mouth.

A late model Chev swerved out from the lane, crushing them into the gutter. The pale smoky sky, golden over the city, tilted and swung.

"Bloody mug," Jack yelled, laying the Norton over with calm artistry. The Chev left them behind, in a snort of arrogant exhaust.

Shirl laughed, a little thrill of fear crawling at the base of her spine. This was the corner, by the silent cop, where she and Roy had come to grief. A big shiny car had forced them over, to sideswipe an oncoming semi. A sharp wrenching swerve, brakes grinding, Roy trying to throw the bike over, the tray slicing at his black head, all over in two or three seconds. She somersaulted into the gutter, the bike turned turtle on its side, the motor screaming at 5000 revs a minute. Roy twitched on the asphalt, hands covered with blood, still clinging to the handle bars, still with his last conscious movement trying to pull the bike over . . . lumps of hair and blood and bone plastered on the edge of the tray.

"These bodgies are a bloody menace," grumbled the cop, reaching over to switch off the throttle. "If I had me way I'd put every motor bike off the road. Anyway, don't look like this one'll ever worry us again."

The truck driver stood by the cabin, white-faced, rolling a cigarette with shaky fingers. The big shiny car had gone. Shirl lay on her back in the gutter, staring stupidly from the pale blue sky to the piece of bone sticking out of her elbow.

And where was Roy now? Wandering round Sydney or up the

bush somewhere with the black crisp curls springing up from the puckered mess of his face, eyes empty and blue as the summer sky above the gutter in Newtown. That was how he'd lain in the hospital ward, only his eyes looking away from her through the white bandages, and the weary voice . . .

"Better call it a day, kid. I won't be no good to you after this."

How fiercely she had come every day with her bunch of flowers or her bag of oranges, to stand at the foot of his white bed. Till he and his mother finally drove her away between them. The little skinny woman in the shapeless cardigan and ankle socks, with her perm growing out, hissing at her from the straight-backed hospital chair.

"Keep away from my Roy, d'you hear? It was a sad day for him when he took up with you. You're nothin' but a filthy harlot. Keep away from my son!"

"Your mother called me a harlot Roy. Your mother . . ."

"Better do as she says Shirl. Better keep away."

"Don't you love me Roy?"

"Don't come back no more Shirl."

"But the baby Roy. What about the baby?"

" 'E's not the father. You know 'e's not the father. Tryin' to pin it on my boy when every Tom, Dick and 'Arry . . ." The venomous little voice hissing, the red roses on the end of the white quilt, the empty blue eyes above the white bandages.

"Okay Roy, I won't be coming back . . . no harlots for you, Roy. Let this greasy ol' bitch keep you warm."

Head flung up, passing through the watery sunlight and polished floors, heels clattering the length of the ward. Don't look back, Shirl. Don't ever look back. If you look back you might turn into a pillar of salt.

They turned into McAvoy Street where the dark bulk of the factories leant ominous and sawtoothed over the Norton . . . Enquiries, Office, Dispatch, Receiving, No Parking, No Vacancies. Down innumerable alleys, glinting with dirt tins, cats' eyes and rusty corrugated iron . . . a lonely flaring neon above a corner shop . . . "Pepsi Cola hits the Spot". Shirl looked down with the old familiar pain in her chest, at the tattoo on her forearm, "SHIRL LOVES ROY". . . . They'd had it done for a lairy joke one Saturday morning in a dirty little joint down by the quay. "SHIRL LOVES ROY" . . . "ROY LOVES SHIRL"

. . . put their brand on each other, something that lasts in a world of impermanence.

"Shirl loves Roy" . . . "Roy loves Shirl" sang the sad summer wind in the chasm of McAvoy Street.

Jack cut the motor and pulled into the narrow alley behind her mother's house. He swung his leg over, thrusting leather gloves into his pocket, helped her off the pillion into his arms, pulling her hard against leather jacket and Stamina trousers, forcing her head back, their mouths soft together in the stinking lane. The blunt black snouts of factory chimneys leaned to watch them, a weary, half-blinded Pom with a grey muzzle nosed and scavenged among the dirt tins, bumping against their legs and growling softly in his throat.

A fat woman, with her head done up in a gauze scarf, two snowy-haired kids at her heels, slip-slapped down the asphalt.

"Will we buy some chips comin' home?" she said in her soft, maternal voice. " 'Night Shirl."

Her huge, white, flabby legs and cotton dress disappeared into the oblong of pale, smoky sky, criss-crossed with telegraph poles, at the other end of the lane.

The light streamed out from the open doorway. Above the sob of the wireless—"I'll cry myself to sleep and wake up smiling. No one will ever know the truth but me"—a harassed, throaty voice cried, "Is that you Shirl?"

The kiss was over. Shirl thrust her hand through the crescent-shaped hole in the high picket gate and worked the bolt loose.

"Let me do the talkin' Jack," she said softly.

"What about that?" He jerked his thumb towards her belly.

"Me trump card . . . only to be used in case of emergency." She grinned.

They clattered across the sunken brick paving into the glare of light, pushing their way through wet, ghostly sheets that flapped in their faces.

Shirl's mother loomed through the steamy kitchen like a bright lorikeet, her hooked nose and swarthy skin beaded with sweat, sleeves rolled up, red, shrunken wool cardigan buttoned tightly across her broad bosom. There was a wet patch across her loose belly, her hands were pink and swollen with hot water, but the arms above the elbow had a girlish white smoothness and roundness, touching in its tenderness. Her mouth went hard when she saw the boy, spiky crew-cut head and leather jacket, blocking the doorway.

"Home early, aren't you?" she said sulkily, turning back to

the washing, bubbling and steaming in the cracked brick copper.

"Jesus Ma, washin' on a night like this. You must be off your rocker. This place is a bloody oven." Shirl sank down by the kitchen table, fanning herself with the *Mirror*.

"It's all very well for you, me lady!" her mother said tartly. "Gallivantin' all over Sydney while I scrub me fingers to the bone. I wouldn't mind a breath of fresh air meself."

She tossed back the heavy dark hair, shot with copper and streaked with grey, that grew in girlish tendrils at the back of her neck. Violet McHendry, forty-five, sharp-tongued, hard as nails, was always fighting a losing battle with life in the grey, warped, weatherboard semi in Maddox Lane. But she still kept, until the day she died of a stroke over her washtubs, ten years later, that peculiar kind of girlishness, that grace of face and voice, that has nothing to do with time.

"Look up the lottery results, will you Shirl. Me stars said it was me lucky week. Me number's 4671."

She took down a bundle of dusty lottery tickets in an old tea caddy—Violet's only dream of escape from Maddox Lane.

"Two off ten quid Ma. Your stars did the dirty on you agen." Violet sighed.

"Kids asleep?" said Shirl. "Why doncha siddown Jack? You make me nervous. No one's got any manners in this joint." She glared at her mother's broad back.

"If you've come in at this time of night to stir up trouble you know what you can do with yourself," Violet snapped. "Come in Jack. Make yourself at home. If Shirl'd get off her fat bum and make us a cuppa tea it wouldn't be a bad idea."

Shirl took the cups down off the dresser. There was a long, official looking envelope addressed to Miss Shirley McHendry poked behind the "Weeties" packet. Her hand paused only a second, her mouth tightened only a fraction. She put the kettle on to boil on the gas stove, sunken into a rusty, sulky despair under a dark fireplace in one corner of the kitchen.

The room was living room and kitchen combined, but it was too small and too crowded to perform even one function efficiently, littered with the tag ends of all the lives that breathed and sheltered under its rusty roof. It was like a stopping-off place where people fling the residue of school and factory, scrubbing brush and dirty overall. In a rummage of school exercise books, *True Love* magazines, comics and unpaid bills, an old clock ticked on the mantelpiece. An ancient couch, covered in greasy blue Genoa velvet, springs bursting exuberantly through the up-

5

holstery, rubbed shoulders with a shiny veneered radiogram. The wood copper and tubs, that doubled as a sink, stood next to the frig and a grotesque carved sideboard.

Violet settled her broad bottom into her chair, pushing her fingers through her coppery hair, full white legs, threaded with varicose veins, spread wide.

"Jeez I'm winded," she said, watching her daughter through wary, velvety eyes.

"Lolly pop, lolly pop, oh! lolly lollipop!" shrieked the wireless.

"For Christ's sake!" yelled Shirl. "I dunno how you can stand that thing blarin' in your ears day an' night. I can't hear meself think."

She switched it off, clattering the cups on the oilcloth.

"You're nervous as a cat tonight," her mother said.

"Jack and me wanta get married Ma."

"You got a one-track mind Shirl," Violet said wearily. "You're too young. If I'd knowed what I know now . . ."

"You'd never've married your ol' man at nineteen. We know." Shirl's brutal young voice taunted and pecked at the mournful bulk of her mother, across the kitchen table.

"Well, you might as well know now Ma. It's a case of have to!"

Violet's eyes swung round to her daughter's rounded belly.

"When did this happen?" she said.

"On Bondi Beach," said Shirl flippantly. "I'm four months. If you had eyes in your head you mighta noticed yourself."

The clock ticked heavily on the mantelpiece. Violet sat, heavy and sombre, one swollen hand hiding her eyes. The boy swung his foot uncomfortably against the table leg. He leaned across the oilcloth.

"I'll look after her Ma," he said quickly. "That job I got at the garage. I'm nearly outa me time."

She brushed her hand across her cheek. "Yeah, yeah, I know," she mumbled. "I gotta think about it. Better go home Jack. Go home now."

He got up awkwardly, shuffling his feet on the worn lino. "See you tomorrer Shirl."

She went with him to the back gate. "It'll be alright," she said exultantly, squeezing his arm. "I'll break 'er down. I'll meet you outside the Registry Office tomorrer, after work. You'll know me by the big grin on me face."

He took her in his arms, shielding her from the narrow gutted lane and factory chimneys, the little shrunken house and the big, shrunken, girlish woman with her shoulders hunched over the kitchen table. The shadows of a crazy, patchworked lattice, hanging on the side of the house, traced tender criss-crosses on Shirl's face.

"Take care of . . . that," he said, stroking her belly gently. "Tomorrer on them big spindles, take care of that for me." His face suddenly lightened with compassion. He strode back to the open doorway.

"Ma," he said quietly. "I'll come over next weekend and fix that lattice for you."

They heard him kicking over the Norton in the lane. Shirl faced her mother like an adversary across the shabby kitchen.

"You're a bright bitch of a thing," said Violet, her mouth twisting on the words. "When you said 'It's a case of have to,' I shoulda said, 'What again!'"

"Why didn't you then?"

"I didn't want to put you in. Does he know?" She jerked her head towards the sound of the Norton, roaring away into the night.

"No, and I don't want him to neither. I'll tell 'im one of these days. Anyway, what's there to tell. It's all over now."

"Even you'd find it hard explainin' away a two-year-old kid," said Violet bitterly.

"I'll settle that problem when it comes up. Listen Ma, this is the only really decent bloke I've ever got hold of. When it come to a pinch Roy was ready to chuck me, but Jack won't do that. He's a good feller, kind, and he really loves me. He's the only one who's ever goin' to marry me. For Christ's sake don't stand in me way. For if you do I'll break you Ma. I swear I will. I'll get back on you somehow if it's the last thing I do." Her lips curved back in a false cupid's bow on her callous little face.

"You're hard Shirl," Violet moaned. "Hard as nails."

"And if I am, who made me like it?" the girl cried from her heart. "Dragged up in this stinkin' little dump, in and out of bloody Welfare homes all me life, inter the factories as soon as I could dodge the Truant Officer."

"God knows I did me best," Violet moaned. "Was it my fault if your father died? Nine kids to bring up and only me scrubbin' out dirty offices from dawn till dark. How could I keep you off the streets?"

"Nine kids, one dead, and five on the State," Shirl taunted. "What a record!"

Violet leapt to her feet like a big cat. She thrust her broad, flushed face into Shirl's.

7

"Don't you sling shit at me," she shrieked, "Don't you throw up at me about the kids on the State and one dead." Her voice broke. She swung her head like a wounded animal to the battered sideboard, heaped with undarned socks, kewpie dolls from the Show, fly-speckled calendar prints of an Indian girl by her canoe, camels moving across a perpetually twilit desert. The narrow, handsome face of her dead son laughed up at her, his wing of deep auburn hair bright against the broad, white, unfreckled brow and leather overcoat. The coppers had come to pick him up for pinching cars the night he died in Sydney Hospital. How she'd cursed them, standing in the little kitchen, her brown eyes dim with grief. He was always laughing and full of life but the young interne said he died of a weak heart.

"Worth ten of the lotta you Normie was," she moaned, sinking back in the chair, twisting her body from side to side. "Worth ten of the lotta you."

"Alright Ma," Shirl said bitterly. "We all know that. He was worth ten of the lot of us. Now will you sign this consent form and for Christ's sake let me get married."

Violet looked at her wearily. "Give me the bloody paper," she said. "And God help young Jack."

Shirl watched her steadily. "You might as well know," she said. "I would of did it without you anyway. Jack and me went to the Chamber Magistrate months ago. We're gettin' married to-morrer."

Violet's eyes were hostile. "And I s'pose you're comin' to dump yourselves in on top of me!" she cried shrilly.

"We'll live in Newtown with Jack's father," Shirl said bitterly. "He *wants* us there. You needn't alarm yourself Ma. Who'd wanta live in Misery Holler with you and the kids!"

Violet rose. Her shrewd eyes raked the thin, painted face of her eldest daughter; the burnished hair, the high, delicate cheek bones, the firm, cleft jaw, the travesty of a cupid's bow drawn on the straight upper lip.

"You're like your ol' man," she said wonderingly. "Nothin' won't ever beat you Shirl. But sometimes I wish there was somethin' a little bit soft or young about you. You're too old for nineteen. It's a cryin' shame. But what could I do about it?"

Shirl pushed her gently between her broad shoulder blades. "Go to bed, Ma," she said. "I'll put the rest of the washin' out."

"There's a letter for you. I stuck it behind the 'Weeties'." Violet paused in the doorway. "I hope it's not more bad news Shirl," she said kindly. She waddled out, walking slopped over on her slippers, favouring her bunions. Shirl waited till she heard the creak of the mattress, then she tore open the envelope. If it was bad news, better to get it over and done with.

For an hour afterwards she worked savagely, wielding the pot stick like a sword, dragging heaps of steamy clothes from copper to tubs, draping them over the lines, the pegs in her mouth to clamp off the tears. The sweat ran off her pencilled eyebrows and into her mascaraed eyelashes. By midnight, with the wet, shiny, innocent face of a little girl, she had finished. Everything was washed, twisted and wrung, and Davie with the swollen, grotesque head on the little spindly body, was dead in her breast, the last of the frosty, official letters in the long, flat envelopes burnt in the copper.

Davie was born seven months after Shirl walked out of Sydney Hospital, leaving Roy to the tender ministrations of his mother. His conception had been planned, a trump card to force Violet's consent to their marriage. But Violet was like a rock. Time, and the big, shiny car in Newtown had done the rest. Shirl worked on the big spindles right up to the night she got her pains, cycling backwards and forwards to the mill, her belly heavy and swollen across her knees. With a grim and terrible humour, she'd told the leading hand she had a growth. He'd pretended to believe her. They were short-handed, Shirl was a good worker, she'd never let the "growth" interfere with her daily output. But when the baby was born she shrank from its great grotesque head and empty eyes.

"Water on the brain," they told her. "Operation may relieve the pressure." That was two years and three operations ago.

"Die little Davie," she whispered, twisting the clothes over the steamy suds, with hands suddenly grown tender and fierce. "Die and rest in peace."

There could be no more operations for the little, swollen-headed boy she had never cradled in her arms. She wouldn't give her consent again. Now was the time to cry "Enough" and let him go back into oblivion, better oblivion than the four walls of an institution, the pain, the futility, the mumbling into idiocy. Sorry Davie, it was all a mistake and you should never have been born. The earth is beautiful, but there is no beauty here for us, cramped between the black snouts of factory chimneys, all our life narrowed and chained between one whistle and the next.

"Poor little bugger," she whispered. "Poor little bugger."

9

It was early on Friday morning when she went to bed. Lovingly she'd pressed the blue silk dress for her wedding, and hung it carefully behind her bedroom door. She'd had it on lay-by ever since that night on Bondi Beach, and the colour exactly matched the blue of her eyes.

Her two little sisters lay tumbled together in the old double bed, their bodies warm and moist with sleep, their lashes tender and gilt-edged on their cheeks. Violet snored softly in the room she shared with Shirl across the passage. The moonlight fell full on her face through the white lace curtains, one broad swollen hand clutching the sheet in uneasy sleep.

Shirl stretched naked on her narrow bed, the moonlight painting shadows on her soft breasts, sheening the blue silk dress behind the door, that same moonlight that shone on the brand new hoarding in the vacant allotment on the corner of Maddox Lane:

> MASONIC HALL
> Next Sunday, 3 P.M.
> TRUE FACTS ABOUT HEAVEN

it proclaimed to all and sundry in the stuffy, concrete heaven of Alexandria.

Chapter Two

☆

THE whistle blew and Beth straightened her back. She switched off her machine and swayed across the mill, thrown back on her heels for balance, unconsciously folding her arms across her belly.

Women came from everywhere, laughing and chiacking down the long, slippery aisles between the rovers, spinners and winders. Relief healed their aching backs, relief loosened their tongues, they ran and pushed and scurried, jamming into the washroom, five minutes to change and scrub up and catch the bus to Redfern, Marrickville, Paddo, Woollahra and all points north, south, east and west.

There was no hot water, no showers. The women thrust their hands, faces, dirty feet into ten cracked porcelain hand basins, standing in a row beside the lavatories. The overflow, and there had to be an overflow with two hundred women in the spinning section, was catered for by a similar row of basins standing unprotected in the centre of the mill.

"Jeez, I'm not goin' to wash me feet in there. Look at all the men standin' round."

"It's here or nowhere luv. C'mon, hurry up or I'll miss me bus."

"She'll get used to it. . . ."

Sure, you'll get used to it . . . feet hoisted over the side, pink and white slips strained over plump thighs, the men hanging round for an eyeful. You're not a woman anymore, you're just an appendage to a machine.

The washroom was thick with women, thick with the odour of urine, sweat, powder, scent and a peculiar, intimate, sickly, stale woman smell.

"Gawd Beth, how the hell are you goin' to get your feet up there. Your belly's in the way lovey. Here, give us your elbow. I'll give you a hoist and for Christ's sake don't slip."

We've washed the worst of the grime off our feet and our faces, we've combed our hair and put our lipstick on, changed out of our greasy overalls, and now we're women again, with kids to collect, husbands to feed, boy friends to cuddle. We're streaming out of the corrugated iron shed, hanging our metal discs on the board, out the tall cyclone gates decorated with a frill of barbed wire, out to wait for the bus on a narrow strip of dried grass opposite the mill. Out at last and the day is only a memory of sweat and fluff and grease and grinding noise, to be added to all the other days, weeks, months and years.

"Yeah, I've worked in the mill ever since they manpowered me durin' the war."

"Jesus Betty, I dunno how you stand it."

"Ah well, you know it's handy. I only live round the corner and I've been doffin' them spindles so long now I can do it in me sleep."

"Eighteen years!"

"Ah well, you know, it suits me. There's only me brother and meself to look after."

"Eighteen bloody years!"

"Ah well, you know . . ." and there she goes, waddling homewards in her dirty blue overalls, with the white fluff accumulated on her dumpy shoulders, mixed with the greying streaks in her hair.

"Ta-ta, Jeanie. See you tomorrer."

"Ta-ta Skin. Don't do nothin' I wouldn't do."

"Ta-ta Shirl . . ."

"Ta-ta Dawnie."

"Ta-ta Beth. Have a good rest tonight, luv. You'll feel better in the mornin'."

"Ta-ta Nell."

Beth leant her aching body against one of the spindly trees, not one over five foot high, planted in badly spaced rows for civic improvement. Every now and again one had given up the unequal struggle, withered, and died.

"Here, sit down on the gutter Bethie, till the bus comes. Spread me newspaper out," said Alice. "Dick had no right puttin' you on that big rover, the way you are. It's enough to bring on a mis. Everyone knows what a cow of a thing it is, always muckin' up on you. She don't look too good, does she Beryl?"

Beth sank down gratefully on the guttering. Alexandria swam in heat haze, dry and shimmering off the rusty corrugated iron fences, the huge silver gas tank, the smudged brick chimneys. A thin wisp of smoke curled into the pale tender blue of the sky. She closed her eyes. It was heaven to get the weight off her legs. The bus came round the corner in a stink of exhaust. Beryl and Alice were on their feet, pushing and shoving, valiantly defending Beth's right to a seat in the crowded bus. They were off, jammed to the doors, Beth straphanging beside them.

" 'Ere, take my seat luv." With a terrible mental and physical effort, old Lil hauled herself to her feet.

"I'm right Lil."

"Go on Bethie, sit down. You look done in." Alice gave her a gentle shove.

"I'm gettin' out at Redfern. It's not that far," said Lil, her varicose veins knotting at the back of her knees. Beth eyed the space left by her skinny little bum doubtfully, and wedged her own broad bottom into the seat.

"Thanks Lil. I'll do the same for you one a these days."

Lil giggled. "Don't go jonahing me now. Thank Christ I'm too old to fall."

The bus sped up McAvoy Street. Lil got out at the park. At the glassworks corner a little, nuggety, snowy-headed fellow balanced on the bottom step with a sheet of glass that reached to his chest.

A great ribald cheer went up from the crowded bus.

"Reckon you'll make it this time Snow?"

"Never say die!"

"Another bloody foreign order. You must be costin' poor ol' Knockout a fortune."

He teetered and wavered, the glass slipped off the step, bounced on the asphalt, shivered into pieces. There was a howl of anguish from the passengers.

"Three fuckin' times I've done it," he said mournfully. "Three fuckin' times an' never got her home yet."

They rolled down Anzac Parade and past the Showground.

"All I can think about is crays," moaned Beth. "A lovely big plateful."

"Why doncha buy some lobsters down Oxford Street?" said Alice sympathetically.

"They cost a fortune. . . . I better not. You oughta see them at home, so cheap, everybody gets them for supper. Crays and a bottla beer. It's the drunks' special for Saturdee night." Beth sighed, fleetingly homesick for the streets of Perth on a hot summer's evening.

Beth's people kept an orchard and a bit of a chook run in the

13

Darling Ranges about ten miles out of Perth. They'd never wanted her to marry Len.

"One of them flash Eastern Staters," her father grumbled.

"Sydney, it's that far away," her mother mourned, screwing up the crowsfeet around her eyes and wiping her hands on her pinny. "And they reckon it's full of white slavers up at that King's Cross. And after all we've done for you Beth. But mothers don't count."

Beth hadn't written about the baby. She didn't want Mum fussing around, whinging about "how much the fare over cost" and "why was Len lettin' her work in her condition. In a mill, of all places. Makin' a show of herself!"

Time enough to let on when the baby was here. Alice leant towards her confidentially, with the sway of the bus.

"Listen Beth. I don't think they'll be keepin' you on much longer. I heard Sister say to one of the girls in the washroom yesterday, it was disgraceful to have you walkin' round the mill like you are."

Beth flushed. "Why don't she mind her own business? Old Nosey Parker," she snapped.

"She's sure to get rid of you, pimp to the management," said Beryl. "She's probably jealous. Looks like an ol' maid to me." She twirled backwards and forwards on the strap, displaying her engagement ring finger.

"Did you see it Bethie?" She thrust out her hand and, quickly, to forestall any breath of criticism, "It's only one diamond. I told Frank he wasn't to waste his money. We can't afford it."

Beth smiled. "It's lovely Beryl. Isn't it lovely Al?"

Alice gave a small, tight-lipped smile that hurt her mouth. She was not much over thirty, but prematurely aged, with a soft, wrinkled face and tiny breastless figure. She did all her living vicariously through her young sister Beryl. It was as if life had passed her by, and she was content to let it go. The sisters shared bed and breakfast in a tiny attic at the top of an ancient stone semi in Woollahra. But when Beryl was gone to set up house with her policeman, life would be dismally lonely, only the old landlady coming in every morning with her hair in curlers, an almost butterless slice of toast and warm tea.

No, Al couldn't rejoice over the single diamond glittering in the crowded aisle. The bus drew in to the kerb. It was the end of the run.

"Ta-ta Beth. See you in the mornin' on the zombie parade. Don't miss the six-thirty."

"Hooray Beryl. Don't stay out too late with the boy friend."

"We never stay out late, do we Al?" Beryl giggled. "Anyway Frank's on point duty tomorrer."

"Oh you and your copper!" Alice gave her sister a half friendly, half irritated push. Together they crossed Centennial Square and disappeared into the maze of little streets running like arteries across Woollahra and Paddington. Here on the borders of Paddington and inner fashionable Woollahra, was the shabby, genteel poverty of bed-sits and bed and breakfast, running downhill into the slummy rabbit warrens of Paddo and the Loo.

Beth swayed across the square, watching the old men playing draughts on the little tables under the poplar trees. The last golden light of summer bathed their white heads in a gentle radiance, a light wind stirred their newspapers. She passed proudly and yet compassionately, conscious of her youth and motherhood. The old men stared after her, jealous of the radiance they could never share again, loafing on borrowed time, unwanted, under the dapple of the poplar trees.

She heard the locusts drumming in the crepe myrtles long before she turned into Moller Street. The sultry air throbbed and vibrated with their song. They were like nerves thrumming up from the shimmering asphalt, growing in intensity under the dark blue shadows cast by the crepe myrtle trees.

Beth hugged the shade all the way up the footpath, hurried from the street into the old, two-storey semi, scabrous with flaky plaster, dim with paperbark baskets of asparagus fern and baked geraniums. The tattered, rusty lace of an iron balcony curved over the street.

It was cool inside with that peculiar combination of mildew, boiled cabbage, mice and polish that always lingers in the residential hallway. Through the half-open door into the kitchen she could see the tea things laid out under mosquito netting. Lou had gone for her Thursday's game of euchre in the gambling rooms over an expensive Pitt Street milliner. The cry of a new baby floated remotely down from upstairs.

Hanging onto the balustrade, Beth hauled herself up the stairs. Only two more steps and she was on the landing, two more steps and she was through the door, two more steps and she was flopped across the bed, with the blessed quiet and peace and privacy of the ugly little room washing around her.

She slept on her back, with her legs flung out, until the first shadows slanted across the washstand, and patterned the floor.

Several times she tried to get up and go to the bathroom, dreaming of the wash of cool water over her skin. Every pore seemed choked with grease and sweat, wool dust furred her throat and antrums. Len had told her always to have a shower as soon as she got home. It took the burden out of the day's toil, he reckoned. But it was like trying to fight your way upwards through swirling water, and each time she fell back, into a well of darkness. Only when she heard Len's step on the landing, the squeak of the door, her eyelids flew open, her eyes and arms embraced him across the narrow room.

And there he was, her beloved . . . chunky shouldered in a cream silk shirt with a half moon of sweat under his armpits, in one hand his leather port holding his working clothes, hurling himself through the air to smother her body with his own.

"Lennie, Lennie," she crooned, rocking his gingery head against her breast. His mouth mumbled on hers, his hands ran over her tired body.

A long time afterwards they heard Lou calling them to tea in the querulous voice that meant she'd lost at euchre again. They lay naked, curled against each other. He smoothed the delicious little wrinkle between her hip and thigh. It was wet with sweat.

"Why do we fit so beautifully together?"

"Look how beautifully we fit together!"

The curve of hip and thigh and shoulder and breast, whitened with shadow, the lilac dusk in the room, the huge, old-fashioned wardrobe, the china jug and basin, the little white plastic wireless, the perfect shadow of the jacaranda tree on the flaky ceiling . . . all this moistened with the breath and kiss of lovers, till it became a sanctuary for love. All this broken into by the querulous voice of the old woman, shrieking in rage and disappointment up the narrow stairs.

"How many times do I have to tell yous. Your tea's gettin' cold." They showered together, as they always did, splashing water in riotous abandonment, while the old woman downstairs shuddered, totting up the gas bill in her head.

Len had never known anything so lovely as the golden-skinned, cropped-headed girl with the swollen belly, cheeks pink from love, gazing at him through the funnel of water. Beth had never known anything so lovely as the deep-chested, white-skinned man with the wet, golden spikes of hair, and the muscly shoulders, spurting water from his nose and mouth.

"Look at them ears. They're filthy," he said, and, as she

16

dodged away, he tenderly slapped her wet, slippery bottom. They leapt and tumbled like big, glittering white fish under the green water. He fondled her breasts, traced the faint blue veins across the great white globe of her belly . . . wet, shining, laughing, they stood in the cracked enamel bath, the spray rainbowing through the electric light.

Dressed and still wet-headed, they ran hand in hand down the shabby staircase, putting on their company faces with their clothes. But how could they hide the glow and tremble of love that made their limbs weak and their voices drowsy? They sat staidly on either side of the white linen tablecloth, spotted with gravy, eyes downcast, smelling of love, glowing with love, while the landlady moved wearily from stove to table with plates of curry and cups of weak tea.

"It's Hughie's birthday tonight," she said, placing a shrunken sponge cake in the middle of the cloth, like a conjurer. "I couldn't get a bigger one for y' Hughie. I was late home from me cards."

Her husband tucked his serviette under his chin. "Lose again Lou?" he said maliciously. "How much was it this time?"

"I lost a fiver and it's not your money Hughie," she snapped. "And if I lost today that means I break evens."

"You said that last week," he taunted. 'How a woman of your age can lose 'er money week after week to a lotta ol' chooks . . ."

" 'Old your tongue Hughie. It's me only pleasure. Slavin' week after week, and you even begrudge me that." Her voice cracked on the edge of a sob.

"Is Polly comin' in for 'er tea?" He jerked his thumb towards the tiny front parlour, changing the subject, satisfied over her tears.

"She's probably sulkin'," Lou said in a loud, hissing whisper. "I told her she'd better get out, bag and baggage, and she threatened to throw 'erself over the Gap. D'you think she might do it? She's mad you know, gone in the head. She don't know what she's doin'."

"I dunno why she 'as to park 'erself on us. I was never that friendly with the ol' man, only usta deliver 'is meat," said Hughie gloomily, stuffing his shrunken mouth with curry.

"You was friendly enough with 'er though when 'er father had a quid or two, and she was always gone on you," Lou snapped. "Hughie always was a ladies' man, though you wouldn't think so to look at 'im now . . . ever since 'e lost 'is teeth. Poor soul, when I think of 'er and 'er sister in the old days. The

17

beautiful Tickner girls . . . they was always so well turned out, and they had their own carriage."

Hughie adroitly turned the conversation into safer channels.

"She's certainly gone to the pack since 'er Mum died. Though they say she starved 'er to death . . . too mingy to spend tuppence. After the ol' man went bankrupt they said there was bags of sovereigns hidden under the floor boards in that old 'ouse of theirs in Redfern."

"Well she hasn't paid me a penny board. All she's done is park 'erself in me best room and clutter it up with a lotta junk only fit for the tip," said Lou darkly. "She's been 'ere three months and without a word of a lie in three months she 'asn't 'ad a bath. How can I ask anyone here with 'er in me lounge room? I'd be ashamed."

"She's 'ad 'er rest. Why don't she go back to Redfern where she belongs? She's lived there twenty years," he grumbled.

"She's afraid of 'er ol' mother's ghost. Reckons she saw it goin' up the 'all. I'd put her out in the street but I don't want 'er death on me conscience. You'll haveta tell her to go Hughie. She'll take notice of you. She was sweet on you once. D'you reckon she'll throw 'erself over the Gap Len?"

Lou appealed to Len, sitting silent over his curry.

"No," he said. "Course she won't. The ones you've gotta watch are the quiet ones that says nothin' about it."

"Have you ast her about the house yet Len?"

Len shifted awkwardly in his chair. "Yeah, we asted her, but she's scared to sub-let. Reckons the agents'll have the coppers onto 'er."

"Keep workin' on 'er Len," Hughie mumbled, curry dribbling down his jaw. "She's bound to crack sometime."

"If she don't throw 'erself over the Gap. She's mad you know, gone in the head. She don't know what she's doin'," Lou said.

"If she does, good riddance, but we won't have no such luck," said Hughie.

The parlour rustled and creaked like a nest of mice, and into the kitchen came a travesty of a woman in a beaded georgette dress, green with age, hitched high above her bony knees. White pulpy skin, dyed red hair, a gauze scarf to hide the bald patch on top . . . green and mildewed with decay, she floated into the dim, greasy kitchen under the pale-green, fly-spotted satin lampshade.

" 'Appy birthday Hughie," she said.

"Sit down. Make yourself at 'ome Polly," he said with heavy

sarcasm. " 'Ave a bit of me birthday cake." He winked at the assembled company. "All dressed up tonight Pol . . . you're a sight for sore eyes. Looks like she just come off the beat in Riley Street."

"Got back early from the Gap Pol," said Lou with false cheerfulness.

The meal proceeded in heavy silence, broken only by the drumming of the locusts in the crepe myrtles, the wail of the baby from the flat upstairs.

"Found anythin' yet luv?" said Lou, looking pointedly in the direction of Beth's stomach, hidden under the edge of the tablecloth.

"No, nothin' yet," Beth blushed and mumbled.

"Two babies in the house is two too many," Lou moaned. "You can't move in the back yard now for the nappies on the line and Mrs. 'Arris always washin', washin', washin'. I said to 'er, 'I wish you'd find another place,' but she just said 'it's hard,' and so it is. But 'e makes good money with his taxi truck and I'm too old to be burdened with other people's troubles."

Beth sighed. Only last week she'd dressed herself up in her blue crepe-de-chine maternity frock, and visited an agent in the Cross, a smart, slick looking young man with hair like boot polish, interviewing his clients in front of a geometric drape in red, yellow and black.

"We've got something here in Redfern," he said. "But I don't feel it would suit you. A bit rough." He looked pointedly at her little blue lace gloves, his fat fingers pensively tapping his chin.

Beth wished she hadn't worn them. "Anythin'd suit us," she cried desperately. "Beggars can't be choosers."

"It's three hundred quid for the furniture," he said. "And of course it's condemned. Might come down anytime with the slum clearance."

"There's not twenty quid's worth here," said Len, in disgust, looking round the three-roomed humpy, sunken sideways with damp and age.

They'd gone back to Lou and Hughie and full board in the two-storeyed semi in Moller Street.

"That's what comes of bein' kindhearted," Lou moaned, bringing on the prunes and boiled custard. "I could get twice as much for these rooms bed and breakfast, and not 'alf the bother."

It was true too, Beth thought. She was goodhearted, she served up a decent meal and plenty of it, her charges were reasonable.

She warmed towards the little dumpy woman with the tight perm and the shabby cardigan pulled over her best dress.

"Never mind, we'll get somethin' before the baby comes," she said cheerfully.

"I know you're tryin' hard luv," said Lou sympathetically. "But there's some as wouldn't 'elp a young couple if their lives depended on it." She glared towards Polly Tickner, slupping and sucking her curry through her loose upper set.

"I'll get a coupla bottles," said Hughie, suddenly expansive under the mellowing influence of another birthday. "I put them up a coupla weeks ago. They should 'ave a real kick in 'em by now." He waddled out, bandy-legged, limping from his varicose ulcer, to fumble and curse under the stairs, where he planted his home brew.

"Why doncha let Len and Beth rent your ol' place off you Pol?" said Lou, putting her cards on the table.

"I'll do what I think best Lou," Polly said slyly. "I got to have somewhere to rest me poor, sick bones."

"Are you goin' back there then Pol?" Lou pressed her advantage ruthlessly. "Mr. 'Arris upstairs 'as got a taxi truck. He'll be pleased to shift you."

Polly sniffed noncommittally, cleaning the gristle out of her teeth with the hem of her dress, baring rolled stockings and blue-veined thighs.

"'Ave a snort Len? Pol? Lou? Beth? . . . 'ave a snort. Best bitta brew you ever tasted Len, absolutely scarlet non pareil. Leaves Tooheys an' Tooths for dead."

Hughie skipped around the little kitchen, a grotesque shadow on the greasy brick walls, filling glasses, froth spurting from the top of the bottles.

"Here's luck," said Len, holding his schooner up to the light. A pale brown sediment floated in the amber fluid. "How old are you Hughie?"

"Seventy-two today," said Hughie proudly. "An' never missed a day's work in me life. Worked butcherin' for the same boss for forty years. Always first there to open up at four-thirty. Never missed a mornin' yet. . . ."

"Scabby ol' bastard," Len muttered.

"Always up at four o'clock winter and summer since I was a boy."

"And always in bed with the chooks," Lou butted in wearily.

"'Ard work never killed anybody. You die in bed."

"Hughie's terrible afraid of dyin' . . . aren't you Hughie?" Lou gave a malicious little giggle.

"I'll never retire. Butcherin' all me life and look what I got to show for it." Hugh held up a gnarled hand with the thumb and index finger missing. "Chopped them orf when I was servin' me time. Coulda been a rich man today if I hadn't worked for wages all me life. Coulda owned half of Bondi by now. I can remember when Bondi was just a heapa sandhills and scrub, goin' dirt cheap. Nobody'd buy it then. We thought it was out in the never-never. An' look at it now." He shook his head over his home brew.

"Hughie never did 'ave any brains," mourned Lou. "I dunno why I ever married 'im. When I was a girl in Sunny Corner all the young fellers was after me. Did I ever show you me photer album?"

She rummaged in the drawer of the sideboard, bringing out photos yellowed with age, girls in white muslin with big hats, the cold, empty, windy streets of Sunny Corner, made glamorous with faded dreams.

"Sunny Corner . . . I'd love to go back there. Everything'd be changed now though . . . not like I remember it when I was a girl."

The three old people sat, gazing at the faded sepia photographs in the kitchen, littered with dirty dishes. Len and Beth slipped away into the hall. Lou scuttled after them.

"Ask 'er again Len," she said, jerking her thumb towards the kitchen and the wizened figure of Polly Tickner, making eyes at Hughie over the rim of her glass. "Wait till she gets 'alf stung and ask 'er again. She might slip you the key."

Len grinned. "Yeah, I'll ask her again, later on."

Lou swayed like the faded palm by the hatstand.

"Look at Lou. She's a two-pot screamer, always 'as been." Hughie doubled up with laughter. The doorbell shrilled.

"That'll be Gladdie and little Esme come for Hughie's birthday. She's got brains my Glad. Takes after me. But never ask about 'er 'usband. They don't get on. 'E's mixed up in the rackets."

A tall, angular woman with a long, mean, hard-bitten face like her father's, strode briskly into the hall. Glad ran an S.P. book in her mother's kitchen on Saturday afternoons. Little Esme, a lissom, buck-toothed teenager with an Elvis Presley locket looped round her neck, scowled down at her grandmother.

"I dunno why we had to be dragged out tonight," she whined. "I wanted to watch TV. There's nothin' to do here Nan."

Len and Beth escaped through the half-open doorway.

"Call in for a drink on your way back," Lou shrieked. "It'll give you your chance to ask Polly again. Glad says I'm hard but I couldn't stomach two babies."

Their hurrying footsteps drowned her voice. Arm in arm they turned the corner, fleeing from the smell of home brew and mice and mildew, fleeing from the muddled, myriad, stagnant, scheming lives of Moller Street.

Chapter Three

☆

BETH stood, gazing perversely and longingly at an impossibly high-bosomed, flat-stomached model in a skin-tight sheath.

"D'you reckon old Polly Tickner'll give us the key?" she said wistfully.

"If I slip 'er a few quid key money, and we can get a Chamber Magistrate to fix it up legal, she might be in it," said Len, mooning over the latest model Holden, enthroned behind glass.

Oxford Street lapped them round with promises, lured them with impossible dreams . . . the whirl of lights, the purr of cars, the distant, velvety roar of the city, haloed with gold. Pressed close together they ambled dreamily through the summer night, eating bananas bought from a street stall, dropping the peel in the gutters as they went.

Streamlined refrigerators, laminex kitchen suites, deluxe washing machines, double beds in polished maple, TV sets . . . a Hollywood Fairytale . . . carpet your home from wall to wall and trade in your furniture, no deposit and easy terms.

Will we buy a truckload of dreams, and carry it back to Moller Street . . . no deposit . . . easy terms . . . stack it all in the little upstairs room and shift out on the landing? Will we erect the dignified double bed, best maple veneers, under the leafy trees in Centennial Park and lie there in connubial bliss, to the envy of the old deadbeats, clasping their metho bottles for warmth, on a heap of newspapers under the Moreton Bays?

Will we set up the laminex kitchen suite, pop-up toaster and electric jug by the bust of Henry Parkes, his frowning brow green with verdigris?

No deposit . . . easy terms . . . everything for baby! High chairs, commodes, playpens, baths, bassinettes, bootees, bonnets, bunny rugs . . . everything for baby. But baby is kicking in his mother's womb . . . he's finished with confined spaces.

No deposit . . . easy terms . . . I've got a kewpie doll with long nylon legs to call me own, who never gets pregnant, but stands under a pool of gold at a street light in the Cross and whistles up the cruising taxis.

"She only pays thirty-five bob rent," said Beth. "We could save on that."

They had already been out one night to reconnoitre round the old house in Redfern where Polly Tickner and her mother had existed for the last twenty years, ever since old man Tickner lost his money. Chained and bolted, with a high picket fence edged with two strands of barbed wire, under a veil of pot plants in hanging baskets, kerosene tins and chamber pots, it presented a formidable appearance.

"There's ten dawgs buried in that front yard," said Polly Tickner, crooking her moonlit finger in the bridal fern. And it seemed to Beth that the ghosts of the ten dogs rose up and howled and fought and bristled over their ghostly bones, among the waist-high thistles.

"Mother never et no more 'n a bird, pick, pick, pick," moaned Polly's voice down the chimney, and the little white supplicating hands begged and pleaded through the picket fence. "Could you spare us a bowl of soup dear?"

A broken shutter, swinging in the wind, bang, bang, banged.

But it was an empty house and Polly was scared to come home. A crowded tram jarred up Oxford Street. "Look," shrilled Beth, clutching at Len's arm. "There's Dawnie from work. She must be goin' out to Bondi. Look, the little blonde one in white shorts. Dawnie . . ." The grind of the wheels drowned her voice.

"Shut up for Christ's sake," growled Len. "You're not out in the bloody bush now. You always make a show of a man . . ."

They walked on in silence. She was cold and withdrawn as the icy models in the shop windows. He peeped under the swing of her hair.

"What's up?" he grinned.

"You hurt me feelings," she said, the glint of tears in her eyes, her mouth trembling.

He put his lips on her hair. "I'll kiss it better." He squeezed her fingers.

Beth giggled. "Now who's makin' a show! The girls at work reckon I'm mad goin' walkin' with you every night. They reckon I'll soon get over that after we been married a few years."

She pressed closer to his side, firmly believing that she would never get over it, but would go walking through the streets of Sydney, through the summer grass in Centennial Park, with the swings creaking drowsily on Sunday afternoons, through this golden dream for the rest of her life. A cocoon was spun around them, and the rest of the world only entered in by virtue of their loving. She swayed along Oxford Street, and nothing could shatter her self-confidence, her warm, all-embracing, maternal calm.

"You're such a kid," Len said to her sometimes, sadly fondling her on his knees. "It seems a pity you've got to grow up."

Their mouths moved together like moth's wings under the black crepe myrtles, the locusts shrilled over their heads in frantic agony.

"Do you love me Len?"

"You know I do."

"Tell me then."

"Words are cheap."

"Tell me just once . . . say something nice."

"Lollies . . . strawberries and cream . . . a big block of chocolate."

"Oh Len, you are terrible."

"That's something nice. Come upstairs and I'll show you how I love you."

They crept through the hall. Hughie, primed with home brew, was lunging round the kitchen table in his tin helmet and rubber truncheon. He'd been sworn in as a special constable during the war. Little Esme shrieked. Lou sat in the rocker, the tears streaming down her cheeks.

"Hughie never did have any brains."

"Look at this Lou." Polly pulled up her skirt to her jazz garters. "Found these stockings in me old trunk, thirty year old, you never see nothin' like that these days."

Lou was thumbing through her old Christmas cards, with maudlin sentimentality.

"All these cards from Sammy Snow," she said. "Every year, never forgets me. 'E's a lovely man, isn't 'e Glad? Boarded with me ten years, sergeant of police, retired now. You'll see 'im next Saturday Pol. Comes down to see me and puts a few quid on the horses with Glad. Never forgets me at Christmas time. A lovely man and always the gentleman." She gazed witheringly at Hughie, cavorting round the rocker.

" 'Ere's one from that tall skinny man who had the top room durin' the war. Hughie reckoned he was a lovely feller. Went off owing Glad fifteen quid in bets and me five quid back rent. A great bettin' man, wasn't 'e Glad? 'Ad a system on the two-year-olds. Never sent 'is address, only the card." She turned it over gloomily. "But I got even with 'im. I kept 'is ration books. I let that back room to a lovely girl this mornin' Glad. New Australian, asted me to call 'er Olga. I told 'er no men allowed in the room, and the look she give me, I could see she was a lady. Hughie, for Gawd's sake don't be such a fool. I dunno how you're goin' to open up the shop in the mornin'. He's usually in bed by seven. Hughie's afraid to go out at night without 'is rubber truncheon since 'e was a copper durin' the war, aren't you Hughie?" She laughed maliciously.

"If you knew what I know you'd keep your wits about you too," said Hughie darkly. "Ol' Snowy Bassett, five times a murderer, sits under the jail wall in the tram shed in Paddington every night. 'E's still got the marks of the 'cat' on 'is back. He lifted up his shirt and showed me. They let 'im out for good behaviour after twenty years, but he can't seem to get used to it."

"Got a good thing for Saturdee Glad. They reckon Georgie Moore . . ." Lou's voice floated up the stairs.

Something soft and fluttering flopped against Beth's ankles on the landing.

"What is it Len?" She clung to his arm. "Turn the light on quick."

"Look, it's only a baby bat," he said. The little, big-eyed creature flopped along on its elbows, for all the world like a crawling baby, trying to scuttle out of the light. Len picked it up carefully in his handkerchief, leant out the bathroom window, and deposited it in the jacaranda tree.

They undressed in the moonlight, and lay on top of the sheets. It was stifling hot in the little room. The sky was like a dark square of silk through the bedroom window. Only the little red eye of the wireless mesmerized them through the gloom.

"How do you know you'll always love me Len?"

"I know."

"But how do you know? You've had lots of girls."

"That's me form, that's all."

The baby squirmed under her belly. She took his hand. "Feel him Len. He's movin'. Can you feel him?"

"Yeah, little bugger wants to boot his ol' man out of bed."

"The girls at work reckon I'll get the bullet pretty soon."

"Time you stopped work anyway. Don't want anythin' to happen to 'is nibs there . . ."

"I'd like to work just a little bit longer. We might be able to save a deposit on a house. The girls at work reckon . . ."

"Go to sleep darl. It's gettin' late. I've got a bugger of a job

26

tomorrer holdin' up rivets between decks on the *Shazadah*."

"Len . . ."

Go to sleep . . . go to sleep . . .

"The casing of Sputnik should be seen in Sydney early on Friday morning and Saturday morning in the north-western sky. Tomorrow it should be seen at 4.36 a.m. at 30 degrees elevation. . . ."

Len leaned across and switched off the wireless. There was a violent shriek from the back yard.

"What was that?" whispered Beth. Len leapt out of bed. Together they craned through the window. In the moonlit path to the lavatory a statuesque blonde wrestled with the grotesque figure of Hughie in tin hat and truncheon.

"Just a liddle kiss, a liddle kiss on me birthday," he crooned.

A shaft of light flooded the path. "H-uu-gh-ee. Glad, bring your father in. 'E's frightenin' Olga out in the garden. 'E never did have any brains."

"Absolutely scarlet non pareil . . ."

"Hughie feelin' his home brew," whispered Len. Beth giggled.

Peace in Moller Street. . . . Polly Tickner kept her light on in the best room till well after midnight, scraping and rummaging through her father's old papers like a cockroach in a sea of litter, turning over cancelled mortgages, bills of sale and bad debts.

Lou lay dreaming, her hair in battleships, her mouth puckered tenderly like a child's, dreaming of Sunny Corner and Sammy Snow, that lovely man, who might have shared her brass-knobbed double bed instead of Hughie.

Hughie snored and yelped in his sleep, his gums fallen in, his teeth grinning from the cup on the washstand, chasing down innumerable Paddington alleys, his rubber truncheon dragging behind him, the ghosts of his conscience crying vengeance at his heels.

Beth stirred and woke once just before dawn, when the baby turned over. Len slept beside her, his arm under her head, his gilt lashes making childlike, defenceless shadows on his cheeks. In the moonlit hall the little bat fluttered and rustled like a discarded love letter. Under the stairs there was a loud report. A bottle of Hughie's home brew blew up and trickled onto the feltex.

At 4.36 a.m. Sputnik whirled across the north-western sky at 30 degrees. The baby kicked and the earth turned. There was the soft squeak of a door opening, a whisper and a kiss. It was Olga, speeding her departing lover into the dawn.

Chapter Four

☆

DAWNIE's hair shone bright as polished brass between the oil-black rovers.

"Better pull your finger out Kennie. Dick's watchin' you."

Her cheeky, pretty little face, a smear of grease on one soft cheek, grinned up at him. For the like of him he couldn't help the quick look over his shoulder.

"Got you tied to his apron strings," she jeered.

"Well, I am his offsider," Kennie said. "Naturally he wants to know what I'm doin'."

"Oh! Naturally," she lisped in a high, affected voice. "Why doncha come down off your high horse Kennie. Got your eye on that pannikin boss's job and you think you're just it."

"Is it a crime to wanta better yourself?"

"Ah, get away from me, you bloody bosses' crawler. You make me heave." She twitched one enticing shoulder, and turned her back on him, threading up the shuttle with skilful, nimble fingers, not bothering to switch off the rover as most of the other women did.

He grabbed her hand. "You'll get your fingers caught in there one of these days. Then you'll have somethin' to squawk about."

"Ah bum!" They wrestled among the whirring spindles, his hands all over her.

"Cut that out!" Her fresh young voice was hard and brittle like breaking glass.

"Aw Blondie, when are you goin' to give me a break? You know I'm crazy about you." He bent his head, trying to kiss the tender curve of her cheek.

"Here's Dick," she whispered. With obvious unconcern they turned back to the machine, breathless, eyes sparkling. Dick's round, weak face peered at them over the top of the rover, his mouth stretched in a lascivious grin.

"Havin' fun in there? Are you young Dawnie's offsider or mine?"

"Just helpin' Blondie out with a bit of a tangle here," Ken mumbled, his eyes fixed on the bobbins, neck turkey red.

"I can see that." Dick's mouth twisted. "Well if it don't break your heart too much to leave 'er, I gotta job for you over the other side of the mill. C'mon, get crackin'."

"Sure, sure Dick. You're the boss." Ken pinched Dawnie's bottom as he passed. "Tonight, how about tonight?" he whispered. "We'll go for a swim out to Bondi. How about it?"

"On the bloody tram I s'pose?"

"That's right. What are you used to gorgeous . . . a naughty on the back seat of a Rolls?"

"Are you comin' or are you goin' to stand there natterin' all day?" Dick bawled.

Dawnie grinned. "You better run. The boss is callin' you."

"I can hear 'im." Ken turned huffily and strode away up the aisle without a backward glance. Thoughtfully Dawnie watched him go. "You wanta watch him, Dawnie." Fat Julie stuck her head round the machine. "He can't keep his hands to 'isself."

Dawnie tied off the wool ends savagely. ''Ah, he's all piss and wind like a barber's cat . . . a real Mumma's boy."

"Gawd your language is on the nose Dawnie." Julie wagged her head sorrowfully. "Are you goin' out with him?"

"I might."

"They're all the same, the men. Only got their minds on one thing."

"Have you got to first base with young Dawnie yet kid?" Dick said.

"No . . . she's a funny kid. D'ya reckon she'd be in it?"

"She's a real tough nut to crack," Dick said thoughtfully. "That Shirl'd be in anythin', but I've noticed it all along with Dawnie. Foul-mouthed and all that but she won't let none of the boys handle 'er. She give young Curly a back'ander the other day, fair across the mush. Dunno what he said to 'er."

Jealousy forked through Ken's body. "It's time Curl got a knockback. He's been makin' it pretty hot." He gazed wistfully up the aisle. "Jees she's a luscious sort though Dick. I'd love to make her."

Dick grinned sympathetically. "When you're as old as me son, you'll know no woman's worth it. She'll be in the puddin' club, and then where'd you be? Anyway I wouldn't get mixed up with a mill girl if I was you." He lowered his voice. "You can go a long way with this firm. You're not one of these logs." He jerked his big, stupid head at the mill. "When ol' Greenie retires

and I'm foreman, you'll be next in line for leadin' 'and . . . a
job for life."

The whistle blew. Dawnie bent down and switched off her
machine. Silence seeped over the mill, thrummed in her ears,
rolled its blank peace over the mind.

"Look," said Dawnie, jerking her thumb over her shoulder.
"Still got his head down and his arse up. Hey Kennie . . . the
whistle blew . . . didn't you hear it?"

She walked to the washroom, queued up behind a mob of
women, sluiced her face and hands with cold water, ran a pocket
comb through her silky blonde hair, beginning to darken at the
roots. She strolled, unconcernedly swinging her handbag, out
the door of the mill.

"Hey Dawnie . . . Hey . . ." It was Ken, running to catch
her up, his hand under her elbow. "What about tonight?"

She looked him up and down with a level stare. "Okay."

He could hardly believe his good fortune. "Where'll I pick
you up?" he stuttered. "I dunno your address."

It was the first time he'd ever seen her flustered. "Never mind
me address!" she snapped. "And I haven't got a phone number
either. I'll meet you outside Museum Station, seven o'clock. It'll
save time. And don't keep me waitin'."

"Save time for what?" He squeezed her arm.

"Cut it out." She jerked away from him. "We're goin' swimmin', aren't we, and if you reckon you're goin' to turn tonight
into a wrestlin' match, we can call the whole thing off, right now."

"Did I say that?"

"No, but it's written all over you."

He stood, crestfallen, as she swung out the gate.

"See you tonight," he bawled after her. She nodded, plodding
doggedly down the footpath, not bothering to turn her head.

Vaguely dissatisfied at their parting, he watched her go. Her
little round buttocks bounced under her overall, the muscly, tan
calves of her legs rippled like silk in the sunlight. A pleasant
thrill of anticipation crawled down his spine. He imagined them
lying on the dark sand behind the rocks at Bondi, undoing the
straps of her cozzie, his hands full of her breasts, her wet body,
the taste of salt in her neck.

The aching sunlight of Alexandria, the dazzle of metal, tin
and galvanized iron, smote his eyeballs. Two bedraggled coconut palms rattled in a dry wind. At his back loomed the barbed
wire encirclement of the mill, smog-blackened bricks, turreted
like a travesty of a mediaeval castle.

"A job for life," Dick had said. Life . . . Jumbuck Mills . . .
Worsted Spinners and Weavers . . . W. H. Holler Pty Ltd . . .
Enquiries . . . Office . . . Despatch . . . Receiving—No Vacancies.
LIFE. . . . "You are sentenced to be imprisoned at Her Majesty's
pleasure for the term of your natural life."

One last glimpse of Dawnie, swinging out of sight between
the smudged brick chimneys, the pale, wispy Australian sky
fragile as hope above her head. He ran to catch his bus.

Dawnie walked home through the long, asphalt lanes of factories, filled with managers' cars, and the steady rattle of
machinery. Past the little semis, with cracked plaster walls in
yellow, cocoa and liver red, defending their privacy from the street
with rows of murderous iron spikes.

Her mother's house was fawn weatherboard, backed onto the
lane, with a paintless, corrugated iron roof, the rusty ends curling
up over the porch.

Hazel was leaning over the gate, her long, silky blonde hair
loose on her shoulders, a cigarette in her mouth, a gorgeous
Japanese kimono half open to her waist.

"Hello darl. Just nick down an' get some fish an' chips for tea,"
she said. "I'm fagged out."

"Jeez Mumma. Get off me back." Dawnie pushed past her.
"And do your neck up. I can see everything you got."

Hazel laughed but she twitched her kim shut. "There's warm
in the bath. I left it in for you," she yelled up the path.

Hazel loved to stand at her front gate watching the workers
straggle home, exchanging a friendly word with this one and that
one, while the air deepened from pale gold to lilac, and a little
wind fanned the pale hair back from her forehead. It was her
time for social contacts and provided there had been no brawls,
or harsh words during the week, a pleasant time when she was at
peace with the world.

"Terrible hot isn't it," she'd say, her beautiful body, lissom and
athletic as a young girl's, draped over the cyclone.

"Terrible muggy Haze. Must be the bushfires up the mountains."

"Reckon we'll get a Southerly Buster tonight?"

"Hard to say. We're gettin' the sort of weather we uster to get
before the war. I reckon it's these atomic explosions. They're
changin' the climate. . . ."

Alexandria was tolerant, and large-hearted. Live and let live
was their motto. They were always willing to forgive and forget.
If the noise and abuse at one of Hazel's regular grog-ups was

31

worse than usual, she just faded away for a week, and went to stay at her sister's in Forest Lodge, only showing her face back in Alexandria when things had simmered down. Memories were short. Alexandria neither approved nor condemned Hazel's behaviour, they accepted her and for that she was grateful.

"She's a good worker," they said, and Hazel slaved in the hat factory, swept the footpath, brassoed the door knocker, polished the hall, kalsomined the kitchen, organized a party, got drunk and took a new lover, all with the same unquenchable, unsatisfied energy.

Married at sixteen, Hazel had three daughters. It was impossible to imagine her a grandmother, but it was true. Her eldest girl, just nineteen, with a toddler at her skirts and a new baby, lived round the corner, the second daughter, sick of brawls and beer parties, had gone fruit picking to Queensland and never came back. Dawnie, sixteen years old, with the maturity of a grown woman, was the baby. Her daughters were all beautiful girls, with their mother's perfect figure, and finely boned, classical features. Hazel had an almost sisterly relationship with her children. They accepted her fatalistically, for what she was, loving her for her courage, her rough tenderness and good humour, rejecting her for her amorality and the booze. Dawnie felt it the worst. It had bred in her an angry pride and fierce resentment, a hurt that found refuge in fierce chastity and a foul mouth.

And Hazel . . . she was squandering the Indian summer of her youth, knowing with brutal honesty that at the end of it lay only the hat factory, the bottle and a cold bed. Yet all her dissipation left hardly a mark on her face and figure. The violet eyes were hard, but they could still warm with generosity, the full mouth drooped a little at the corners, the curve of the soft cheek and chin was faintly coarsened, the pale hair brassy in bright sunlight, but the white-skinned body remained firm and alluring as a young girl's.

"I'll make a cuppa tea Dawnie," she called, moving briskly around the kitchen, straightening the china dogs and the photos of her grandchildren on the dresser. Sunlight danced in the starched lace curtains, shimmered on the peacock blue and scarlet of her kim, gilded the loose gold of her hair.

"By the way darl . . ." she paused, her bright head cocked towards the bathroom. "I'm havin' a few friends in this evenin' . . ." Keep it dignified Haze, she thought cynically. What you really mean is you're turnin' the joint into a brothel tonight.

"Did you hear me Dawnie. I'm havin' . . ."

"I heard you." Dawnie came out in snow-white shorts and shirt, rubbing her soft hair in a towel. "Why doncha cut it out Mumma?" Her weary little face twisted with helpless anger.

"You're turnin' into a real nark," Hazel said sulkily, keeping her back to her daughter.

"Thank Christ I'm goin' out. Who are you plannin' to share your bed with this time, or is it a big surprise?"

Hazel whirled round, eyes blazing, the teapot swaying dangerously in her hand. "Ah, shut your dirty little mouth or I'll shut it for you."

"Lissen Mumma." Dawn stuck her bottom lip out. It was trembling a little. "You better cut out your trollopin' around or I warn you I'll shoot through like Norma did and leave you on your own."

"Do what you bloody well like," Hazel said. "I'm not goin' to have a bit of a kid tellin' me what to do."

"Have it your own way." Dawnie sipped at her tea, her shoulders slumped, her voice tart as a lemon drink. Hazel stretched herself on the day-bed, playing for time. Her kim fell open, and she lay, admiring one graceful leg, marble white in the filtered sunlight.

"Who's the boy friend?" she said slyly.

Dawnie's elaborate unconcern with boys worried her. It was something completely outside her range of experience.

"None of your business!" Dawnie snapped.

"Bringin' him home for a drink after?" Hazel narrowed her eyes under the high, curved, golden brows.

"What for? So you can get your paws on him. No thanks. Do you want two pieces of fish or one?"

"One an' two-bob's worth of chips. Take the money off the top of the dresser. And Dawnie . . ." She got up, putting out her hand with an oddly helpless gesture . . . "don't be crooked on your old Mum."

Her daughter gazed at her with disenchanted eyes.

"Jeez Mumma you're a bitch of a thing." She banged the fly-wire door behind her.

Hazel watched Dawnie stride down the pavement like a flaxen-headed boy in her shorts and shirt, her hair tied back in a wet pony tail, her body outlined in a tender, radiant, golden haze.

She moved aimlessly round the room, flicking at the fine dust that always sifted through the air of Alexandria and settled on her furniture. Muttering to herself she took the polish tin off the shelf and redid the lino, rubbing and buffing, down on her hands and knees till the cheap felt base took on a glow that reflected the sun. But no matter how she scrubbed and rubbed, like Lady Macbeth the spot on her conscience would not be erased. All she could see in the shining floor was her own beautiful, petulant, brilliant image, all she could hear was the harsh, weary voice of Dawnie echoing through the spotless rooms: "Jeez Mumma you're a bitch of a thing."

A wayward blowfly buzzed against the hot glass of the window. Hazel stalked it warily round the kitchen, pounced on it with a vicious burst from the fly spray. . . . "Got you you bugger." It tumbled, buzzing in its death throes, onto the window sill.

Triumphantly Hazel surveyed the little room, heavy with the stink of fly spray. I got a real thirst up, she thought. I'll just crack a bottle now, while Dawnie's up the street.

Dawnie, Museum Station, the streets of Sydney were bathed in a sultry, pinkish glow.

"So you didn't stand me up Blondie?" Laughing exultantly Ken swung her onto the footboard of the Bondi tram, packed with a sweating crowd. They lurched down Oxford Street, strap-hanging, giggling with the joy of young things let loose on a summer's night.

"Isn't it fabulous," said Dawnie dreamily, and Ken wasn't sure if she meant the night, the ride, the promise of cool water or his arm round her waist. Lighted shopfronts whirled past, cars tooted and changed gears, people were vague, blurred shadows on the pavement, he felt the warmth of her body as they swayed together. The tram took on an intoxicating holiday atmosphere. A mob of kids, cozzies and towels tucked under their arms, swung and whistled, defying death, hanging by their toes over the road. The trammie, sweaty and dusty from a long hot shift, grinned good humouredly, edging his way along the footboard. . . . "Fares please."

"If you keep lookin' at me like that I'll run off with you, and never bring you back," Ken muttered in Dawnie's ear. She dropped her eyes in delicious confusion. His heart thumped. This was a new Dawnie, not the coarse, brittle mill girl with a smudge of grease on one cheek, but a warm, round, glowing female with demure eyes and enticing buttocks, like the girls in the Pepsi ads. His body ached with impatience to get her away from the summer crowds into the darkness behind the rocks, unzip her shorts and enjoy all her ripeness.

The sun sank in a blood-red ball balanced on the roofs of the city. They smelt the tang of the sea, drowning the stink of asphalt, hot tar, exhaust and sweat. It was Bondi, a great, dark, silken, heaving surf in the heart of Sydney. They followed the crowds, streaming off trams and buses, laughing, pushing, moving like a great weary wave across the lawns, moving inexorably, patiently, thankfully, towards the thump of breakers, the moonlit curl of white on the sand. The milk bars and hot dog stands were jammed with people, dazzling girls in skin-tight bathing suits, clinging to the arms of brawny, godlike, brief-trunked young men, kids with wet heads and sandy costumes darting through a forest of legs, sand gritting under bare toes, the smell of salt, juke boxes blaring out across the sweaty asphalt . . . dum tiddly um tum tum BOOLAH. . . . Ice Cold . . . Shelley's famous drinks . . . Street's ice cream, the cream of the coast . . . Rockets, chocolate-coated Sputniks . . . pedal pushers, sloppy joes, faded jeans, crew cuts and pony tails . . . dum, tiddly um tum tum tum BOOLAH. A string of cars turned into the Promenade, women in cotton beach dresses shepherded mobs of kids between the headlights. There wasn't an inch of space on the sand.

Hand in hand Ken and Dawnie picked their way delicately between the sprawled bodies, old and young, fat and thin, rich and poor, all shapes and sizes huddled under the deep blue starry roof of the sky. Bondi in a heat wave was a great leveller. Multistorey flats and luxury hotels, ablaze with lights, craned out over the surf, clinging to the craggy black rocks that marked the boundary of the beach. Farther up the hill the houses of the rich and successful gazed disdainfully out to sea, the whole, wild, magnificent sweep of the coast caught in their picture windows. An old woman in a shabby black dress pulled up high above her knees, paddled happily on the edge of the surf. The golden boys and girls stretched their immortal limbs along the sand beside their portable radiograms . . . Dum tiddly um tum tum tum BOOLAH . . . OH! God, let us cling to the beloved fairytale, the rim of golden sand against the creaming surf, the sun bronzed gods and goddesses drinking Pepsi in the moonlight . . . let us forget the stink of smog in the summer night, let us forget the grease under our finger-nails . . . boy wanted sixteen years . . . nobody over twenty-five need apply . . . No Vacancies . . . and golden boys and girls all must, like chimney sweepers come to dust. . . . BOOLAH!

On the bleached wooden slats of the change rooms, Dawnie inched herself into a scarlet costume. She swaggered out, chin up, eyes self-conscious. A group of handsome, bare torsoed youths, pale blue jeans hanging on their hips, cigarette butts hanging between their lips, whistled appreciatively.

"C'mon, let's get out of here." Ken grabbed her elbow, casting pugnacious looks of jealousy over his shoulder.

"That's a flash lookin' outfit." He threw a grudging, half-embarrassed glance at her body.

Long and lanky, with a mop of auburn curls, good legs and a back covered in freckles, Ken stalked to the rim of the sand, then flung himself with skill and grace into an oncoming breaker. Heads sleek as seals, shining bodied, they duckdived and skylarked, washing the grime of the mill out of their pores, relaxing on the dark pull and swell of the ocean like a mother's breast. They were coastal dwellers, handling the surf with confidence and good timing, daring, but watchful for sharks, rips and dumpers.

"I'm goin' out to get a shoot," Ken yelled. "Comin'?" She followed him out, a little more warily. She was not as strong a swimmer as he. "Now," he yelled. Dawnie rode the breaker up onto the sand like a veteran, head down, tail tucked in.

"Not bad," said Ken, with lordly condescension. They lay on their towels, staring up at the sky, sifting sand through their fingers. Ken rolled over, playing idly with her hand. "Let's go for a bit of a walk," he said casually.

They strolled along the beach, arms round each other. He was violently conscious of his hand just underneath the curve of her breast. The crowd was thinning out now. They climbed the rocks, past the pool where older, stylish women and men with big, self-satisfied bellies lounged, watching their children . . . teaching the ten commandments of their kind, "Oh, you can do better than that darling. You *know* you can beat Kimmy if you try . . ." round the path . . . a few fishermen outlined against the swell of the sea . . . the boom of the surf, seagulls crying and wheeling out of the darkness . . . white sand crunching under their toes.

"Here's a good place." They sat down, self-consciously staring out to the horizon. Ken lit a cigarette.

"I didn't know you smoked."

"Ah, I don't smoke too often. Only when . . ."

"Only when what?" She laughed at him.

"Only when I'm a bit nervous."

"You nervous. What the hell've you got to be nervous about. D'you reckon I'll bite you?"

He glanced at her under lowered eyelids. "When a feller's

pretty sure he's goin' to get a knockback it takes a lot of nerve to try."

"Why try then?" she said cheekily. Savagely he stubbed out the butt in the sand, slid his arms around her, tipped her back, and kissed her violently. His voice was muffled in her neck.

"Because I want to try, that's why. A feller's gotta try with you Dawnie . . . he's just itchin' to try. You're such a good sort."

"Yeah I know," she said tiredly. "That's how Mumma started, and now she don't know when to stop." She turned on him fiercely. "And I've made up me mind, there won't be two harlots in our family."

Ken was shocked. His own mother was a widow, grey-headed, middle-aged when he was born. He thought of her as an ageless, sexless being, stiff legged between two soughing palm trees in her crumbling weatherboard on the shores of Botany Bay.

"Where's your ol' man?" he said.

"He's a seaman. Mumma and him don't hit it off, so he don't come home too often, just sends her kimonos from Japan. It's better that way." She thought of her father, that tall, gaunt-shouldered man with the blue Hawaiian dancing girl tattooed on his chest, who appeared on the back doorstep like a ghost out of the past, mooched around the house for a few days and then was gone again.

A dance band syncopated from the beach. She jumped up, rubbing the sand off her legs.

"Why doncha take me to the dance," she said grinning. "You won't do any good out here. And I've gotta lot of time to fill in tonight."

"Jesus, you're a cold little bitch. Cold as ice." He stared up at her gloomily.

"C'mon, lover boy." She put out her bony little hand, and yanked him to his feet. He pulled her hard against him, feeling the roundness of her thighs, the press of her nipples through the wet material.

"Stay a little while," he whispered, fiddling with the zip of her costume. Dawnie wrenched herself out of his arms, running down the path between the rocks, her head bobbing, white as lint, in the moonlight.

He swore, stumbled after her, knocked his toe on a rock, grimaced with pain and frustration. "You're a teaser," he muttered, "a bloody little teaser."

The surf crashed, the dance band throbbed, blobs of coloured fairy lights streamed out over the sand. They circled the open-air dance floor in a sort of dreamy daze, only coming to life when the tempo thudded, hotter, sweeter . . . "My heart was achin' that night at Harry's . . . plentya booze and the jazz, the jazz . . ." hot and sweet and restless, dust and sweat and sand and sea, shuffling feet and moths sizzling against the fairy lights . . . "Another day older and deeper in debt" . . . "if you got the money honey I got the time" . . . boy wanted sixteen years . . . nobody over twenty-five need apply . . . No Vacancies . . . Dum, tiddle um tum tum tum tum BOOLAH!

Now Ken was allowed to hold Dawnie close, put his lips against her hair.

"You got a steady Dawnie?"

"Lissen Ken, if I had a boy friend he wouldn't be a poor kick-me-Charlie like you."

"What d'you mean?"

"Always suckin' up to the boss," she jeered. "Why doncha get yourself a decent job instead of standin' over a mob of women?"

Ken's eyes were hostile. "A feller's got to look out for number one. I been promised the leading hand's job when old Greenie retires. It's a job with a future . . . a job for life."

"What a future," Dawnie laughed. "A job for life, me bum. Who's been fillin' you up with all that bulsh. Dick I s'pose?"

"Dick's a good feller, nothin' wrong with Dick. He's no stand-over man."

"No, but he's a terrible pimp, ain't 'e?"

"What are you comin out with me for if I'm such a no-'oper?" Ken glared at her.

"Ah, you're not a bad poor bastard," she sighed. "But you don't know nothin'. You're just a poor, inoffensive Mumma's boy."

"And you're real smart, right on the ball! How old are you Dawnie?"

"Sixteen and don't go pimpin' to Dick about it. I'm not slavin' me guts out for a kid's wage."

Tireless legs whirling to a stop, the orchestra packing up with dark rings under their eyes, youth streaming out onto the cool sands of Bondi. Silence, darkness, loneliness, lights out in fairy-land . . . pedal pushers, sloppy joes, jeans, crew cuts and pony tails . . . scuffs and thong sandals. Lights out in the luxury pubs, craning like great white seabirds over the swell of the sea, lights out in the fabulous rented flats, lights out in the houses of the rich and successful, lights out in dreamland.

"Back to work tomorrer" and tomorrow is a hangover in your

mouth already. By the waters of Lemon I sat down and wept. BOOLAH, BOOLAH, BOOLAH.

"Let's sit here for a while," Dawnie said. "I can't go home yet."

"It's gettin' late Dawn."

"What, got cold feet. Will Mumma take the strap to you?" she jeered.

"Jesus you're hard to get on with Dawnie. Better go home."

"No," she jerked her arm away. "Please yourself but I'm stayin' here."

"You can't stay by yourself." He looked down at her uneasily. She flopped stubbornly onto the sand, hugging her arms under her breasts.

"What's up kid?" He squatted beside her, putting his hands on her shoulders, gently tipping up her chin.

She shivered in her light shirt. "I don't wanta go home, that's all."

"Wanta stay with me for a while, like me a little bit better?" he stroked her hair.

"Maybe."

They lay together on the sand. "Cold?" he whispered.

"A bit."

"Come over closer then." She edged nearer to him like a timid, stray cat.

"Gawd you're shy. . . . Who'd ever of guessed it. Dawnie, the toughie, Dawnie the big mouth." He scooped her expertly into his arms, pressing his lips hard against hers, undoing the buttons of her blouse with shaky fingers.

"Listen Ken," her voice came smothered against his shoulder. "We can't stay here all night. Let's go into town and get a room somewhere?"

The sky tilted and rocked. "What you say kid?"

She sat up, patting her hair into place, face expressionless, only her hands trembling and fluttering like moths against her hair.

"Do you want me to spell it. Let's go into town and get a room for the night." There was a long pause. She stood up, shaking the sand out of her clothes. "Well?"

"Yeah," he said. "Yeah, sure. Good idea." In the scooped, shadowy hollows left by thousands of feet, they plodded across the deserted beach.

"Jesus, you've got me beat Blondie. I can't get the strong of you at all." Together and in silence they climbed onto the promenade, swung onto a late city tram. The moon was cold on the water. A lonely fisherman cast his line into the moonlit sea.

39

Chapter Five

☆

"Doubles or singles. One night only."

"This'll do us," said Ken in a new businesslike voice. He looked down at Dawnie critically. Face scrubbed clean of make-up, a rime of salt on her blonde lashes, she looked like a weary child. "Better put some make-up on kid. They don't want no trouble and if they think you look under age they steer clear."

Dawnie made up her face in the light from a neon sign, switching on and off above their heads, turning their skin a peculiar corpse-like shade of green. . . . "New and Second Hand Clothing, lowest prices in Sydney. Licensed Dealers in Old Wares."

She followed Ken up the breakneck flight of wooden stairs, turning sharply and discreetly off the street as if they didn't want to advertise their presence. High up on the landing above their heads a single, fly-spotted fifteen-watt globe burnt dimly in satirical welcome.

The man behind the desk had three strands of hair oilily plastered across his scalp, a dirty shirt and dingy eyes. Ken lost much of his self-confidence under that cynical stare.

"We'd like a room for the night," he muttered.

"Got your luggage with yous?" The weary glance travelled from Dawnie's tote bag to the cozzies and towel rolled under Ken's arm.

"We just got in from Central," Ken lied. "Been workin' up the bush. We cloaked our luggage, just brought our overnight things. Too heavy to lug it all round the city."

"Yeah, yeah. That'll cost you a fiver, feller. Betta sign the book."

He stuffed Ken's fiver in his pocket. Ken signed with a flourish. "Mr. & Mrs. K. Betteridge."

The man drew him aside on the landing. "Hope you know what you're doin'. Not cradle snatchin' are you?"

Ken stiffened. "She's eighteen," he lied.

40

"Yeah! well, have it your own way. We don't make no trouble for the guests and we expect the same treatment. And we don't like 'em under age, draws the crabs."

He shuffled up the greasy seagrass runner, jangled his keys, opened the end door and switched on the light. He unclipped one key from the ring and handed it to Ken.

"Here you are. Cheap at half the price." His eyes ran up and down Dawnie's body with lascivious enjoyment, undressing her as they went.

"Hey!" Ken's fist doubled up against his side, his eyes hostile. "You wanta watch yourself."

Dawnie kicked his shin. "Aw shut up," she whispered fiercely. "What d'you expect in a dump like this. D'you wanta get us lumbered?"

"Got brains too." The man winked at Dawnie. "Just leave the key on the desk when you've finished, if I'm not around." Wearily he shuffled back down the passage, his worn sneakers making only a faint whispering sound under the naked globe.

They were alone in a room notable only for its extreme ugliness, its sense of the transitory, tragic lives of all those who had spent a fiver's worth of privacy behind its doubtful walls. It was furnished with a sagging, iron-framed double bed, a raggy white cotton quilt, a navy blue blind torn off its runners and concertina-ed sideways, cup hooks on a bleary wall, a scratched chest of drawers. Someone had chalked up an obscene drawing of a woman with painstaking, anatomical details and no face. There was a strip of worn brown lino by the bed, and a sign, "Please lock your door" but the lock was broken.

Ken looked around warily. "Homey isn't it? Better if you couldn't see it at all." He turned off the brutal, naked bulb. A neon sign switched on and off through the narrow window, staining floor and bed now blood red, now a livid green.

Ken stretched his lanky frame gingerly on the bed. The mattress gave a protesting wheeze and hit the floor. "Well sprung," he grinned. "Nothin' but the best for the customers."

He looked up. Dawnie was standing by the door, a small white blob of loneliness and terror. He stretched out his hand.

"Come over here kid." He patted the side of the bed. "I won't eat you."

She moved hesitatingly towards him, seating herself very primly on the edge of the wire mattress, wincing as it bit into the tender flesh of her thigh.

"Jeez it stinks in here Ken."

41

"Yeah, it's on the nose alright. Stinks of bugs. All these amateur brothels have 'em. Go with the furniture."

Dawnie winced. "Snuggle up a bit closer kid," he said. "You look a bit lost over there."

They lay stiffly, side by side on the greasy quilt, gazing at the headlights sweeping across the ceiling, the muffled noise of trams, jarring and switching points in Elizabeth Street.

When he turned to look at her the light from the neon sign glowed in the hollow of her throat, stained her pale hair and white shirt a livid, fiery crimson. He rolled towards her, crushing her into the mattress, choking her cries with his mouth, undoing her shirt. Her little breasts quivering now green, now red, filled him with frenzy. She fought him grimly, silently, with nails and teeth, and because he didn't want to hurt her, she escaped to the other side of the room, standing with her chest heaving and panting, her hands over her breasts, seeming suddenly no longer a woman to take to bed, but a hurt, half-grown child in her bra and panties.

He lay, breathing hard, his hands balled into fists, his mouth twisted. He shook out a cigarette and lit it with shaky fingers, watching the smoke curl up in the half darkness.

"What's the game kid?" he said harshly, angry because his voice broke on the last cynical syllable. "Playin' hard to get?"

The silence unrolled between them. Quite clearly he could hear the electric trains swishing into Central. A car backfired in the street outside.

"I'm sorry Ken." She spoke in a tired, humble voice, pitifully unlike the brash, self-assured Dawnie of the mill.

"What's up with you? What are you rubbishin' me for?"

"I can't do it, that's all. I thought I could but I can't," she said wearily.

"Well it's a great time to find that out when you're in bed with a feller."

"I never done it before," she said.

"Most fellers worth their salt'd hold you down an' do you anyway, once they got this far. You're takin' an awful risk Blondie." Silence. . . . "Aw well," he said irritably. "For Christ's sake take your bloody clothes and quit standin' there half in the nuddy." He tossed her clothes towards her and they fell into a white, twisted heap at her feet. Silently she dressed herself, and stood awkwardly by the door, ready for flight, her tote bag in her hand.

"I'm sorry Ken."

"If you don't quit sayin' you're sorry I'll throw you down on the bed and have another go at you," he snarled. "C'mon let's get crackin'."

Together they flapped down the seagrass matting onto the landing. The dim light still burned with sickly radiance above the narrow stair. The desk was deserted. Ken dropped the key distastefully on the scarred veneer.

"A bloody dear fiver's worth," he said in a loud, sneering voice, but Dawnie had fled down the stairs. He followed her out into the almost deserted street.

"What's the time?" she said, twisting her hands together, not meeting his eyes.

"Two o'clock. What's up? Got another meet on?"

"I'm goin' home now," she said awkwardly. "See you later." She turned on her heel but he grabbed her elbow.

"Not so fast smarty. What was all this? Just a bit of fun to fill in the evenin'? You certainly played me for a sucker."

She turned on him fiercely. "I was on the level in there but I couldn't do it, that's all. Do you want me to write you a letter about it?"

He stared at her gloomily. "I never met a sheila like you in me life," he said. "I just can't get the strong of you at all. Anyway now we've got this far I'd better take you home. If I leave you wandering round here at this time of night you'll end up bein' raped. Not that you don't deserve it."

"You can't come home with me and that's flat."

"Why? Doncha ol' woman know you goes out with boys."

"Funny aren't you?" Dawnie said bitterly.

"Well, what's up then?"

"You won't be satisfied till I tell you the whole story." Dawnie stared at him coldly. "So here it is. Me Mum goes on the booze every now and then, gets blind paralytic, don't know what she's doin'. There's a party at our joint tonight. There'll be booze tricklin' down the hall, broken schooners and smashed noses, fellers runnin' their hands all over you." She glanced up at the station clock. "She'll be just about easin' up now if the coppers haven't got wind of it. I'm sick and tired of puttin' up with it. Anythin' was better than goin' back there tonight."

"Even me," said Ken.

"Yeah, even you. I meant to play square with you but all I could see was Mumma slobberin' over one of her boy friends."

"Thanks. D'ya reckon they'll have quietened down by now?"

"Yeah, it always starts to ease up about two o'clock. They

gotta get to work in the mornin'. By the time I get home it'll be all over."

"C'mon then," he said. "We'll grab a taxi. Might as well finish the evenin' in style."

"I'll pay half," she said, scraping her sandals awkwardly on the gutter.

"If you insist. Conscience money?" He grinned. "C'mon Blondie. I gotta do the right thing by you, even if you did use me up." He stepped out into the middle of Elizabeth Street, his shrill whistle cutting through the silence. A cruising taxi pulled over, took them to its warm upholstery, and bore them through the empty streets, past muffled figures in shabby overcoats huddled on park benches, wrangling couples under pale street lights, a fuddled drunk weaving home, here and there a lonely worker coming off night shift, carrying his kitbag through the silent city.

"How the hell are you goin' to get back to Botany tonight?" Dawnie said. "It'll cost you a fortune."

"I'll make it okay."

"You better stay the night at my place."

"Got a spare bed or do I share yours?" He nudged her ribs.

"Ah! cut it out. You can sleep on the day-bed."

"What'll your Mum say?"

"She's probably shot through, gone to me auntie's in Forest Lodge. She usually does, till the neighbours cool down."

"So we won't even have a chaperone?"

"Fat lot of chaperoning Mumma could do after a night on the grog."

"You don't wanta push me too far you know Blondie. I'm not as meek and mild as I look."

She smiled up at him, the narrow, pale face and high-bridged bony nose, the sensitive curve of his mouth.

"Ah, you're not a bad poor bastard," she mumbled sleepily. She laid her head back on the upholstery, closing her eyes. His heart ached at the soft shadow of her gilt lashes on her cheek, the weariness in her slumped body.

"Here," he said, pulling her roughly against him. "Put your head on me shoulder. I'll wake you up when we get home."

Dawnie sighed and snuggled closer like a trusting child. "We get off at Byrnes Lane, corner house," she murmured.

"Alexandria you said. Which part matey?" The taxi driver kept his eyes turned tactfully to the road.

"Byrnes Lane," said Ken, settling Dawnie's head more easily on his shoulder, taking her rough little paw in his hand. The factories

44

lining the road were silent now, high cyclone fences, blank netted windows, chimneys leaning their black, smokeless snouts satirically to watch as he sped homewards, the sleeping Dawnie, golden-headed, on his shoulder. "A job for life . . . a job for life," sang the tyres skidding on the tramlines. "Pepsi Cola hits the Spot" flashed the lonely neon on the corner of McAvoy Street.

"Seen that Sputnik yet?" said the taxi driver. "I missed it every time and been on night work for a week. Oughta be a good view tonight though. Not much cloud about." He stuck his head through the driver's window. "Reckon she comes over four o'clock. Wonderful world we're livin' in son. Well here she is. Byrnes Lane."

"Corner house," said Ken. "Wakey, wakey kid, it's 'ome sweet 'ome."

The house was dark and silent; no groggy figures weaving down the front path, no sounds of pugnacious repartee from the lounge. Dawnie, sleepy-eyed and stiff with weariness, sighed with relief.

"They musta give it away and all gone home," she said, creeping carefully between the dirt tins on the kerb. "I'll just take a dekko inside. You never know when you might collect a bottle out the kitchen winder."

Ken swung her gently around. "How about a kiss, just between friends?"

She stood on tiptoe, placing her cool lips on his, one arm wound round his neck. They kissed chastely and innocently in the pale moonlight of the lane, leaning and groping a little towards each other out of their loneliness.

"No hard feelin's kid," he said huskily, the silky strands of her hair tickling against his mouth.

"No hard feelin's." She slid her fingers through the crescent-shaped hole in the back gate, carefully eased the bolt back and flitted like a little white ghost through the brick-paved yard. She switched on the kitchen light, gazing at incredible chaos. The house stank of beer. It lay slopped and puddled over Hazel's once gleaming lino. Dawnie picked her way like a cat through heaps of broken glasses and beer bottles. In the hall the pink satin lamp-shade swung brokenly by one dainty tassel. The globe was broken. Someone, not long ago, had heaved a glass of beer, a head had ducked, and the stain oozed down the wallpaper. There was not a sign of life anywhere.

She stood uncertainly in the hall, gazing warily towards the front door. The filtered light from the street lamp crept through the glass panels, and patterned the floor. The clock ticked in the lounge. A bed creaked, somebody groaned. Dawnie held her breath. She tiptoed to the half-open door into her mother's room. The moonlight fell full across the bed, lingering on Hazel's small exquisite, wanton face, one eye tight shut and turning blue.

The strap of her slip had snapped, the bodice fallen down, exposing one perfect white breast. Her golden hair spilled out over the dark, muscly shoulder of the man who shared her bed.

"Thass you Dawnie? Thass you darl?" The pink lips mouthed the words. Hazel tried to struggle up, but fell back, eyes closed, breathing heavily.

"Whassa row? Whassa matter Haze?" The man beside her rolled over, groaning loudly.

Dawnie fled, stumbling through the litter of broken glasses, the winking eyes of the beer bottles, the sloppy puddles of beer. The gate creaked behind her and she stood with her back against the corrugated iron fence, facing the lane.

"Well, everythin' okay?" Ken put out a caressing hand to draw her towards him.

"Keep away from me," she spat.

He recoiled, bewildered at the venom in her voice.

"What's up? For Chrissake what's happened now?"

"Mumma says you can't stay."

"But I've sent the cab away," he protested.

"Walk down to McAvoy Street. You'll soon pick one up. Here . . . " she fumbled in her bag, thrust a pound note at him. "It's the best I can do, till pay day."

He struck her hand away. "Keep your bloody money." He turned on his heel, striding down the empty lane through the picket fences, head and shoulders pushing angrily against the blurry sky.

"Ken," she called. "Ken, hey Ken." She started after him, stumbling and barking her shins on the dirt tins, her breath sobbing in her narrow chest. "Hey wait for me."

"Ar, you're a bitch of a thing," he snarled. He didn't turn round. She walked back and stood, leaning against the gate, listening to the saw and scrape of corrugated iron working loose in the wind. Next door a window slid up. A cautious head in battleship curlers poked out over the lane.

"Dawnie, that you luv?"

"Yeah, it's me Mrs. Wheeler."

"Jus' wanted to tell you luv. The party's over. I think your Mother's shot through. The john 'ops have been nosin' around.

46

Some nark musta phoned them up. But it's been quiet in there over an hour."

"Thanks Mrs. Wheeler."

"Go in an' get a good night's rest now the coast's clear. You're alright aren't you luv?"

"Yeah, I'm okay."

"Righto. Sweet dreams luv. See you tomorrer."

"Yeah. See you tomorrer."

Sweet dreams for Dawnie . . . sweet dreams in Byrnes Lane.

A half-starved, stray kitten came smooging and groping against her legs, hopefully cadging for food and love. Dawnie picked it up, hugging it fiercely against her breast, till it struggled and spat, miaowing to be free. Her tears wetted its skinny head.

"Jeez, you're a bloody little cry baby," she murmured, carrying it carefully with her into the yard.

Sweet dreams in Byrnes Lane.

The milk train shrieked from Redfern Station, the night shift whistle wailed from Metter's foundry, weary footfalls, turning homeward, echoed down the lanes and streets of Alexandria. Sweet dreams . . . Hazel moaned in her sleep.

"You're not goin' to use my body. Don't think you're goin' to use my body, you bastard."

With an aching, speechless grief Dawnie sat nursing the stray kitten on the moonlit step.

Chapter Six

☆

AL and Beryl crossed Centennial Square, their faces pencilled by the steeple-thin shadows of the poplar trees. The pensioners played draughts at the little tables, nodding and muttering, mottled with sunlight, their paper-thin bones wrapped in old, out-the-elbow coats, even though the sun was still hot.

Their eyes were sockets of loneliness, their features bleared and runny with time like the disfigured plaster busts in Centennial Park. They were so isolated, so outside time and life that Al shivered as she passed. A breath of their loneliness wafted into her mind like the shadow of the poplar leaves. Who was there to care if they took an hour, two hours to make one move in the endless games of draughts, played day after day, weekdays merging into weekends, under the poplar trees.

She hurried from shadow to shadow like a child playing hop-scotch, mesmerized by the dim, blue, perfect leaves swaying on the asphalt under her feet.

If my feet don't touch the shadow then Beryl won't marry her policeman this year and we'll live happily ever after in our attic in Oxford Street. . . . So desperately she sought a reprieve from time, and as her feet touched the dipping shadow, knew with fatal certainty that there was no bargain she could strike to hold it back.

She looked almost bitterly at young Beryl, with her big, soft-limbed body and rosy cheeks, gambolling happily through Wool-lahra, moist eyes turned inwards on her own happiness, secure in a future clasped in the arms of her policeman.

Alice saw herself unwanted, set adrift like the old men in the square, existing out the years on tea and toast in the little attic above Oxford Street, putting out crumbs for the pigeons on the window sill.

She shook herself impatiently, filling the dreary holes in her mind with the safe, everyday business of living . . . groceries and meat to buy, the dinner to get, whether they needed another loaf of bread before the shops shut.

48

"What would you like for tea Bub?" she cried wildly, falling back on the old family pet name, breaking in brutally on the reveries of the rosy-limbed maiden striding at her side.

Beryl came back from her dreams of a white wedding with the organ playing "I'll walk beside you" and Mum howling in the front pew.

She blushed, glancing shyly sideways at her sister.

"I asted Frank to tea tonight," she said. "Poor feller he's havin' a real rough trot at his place. The old landlady's a tartar, serves up the same tea leaves for a week, just stews 'em up in a pot, keeps them in a little bag in the tea caddy."

"I wished you'd told me before," Al said sulkily. "We coulda prepared somethin' decent. Now it'll be rush, rush, rush. Well you'll haveta chip in and give a hand that's all."

"Anyone'd think I was a bludger," Beryl said shrilly, indignant at the injustice of it all.

"Don't forget you've been sittin' on your bottom all day. It's a bit different to the sorta work I do in the mill." Al wiped one tiny wrinkled hand across her forehead.

"It was you that wouldn't let me get a job in the spinnin'. Remember?" Beryl snapped. "Reckoned it was too rough and too hard. And now you're moanin' because I get it a bit easier than you." She glared at Alice.

"Aw give it a bone," said Al wearily. "We'll have a salad and a pine for after. Betta get a coupla chops for Frank. Men like their meat. Clarry always usta say, 'It ain't a meal without meat.' Get the chops down the corner. He's cheaper." She vanished into the greengrocer's, her heart sore, as she trampled over bruised lettuce leaves. It was true what Beryl said. She hadn't wanted her baby sister to go into the spinning. It was a tough job . . . alright for her, she'd been there since the war, she was used to it. They were all good mates even though their language was a bit crook at times. But it was better for young Beryl in the packing, a better class of girls, and the work was easier, though she couldn't stand it for two ups herself. The packers turned their noses up at the mill girls, a lotta snobs, always pimpin' and runnin' to the forewoman.

The young Italian with the flashing smile and melting brown eyes filled her string bag with her purchases.

"Stinkin' 'ot," he said cheerfully. "Too 'ot for the work luv, better for the beach." He sniffed the air wistfully as if he scented the spume of surf rolling up Oxford Street from Bondi.

Al let herself into the narrow-gutted semi in pale, crumbling stone, shoved in between the butcher's shop and the iceworks, its plaster cracking from the tight squeeze. It presented a façade of pathetic, ancient, Victorian respectability . . . the high-pitched slate roof that never knew the gentle obliteration of snow, the sunken front step and carved lintel, the inevitable starched lace curtains, grey with dust drifting off the tramlines.

She climbed the corkscrew staircase, her nostrils wincing at the familiar stink of mould, mice and phenyle. Their little bed-sitter lay under the angle of the roof, suffocating from lack of air. To-night its dreary shabbiness filled her with a distaste as bitter as the phenyle in the toilet on the stairs. She flung up the tiny window, looking down on the myriad crooked roofs of Woollahra, jammed together over the bustling commerce of Oxford Street.

"My God it stinks in here," she said. A thin layer of dust covered the furniture, for no matter how tightly the landlady shut their window, the dust seeped and crept under the warped frame, lying like the dust of time and weariness over the room, over their hopes, over their youth, that withered like the hydrangeas leaning their ancient, blue faces over the spiked railings.

A pathetic attempt had been made to turn the attic into a bed-sitting room, but it was so far removed from the business-girl's dream in *House and Garden* that it would have been kinder if the attempt had never been made.

The floor was covered in a cracked felt base, the pattern of pink roses on a dirty fawn ground, fading into a blessed oblivion. A couple of raggy pink chenille mats were placed strategically beside the beds . . . narrow iron frames camouflaged with washed-out pink calico covers. A corner curtained off with badly dyed calico served for a wardrobe. There was a scarred chest of drawers, an old-fashioned blackened grate with a surround of green tiles and pale tulips. It would have been sacrilegious to light a fire there. A dark green, pressed metal ceiling in a design of fleur-de-lys, cocoa brown wallpaper, a cracked porcelain sink, a chipped electric stovette . . . how depressing it all was. A mirror on the wall was so placed that the window light struck mercilessly across it, cruelly revealing every wrinkle, every blackhead, every open pore. With youthful self-confidence Beryl faced the mirror every morning, flouted her peach-soft cheeks before its ruthless stare, but Al crept past in a faded chenille wrapper, eyes averted, head turned away, lest she should start the day with a sallow, middle-aged widow for company.

The room obliterated Al, her delicate, fine-boned face, the soft, mousy hair, the pale almost transparent skin. She became plain and withered, drained of all colour, her slight, graceful body flat-chested, hipless and sexless. And she wondered for the hundredth time if she really ought to start taking the green, poly-haemin tablets her mother sent her because "you always was anaemic Al".

She heard Beryl's step on the landing, and she rushed in, bursting with vitality, slinging the chops on the table, bringing the room to life like a beautiful unplucked rose, sweat beading the pencil of down on her upper lip.

"For Gawd's sake turn on the wireless," she laughed. "The place's like a damn morgue." She switched on the little red mantel model Frank had given her for her last birthday.

"You call me sugar lips,
How I'd love to get you all alone."

She murmured and swayed and crooned to the hermaphrodite tenor voice on the air.

"You have the shower first," Al said, gentle with love again. "You'll wanta look nice and fresh for Frank when he comes."

"What'll I wear?" Beryl sucked in her crinkled pink lips, ruffling through the dresses in the "hanging wardrobe". "The sundek or me new nylon?"

"Wear the pink nylon," Alice said, chopping lettuce and slicing pineapple with nimble fingers. "Frank hasn't seen you in that."

Beryl rummaged through the drawers, dragging out bra and scanties, nylon stockings and girdle, black patent leather sandals, toilet soap and talcum powder.

"You call me sugar lips,
How I'd love to get you all alone."

She went singing out to the bathroom, the pink nylon dress in a froth over her arm. When Frank tapped on the door she hadn't finished dressing and Al was dishing up chips, chops and salad, her hair sweaty on her forehead, her face mottled from the stove.

Frank came in like a great, overgrown calf, beefy face raw with sunburn, red-gold curls crinkled tight on his round skull, hands hanging big as frying pans at his sides. His navy blue pinstripe suit was too tight, and his neck bulged over his collar. He sat gingerly on the edge of Beryl's bed.

Every inch a copper even out of his uniform, Al thought disgustedly, trying to swallow dislike and resentment like a quinsy in her throat. What on earth can Beryl see in him! But when Beryl came back from the shower, the pink nylon strained seductively across her full breasts and belly, she had eyes for nobody else, hanging and fawning on his words as if he uttered the wisdom of Solomon.

"Well sit up," said Al brightly. "Dinner's on." Frank helped her carry one of the beds up close to the table for a third chair. Beryl and he sat on the two chairs, thighs pressed close together, eyes heavy with love.

I wonder if she's alright, Al thought, glancing furtively at the rounded belly, but then she dismissed the suspicion as unworthy. Bub had always been built solid. Anyway she wasn't that sort. She had her head screwed on the right way.

"How about comin' with us tonight Al?" Beryl said, snuggling closer to Frank. "We're only going to the local. Rock Hudson's on. We'd like her to come wouldn't we Frank?"

"Yeah, why doncha come along. Should be a good show." Frank's enthusiasm was pitifully forced.

"Think I'll have an early night, go to bed with the *Women's Weekly*," Al said cheerfully, hating him for his charity. "It was stinkin' hot in the mill today." .

Frank looked relieved.

"You oughta get out of this dump," said Beryl sympathetically. "You know it's no good for your asthma. Wait till Frank and me gets our little place. We'll have a second bedroom just for you Al. Won't we Frank?"

But Frank didn't answer. His mouth full of chop he gazed steadily out the window into the wispy summer sky.

"When are you thinkin' of gettin' married?" Al said, her hands trembling on the tablecloth.

Beryl gazed adoringly at Frank, waiting for the master's verdict.

"Oh! I dunno, six months or so," he mumbled, running his fingers round the back of his collar. "We gotta have somewhere to live first. I thought we might put a deposit on a house. Although now I'm not so sure."

"Why darl, what's up, what's the matter?" Beryl cried, her voice shrill with fear. "You haven't lost your job?"

"No, nothin' like that. In fact they're addin' to the force." His slow face puckered with worry. "But I've been thinkin' of turnin' it in luv."

"Turnin' it in," Beryl's voice rose in an indignant shriek. "Why it's a steady job, a job for life Frank. You told me that yourself."

Frank looked at her with the large, wet eyes of a young bullock waiting in the slaughter yards. He gazed uneasily round the table, fiddling with his knife and fork.

"Yeah, I know darl, but things are gettin' a bit tough. They're puttin' the screws on. . . ."

"What sorta screws?"

"Well I dunno. I don't object to a bit of rough stuff if it's necessary, but when it comes to kickin' a feller half to death, well, I don't like it, that's all."

Al's pale blue eyes came up in a level stare.

"Doncha read the papers?" she said scornfully. "Everybody in Sydney knows the coppers are a lotta thugs. You should hear the girls at work. They reckon the only good copper is a dead one."

"Al!" Beryl's hurt young voice rose in protest, trembled to a stop.

"I'm sorry Bub, but you know as well as I do, in our family there's no love lost on coppers."

They went on eating steadily, working their way through cups of tea and sliced pineapple. Only the muted murmur of the wireless and the alarm clock ticking on the chest of drawers, broke the uneasy silence.

"How could Frank help it," Beryl burst out. "He hasn't got a trade. It was the only job he could get with any sort of a future in it, when he came down from Forbes."

"The only future he's got is a bash over the skull one of these dark nights," Al said tartly.

Frank rose heavily, trying to keep the shreds of his dignity together. His voice was icy with dislike.

"You wanta be careful talkin' like that about the force Al."

"Oh! Al's like Dad, always was a bit of a red ragger." Beryl laughed shrilly.

"We better go if we wanta bit of a walk in the park first," he said.

Beryl looked pitifully at the stack of dirty dishes on table and sink.

"Oh go on," Al said. "I can do them. There's not much here. Go on and enjoy yourselves."

Beryl almost ran out the door, dragging Frank with her.

"We'll be back early Al," she called guiltily from the landing. "But don't wait up for me. Get some sleep."

Al, her hands soaking in the dishwater, heard the heavy boots thud, thud, the stilt heels rattle down the uncarpeted stairs. Beryl's fresh young voice wafted up from the hall.

"Al's turnin' into a real crank."

"She wants a man, that's all that's up with her!" The front door banged.

"You call me sugar lips,
How I'd love to get you all alone."

The loneliness advanced wave after wave up the stairs, onto the landing, through the door. Thoughtfully Al twisted the thin embossed ring, nine carat gold, on her wrinkled finger.

"I wonder if he'll have the guts to toss it in," she thought. "But he hasn't got a trade, he hasn't got nothin', just a great ignorant, overgrown cockie's son, and no room for him on the farm."

She washed and dried the dishes, worrying about Beryl, worrying about the walk in the park. Wonder does he ever put the hard word on her? Beryl's such a kid. How can she know right from wrong? I oughta have been more of a mother to her.

The burden of responsibility sagged her thin shoulders. It had always been like this . . . the eldest always copped the short end of the stick. It was "Ally do me pinny up . . . Ally I wanta go to the dunny . . . Ally what about them messages . . . Ally watch them kids near the river . . ." Ally the eldest of seven and Mum always sick with her womb dropped since the seventh.

Al had been born in Forbes, grown up into a pale, leggy little girl in the depression. She remembered the humpy by the Lachlan, her empty belly rumbling, cramped and cold in the big double bed with her brothers and sisters tumbled around her . . . the rushing of the river water in the night, the wind tossing the gums.

Never enough blankets to go round, never enough tucker to go round, never enough dole to go round and Dadda couldn't get a job bag sewing or fencing on the wheat silos, or the roads; not anywhere in the whole wide, brown Southland was there work for the freckled, calloused, useful hands that had spelt security for her since she was born.

It was better in the summer when they could run barefoot on the river flats, diving and splashing in the quiet brown pools of the Lachlan. You were never cold in the dry summers of the wheat and sheep country. But a diet of soup bones and stew that was mostly potatoes, took their toll. Al never grew very big and the sharp, protruding bones of skull and face marked her all her life as a "Depression baby".

The happiest time of her life was the early war years when she met and married Clarry Brewster. He was an airgunner stationed at Parkes. She was working in a milk bar at Forbes when Clarry strolled in one night with his forage cap perched jauntily over a big, hooked nose. He wasn't much to look at, a little, fine-boned feller with a swarthy skin and big, leathery hands. The Brewsters owned half of Condobolin, with big properties up and down the Lachlan. They had a reputation as snobs, skinflints, wowsers. She didn't know for a long time that Clarry was one of the sons. He didn't get on with old man Brewster. When he married her, against the bitter opposition of his family, his father cut him out of the will. It didn't make much difference. He'd only ever been an unpaid labourer on one of the properties.

"When I'm gone this'll all be yours son," the old man used to say, sweeping his hand over his rolling acres. But it was like pie in the sky to Clarry, slaving from sun-up to sundown, on pocket money. Besides the Brewsters were long livers. The old man looked good for another thirty years.

"When the war's over we'll go to Sydney," Clarry used to say. "I'll get a job with one of the big agricultural machinery firms. We'll be sittin' pretty, with a War Service Home. The war's been a real godsend to us Al."

He was posted to New Guinea, and shot down over the Owen Stanleys two months later. The War Department notified Al that she was a widow.

Forbes became a place of tragic memories, the little bedroom in the humpy by the Lachlan haunted by a ghost in a blue forage cap. If only there'd been a baby, but there was no baby, only a barren ghostly memory on the wind . . . "the war's been a godsend to us Al. We'll go to Sydney . . ."

"I'll have to go away Mum. I'll go to Sydney, get a job."

"Al you couldn't leave me. Not sick with this crook back and . . ."

"Let the girl go Mum," Dadda said. "She's got to make her own life. She's not a baby any more."

They wore their best clothes to see her off at the station, just as they had when she'd married Clarry in the Baptist Church. That was to please her mother who wandered from religion to religion, seeking solace in heaven, because there was none for her on earth.

She had already been saved by the Salvoes, baptized into the Plymouth Brethren, had the "right thought" with the Christian Scientists, changed her Sabbath for the Seventh Day Adventists. As she got older she tended to become more orthodox and called herself a Baptist.

Al leaned out of the train window till the last minute, waving frantically. The last thing she remembered was her mother's old black hat with the pink roses askew, bobbing against the great, flat empty landscape, her big knuckled hands, roughened and red with toil, wringing against her black serge skirt.

She got a job in the spinning mills and only went home for her yearly holidays. The smog and the fine, white wool dust coated her lungs, she choked with catarrh and loneliness in the little attic over Oxford Street. By the time the war ended she was having regular attacks of asthma. She was pleased when Mum suggested she might take Beryl back to Sydney with her.

"There's nothin' for a pretty girl like Beryl here Al. I'm frightened she might end up in trouble. It'd kill your father."

Al fixed up a job for Beryl in the packing department at the mill. The landlady in Oxford Street moved another bed into the attic, and added a bit extra on the rent for Beryl's breakfast.

Al was happier than she'd been for a long time. She seemed to snap out of the numb stoicism that had helped her live through the years without Clarry. She found an outlet for starved, maternal love in pretty Beryl. They went everywhere together. She began to realize how dull and lonely it had been in the attic before her sister came. Beryl was full of life. She loved pretty clothes, dancing, going to the pictures. Week after week she trotted up escorts for Al, but Al couldn't even pretend to be interested. The memory of Clarry was dim, growing dimmer every year, but she felt as if her youth had died with him. She was content with Beryl for companionship.

Then one night came the knock on the door that was to write finish to all her happiness. . . . A young policeman, red-gold curls spilling out from under his cap, stood blushing on the doorstep.

"I come to see Beryl," he stammered. "Tell her it's Frank."

Frank was a Forbes boy, youngest son of a local cockie. He and Beryl had gone to the "public" together, partnered each other at the local "hop", shared clumsy kisses on the banks of the Lachlan.

In two months they were engaged. Beryl refused to go home for her holidays, she said she wouldn't leave Frank, so Al was left to face the music alone.

She told them sitting on the front step in the soft, spring darkness, the river tinkling at the foot of the garden.

"To think a daughter of mine'd marry a bloody copper," Dadda said sorrowfully. "Well I would of thought you had more sense than that Al."

"I couldn't do nothin' about it Dadda," Al said. She and Dadda had always been closest. They even looked alike, both little and skinny and tough, with washed-out blue eyes.

"You got no right to interfere," her mother snapped. "He's a good livin' boy, and if he wants to make somethin' of himself I say good luck to 'im. There's nothin' for young people here, nor old ones neither." She stared bitterly at the ragged, spectral gums peering over the fence.

"Make somethin' of 'imself," her father laughed scornfully. "I've never met a copper yet was any good. They're all a lotta animals, and I'm buggered if I'll be a father-in-law to one."

"Do what you like," said her mother. "But I'll be right in the front pew for the weddin' march, in me best hat. I wonder could I get it reblocked again Al? We'll have 'er done in the Baptist . . ."

Al stacked the dishes in the open shelves under the sink, gathered up pyjamas and dressing gown, and padded out barefooted to the bathroom. It was wonderful to relax in a hot bath, soaking out all the sweat and grease and aching irritation of the day. The landlady moaned if they filled it up too full, but tonight Al didn't care. Recklessly she ran the taps till the room was muggy with steam, finished herself off with an ice-cold shower.

When she came out, wrapped in her pink, chenille gown, cheeks glowing, her hair in little, damp, fluffy wisps against her neck, she was whistling to herself:

"You call me sugar lips,
How I'd love to get you all alone."

A man cleared his throat in the shadows on the landing. Al jumped. "That you Miss Brewster?" It was the new boarder from the end room down the hall. "I seen you on the stairs a few times."

"*Mrs*. Brewster," she said coldly, clutching her dressing gown modestly up to her throat. The fifteen-watt globe, beloved of landladies, burnt dimly. The man smiled. It seemed to soften all his face. Al had never taken much notice of him before. She wasn't interested in men. Beryl said he was a wharfie. But now in some funny nostalgic way he reminded her of her father. The big, freckled hand leaning on the door jamb, mottled with sun-cancers, calloused with labour, tugged at her heart.

He was medium height, sandy-haired, with high, scraped, almost transparent cheekbones, an adam's apple working up and down in a thin throat, eyes as pale and washed out as her own.

He bent towards her, eyes warily on the stairway. "Dunno if you've heard yet, but our ol' faggot of a landlady is tryin' to get vacant possession so as she can sell the place over our heads."

Al stiffened. Here was a new fear to contend with.

"Don't worry," he said quickly. "She can't do nothin' till she finds us suitable accommodation. But you wanta know your rights, and don't let her put nothin' over you."

57

He smiled again, that peculiar, luminous, touching smile, that showed one broken tooth in front.

She knew suddenly that she trusted him. They were in league against the vague, lurking shape in hair curlers, who exploited them both with her weak tea and cold toast.

"Thanks for the warnin' Mr.—."

"Waters, Steve Waters. It's okay. I picked you for a battler like meself."

She heard the echo of Dadda's voice. "Battled all me life Al and for what . . . a humpy on the Lachlan."

"You don't wanta get behind with your rent," Steve Waters said. "That gives her a perfect alibi. A fortnight behind and outski. And the law's on her side."

"Oh, we never get behind." Al was inclined to stand on her dig a bit. Get behind with the rent indeed! Who did he think they were, a couple of no-hopers?

"It's easy enough," he grinned crookedly. "Specially when you're outa work or on short time, and there's plenty a that nowadays."

"Ah, we're apples at the mill," Al said jauntily. "I been there for donkey's years. Always plenty a work if you know your job."

He smiled wryly. "I been slingin' a hook for a few years meself. I thought I was sweet as a nut but now I'm not holdin' too well at all."

Al watched him, a little pucker forming between her brows. "I remember the last time," she said slowly. "You don't reckon it'll happen again, Mr. Waters?"

"I've had three days' work every week for three months," he said. "As far as I'm concerned Miss . . . Mrs. Brewster, it's happenin'!"

They stood together, wrapped in their own memories of hungry bellies, hand-me-downs, bitter cold and bitterer humiliation. He chuckled, crooking his thumb downstairs.

"I been round drummin' the boarders. Ever heard the sayin' 'Unity is strength'? The ol' girl's awake up, been watchin' me like a hawk. Reckons because I'm a wharfie I must be a Commo."

As if to prove his point, a querulous voice floated up the stairs. "That you Al?"

Al fled taking with her the memory of his chuckle, his amused eyes watching her escape down the hall. She was flustered and disturbed by him. For a moment she thought she had surprised admiration in his eyes. She looked at herself in the unflattering mirror, smoothing her hair back from her narrow, white fore-head.

Why, I don't look like me at all, she thought wonderingly. I look like somebody else. And with flushed cheeks and bumping heart she remembered who that someone else was . . . the slender girl who'd lain in Clarry's arms in the old three-quarter bed in her father's humpy.

She turned off the light, switched on the wireless, lay restlessly on top of the sheets, hoping the landlady wouldn't come poking into her privacy, with some whinge about the other tenants.

"Today, officials of the Textile Workers' Union gave warning of a large scale recession in the industry. In an attempt to cushion the effect, the union has consented to a plan put forward by the employers for a weekly roster of textile workers, and this is already in operation in some mills. Each worker is rostered on a two to three day basis, thus ensuring no lay-offs and some work for all. The Secretary of the union said that there was no real cause for alarm, the recession was caused by the influx of cheap Japanese textiles into Australia, a general tightening up in the overall economy and the usual seasonal factors . . ."

Al stiffened on the bed. Her hands went out and slowly twisted the dial, twisted it anywhere away from the voice spelling out doom . . . sugary doom, dripping with honey . . . "they call me sugar lips".

Oh Gawd! not again, she thought. I'm too old and tired to go through it all again. And young Beryl and Frank and that feller out on the landing, Mum and Dadda, the young ones at home, the girls at the mill . . . why can't we be left in peace? If there's a God why don't he just leave us in peace?

She fell asleep to the taste of her own tears, salty on her lips.

Hours later she awoke to a jarring sense of shock. The moonlight was a deep, shadowy blue in the room, over the night sky a full moon floated, its round, puckered clown's face twisted into a cynical smile.

The ice-saw ground, shuddered, jarred through the old house, the high, weird shriek of steel on ice cut through the ancient walls like paper, cut through the layers of her brain like a surgical instrument, laying her nerves bare and shivering. The iceworks was working night shift again. For Gawd's sake isn't it enough all day, without this yammering all night. She put her head under the pillow, stuffed the blankets into her ears, but it was no good. Then suddenly she was sitting bolt upright, her heart thumping. **Beryl, where was Beryl?**

59

The twin bed was empty, smooth, unrumpled in the moonlight, no dark, curly head turning to meet her on the pillow, no voice husky with sleep to murmur: "For Chrissakes Al lissen to that iceworks."

She looked at the luminous dial on the clock . . . 2 a.m. What on earth could they be doing out till this hour? And Bub had said she'd be back early. Al crossed to the window, peering up and down the deserted street. A gentle wind, blowing off the sea, stirred her hair. What was that? Only a stray dog nosing in the gutter. But that farther over . . . two figures, arms entwined, crossing the road, pausing under the street light . . . Beryl and Frank. The gate closed. The shadows merged passionately together by the hydrangea bushes. Al faded out of the window, and climbed back into bed, muttering to herself.

"If she wants to make a fool of herself, let her. She's free, white and twenty-one." Before she went to sleep with the grind of the iceworks in her ears, she wondered if it really did Beryl much good to be any of those things.

"Yeah it's a free country," Dadda had said, "we're all free to starve in it."

When Beryl crept in, her shoes in her hand, Al was already gently snoring, her head tipped back like an asthmatic.

Over the crooked roofs of Woollahra the moon sailed, poking her face in at the window in Moller Street where Beth lay, smiling gently in Len's arms, where the tiny bat fluttered and crept from the jacaranda tree onto the landing . . . on over the sleeping city to crease the folds of Shirl's wedding dress with moonlight, to weep with Dawnie over her stray cat in Byrnes Lane. At 4.36 a.m. she gazed with jealous awe at this celestial interloper whirling through space at 30 degrees elevation.

At dawn while Al and Beryl still slept soundly, a little man in a stiff, starched collar and a high-crowned felt hat squatted outside the iceworks in Oxford Street and printed in perfect copperplate the one word . . . ETERNITY.

Chapter Seven

☆

LIL dragged slowly home down Botany Road. This muggy weather was playing up with her veins. Big, red semi-trailers roared and revved up the glittering asphalt ribbon, handling loads of wire, wheat, beer crates and machinery. Trams clanged and jarred, the dust rose and settled, settled and rose, vaporous, acrid with bubbling tar. Tyres sang, taxis edged in and out the traffic. Workers drove home from the factory belt of Alexandria, Rosebery, Botany in eight-year-old Fords, Holdens, Plymouths and Chevs. Triumphs, Nortons, B.S.A.'s spluttered at the traffic lights. All the streaming commerce of the city flowed in a dark, sluggish vein between the rows of frowsy semis, sheetmetal works, bottle merchants' case factories, oxywelders, ironmongers and disposals.

Lil wasn't used to moving slowly. A wiry, brisk little woman, her face networked with as many lines as a road map, she walked, head cocked sideways like a cheeky spadger. Slow movement, laziness, inefficiency, annoyed Lil. She always had to have her hands busy with something.

I'm even becomin' a nuisance to meself, she thought irritably. Gettin' too long in the tooth for work, but she was buggered if she'd scratch along, half starved on the pension. She'd seen too much of it . . . old women, gasping in the shade in Redfern Park, broken sandshoes, discoloured ankles, scabby looking dresses picked up in the pop shops. Gawd knows where they'd been, might have the pox all over them, but they sold for five bob.

Lil liked to be independent. She'd never cried poor mouth in her life, and she was too old to start now. She'd work till they carried her out, feet first, and there'd be enough left over for a Labour Funeral.

Carefully her eyes swivelled away from "No Vacancies" . . . "No Work . . . Please do not apply" . . . coming out like a rash on the factories. They'll never put me off she comforted herself. I been with 'em too long. It was her last great illusion.

61

Against the pale-blue, smoky pall of Redfern, the city buildings loomed up like giant cliffs in perpetual shadow. Lil turned left, following a mass of low-lying cross streets and dingy lanes, dignified by the name of Waterloo.

On one corner of Riley's Lane, the soot-blackened shell of an old church had been converted into a factory storeroom, only the cross removed in the interests of piety. On the opposite side, a tiny corner store, jammed into a wedge-shaped block hardly big enough to swing a cat, hopefully announced "Curran's Cash Grocery . . . Take Vincent's APC with Confidence". A few shrivelled oranges were embalmed behind the fly-speckled glass, prudently protected by a screen of heavy-gauge, rusty wire. Behind the counter a weary sign, up since the last Depression, announced to the customers of Waterloo "PLEASE DO NOT ASK FOR CREDIT AS FAILURE TO GIVE SAME MAY OFFEND."

A little Cockney woman with skinny shoulders and bobby pins in her hair, came out of the dim cave behind the shop.

"Oh it's you Lil," she said, standing with red hands folded patiently on the counter. "Been terrible 'ot?"

A blowfly buzzed exhaustedly against the window glass. "What can I get you luv?"

"Give us a tin of baked beans an' a loafa bread. Can't be bothered cookin' much these muggy nights. It's not worth it if you're on your own."

"You want to keep your strength up though Lil. Specially at your age. 'Eard anythin' from 'ubby lately?" The sharp little eyes burrowed beneath Lil's horny exterior.

"No, an' good riddance to bad rubbish." Lil scooped up her parcels, anxious to escape the inquisition.

"It's a shame I always say when a woman's left without a man. But it always seems the best is taken. My 'ubby now, never a cross word between us, passed away without a murmur in the back room there. Toiled all 'is life. Always said 'ard work never killed anyone."

"Dunno about that. I'm half dead meself t'night," Lil said.

"It's too 'ard for you in that mill. I knew mill work in the old country. You wanta get out of it while you've still got your 'ealth Lil. Go on the pension, pick up a couple of quid cleanin' or somethin' light like that."

"No," said Lil stubbornly. "I'd only go through me savin's and end up out at the Ol' Women's Home. And I couldn't stummick that."

"You're bein' silly about it dear. Why I knowed one woman

—all 'er life she was scared 'alf out of her wits of the Ol' Women's 'Ome. 'Ad her pride too I s'pose like most of us. But she found out different. They was lovely to 'er Lil. Even when she was dyin', right up to the last, they fed 'er warm milk out of an eye dropper. You don't wanta worry luv. . . ."

Lil escaped into Riley's Lane. "Bloody ol' crank," she muttered.

Riley's Lane . . . a running sore, littered with orange peel, empty milk bottles and old papers. A damp dead-end lined with two-storey weatherboards, built straight onto the road, hump-backed, sagging with time and rot and cynical neglect. The crazy, toppling balconies hung over the lane, defying the laws of gravity. The incredible patched fences of corrugated iron were kept partially upright with paling cross pieces. A puff of wind in the night sent the loose, rusty iron flapping and scraping in a mournful music. On washing day each back yard accommodated one double sheet at a time. And over it all swung the limpid Australian sky, cotton-woolled with cloud. It was hard to raise your eyes above the level of the toppling balconies of Riley's Lane, better to mix a bottle of pinkie and drown your sorrows in the dry, yellow grass behind the bottle factory.

The landlady was coming sly-eyed out the front door. She was on one of her periodic swoops to see that the tenants weren't using too many electric appliances secretly in their rooms. She was a typical Redfern landlady . . . good black suit, a little black hat with a veil, coquettishly softening a face all sag and pucker like a papier mâché mask. Her lower set joggled in her jaw, her stockings concertina-ed on skinny ankles, a cheap, blonde fur stole trailed over one arm.

"Afternoon Mrs. Kelly." The eyes round and hard as pebbles looked past Lil as if she was litter in the gutter. "Still in work. You're lucky aren't you?" Her tone implied that anyone employing Lil would do so only out of charity. She stood, blocking the doorway with her squat body, making it impossible for Lil to pass through without shoving her aside.

"I hope we haven't 'ad any more trouble with your 'usband lately?"

Lil set her stringy shoulder against the door jamb. " 'As anyone complained?" she said sharply.

"Oh no, now I never said that Mrs. Kelly, but after the last time . . ."

"The roof's in a terrible condition ain't it?" said Lil, gazing sorrowfully at the corrugated iron, rusted into a network of holes.

"I hope you can see your way clear to gettin' it fixed before the winter sets in?"

The stony eyes glazed under the dotted veil. "The iron's the trouble," the landlady moaned. "So dear now and rents are that low I can't afford to keep the places in repair. The Guvment won't let us raise our rents, so everyone has to suffer. It's terrible Mrs. Kelly. There's no incentive to better yourself in this country any more. S'pose they'll be pullin' them all down soon, and I won't get no decent sort of compensation. It's hard for a widder . . ."

Lil pushed past her, and climbed up the rickety staircase. The wall had once been painted a pale blue, but now the plaster was mushroomed with furry green and brown fingers. Lil was glad she had the top room. There she only had to cope with the rain, downstairs the tenants struggled with an insidious creeping fungus that furred the walls, and rotted the floor boards. The house had been built without a damp course on an old swamp. The legacy of a sharp, musty stench filled the rooms from top to bottom, sent the kids to bed with bronchitis and pleurisy half the winter.

Upstairs Lil had a view. Across the crooked slate and corrugated iron roofs of Waterloo and Redfern the Housing Commission flats stood like a dream of luxury amidst green lawns. The sunlight slanted golden against their solid brick walls, a rainbow of mist from the water sprinklers circled them with enchantment. The tide of change crept over Waterloo and a legion of landlords standing shrieking like Canute with the water lapping at their shoes, could not halt the march of those golden-walled palaces, with canaries swelling their throats in little gilded cages on the balconies.

But it was not much comfort to Lil. She would never dare to take on that rental, not at her age, with the wage she was getting. And the family downstairs with their four kids and Arthur on the basic wage at Eveleigh, what hope was there for them of a sunlit Government palace to call their own at £4.15.0 a week, and out on your ear if you got behind. Besides, the flats were for childless couples or one-child families. Redfernites were lusty, uninhibited and virile. They believed in populating the country. A double bed in a mouldy room was the only answer for them, and when the council bulldozers knocked it head over heels, there was a hut in Herne Bay or Hargrave Park. The encroaching tide of progress was regarded with mixed feelings in the narrow lanes and streets of Waterloo.

Lil's room had double glass doors, with the bottom panels

boarded in, opening out onto the balcony. She dragged her bed out there in the summer, but the floor was getting so rotten she sometimes wondered if she wouldn't finish up sitting in her nightie in Riley's Lane, bed and all, one of these stifling nights.

Lil had a gas ring, and an icebox she'd bought herself. There was an old gas stove and a sink on the landing for the use of all the tenants. Out in the bricked-in back yard a washhouse with a couple of tubs and a fuel copper was housed under a corrugated iron shed loosely nailed together. In a little lean-to beside it was a chipped enamel bath and a toilet with a cracked wooden seat that pinched your bottom. The fellow downstairs had put in a chip heater and rigged up a shower. Hot water was not something that the landlords of Riley's Lane cared about. Lil had often thought she might buy herself one of those little electric stovettes and a frig on time payment, but she knew there'd be so much trouble with the landlady it hardly seemed worth it. As it was she concealed a one-bar radiator to warm her meagre old bones on winter nights and in the early mornings. It had to be quickly stuffed away under the bed when she heard the landlady's sharp little heels clipping along Riley's Lane.

She had bought herself a nice bit of pink and blue lino to cover the floor, and kalsomined the cracked plaster. But the roof was beyond her. All she could do when the rains came was to push her bed into a dry corner and listen all night to the melancholy sound of the drips rattling in her strategically placed saucepans.

Lil heard a cautious step in the hall below. It was Marge, downstairs, creeping back home. She seemed to have a sixth sense of her landlady's visiting days, and gathering up her four kids fled from the rasping whine and the prying nose, long before it poked its long white tip round the corner of the lane.

"That you Lil?" she hissed softly up the stairs. "Keep quiet you little faggots."

"Yeah, it's me luv."

" 'As the ol' bitch shot fru yet?"

Lil peered down the shadowy stairwell, seeing the round, pale face framed in russet hair, the four little white faces gazing upwards, clinging to their mother's skirts.

"Jus' this minute gone."

"I'll come up then." She turned fiercely on the little faces. "Yous can go out an' play in the lane and mind, no fightin' or I'll be down to tan your bums for you."

She watched them go, tenderness in her eyes. "Sit right down in your chair and I'll put on a cuppa," she said.

65

Lil did as she was told. It was nice to be waited on for a change. "You're a godsend Marge."

"You look done up, and no wonder. What a stinker!" Marge filled the kettle from the landing. The smell of gas tainted the little room. "Pooh! your gas ring's leakin' luv. Well, what did the ol' bitch haveta say for herself today?"

"Whingin' about the Housin' Commission," Lil said briefly, fanning herself with the *Mirror*. "I told 'er about the roof agen."

"Fat lot uv notice she'll take. She don't care. You know we ought to get the health authorities onter her. Little kids livin' in a place like this!"

"If she fixed the roof she'd only put the rent up," Lil said.

"Yeah, I s'pose. Arth says they retrenched a few more off the railways yesterday. Things is bad y'know Lil. Your job holdin' out alright?"

"Yeah, it seems to be."

"I hope so." They sat either side of the little deal table, sipping the scalding hot tea. "All I'm scared of now is fallin' agen. I says to Arth last night, 'If you put me in the family way agen I'll bloody well drown meself.' I got somethin' from the chemist last time, cost me twenty-five bob, and there's young Cheryl toddlin' round now, large as life. Not that I'd be without her, now she's here."

She got up, gazing wistfully across the rooftops at the Housing Commission flats.

"Gee, it'd be swell to have one of them. They've got them fixed up so nice inside too, little frilly, organdie curtains. But you might as well cry for the moon. You got a good view up here Lil. A bit of a breeze too."

The sound of shrill angry voices rose from the lane. "There's them bloody kids, at it agen." She stood dreamily in the doorway, her strong graceful body outlined against the light. In her smooth, white armpits the dark hair glistened, curly and wet with sweat. "I s'pose we'll all end up in one of them housing huts. Not that I'd complain. Anythin' to get outa Waterloo. But the fares'd be terrible high for Arth. And how we'd ever pay the rent if we got in the ballot for a Commission house I dunno." She laughed wryly, yawning and stretching in the sun like a big reddish cat. "Still as Arth says . . . cross your bridges when you come to 'em luv."

She nattered on, her tongue unloosed from the long, lonely hours spent in the house, with only the kids to talk to. The

66

shrieks rose louder, a stone thudded against the weatherboards, the walls shuddered under the impact.

"My Gawd!" Marge plonked her cup of tea on the table. "Never a minute's peace with the little buggers. See you later luv." Her shoes clattered on the wooden steps, the lane resounded to slaps and yells. "Wait till your Father gets home."

A woman shrieked from next door. "Why doncha control your bloody kids!"

Lil went downstairs for her cold shower.

A pale, greenish dusk trembled over the rooftops, tiny stars pricked behind the chimneys, golden lights switched on, hazy behind the window curtains, cooking smells wafted down the streets and alleys of Waterloo.

Lil ate her baked beans on toast, listening to the sounds floating up from the street below, kids playing hopscotch, a tennis ball thumping regularly against weatherboards, footsteps dying away, a tram passing in Botany Road. The room was full of the dim, greenish light, softening its ugliness, only the glow of the gas ring, with its little pointed star of flame, burned merrily under the kettle.

Marge came up on the landing, banging her pots and pans about, yelling down at the kids. Lil could hear the shower going in the back yard as Arthur washed the grime of Eveleigh Railway Workshops down the plughole. She was at peace. This was home, the noises friendly and familiar. You could never be lonely in Waterloo, always conscious of the myriad lives woven and interwoven with your own, breathing, battling, loving, fighting, suffering in the stifling summer dusk.

After dinner she washed up and went to sit in her old wicker chair by the french doors, smoking a cigarette, watching the moon come up in a great, glowing ball, climbing higher and higher, whitening under her eyes. Marge carried her dishes up the stairs, and washed up on the landing, singing gently to herself, the baby Cheryl whinging softly round her legs. Doors slammed, somebody put their milk bottles out, the air was full of the soft murmur of talk, the creak of chairs, hands slapping at the mozzies, as people migrated to the pavements for a breath of air.

Lil went to bed early, thankfully stretching out on the sagging wire mattress. Mosquitoes droned over her head, cars tooted, cats wailed from the picket fences, dogs set up a wild hullabaloo under the street light, but Lil slept like the dead, rejuvenating her weary old body for another day in the mill. Friday . . . tomorrow was pay day. You couldn't take a sickie out on pay day. The chairs scraped in over the doorsteps, the lights went out one by one in the little houses ready for an early start in the morning. Workers lived in Waterloo and Redfern.

"For Christ's sake, natter, natter, natter, can't a man get a winka sleep," Arthur muttered and tossed in the double bed downstairs. A stick tapped mournfully down Riley's Lane. It was an old pensioner with cataracts growing over his eyes, retiring for the night on a bed of newspapers in the vacant block. The rats came out to frisk and scavenge in the moonlight, rustling amongst the orange peel, a little breeze chased the discarded paper up the gutter. Waterloo slept the sleep of the innocent, the weary, the wronged and the just.

It was two o'clock when Lil heard the thick voice under the balcony. She lay tense, not daring to move in case a creaking spring betrayed her.

"Lil, is that you Lil. I know you're there Lil. Lil . . . bloody bitch. *Lil!* By Christ if you don't bloody well come down and let me in I'll give you a smack across the mouth. *Lil . . . Lil. . . .* Ah! you bitch of a thing. I'll fix you."

He weaved across the road, collecting a swag of empty milk bottles under his arm. Thud . . . the first bottle struck the ancient walls like a depth charge. The house shuddered and shook itself like an old rat in mortal combat. Thud, thud, thud, the crash and tinkle of glass; a deathly silence in Riley's Lane.

"Lil . . . Lil if you don't show your ugly mug on that balcony I'll brain you with a bottle. One, two . . ."

With a sudden lightning movement Lil flung a dish full of cold water into the lane, drowning the persistent voice under the street light. He stood there, spluttering, a pathetic, dripping little figure, shaking the water out of his eyes, gazing sadly at Lil, outlined like an avenging angel on the rickety balcony.

"I didn't think you'd do it to me," he said. "I didn't think you'd do a dirty trick like that Lil." He stumbled off, not without a special dignity of his own, boots squelching, leaving a trail of water at every step. The street was silent. The rats crept out of hiding. A cautious head poked out of the window downstairs.

"You alright Lil," whispered Marge.

"Yeah," said Lil.

"Reckon he'll come back tonight?"

"No he won't come back."

68

Marge wondered if that was a sob she'd heard in old Lil's voice. Must have imagined it she thought. She hasn't got no tears to spare for that drunken old sod.

Lil lay down again but she couldn't rest. Some part of her followed the dripping little figure down the streets and alleys of Waterloo, some part of her guided his uncertain footsteps from the unseen gutters, the marauding coppers, the cruising police car. The flattened nose, the cauliflower ear, the scarred grey head floated above her bed like a weary ghost. Kel had done a lot of pugging round the sideshows in the country towns. There was one time they'd had their own show. Lil had gone with him. She was a real drawcard in those days, in the ticket box and the hoopla stall. She even had a contortionist act of her own. Kel was a good feller, except when he was full, but he got full more and more often. The show folded up, Kel did all their savings at Thomo's. The booze really got him then. He was always hanging round the plonk shops half sozzled, cadging a drink off anyone he met. He'd drink anything they reckoned, plonk, pinkie, straight metho.

For a while he used to take a bag of snakes out to La Perouse on a Sunday and do a bit of an act for the weekend crowd, but it got so he'd forget where he put his snakes. The night Lil found them crawling about under the bed, she left him to it, but wherever she was he seemed to find out, and come wandering back to haunt her with the memory of old dreams and vanished love.

"I won't ever be free of you Kel," Lil murmured wearily. She jumped up and pulled on her dress. Slippers in her hand she sneaked down the moonlit stairs, hugging the wall like a shadow. A bed creaked. Arthur and Marge gasped and struggled together in the act of love.

"For Gawd's sake be careful Arth. Arth be careful luv." Marge's hoarse whisper pierced through the thin walls.

Lil unlocked the door and slipped out into the street. "Poor feller, he'll catch 'is death of cold in them wet things," she muttered and argued to herself as she shot up Riley's Lane. A cheeky rat sat gazing at her from the gutter, a crust of bread clasped in his tiny paws. Lil paused under the street light on the corner, looking up and down Pleasant Terrace. Then she set off with a steady stride like a young girl, putting streets and alleys, asphalt valleys and hills behind her and the slumbering inhabitants of the lane. The rat watched her go, his sharp inquisitive eyes glinting like tears in the moonlight.

An old woman slumped in a doorway of Pleasant Terrace,

sobbing broken-heartedly, a dirty white Pom nosing round her ankles. "The dirty bludger pinched me bottle of meffo luv," she mumbled to the uncaring stars.

The door opened, a pyjama-clad figure stood outlined in the electric light. "Better go in now Mum," said a kindly voice. "'Ere, I'll give you a hand home."

The old woman tottered off, leaning heavily on the arm of her good Samaritan. The little Pom followed, snuffling faithfully at their heels.

"Pinched me meffo. Pinched a full bloody bottle." Her weeping blew up the street on the summer wind. A weary roar shook Riley's Lane from end to end.

"Gotta be up at sparrer's fart tomorrer. Don't you bastards own a bed?"

The baby Cheryl cried bitterly from her cot pushed underneath the window to catch the air.

The old man coughed and hawked in the dry, moonlit grass behind the bottle factory.

A long time afterwards Lil dragged slowly up the lane. She went inside, leaving the front door carefully ajar.

Chapter Eight

☆

"LEAVE THIS MACHINE CLEAN . . ."

Grimly Jessie propped the rough, cardboard notice on the rover. With tightened lips she threw her hand towel over her shoulder. Dragging one stout leg behind her, she went to change her overall in the washroom, nearly colliding with fat Julie on the way.

"That'll fix her," Jessie said savagely. "Every mornin' it's the same story. I've let her get away with it too long. She never so much as puts a grease rag near me machine, and I keep it shinin' like me own kitchen floor at home. You can't work with dirty tools me ol' man always says, but that bitch! Ah, she's a dirty faggot!"

"I dunno what they do on that night shift," Julie grizzled. "Must be the biggest bludge on earth."

"She never fills up for me neither, just lets the machine run out. And there am I, workin' me guts out to make sure the rows are all full up for her, before the whistle blows. The rotten thing!"

"Why doncha put her into the foreman?" Julie said indignantly.

Jessie looked shocked. "I couldn't do it. I've never been a boss's pimp in me life. Ah, well I s'pose there's a nark on every job."

Hips rolling, they disappeared into the washroom, peeling off their sweaty overalls, standing bare-armed in pink swami slips, a roll of fat over the tops of their corsets. Jessie thrust her big, red, freckled arms into the cold water, watching the suds thicken and turn grey with grease.

"Give us a lend of your nailbrush Jule," she said. "I can't get this flamin' grease out from under me nails. I'm ashamed to go out in me son-in-law's car at the weekends with these nails . . . haven't got the nerve to take me gloves off."

Dick stood, surveying Jessie's handiwork with an approving smile. He nudged young Ken in the ribs.

"Old Jessie's got the right idea. She'll make the bludgers sit up and take notice. I oughta make her me offsider."

He glanced slyly sideways, but the kid wasn't listening. He was watching young Dawnie strolling across the mill for her wash.

"You look like a dog after a bitch," Dick said disgustedly. "Go on then, the whistle's gorn, why doncha chase her. You won't be any good round here till she gives you a bit." He gave Ken an unfriendly shove in the back.

It was part of the unspoken policy of foremen and leading hands to sow discord between the day and afternoon shifts. While the women worked out their grudges on each other, they forgot the cold water in the washroom, the broken bobbins, the antiquated machinery. Dick was always egging on the older, more experienced hands who "took a pride in their work". He liked to see them bouncing the slipshod newcomers, the inexperienced housewives, who worked on a more or less casual basis, ready to give up when "the kids were crook" or "me ol' man's on night work now".

The women didn't often fall for it, only occasionally when the pace was on, the heat terrific and the provocation great. Then the tension snapped in raised voices and bitter passing feuds in the aisles between the roving machines, when the afternoon shift came on at four o'clock.

Dick would go off to have his supper, chuckling to himself, well pleased with the anger that didn't break over his own baldy head. He liked to get even with the women too. He resented their companionship. For no matter how hard he tried they would never accept him as one of the mob.

"Yeah, Dick's pretty easy goin' but . . ." And in that "but" was expressed all their unshakable distrust of the pannikin boss, the boss's man. Dick had crossed the dividing line, not for him the spare mug of tea, the murmured confidences, the quick helping hand to cover up a blue. He was out on his own in a no-man's land . . . the pannikin boss, the lowest of the low in a world where dog ate dog.

"All a moba bastards," he'd rumble into his beer after work. "All a moba bastards," and it made his feel better.

Jessie and Julie went home together every night, bottoms waggling under their cotton print dresses, Julie shortening her step to accommodate Jessie's bad leg.

"Been crook ever since the last two," Jessie confided. "Varicose veins right up to me crotch. You shoulda seed me with young Maxie. I had a left leg like a balloon all the way down to me ankle."

By the time they reached the corner opposite Metters they were both red in the face and short of breath. Julie looked back wistfully at Dawnie making her date with Ken, the sunlight circling a halo around her silken little head.

"It'd be nice to be young again," she said. "Though I told Dawnie she better look out for that Ken. I bet he's hot stuff."

"If she was my daughter I'd turn her up and tan her bottom for her," said Jessie indignantly. "All that filthy language she uses. And she looks as if butter wouldn't melt in her mouth."

"Ah, she's not a bad kid underneath all that. It's not her fault. It's the way she's been brought up. But that Ken won't do her any good. Did you see those photers he was handin' round yesterday. Filthy things they were. A girl with nothin' on, sittin' with her legs spread apart. I coulda smacked the dirty thing's face, sittin' there smilin' as if she was doin' a great stroke."

"I'd hate my Maxie to be cartin' things like that around," said Jessie. "I found a French letter in his pocket when I was doin' the washin' last weekend. He got a real tongue bangin' I can tell you."

Julie blushed. "I dunno what Don would say if he could hear how I talk at the mill. He'd give me a smack under the ear. I never even knew any dirty jokes till I come here."

They hoisted themselves onto a city-bound tram, settling back in the seats, stretching their tired, thick legs out in front of them. Jessie relaxed like a bag of wheat. Weariness spread through her muscles like a physical pain. She half closed her eyes, conscious of the hot wind off the asphalt fanning the hair back from her forehead. Drops of sweat trickled into her eyebrows. Her dress was sticky across her back, plastered dark and damp against the leather seat. Her breath rasped and wheezed against her chest. She wiped her broad red face with her handkerchief.

"You alright luv," said Julie anxiously.

"Just let me get me breath," Jessie gasped. "It's me blood pressure. Plays up with me these hot days."

"You oughta take a rest," Julie said. "The money won't be no use to you out at Rookwood."

They caught the Tempe train at Central, bought a paper from a shapeless woman in a big white pinny, with a voice

73

famous all over Sydney . . . a hoarse, tireless bellow echoing down the shadowy steel and concrete gullies from the Railway to the Quay.

Jessie half drowsed in her seat, hardly conscious of the jarring stops and starts, the stations whirling past, the clacking of the wheels on the hot steel rails. Under her drooping lids the familiar landscape slid past, smoke-blackened loco sheds, steam trains gleaming and panting in the yards, a cleaner with a black face and a glistening, sweaty, beautiful body whistling to the girls hanging out the windows. The rails glittered in the sunlight, criss-crossing in a crazy maze. Overhead bridges, brief tunnels, dusty clipped privets, dirty brick stations, green seats, yellow hoardings, abandoned brickpits full of muddy water and rusty tins, clicking past like a camera shutter in a familiar, reassuring pattern, crying . . . crying . . . Here . . . Here . . . Rest . . . Rest . . . Home . . . Home.

Castor oil plants grew rank beside the picket fences in back yards thick with grey washing backed onto the railway line.

"How is your daughter, the one that had the baby, gettin' on?" Julie said.

Jessie fumbled in her purse. "Real good. And the kid's a little tiger. Didn't I show you the photers. Takes after our side. Got a nose the spittin' image of my Bert."

Julie gazed admiringly at a blurred photograph of a tall plump young woman holding a small, indeterminate looking baby.

"Lovely isn't he. Does she take 'im to the clinic?"

"Yeah, but she don't take no notice of what they say, just takes the dummy out of his mouth before she goes in. The Sister's a real crank. Linnie jus' comes an' asks me if she wants to know anythin'. 'You've reared six Mum,' she says. 'You must know somethin' about it.' Well here we are. Tempe at last."

TEMPE . . . JUNCTION FOR THE EAST HILLS LINE.

They hurried onto the platform. Jessie winced at every step. "Gets you right in the kidneys don't it," she said. "Well, see you tomorrer luv. Hope you can get some rest with young Johnny tonight."

Her face puckered with sympathy. She grabbed the handrail and climbed groggily onto the overhead bridge, lost in the crowd, milling past the ticket collector, lost in the frayed grey and fawn trouser cuffs, the cotton dresses, the shirt sleeves, the sports coats, the skin-tight, grease-stained jeans, the kitbags, the rolled-up newspapers, the legs going up the ramp, pink legs, brown legs, white legs, fat legs, skinny legs, muscly legs, nylons . . . tired legs, weary legs, legs that stumbled against the step, legs that mounted up towards the blue rush of the sky. . . .

"Where'd you get that locket thing with the chain on it?"

"Only two and six at Coles."

"Really, isn't it f-a-a-b!"

"So I says to the foreman, 'Lissen feller, you got anythin' else t'say I'll see you out the gate."

"So what happened Syd?"

"He never showed up."

> "Hes got you and me brother in his hands,
> He's got you and me sister in his hands
> He's got everybody here in his hands,
> He's got the whole wide world in his hands."

The music poured into their ears from the open door of the record bar. They neither paused nor faltered but streamed on, over the bridge, and dispersed into the dreary suburbia of Tempe, crouched over Tempe tip and the blue glitter of Cook's River threading its way out to Botany Bay.

Two old mates sat under the shadow of a petrol hoarding, old-fashioned velour hats tipped over their eyes. One was a skinny little fellow with skin as thin and white as tissue paper, the other a red-faced old timer with a bushy white moustache, buttons straining over his paunch, the crown of his hat pushed up round and hard like a Clay's vaudeville comic. Two of the original river mob, the Tempe mud rats living out the last of their brief, hard days under a hoarding by the eternal Cooksa.

A little girl with a dusty seat on her shorts and gravel rash on her knees, steered her scooter in a wide arc round the corner, her tongue pressed hard between her teeth.

" 'Ooray Mrs. Packer," she yelled.

The little girl had a round, red, sweaty face, and fair braids, bunched on top of her head with a big pink bow. She reminded Jessie of her daughter Linnie when she was the same age.

" 'Ooray luv," she said.

How wonderful it was to turn into your own street, to hear the lawnmower whirring, the gentle rustle of the sprinkler on the hydrangeas, to smell the swathes of new-mown grass steamy in the sunlight, and see young Maxie, shirtless, the sweat trickling down his smooth, bare chest, pushing back his fair hair under the spattered shadows of the old palm tree.

"Hi Ma," he called. "I've nearly finished."

She leant against the gate to get her breath. "It's a long pull from the station," she said apologetically. "Don't overdo it son. Leave it go for a while. It's too damned hot."

"What d'ya think I am . . . a weaky," he said. The motor started up again, whining its way round the side of the house.

"I'll call you for a cuppa in a minute," she yelled.

The old man sitting in the shade of the back verandah raised his head as she came round the corner. His big, blotched, knob-knuckled hands were folded quietly in his lap.

"That you Jesse?" he said.

"Who was you expectin'. Your girl friend?" She flopped down in the wicker chair beside him. "A real stinker ain't it? How've you been luv?"

"Sit there," he said. "Don't move. I got the kettle on."

She tried to protest, to rise up and go inside, to put out the cups with nimble fingers, cut the cake, measure the two and a half spoonfuls from tea caddy to teapot, fit the knitted cosy over the top . . . the simple little tasks that flowed automatically on from the other after the years of housekeeping. But her body refused to move. She lay spreadeagled in the shadow, safe, relaxed at last in her working man's castle. The quietness of the garden, the criss-crossed shadow of the lattice on the lawn, the sound of a pigeon cooing high up on the telegraph wires, lapped over her like soft, green water, loads of it, sinking and swirling, dappled with sunbeams.

When Bert came out, carrying the tray carefully, with a white doily under the cake plate, she was fast asleep, slipped down in her chair, swollen legs sprawled across the verandah, mouth open, grey hair poking through the wicker work.

He stood listening for a minute. "Jesse," he said softly.

A little motor boat chugged gently up Cook's River, a swirl of foam in its wake, the white smoke drifted up lazily from the tip, the pigeon cooed and cooed, swinging against the blue drift of the sky.

"Jesse," he said again. He tiptoed inside, feeling his way with the certainty of long memory. "Better finish up now son. Your mother's asleep," he said softly, sticking his sightless white head out the bedroom window.

Jessie snored on till the golden light slipped down the sky behind the lemon tree, and the blue shadows of the little boats lengthened on the river.

After tea they sat in the cool on the back verandah, slapping at the mozzies, listening to the locusts drumming in the oleander bush.

The wireless droned in the background, the light from the kitchen streamed out making a pool of gold on the lawn. The night was full of the soft thud of the moths bumping their bodies against the flywire door. Max came out with his kitbag, and roared away into the dusk on his B.S.A. He was an apprentice fitter just started night work at the 'drome.

"Have you got a clean hankie luv?" Jessie yelled after him, but only the splutter of the exhaust answered her, rolling back up the street.

"Lissen," she said, cocking her head on one side. "I can hear Linnie comin'."

"You're always imaginin' things," the old man murmured. "If it was Linnie she'd be in Reg's new Holden."

Jessie eased her bulk out of the chair. "I hope there's nothin' wrong," she said anxiously.

The high heels clipped up the gravel drive at the side of the house, and Linnie came round the corner, the baby asleep in a blue bunnyrug, dragging down in her strong, sunburnt arms.

"For Gawd's sake what are you doin' with that child, out at this time of night?"

Linnie stood in the light from the kitchen door, her eyes red with weeping, her lower lip thrust out. Jessie was reminded of the stubborn little girl with the scooter.

"Never mind Lynne," she said quickly. "We can go inside and put the baby down. And you look as if you could do with a cuppa tea."

Lynne followed her into the front bedroom. The baby yawned, showing its pink, toothless gums, stretching up its small, red, tightly clenched fists.

"He looks lovely Lynne," Jessie said tenderly. "He's a real credit to you."

"Reggie's mother don't think so. She's always sayin' me milk must be too thin, and how skinny he is compared to what hers was."

Linnie stood, looking down at the baby, her hands clenched like his at her sides, her lower lip trembling.

"What's up luv?" Jessie said softly, rocking the baby up and down on the kapok mattress.

"Oh, I dunno Mum. Everythin's goin' wrong," Linnie said desperately. "We jus' fight like cat and dog all the time and the baby howls and I bawl, and last night Reggie hit me."

77

Jessie stiffened. A fierce maternal hatred against Reggie who had dared to lay a finger on her child, flooded through her body. She remembered she had felt just like this when her kids had come back, eyes blackened, lips gashed, lumps as big as pigeon's eggs on their foreheads, after a stoush with one of the rival gangs who roamed the mudflats.

She laughed, remembering how she had rubbed embrocation on the bruises.

"It's nothin' to laugh at," Linnie snapped. "I wish I could see somethin' funny in it." She laid her head down against the old-fashioned four poster bed and wept.

"Now look here Linnie," her mother said, giving her a hankie out of her pinny pocket. "Have a good howl and you'll feel better."

Linnie lifted a tear-stained, scowling face. "I'm not goin' to howl jus' to please you," she sniffed.

Jessie grinned. "That sounds more like my Linnie," she said. "Got a bit of stuffin' in her. Now sit down here on the bed and tell me what's been going' on. Has the ol' girl been makin' it hard for you?"

"She's an ol' bitch," Linnie said bitterly. "She sticks 'er nose inter everything. Wants to run our lives for us. It was alright when we was both workin'. But now I'm home all day with the baby . . ."

"Well you'll have to shift out, that's all."

"And where'll we shift to?" Linnie snapped. "It's not like when you was young. Houses to burn. We might've put a deposit on a place but Reggie bought a car instead. Reckoned if he had to travel miles to get a job he needed a car. Never mind about me and the baby breakin' our hearts for a roof of our own."

The baby began to cry. Jessie picked him up and rocked him gently in her arms. "Don't Reggie want to shift?" she asked.

"Not him. Why should he? He's got his ol' woman waitin' on him hand and foot. He's on a real good wicket." Linnie blew her nose hard in the borrowed handkerchief.

"Does he know you was comin' here tonight?"

"I told him we wouldn't be there when he come home from work."

"An' what did he say?"

"He jus' said, 'Suit yourself.' That's all, jus' 'Suit yourself.' He don't care two hoots about us Mum."

"Well Linnie, you know what it says in the marriage service— 'Forsakin' all others I cleave unto you.' "

"Yeah and that goes double. The only one he cleaves unto is his bloody ol' woman." Lynne put out her arms for the baby. "It's time for his feed. He's 'alf an hour over already." She unfastened her blouse, the baby began to whimper and make sucking sounds with his lips, turning his head blindly from side to side, nuzzling against her breast. She pressed the dark, swollen nipple into his mouth. He fought and wailed, his little face red with temper. Then he began to suck, arching his back, smacking his lips, throwing his whole body greedily behind the action. A trickle of pale blue milk ran out the corner of his mouth.

"He's a real tiger for his tucker," Linnie said, smiling wanly through her tears. She turned fiercely on her mother. "I tell you Mum, I'm not goin' back to that house. If Reggie wants us back he can come an' get us."

"And what if he don't come," said Jessie, looking thoughtfully at her daughter. "Don't you reckon that little feller there needs a father."

Linnie dropped her eyes, pouting her mouth. "Ah Mum, you don't understand. You and Dad always get on so well."

Jessie laughed. "And d'you think it was always like that. D'you think we didn't fight and squabble when we was younger. D'you think we never had mother-in-law trouble or your father never give me a black eye? Well, take another think young lady. Nothin' in this world that's any good was ever got the easy way. Anythin' that's any good has always been fought for."

Her daughter looked at her in amazement. "You sound like the Commos Mum."

"I don't care who I sound like," Jessie snapped. "Your Dad and me's been through some pretty terrible times. And the worst was when that bit of steel flew orf the emery wheel and he lost the sight of his eyes. He made my life hell there for a while, poor feller. Anyone'd of thought I was the one that blinded him. And I made the mistake of babying him. Treated him like an idiot in his own home. One day he pulls me up. . . . 'Lissen here Jesse, just because I ain't got me eyes don't mean I don't wear the trousers round 'ere any more,' he said. 'Seems as if you don't give a woman a back'ander once in a while she gets to thinkin' she's the boss.' And he meant it too."

Linnie dropped her head onto her chest, the tears spilling out over her cheeks. "I'm not goin' back to that house Mum. I'm not goin' back I tell you." She jerked the breast out of the baby's mouth. He screwed up his face and yelled.

"Now lissen," Jessie said fiercely. "I'm ashamed of you carryin' on like a spoiled kid. You'll curdle your milk if you keep it up. Sit there and feed that baby like a decent mother, and I'll put a cup of tea on."

She got up and waddled to the door. "Now you're here you better stay the night and we'll talk about the rest in the morning. But no more about it tonight. I won't have your father worried, do you hear."

Linnie nodded dumbly. "When you're ready come out and get it," her mother said. "And don't hurry that baby. He needs his nourishment."

Linnie sat for a long time staring vacantly out the bedroom window. The baby stopped sucking, her long pendulous breast fell out of his open mouth, he slept, sweat beading his crinkled upper lip. It was pleasant to be back in the old house where she'd lived all her life. Just down the road a bit was Tempe School with the boys still coming out at playtime in their wrinkled jeans, stoushing each other over the head. The little girls bowled their hoops in the summer dusk up the hilly street where she was born. Down below in the river were little islands, with a dead tree or two leaning over the water, where Mum had told her they used to go on boating picnics in the old days, dressed up in their straw hats and middy blouses.

She understood this place, she was part of it. The hard-faced Tempe men and women reared on the river bank were her mob . . . the Cook's River mob. When Mum told her what to do she didn't resent it, somehow it wasn't like taking orders from Reggie's mother. Absently she pushed her breast back into her blouse, but she didn't get up.

Jessie stuck her head through the flywire door.

"I'm makin' a cuppa tea now Bert."

The old man still sat, staring out over the moonlit garden, rolling a cigarette.

"Come on out here a minute," he said. "What's goin' on in there?" She hesitated. "C'mon," he said impatiently. "I'm 'er father aren't I?" She came out and stood beside his chair, biting her lips. "She's 'ad a row with Reg," she said softly, looking over her shoulder. "Reckons she won't go back."

"I thought they was makin' a real go of it."

"She don't get on with the old lady."

"Ah, so that's the way it is . . ." He paused and lit his cigarette, inhaling deeply. "What d'you think about it?"

"I told 'er she could stay the night."

"Wonder will 'e come after 'er?"

She sank down with a creak in the wicker chair. "That's just what I'm bankin' on Bert. I reckon we oughta let her sleep in our double bed tonight. We can easy doss down on the two divans in the lounge room."

"And what if they decide to stay?" he said.

"It's no good livin' with your in-laws," she said stubbornly. "It never works. We proved that ourselves. Your mother . . ."

He grinned. "Now don't start on my ol' woman," he said. "She's been in 'er grave for twenty years."

"Well, she nearly bust up our marriage before they put 'er there," Jessie snapped.

"Alright, alright, I admit the ol' girl was a bit of a tartar. So what happens if they stay?"

She leaned forward putting one worn hand on his knee. "You've gotta talk to Reggie, Bert. You've gotta make him see. They must have a place of their own. We could lend them a bit. We got our savings. I only wish it was a bit more. We haven't been able to do much for our kids Bert."

"If this hadn't happened to me," he said bitterly.

"Oh, I'm not blamin' you luv. It's just how things turned out. It's no good cryin' over spilt milk. We never cried poor mouth in our lives. But if we could see our way clear to helpin' Linnie and Reg and the little codger. We've 'ad our lives Bert . . ."

"Did you make that cup of tea," he said, taking her hand in his. "Let 'er sleep in our bed tonight then Jesse, and we'll see how things shape by tomorrer."

By the time Jessie had Linnie and the baby settled down for the night it was ten o'clock. Never mind, she thought, I had that bit of a doze off before tea. That'll keep me goin' for a while. She wished she could take a sickie tomorrer, but it was pay day. I better show up on pay day she thought, pulling her nightie on over her head.

She leaned out the lounge room window straining her eyes for Reggie's Holden swerving round the corner.

"I'll leave the back door unlatched," she said softly. She stood on the verandah, watching the infernal fires of Tempe tip gleam through the night like a myriad evil, little, red animal eyes. The smoke rose in long, curling tendrils into the dark sky, the stench of burning rag, rubber and rotting vegetables hung in the still air.

In the Depression there was a famous two-up school out on the Tempe tip. They used to pile up walls of rusty kerosene tins, and crouch down in the hollow, with a cockatoo on the muck heaps against the skyline, to watch out for the coppers. But the coppers used to stroll over, disguised in old clothes, and pinch them all.

It wasn't healthy to walk alone on Tempe tip even in broad daylight in those days. Jessie's kids always knew enough to beat it in the opposite direction if they saw a rival gang coming. You could see figures moving for miles across the mudflats. If you were stiff enough to be caught they'd frisk you, blood your nose for you, perhaps drag you round on a rope for a while till they got sick of it, then boot you up the bum and send you home.

But now the Tempe tip was haunted only by the old men and the birds . . . the old men with their bony black dogs scavenging for scrap iron, the birds scavenging for rotting vegetables. Flocks of pigeons and seagulls swept over the tip in dense clouds, swooping and shrieking among the acrid smoke, beating the air with the rush of their wings. The shadow of the crows skimmed cawing over the rusty truck cabins, the abandoned frigs, the kids' pedal cars, prams, hospital waste and trusses. A blue Genoa velvet lounge chair, with orange stuffing spilling out of its guts, was white with shags' droppings. It stood lopsided with a kind of pathetic gentility among the squawking birds.

A great white moon rode over Cook's River and the little humped hills of Tempe. At the foot of the street the shadow of a dead tree shivered in the water. A man had hanged himself there once years ago.

Jessie could hear the sound of the trains shunting in Tempe Station, a Super Constellation warmed its engines up at Mascot 'drome. A muffled sobbing came from the front bedroom. It was Linnie, crying her eyes out in the lonely double bed.

She fought a terrible need to pad down the hall and take Linnie in her arms, comforting her as she had when she'd broken her doll or barked her shins. No, she thought fiercely. I mustn't coddle her. She's gotta learn to grow up. Maybe I've been too soft with her. It was hard to believe the tall, buxom woman with the swollen breasts was her pigtailed daughter Linnie.

"For Christ's sake why doncha come to bed woman," Bert growled from the divan in the lounge. "All your watchin' won't bring Reggie round that corner."

"Lissen," she said. "Thank Gawd. He's come." The Holden turned into the side passage, the headlights swept across the ceiling. Reggie's shoes crunched on the gravel drive.

Jessie stuck her head out the front window. "That you Reggie?" she whispered.

"Yeah it's me Mum." He crossed the lawn and stood gazing up at her, his face white in the street light.

She grinned. "Lookin' for someone?"

He didn't grin back. "Is Linnie here?"

"Yeah, she's here. She's in the front bedroom. You better stay the night. It's pretty late. Too late to drag the little feller out now."

"Thanks Mum."

"Oh and Reggie . . ." she paused.

"Yeah."

"Go crook on her luv . . . but not too crook eh?" This time he grinned back.

"Okay Mum."

She listened to his footsteps tiptoe up the hall. Then she stretched herself out on the divan and pulled the sheets up to her chin. For a long time there was only the murmur of voices from their bedroom. Then the bed creaked. Eventually it began to creak with a gentle rhythmic pattern.

"Them springs need oilin' bad," Bert growled.

Jessie giggled. "Bert."

"What?"

"I'm comin' over inter your bed. It's too lonely here."

"You'll never fit. Anyway it's too hot," he grumbled.

"I'm not *that* fat. Jeez you're a real nark luv."

"Ah, alright, come over then," he said grudgingly.

She squeezed her big body alongside his hard, spare hips. He reached out and put his arms round her.

"Do you reckon they'll stay?" she murmured against the hairy warmth of his chest. "It'd be nice t' have a baby in the house agen."

"You're bloody hopeless," he said. They giggled together like a couple of young lovers.

"I hope she remembers to give that baby 'is night feed," Jessie whispered anxiously.

The palm tree soughed in the wind off the bay, its long fronds scraping and rummaging in the gutters of the old house. The tears dried on Linnie's cheeks. The baby snuffled in the crook of her arm.

On the opposite side of the river Saint Magdalene smiled in the garden of the Home for Fallen Girls, otherwise known as

Tempe Laundry, raising her white plaster arms in enthusiastic benediction. The fallen girls lay quietly, their little red hands, chapped with washing soda, folded gently above the sheets, their institution nighties buttoned tightly up to their necks, dreaming of sweethearts and marriage and a fat baby nuzzling for love at their narrow little breasts.

Chapter Nine

☆

A LITTLE, snub-nosed girl with a thick body and eyes like brown pansies, came singing and swinging to herself through the rows of roving machines. Only her parted lips betrayed the song. The noise of the mill roared out of the summer like waves beating and thudding against the mind, drowning all subsidiary sound with ruthless ease.

"Hey Patty, what are you doin' outa your section? You'll cop it. The whistle hasn't gone yet."

The hoarse whisper was tuned exactly one octave above the roar of the machines.

Patty jumped and looked guiltily behind her. Julie's grinning, moon face blocked her passage down the aisle.

"You nearly give me heart failure, Jule. I thought it was that sneaky Dick. I wanta get away early tonight." She tossed one dark switch of hair over her shoulder.

"Why, what's on? Gotta audition on TUW or somethin'?" Julie's little eyes poked and pried, desperately trying to relive some of the glamour of her youth in this little, freckle-faced girl, scratching one bare ankle with her shoe.

"Naw, just a dance out at Newtown. But I might get a chance to sing solo with the band. One of me brother's mates is the drummer. They send a talent scout out there sometimes. Might lead to somethin'."

"Yeah, you wanta try everythin'. That's the only way to get on." Julie sat down on the rickety box. It wheezed and crumpled under her weight.

"I'll be on Rumpus Room on Fridee night though. Don't forget to listen."

"Gee that's good Patty. Are you goin' to get paid for it?"

"No, they don' pay you for nothin'. Just a bottle of Pepsi Cola. I come between the Pepsi ads."

"I'll tell Don an' the kids. We'll all lissen in. What number are you singin'?"

" 'Three Coins in the Fountain'. You know! Frankie's number. It's an oldy, but it suits me voice . . . Eric Elliott, he's the compère, he's been lovely to me. He suggested I sing it, said I had a lyric quality." She mimicked the tone. "He reckons I could have a future but me voice needs trainin'."

"Pity your Mum couldn't get you a bitta trainin', luv." Julie kept one wary eye on her whirling spindles. "Don't want them muckin' up on me before the whistle blows," she said. "They've been too good to be true this arvo."

"There's Berenice Follett near Newtown Station," Patty said. "She told me she'd take me at a reduced rate, if she got a bit of kudos outa it."

Patty swayed to unheard music, her half-closed eyes drowsed and dreamed over the greasy concrete floor, the hunched, overalled women, wool fluff powdering their shoulders. Blurred and distorted through a fine, damp mist of steam, they sweated and scurried between bobbin box and rover, like nightmare figures in the grip of some awful compulsion.

Reality faded away and she was standing in a golden glow clutching a microphone, a white satin gown sliding down off one shoulder, a gardenia in her hair. If Shirley Bassey could do it, why not Patty Maguire? She was a factory girl, too.

"Berenice? She still teachin'?" Julie gave a shrill, contemptuous laugh. "My Gawd she must be pushin' fifty. She was teachin' when I was a bit of a kid. How's she lookin' now?"

"She looks pretty good," Patty said. "Still got her smashin' figure. Teaches tap an' ballet too."

"Ah, well good luck to her. You could do worse than Berenice. An' she's got the good connections. Usta live with one of the top radio announcers. I wished I was still in the game. I'd a pushed you luv." A bitter smile creased Julie's sweaty cheeks. "Never think to look at me I was a top liner in me day. Acrobatic dancin' was me speciality. You don't wanta do what I did Patty. Fall for some feller and that's the end of the penny section. Once you give up your exercises, you run to fat. I could be makin' a packet now, if I'd kept at it."

"Ah, I won't be gettin' married for years yet," Patty said with lofty condescension. "I'm not that interested in boys. Did I show you the lovely photo I got of Frankie?" She dived into the bosom of her overall, and pulled out a glossy, autographed print of Sinatra.

"Looks a bit worn on it, don't he?" Julie grinned. "And who wouldn't after Ava Gardner and Lauren Bacall?"

"Frankie still leaves the rest for dead," Patty said indignantly. "They're always pickin' on him in the papers, but like Dad says, it's only the capitalists. He's real progressive minded. Goes round talkin' to the high school kids about race riots, and all that. Ain't he got lovely eyes? Sorta meltin'."

"Ah you and your Frankie," Julie grinned. "I'd rather have Bing."

"Bing!" Patty looked disgusted. "He's got no guts. We still meet at the Sinatra Club. Some of the kids have dropped off, an' gone over to Elvis Presley, but it's Frankie for me."

"Sing me that number," Julie said. "Dick won't be round now. Go on, I'd love to hear it. I've filled in for the night. I got no more worries till the whistle goes."

Patty draped herself over the side of the machine, took a deep breath and began to sing. Softly her voice beat under the throb of the mill, tender as a child, quivered and rose up and stormed the sky.

> "Three coins in a fountain,
> Which one will the fountain bless.
> Just one wish will be granted . . ."

The whistle blew in a long shuddering wail, as if it wept for Julie, sitting with her heavy thighs spread over her deal box, the tears wetting her cheeks, as if it wept for Patty singing like a little, caged, warm-throated bird in a shaft of sunlight through the high, barred, factory windows.

"Ah now that's mucked it," Patty moaned. "I'll have to get inter the wash queue and miss me early bus."

Jean and Patty left Lowe's bus at Erskineville Road. You could pick them for sisters a mile off . . . the same stubby bodies, the same wide-spaced eyes, the same long, loose, swinging brown hair. But Jeanie was already beginning to lose the bloom of youth. An unhealthy, blotchy red stained her cheeks, her hips swayed heavily as she walked.

The kids were still straggling out the gates of Erskineville Public School, built 1882, with the bell tower and all its cream plaster and brick dignity.

"See you later Nance?"

" 'Ooray."

School bags and bobby socks, skinny legs and rat-tailed hair. It didn't seem very long ago since Patty had been one of those little girls ambling along, arms entwined, swapping giggles and confidences and sticky lollies. They'd dawdle down past the barrowman, past Erskineville Station, brown weatherboards furred with soot, the *Daily Mirror* . . . "Doctor tells of Seven Stab Wounds" . . . the *Sun* . . . "Free House Contest Offer". They'd hang over the picket fence watching the electric trains rushing out from the shadows, the sunlight sliding like liquid along their roofs, the steam trains puffing and shunting onto the branch lines. The sky behind Silver Street was dark with smoke, thin spirals of smoke pluming into great white cauliflowers, dense grey clouds wiping their smoggy fingers on the little houses.

Yet surely it must be a lifetime ago and the little, brown-eyed girl in the navy blue tunic would soon be like Jeanie, plodding at her side, her thighs chafed with sweat, would soon be like the broad-hipped woman in the old weatherboard, shading her eyes against the sun dazzle, waiting for them coming home from work up Silver Street.

Generations merged into each other and time lost its meaning. The struggle to live out your days blurred your dreams. Powerless, you watched them sliding away like the sunlight on the roofs of the trains, never to come back again, lost forever . . . lost . . . lost . . . only to be born again in the hearts of the little girls leaning over the railway fence chucking orange peel onto the rails.

Kids in faded jeans, their hips weighed down with cowboy holsters, skidded around the three spindly trees in the little park, nicked out of the corner.

A woman came out with a mop and sloshed a bucket of soapy water over the cracked tiles of her front porch.

A little girl with a blonde pony tail skipped down the road. A boy played marbles against a brick wall, whistling between his teeth.

"Here come the kids," Jeanie cried, her face alight with eagerness. Jammy-faced, with the strong, sweaty smell of children in summer, they hurtled into her skirts.

"Pooh, you stink." Jeanie wrinkled up her nose, laughing at them, holding them tight. "Have you been good for Nana today?"

They went in the gate of the old yellow weatherboard, its tiny front garden crammed with flowers in pots and tins, creepers climbing up chicken wire, geraniums struggling for life in a narrow, damp, bricked-in side passage. The back yard ran down to the railway line and Peggy Maguire's washing was always streaked with little wisps of soot off the passing trains. The old house shook to their thunder, night and day they clattered and puffed, shunted and shrieked, till life would have seemed empty without their urgent sense of coming and going, a myriad lives hurrying past the back door.

Jeanie's kids loved Nana's place. Hanging over the back fence they watched the "lectrics" that went "lec, lec, lec", the diesels and the spectacular "steamies" that never lost their novelty.

The front door was open and the sound of the wireless poured out onto the pavement. A graceful, wide-hipped woman with loose, wavy, grey-streaked hair stood on the front verandah, shading her eyes with her hand, in an attitude that had become as eternal for Patty and Jean as the Statue of Liberty.

"They been drivin' me off me rocker," she said to Jean, scowling and grinning at the two kids. "Specially Jimmy. I s'pose it's the heat. You can't blame the poor little sods."

A Major Mitchell parrot blinked and bobbed in his cage, a big white conch shell, glistening with sunlight, curled against the wall. The doorstep was blacked and shiny, the inevitable white lace curtains stiffly starched, the hall runner polished to a dangerous smoothness. It was just as it had always been in Silver Street.

They trooped inside, sprawling round the kitchen table. Jeanie moved a pile of books and magazines off the chair. She knew she would have to get up in a minute, wipe the kids over with a flannel and set off on the long trek to Fivedock. But just for twenty minutes, perhaps half an hour, she was content to stretch out her legs, close her eyes and let the ache drain out of her toes in the dimness of her mother's kitchen.

"Here, get this inter you," said her mother brusquely, watching her out of the corner of her eye. "You're a bloody fool, Jeanie. If you keep this up you'll never live to enjoy that flash house at Blacktown."

She planked the cup of tea down in front of her, slopping it in the saucer.

"Ah Mum, give it a bone." Jeanie kept her eyes tightly closed against her mother's anger, just as she kept her mind tightly closed against her mother's ideas.

"Someone's gotta talk sense to you," Peggy said. "What good does it do Jeanie? What are you and Alec tryin' to do?"

"Get a decent roof over our heads and some sort of a life for ourselves, that's all," Jeanie said wearily. "Is that bad, to have a bit of ambition?"

"Ambition." Peggy snorted. "Didn't your Dad and me have

ambition. A fat lot of good it did us. I dunno. You kids never seem to have learnt nothin'. Patty thinks she's goin' to be another Shirley Bassey and you're dreamin' of bein' a property owner. Don't you never learn?"

Jeanie leaned forward, opening her eyes, looking at her mother without pity. "What can we learn off you Mum? To give up without a try? No thanks. If you and Dad wanta rot in Erskineville, that's your look out. But not for this pigeon."

The angry tears stung in Peggy's eyes. "Rot you say. We don't rot. You never rot if you've got the guts to fight. But you and Alec have got another answer. Alec's one a these overtime kings and . . ."

Jeanie stood up, her neck blotched red, hanging onto the table for support. "You leave Alec out of this. He's no Commo, if that's what you mean. Just because he's got a bit of sense about him. We'll live our own lives Mum, without any help from you." They glared at each other across the sunlit kitchen. The kids pressed closer to Jeanie's skirts, wide-eyed, starting to whimper. "Now you've made the poor bloody kids cry," Jeanie shouted fiercely.

Peggy dropped her hands onto her lap. "Alright," she said bitterly. "I've had me say. But don't say I never warned you. You think you're sittin' on top of the world, but you're ridin' for a fall me girl. You're too big for your boots by half, and by Christ, when it comes it'll be a beauty."

"I'm goin' home," Jeanie said. "Home for a bitta peace and quiet. There's none here and never has been."

She flounced into the bathroom. The kids yelled in protest as she scrubbed at their faces and knees with angry hands. Patty gazed dreamily at the blowfly tangled, buzzing, in the lace curtains. "It's no good naggin' at Jeanie, Mum," she said. "She thinks she'll solve all the world's problems with that little house at Blacktown."

"Always slingin' off at your father," Peggy said sombrely. "And when I remember him draggin' home week after week with those blasted dole tickets, and all the years of strugglin' on the wharves . . . ah, I could slap her smug little bottom."

"She just don't understand Mum, because she don't want to," Patty said from all the superior wisdom of her sixteen years.

"How can't she know?" Peggy cried out, beating her hands together. "How can't she? She lived in this house didn't she? She saw your father blackballed. She saw it when he came home with his nose all smashed in, she wore the welfare shoes, she ate the damn thin soup day after day . . . why don't she know?"

"She's afraid," Patty said softly. "She's afraid Mum."

Jeanie came back leading the two kids by the hand. Their little scrubbed faces were subdued and sulky.

"And another thing Mum," she said, going into the attack. "I've been meanin' to talk to you about Patty. What's all this about her goin' to work in the jammy?"

"If I wanta work in the jammy I can, can't I?" Patty snapped.

"You're too young and silly to know what's best for you," Jeanie said loftily. "But it's up to Mum and Dad to have a bit of sense."

"What difference does it make?" said Peggy wearily, brushing her hair back from her white forehead. "The mills are all closin' down."

"There you go again. You're beaten before you start. You're hopeless Mum. Patty's got a good trade. I only wished I'd been given a chance to get one." She glared up at her mother. "There'll always be work in the weavin', if only she finished her time."

"D'you reckon?" Peggy said sarcastically. "Well, it's up to Patty to decide. If she wants to work her guts out for a kid's wage and the sack at the end of it, she's welcome. I don't care where she works as long as she sticks up for her rights."

"Ah, you make me sick," Jeanie snapped. "I might of knowed it was useless tryin' to din any sense into your heads. You're a bunch a no-hopers . . ."

"I know . . . a buncha dirty Commos," said her mother quietly. "I never said that."

"No, but you meant it. Well, we won't fight about it no more Jeanie." They stood staring at each other in the shabby little kitchen, memories tugging between their eyes . . . all the days and months and years of struggle, the lay-off and the sackings, the strikes and the pickets, the handouts and the hostile eyes . . . "there go the Commo kids" . . . "yeah, can't you pick the type" . . . the scrawled letters on the footpath outside . . . "dirty Commos live here."

A train roared past and pulled into Erskineville Station. The little house shuddered. Jeanie put out her hand. She smiled crookedly, her brown, honest eyes on her mother's face. "You'll never make a Commo out of me Mum," she said. "I saw too much of it when I was a nipper."

Her mother bent and kissed the kids. "Take care of your-selves," she said softly. "See you tomorrer."

"Thanks for the cuppa Mum."

The gate banged behind them.

"Thank Christ she's gone," said Patty wearily. "She was be-binnin' to get on me tripe."

"I run a bath for you Patty," her mother said. "Better get in it. Your new cotton's laid out on the bed. I starched your petti-coat, stiff as a board, and it was a cow to iron."

For a long time afterwards, Peggy sat at the kitchen table press-ing her broad white hands together, staring out the window, seeing only a little girl with a tear-stained, grubby face and a desperate voice.

"Don't go up to school Dad. Don't go up to school. I don't care if they take me out of High, but don't go up to school. Please Dad."

"I'm goin' up whether you like it or not," Tom Maguire roared. "I'll tell 'em why me daughter's got no school uniform. I'll tell 'em why me kids wears bloody sandshoes . . ."

"Don't go up to school, please Dad. Don't go up to school."

She pressed her hands to her eyes but the image stayed there, pleading and crying, the velvety brown eyes shadowed with an-guish, the little white face trembling like an image seen through a mist of tears.

A moonless night, a pot of white paint in a deserted lane . . . "Alright Jeanie. No coppers watchin'. 'Op to it luv. Now . . . 'Re—lease Sharkey' . . . Ah, you duffer, that's not the bloody way to spell bloody Sharkey. S—H—A—R— . . ."

Peggy crossed the room and turned the wireless up.

"The casing of Sputnik should be seen in Sydney on Friday and Saturday morning in the north-western sky. Tomorrow it should be seen at 4.36 a.m. at 30 degrees elevation."

"I must get up and have a look for it," she thought. "Tom'll wake me when he comes off shift." She started to peel potatoes and slice onions for tea, but her heart followed Jeanie down Silver Street, onto the station, all the long weary miles to Five-dock with the kids grizzling at her heels, the little dream fibro glowing above the factory chimneys like a mirage of happiness.

"I hope she gets it," she whispered, slicing onions savagely into the frying pan. "I hope she gets it," and fiercely, though she'd stopped believing in God years ago, "Oh, God, let her have it."

"If you leave me I'll be a lonely one,

Dontcha know you're me one and only one" yelled the wireless.

Peggy wiped the back of her hand across her eyes. "Bloody onions . . . always did make me bawl," she said.

A voice cooed gently in her ear: "Do your hands tell what you do, instead of how lovely you are," it said.

"Let's go to the Hop. . . .
Oh! baby let's go,
Let's go to the Hop.
C'mon let's go . . .
Oh! you c'n rock it, you c'n roll it,
You c'n swing it, you c'n groove it,
You c'n really start to move it
AT THE HOP . . .
Let's go to the Hop,
Oh! baby c'mon . . .
LET'S GO TO THE HOP . . ."

Flock nylon, rustling taffeta, starched cotton over a roped half-slip, drainpipe trousers with a lurex thread, tropical shirts, char-grey and Sinatra red . . . Brylcreem and crew cuts, Wild Poppy behind your ears and in the cleft of your new breasts. The Yank compere sweats in the middle of the hall, the hula girls jiggle lewdly on his fat bum. The trio warms up to it, half steamed already, the dust rises off the floor and floats in a steamy haze down the long, golden arcade of light and sound and sweat . . . forgetfulness and romance and Wild Poppy sousing the dust with scent . . . LET'S GO TO THE HOP . . . Oh! baby let's go.

The boys hang round the entrance, stamping cigarette butts into the floor, swopping dirty jokes, eyes narrowed to survey the talent. Youth fortifies itself at the milk bar, chrome and laminex and a sad-eyed Greek rattling up the change in the till. The juke boxes across King Street all play a different tune. Jalopies with lurid yellow signs huddle against the kerb, motor bikes roar up beside the tramlines, pull in behind the jalopies. Youth converges like ants to honey.

"Gotta bit of leg opener in the back seat of the heap . . ."

"Oh! baby c'mon . . ."

Lips half open, they mumble and lounge and spit and shuffle, pretending to a sophistication that doesn't exist.

"Look at that one. Reckon she'd be in it?"

"I got 'er pants half off already."

OH BABY C'MON LET'S GO . . . LET'S GO TO THE HOP.

The factory grease stubbornly clogs under their finger-nails, premature wrinkles bunch in the corners of their eyes, their bodies are hard and stringy and muscly and tough with work, when they smile the smile slips over their faces, and lingers in

93

their eyes, sardonic and vulnerable, tender and brave, as a boy whistling in the dark.

Patty and Val tripped into the hall, heads held high, eyes blind to the comments and the nudges at the door. Val was a little blonde with a pony tail and a pert bottom. She worked at the jam factory. But tonight in black taffeta, a transparent, frilly blouse with only a bra underneath, she was transformed. In her starch cotton with a blue Alice band in her swinging hair, Patty felt gauche and childish beside the scented glory of Val.

The girls sat primly round the walls, hearts beating like tom-toms in unison, waiting for the lordly males to notice them. If none eventuated they fled to the washroom and wept into the toilet, jerking the chain to cover their sobs, powdering their noses fiercely a hundred times in front of the smeary mirror, sweeping back into the hall, with frozen, disdainful smiles painted carefully on their little, pink faces.

The males strutted and whistled at the doorway, unsuccessfully hiding a terrible sense of their own inadequacy.

"If I asted that little sort in the pink dress wonder would she give me a knockback?" . . . sidling desperately across the floor, and when the dance was over, rushing back in a frantic stampede to the safety of "the boys" round the door. The ones who came with regular partners were the lucky, the envied of the bunch. They danced every dance together, cheek to cheek, body fitted to body, eyes glazed. In the intervals they flocked to the milk bars or sneaked down side streets, embracing with passionate longing in narrow lanes and tiny parks, naked with space under a pitiless street light.

> "Sugar in the mornin',
> Sugar in the evenin',
> Sugar at suppertime.
> Be me little sugar
> An' love me all the time.
>
> Honey in the mornin',
> Honey in the evenin',
> Honey at suppertime.
> Be me little honey,
> An' love me all the time."

The starch went out of Patty's blue cornflowers. Her new cotton hung limply against her sturdy legs. The sweat trickled down her back, the Alice band slipped sideways over one ear.

She rocked and rolled and jived from one embrace to the other, from one knee to the other, always popular because of her marvellous sense of rhythm, her good humour over squashed toes and fumbling dance steps. But most of Patty's partners were expert dancers. Their energy was prodigious . . . the restless, seemingly bottomless energy of youth, squandered so cheaply, till one morning they would wake bleary-eyed for the "zombie parade" at six o'clock, and realize that youth had gone, drained away in the factories, ground away on the ceaseless, pitiless treadmill of existence.

Never again would they roar down the Darke's Forrest straight, the coppers on their tail, their white silk shirts flapping in the summer wind, never again would they dance till the dawn paled over the warehouses and the factory chimneys.

They would turn over in the double bed, listening with a kind of weary, cheated amazement to the sound of the boys and girls laughing down the street at three o'clock in the morning. "How do the bastards do it?"

But now Patty danced like the mermaid in Hans Andersen's fairy tale, knowing that the pain and the sharp knives waited under the slushy floors of the jammy, under the asphalt pavement of Silver Street, but with no alternative but to dance her way to that dreary destiny.

> "Wake up liddle Suzy,
>   Whata we goin' to tell your Momma?
>   Whata we goin' to tell your Poppa?
>   Whata we goin' to tell your friends?
>   WAKE UP LIDDLE SUZY . . ."

The lanky, white-faced drummer, his fair hair hanging childlike in his eyes, leaned over the platform, mumbling out of the corner of his mouth.

"I fixed it for you Patty. You're on, next number. What'll it be?"

"Thanks Shorty. Make it 'Santa Catalina'."

Patty trembled, the palms of her hands were wet, her knees gave as she climbed onto the dais. The words of the song ran a rat race round her head. She fixed her eyes on a mouldy spot on the ceiling, opened her mouth a couple of times, took a couple of deep breaths. The drummer led in, the tinny piano followed, the sax wailed. The first couple took the floor.

"One bar an' come in honey," the compère muttered in her ear. The dancers circled in a dusty haze at Patty's feet. She clutched the mike with sweaty hands. Where was the clinging satin, the gardenia in her hair, the flattering spotlight glow?

"Twenty six miles across the water,
Santa Catalina is awaitin' for me" she mumbled, licking her lips. The compère looked worried, adjusted the mike. The drummer covered up. He shot Patty a gentle grin of encouragement. "Get the beat kid," he whispered.

The dancing feet shuffled, the drummer thudded out the rhythm. Patty closed her eyes, flung up her head, swayed her body, got the beat.

"Forty kilometres in a leaky ol' boat,
Any ol' thing that'll stay afloat,
Santa Catalina . . . the island of Romance . . ."

The feet flew, the dust whirled, the drummer's fair hair banged up and down on his wet forehead, the light globes swayed. Long spindly shadows dangled across the ceiling. Outside the trams ground sparks off the rails, the trains rushed with a demented wail through Newtown Station. Four months gone and just starting to show, Shirl roared up King Street on the back of a second-hand Norton.

The stubby little girl stood, thick legs planted wide apart, breasts swelling up and down under the scooped neckline of her cotton frock. Patty had the beat. She'd always had it, since she was born to the shriek of a factory whistle in Silver Street.

"Twenty six miles across the water
Santa Catalina is awaitin' for me.
ROMANCE, ROMANCE, ROMANCE, ROMANCE . . ."

The drummer grinned and shook hands with himself. The Yank compère squeezed her arm. "You was swell honey. Come again some time."

"Now put your hands together for the liddle local gal . . . Patty Maguire from Erskineville . . . a honey of a voice Patty. See you roun' sometime Patty."

"Jeez you was real good Patty," Val said, wide blue eyes swimming in ecstasy.

The moment was over, the glory of the night had gone.

"I promised Mum I'd leave early tonight," Patty said, ruthlessly dousing the light in Val's eyes. "She reckons I've had too many late nights."

Val was horrified. "But Patty it's only just started."

"I'm leavin' at eleven o'clock," Patty said stubbornly. "You can stay on if you like."

"You know I don't wanta stay on me own."

The orchestra swung into the next number.

At eleven-thirty Patty and Val left the dance hall and walked towards Newtown Station. Inarticulate Romeos lurked by the kerb, their bikes hotted up, their blood running fierce and hungry under their leather jackets.

"How about a ride girls?"

"Wanta be in it you sheilas?"

"Goin' my way luv?"

"How about a lift gorgeous?"

Patty stuck her little freckled nose up in the air. She grabbed Val fiercely under the elbow and propelled her up King Street at a half trot. "They're only a mob a lairs."

Val hung back, her voice shrilly defiant, her mouth sulky. "You're gettin' too big for your boots Patty Maguire. Doncha try to run my life."

"Ah, shut up," Patty said. "You give me a pain. Go ridin' with one of them bodgies and you'll be lookin' for just what you get."

Val glanced out of the corner of her eye. "They look alright to me."

"Sure!" Patty loaded her voice with elaborate sarcasm. "Well, why doncha have a ride then, if that's what you're dyin' for?"

Val stood stock-still in the centre of the pavement, tugging her arm free. "That's just what I think I'll do," she cried shrilly.

The bike puttered up the gutter, and stopped beside them. "Climb on kid. What are you waitin' for?"

Val giggled. "You'll take me straight home woncha?"

"Sure. Where d'you live?" He gazed fascinated down the front of her sheer blouse.

"Erskineville."

"Whaddabout your girl friend. Don't she wanta be in it?"

"Comin' Patty?"

Patty shook her head. She didn't turn round and Val roared away, plastered to a leather coat with an elaborate yellow tiger stencilled across the back. On the side of the bike was a neatly printed inscription, "N.N.N.R.H." . . . visible to the discerning eye, but not too visible for a prowling copper.

"What's that mean?" Val whispered doubtfully in her escort's ear.

He grinned. "No naughty, no ride home. Hang on kid. We'll give 'er a burst."

Val was swept away, her pony tail bobbing, her little white face rigid with shock in the blink of a blue neon sign.

> "Wake up liddle Suzy,
>   Whatta we goin' to tell your Momma?
>   Whatta we goin' to tell your Poppa?
>   WAKE UP LIDDLE SUZY . . ."

"Val," Patty shouted. "Val."

She turned and trudged onto the station, rubbing shoulders with the picture crowd, coming home. But she was lonely, as lonesome as the white, scarred face of the moon riding through a film of smoke above the slate roofs of Newtown.

> "Twenty six miles across the water,
>   ROMANCE . . . ROMANCE . . . ROMANCE . . . ROMANCE . . ."

"Wakey, wakey Peg. Here comes Sputnik."

Peg came out of a blur of sleep to feel the big hand shaking her shoulder. She groped upwards and her fingers closed on the familiar, thick, warm flesh, the calloused pads on the palm.

"Ah Tom, I'm too sleepy. I waited up for Patty."

"C'mon Peg. This is history. You're goin' to tell your grandchildren about this. You'll be whingin' if you miss it."

Grumbling she struggled into her dressing gown, and followed him out into the back yard.

"Dunno how you can be so bloody enthusiastic at half-past four in the mornin'," she said.

But he was already peering upwards, bulky shoulders and grizzled head outlined above the picket fence, scanning the night sky, pricked by its multitude of stars, with only one man-made star, a pathfinder, swinging on its solitary orbit.

Millions of heads turned in breathless wonder to watch its lonely flight, millions of hearts in the streets of the world beat a little faster, but none faster than the heart of Tom Maguire, Sydney wharf labourer, his thick, calloused hands gripping the back fence that hung over the Erskineville railway line.

He grabbed her shoulder. "Look Peg. There she goes. Look." His stubby forefinger pierced the sky in triumph, shot with the impetus of joy over the roofs, the factories, over the smoke and the smog, over the steam train, with a burning bush of sparks, hissing beneath the embankment.

And with his finger went a host of fingers, white, black, brown and yellow, stubby fingers with grease under the nails. *"There she goes."* It was a song pouring like a ladle of boiling steel from the throats of the world's toilers. Shadowy and triumphant, they stood, pressing against Maguire's back fence, in the path of light from the flywire door.

The little star moved slowly across the sky, taking with it the hope and joy of man.

"Get Patty," Tom roared. "She mustn't miss this. Get Patty."

He stumbled up the yard, and tripped over the clothes prop.

"Jesus Christ what's that bastard doin' there? A man could brain 'isself."

Peg helped him up, her shoulders shaking. "Why doncha look where you're goin', y' great galoot."

'Get Patty," he said, tenderly feeling his shin.

"Let her sleep. The poor kid's gotta be up before six."

"She can stay up all night dancin' to those silly Yankee pop tunes," her father said. "And she misses Sputnik."

"There'll be other nights," his wife said. "Let her sleep. I'll make you a cuppa." She put out her broad, heavy hand, and they went, fingers interlocked like children, into the little house.

"Well, how was it tonight?" she asked, as she'd asked a thousand times before.

"They're really rippin' it in," he said. "The boss has got all the militant gangs marked with a red ring. We been sat in the hot seat from the word go."

"How much will you bring home this week?" she said, frown marks creasing her brow.

"Twelve quid."

"And the week before six and the week before that eight. We might as well be back in the Depression Tom."

"The Groupers get all the good bait," he said. "And it's too bloody often to be just coincidence. All the confirmed, habitual militants get sat in on the jobs with no money and no future."

He looked at her tall, strong body narrowly. "You're bein' terrible close-mouthed about what happened at Crown Street."

She poured out the tea, her face averted. "It's just what I thought. I'm two months."

He sat back in his chair, grinning. "So there's life in the ol' feller yet?"

"It's not funny," she snapped. "Not at my age. Gawd knows what Jeanie'll say."

"Let her say what she likes. What'd they think about it at Crown Street?"

"They said it was a change of life baby. I got a bit of blood pressure and I had that trouble with me kidneys when I was carryin' Patty. But that was sixteen years ago. I'll be alright."

He sat, stirring his tea, smiling to himself. "Won't the gang be jealous. Reckon I'm an ol' man. They can't keep a good militant down."

"I don't see nothin' to laugh at." Her voice trembled.

He looked up, knitting his brows. "Are you sorry about this Mum?"

"I dunno whether to be glad or sorry."

He took her hand across the oilcloth, gently playing with her fingers. "We'll call him Sputnik," he said softly.

"Over me dead body you will. You're mad. You wanted to call the others Lenin and Stalin. If I hadn't put me foot down . . ."

"C'mon," he said, pulling her to her feet. "An expectant mother should get her beauty sleep, and it's a fat lot you'll be gettin'."

Arm in arm they walked down the moonlit hall, her head against his shoulder.

They lay awake for a while in the old, iron-knobbed double bed, staring into the dark.

"You know Peg," he said. "We put that Sputnik up in the sky."

"What, you an' me Tommy?" she mumbled. "That's a pretty tall order."

"All the things we done, the fights we fought, the months on short pay, the hard times and the battlin'. If we hadn't done it the Soviet Union wouldn't a got that satellite up there. They'd a been too busy fightin' a war. Even if they'd got it up those bastards of Yanks would of shot it out of the skies. But they couldn't get away with it. It's us, the power of the workin' class that's keepin' it afloat."

She didn't answer. She was already asleep, her dark, greying hair tumbled against the pillow, her lashes long and youthfully black on her cheeks.

He lay there for a long time, thinking, following Sputnik in his mind, through the lonely reaches of the sky. Funny, he thought. Funny how I've battled all these years, gettin' labelled a Commo, and I never joined the Party. All the times I been asted and I never joined. He tried to explain to himself why this was

100

but his mind was foggy with weariness and the desire to sleep the clock round.

At first, when he was young, he'd thought he wasn't good enough. He'd believed you had to be a man of a special breed to be a Communist. But later he'd come to see that the Communist Party was full of men like himself, with all their weaknesses, their strengths, their vanities and their virtues. The only difference between them and the rest of mankind was that they'd seen the need to change the world, and, in doing so, had begun the long, painful, bitter process of changing themselves.

And now as first light streaked across the Sydney sky, he knew why he'd never joined the Party. He hadn't wanted to relinquish himself, that individuality, that wild, thrusting, rebellious spirit that had always marked him apart from the "weakies" and the "crawlers".

He'd wanted to be free to be himself, not bound by the discipline and the rule book of any Party, not committed to follow a policy that he didn't always fully support, or men he didn't always fully agree with.

And it had all been an illusion. He had never been free. He had always been part of that great army of toilers that had helped to put Sputnik into the skies of the world, and would fight to keep it there.

No man was free to be himself, no man dared to be alone. All men only existed in relationship to other men. It had taken him thirty years to find out what he had always really known. And so tomorrow he would go up to his mate Les and say: "Well you got a new recruit to your Party. And you never done it you log. It was Sputnik what recruited me. Nothin' less than a satellite."

No man could fight alone . . . he struggled with the thought and then fell asleep, sprawled across the double bed, his arm flung out under Peg's heavy head, her body fitted into the warm hollow of his side . . . ROMANCE, ROMANCE, ROMANCE.

Chapter Ten

☆

VIC was drinking with the flies. He'd been drinking too long
and his eyes were brown and wet and soupy as a spaniel's.

Little groups of workers nattered and argued and hung over
the bar, but they gave Vic a wide berth. Surly and morose he
stared into his beer, and the more he drank the worse he felt.

Through the open doorway he could see the lounge, packed
and noisy, hazy with smoke. The bars of the fluorescent lights
were pink and lemon as lolly sticks.

A big, thick-shouldered truckie in a three-piece pinstriped
suit snapped his fingers, roaring with healthy gusto into the mike.

> "Tutti fruit toot,
> I wanna tutti root toot,
> Tutti fruit toot,
> I wanna tutti root toot."

The mob cheered and stamped. Full of self-confidence, he
came back for an encore.

> "Tutti fruit toot
> I wanna tutti root toot . . ."

"Time gents please." Sick to the bottom of his guts Vic pushed
his schooner across the bar.

"Time gents please." He staggered out under the red and
blue neon sign. It shuttered on and off . . . on and off . . . flicking
against his eyelids. A car nearly hit him as he lurched off the
gutter.

"Bastard's mad," he whispered, hardly moving his lips. "Bastards'd kill a man."

He drove round aimlessly for a long time, circling the bay.
The lights jiggled up and down like yo-yos on the other side of
the water, the flare stack on Bunnerong licked a reddish tongue
into the night sky. A line of cars crawled in a golden daisy chain
along General Holmes Drive.

He bought fish and chips and herked them up again on the moonlit sand. A few couples wandered up and down the wet, phosphorescent edge of the waves. He waited till they passed, then had a leak behind an old boatshed wobbling over the water. When he came out, buttoning up his fly, the beach was deserted, silver and solitary, everything so still that even the pines along the waterfront drooped in soundless, deep green, muggy shadows. Everything was so still, yet everything screamed and retched with horror, bunching and kicking in his mind.

He wet his trouser cuffs in the dark suck of the tide, trying to decide if it would be easier to drown himself. But it wasn't easier. He lay on the warm sand, his shoulders trembling, his legs drawn up. The ulcer in his belly burned like a ball of fire. The tears scalded his lips and he licked them away with his tongue. His finger scrabbled at his once-white shirt, sticky with vomit.

"I lost me guts," he muttered. "I lost me guts."

He got up and crawled behind the wheel of the grey Holden. There was a neatly printed sign on the windscreen:
"Pasadena Driving School,
22/- per hour".

"It'd be just me luck to be pinched by a mug copper," he said. "Jus' me bloody luck."

He drove home without much trouble, doing all the right things by instinct. He often boasted he could drive a car in his sleep. Practically did since he'd been working the clock round. It wasn't unusual to find himself nodding off at the wheel.

The motion of the car soothed him, the pain that had seemed impossible to assuage deadened like oil of cloves in a nagging tooth. He lapsed back into his old protective habit of wiping his mind clean, gritting his teeth and putting up with it. After all who was he to expect happiness? He'd never had more than a tantalizing taste of it. Long ago in the Boys' Home he'd learnt to expect nothing. Long ago when he was a little, raggedy State kid, passing from one weary foster home to the other, he'd learnt to show nothing, feel nothing if you were to survive. He shared, with the legitimate children in the family, the soup bones, three times boiled, the sagging iron bedstead, the loveless cuffs that hid the desperate love.

"We wanna piece of bread an' jam Ma."

"Get out in the yard and play. You're always pesterin' me. It'll spoil your tea."

It'll spoil your tea . . . tea was the leftovers from last night's meal. On his ten bob a week State money they had all starved together. There was only one difference. They belonged, they would stay, but when times got harder, or, by some miracle, perhaps a little better, he would go on to another crowded bedroom, another worn strip of lino on the floor, another nagging woman, ground thin on poverty and despair.

His was an economic relationship, brutal, only resorted to in the interests of survival. Even an occasional soft word, an occasional comradely arm across his shoulder, couldn't change it. You only took State kids when you were on the bones of your arse. Their miserable ten bob a week from the Government helped to feed your kids and kept *them* out of a Home.

The boundary lights on the 'drome were like blood-red lips meeting in a chain of fiery kisses. He drove through Mascot and Botany, smelling the familiar stink of the tallow and hides in the tanneries. Once across Cook's River the air changed, it got thicker, soupier, the smog settled down on the inner suburbs, your breath started to labour in your chest.

He stopped in the grinding shadow of the wire factory. They were working night shift, doors wide open for the hope of a breeze from the street. The gutters were jammed with workers' cars. Farther up the road a giant press pounded in the Sydney Morning Herald Building. The little houses shuddered.

They were all purply-blue brick, and all respectable; streets of them built of cheap blue commons in the Depression. The one next door to Vic was owned by a compositor called Danny. His wife had left him with three kids, and only an old, cranky mother dying of a cancerous lip, to look after them. He drowned his sorrows in home brew, while the kids went to the convent and she went to confession, belting the kids off to Mass and Benediction. Danny seldom mowed the lawn or fixed the house. It needed new guttering and various things kept falling apart or rusting through, but were never replaced.

Against his back fence lived a night watchman, and on the other side a foreman at Eveready's. Rosebery was a hybrid mixture of honest workers, top-off men and crawlers. It straggled on the edge of Redfern and Waterloo, turning its nose up at "the slums", pathetically proud of its green squares of lawn, and the strips of grass springing up beside the footpaths. Its inhabitants had emancipated themselves by hard work, or luck or other means, out of the sub-standard, yardless semis, exchanged for that cheery, extroverted pavement society, a brick wall, a lemon and a peach with fruit fly in the back yard. It was not unusual for the children of Redfernites to shift into Rosebery if their pay packets could stand it. Thus, even if they never really owned the home and the rent was double that paid by their parents in "the old house", they changed from rent payers to home owners in one generation.

The result was streets of smug, little, brick, detached cottages, jealous of their precious privacy, often bought so dearly; streets of an unrivalled dreariness, a smog hardly less thick than the smog coating the lungs of the less fortunate in Redfern, Waterloo and Surry Hills.

Such was the house inhabited by Vic and Maisie, their twin sons and Maisie's fat old mother, rescued from a windowless room at the back of the meatworks, to look after the babies and act as unpaid housekeeper.

It was a sombre, blue, brick house with two dwarf poplars standing stiffly erect on either side of the porch. The old woman had made an effort, pottered about and planted a few straggly Red-hot Pokers in a tiny front bed. It would have been better if she'd left it alone. Although everything was in reasonable repair the house had a neglected look, as if it was only used as a place for sleeping and eating, as if nobody really lived there. They had all forgotten how to live a long time ago. Not that they had ever really known. And there was nothing here to teach them.

A plane tree grew in the side passage. It clogged the gutters with dead leaves in the winter time and Vic swore and threatened to cut it down. But in summer it was the only beautiful thing about the house—shaking a rustling mantle of green shade over the ugly walls. It spread over the picket fence into Danny's yard and the little boys climbed up and sat swinging their bare toes against the blue sky, happy for once out of reach of their grandmother's strap, even, in their happiness, out of reach of her tongue.

Lights burned behind the closed holland blinds. Vic lit a cigarette and turned the wireless on to get the time. Wearily he heard the signal go for ten o'clock. Wonder if she's home yet he thought.

He'd sleep in the car, just as he was. It was better than going inside and listening to the malicious whinging of the old woman. She always enjoyed it when he and Mais had a blue, and they'd have a blue tonight alright. He could feel it building up like summer lightning in his mind.

Ah! Jesus he would a shot through long ago but an honest worker don't desert his kids. The live green eye of the car radio mesmerized him in the stuffy dark. He slumped forward. His head dropped against the steering wheel, his shirt came away, sticky with sweat, from the vynex seat cover. The rich, sexy voice of Elvis Presley entreated him . . . "Wear my ring around your neck" before he fell asleep.

Skinny and grey-faced as a telegraph pole Maisie stood under the street light waiting for her tram. Because she was bored and it was something destructive to do, she scratched at the poster on the pole with her dirty finger-nails. They made a small, scrabbling sound like a rat at work in a cupboard. The poster said: "Vote Communist. For the People's Welfare", but she hardly read it. It didn't register. Nothing registered but the longing to get home and fall into bed, sour with sweat, just as she was.

The knock-off whistle went at nine o'clock. She'd worked an extra five minutes on the reelers before she switched off, just as she always did. She made certain of her bonus that way and got in sweet with the foreman. She'd worked it all out. That extra five minutes was worth it for the sake of the few mingy perks she got out of it. For this she was willing to endure all the snide remarks, the hatred and the contempt of the women on the afternoon shift, that built up week by week. What was five minutes on a shift that started at 7 a.m. at Vickers in Marrickville and finished at 9 p.m. at the Jumbuck Mills in Alexandria? Everything was grist to Maisie's mill, and even if the wheels ground slowly, she was possessed by an almost demoniac patience.

When the tram came she rolled a cigarette, stuck it in the corner of her mouth, laid her head back on the seat and closed her eyes. She still wore her blue overall, stiff with dried sweat, streaked with grease marks where she'd wiped her fingers on the skirt. Maisie's machine was always the filthiest in the mill. At Alexandria she always left it for the day shift women to clean up after her; at Erskineville she left it for the afternoon shift. The foremen never complained.

"Maisie's a good worker," they said. "Wish there were a few more like her round the mills. She's no clockwatcher."

It was true. Mais was no clockwatcher. She worked through her tea break, only taking time off to swig half a packet of Bex with no noticeable results. Certainly her temper never improved. She was a very tall woman about twenty-eight, with flat breasts and a filthy tongue. She wouldn't have gone much over seven and a half stone. Slouching between the winding machines she looked like some dirty, uncouth animal, her hair shorn in dull rats' tails against her head, her voice nasal with catarrh, a cigarette butt dangling incessantly between her lips.

Why did Mais work two jobs? Why was she willing to turn herself into a sexless creature, an automaton that sweated and stank and swore from one mill to the other? They said she had a husband, two lovely kids, a nice house at Rosebery. In a rare moment of friendliness she'd even passed a photo of her twins round the mill. It was hard to believe that such rosy-cheeked angels could have been wrenched from the skinny loins of Mais.

The women could have understood and half forgiven it, even the missed tea breaks, the extra five minutes pinched before and after the whistle blew, the feverish counting of tallies, the greedy, nicotine-stained fingers flying over the reeling machine; they could have forgiven all that if there had been a valid reason. Fatherless kids, a deserted wife, a sick husband, anything. But there was no reason, or if there was, Mais never gave them one. It was impossible to forgive her, so they hated her for jumping up the tallies they were expected to make, hated her for having a word in the ear of the leading hand, and arranging for the machines to be speeded up, hated her for ignoring their hard-earned tea breaks, the few lousy benefits they'd managed to wring from the mill owner's tight-sewn pockets.

For how could they see the mirage that beckoned Mais down the long greasy aisles between the reeling machines, how could they fathom the dream that turned her eyes into black holes in her paper-white face, the dream that sent her fingers reeling feverishly over the skeins of wool? For Mais was reeling a dream into reality—a dream of a residential in King's Cross and emancipation forever. For that she was willing to earn the hatred of the women. They were never real to her anyway, only dim, shadowy figures accompanying her on her way to the stars. She knew every step of the way, every move was meticulously planned.

The first step was already accomplished. The house in Rosebery was paid off. With a little extra capital she would sell it and invest in a corner grocery, one of those myriad little shops that took their pickings from the factory workers. From there they would ascend to the King's Cross residential, and from there there would no doubt be further heights to scale. She would never stop. The habit had grown too fixed, the hands too greedy.

If Vic remained passive she would drag him up with her, if

he was a stumbling block on her mighty climb she would dispense with him. He was the one chink in her invincible armour. Because she had once loved him in her way, he had the power to hurt her, to wound her self-esteem, and she hated him for it. Through his contemptuous eyes she sometimes saw herself for one frightening instant, saw what she had become, saw the transformation of the tall, skinny girl with the nervous, lonely eyes hidden under her wedding veil, and knew that for that girl there could only be a long and painful returning.

Yet for this dream she was willing to destroy herself, and destroy her family. And why was she doing it? Why? If you'd asked her she couldn't have answered. It was as much a part of her as her bones and her blood, as much a part of her now as the wheeze on her chest.

A long time ago when she was a little girl, her mother had owned a corner shop in Tempe. Late in life she had married a telegraph linesman without money or prospects. They had lived out a lifetime of bickering and hatred together "for the sake of the children". Then, twisted and warped to a caricature of themselves, they parted to scrape out a lonely old age in little back rooms on the pension. Long before this the corner shop had gone broke, but Maisie had been brought up on this dream of her mother's past affluence . . . the time "when we owned the pub in Kalgoorlie" and how "I built up that business in Tempe." She had grown up with that goal engraved on her mind forever. She could even smell the lollies in the glass jars on the counter. Hollywood never beckoned so alluringly as that shabby little corner shop in Tempe.

She got off the tram at Sweetacres. Vic heard her footsteps slopping along the pavement. Her walk always maddened him. It was slovenly, insolent and rotten, just like she was. He sat quite still, his shoulders hunched, nerving himself for the blow of her voice, half hoping she'd pass by without noticing him, half hoping that she'd give him the chance to flay her with his tongue. She crossed the road. His fingers trembled on his cigarette, his body tensed. She stuck her head in the driver's window, her lips drawn back from her teeth. He could smell the stale sweat saturated under her armpits.

"Why doncha come in, you bastard? Haven't you got the guts to face me? Why doncha come in then?" she said in a low, vicious whisper, low enough so the neighbours wouldn't hear.

"And lissen to your naggin' tongue, you filthy bitch. No thanks."

"You're rotten drunk," she sneered.

He puffed the smoke slowly into her face. "And you pong. Why doncha go and wash yourself?"

She turned and slopped up the front path, slamming the gate behind her. He heard her fumbling for her key, but he didn't turn his head. He was buggered if he'd go in just yet, make a fool of himself stumbling through the lounge room, skirting the mattress laid out ostentatiously on the floor. Mais always shifted her bed into the lounge after they'd had a blue. Well let her sleep there, let her snore her head off. He wouldn't be there to listen so the gesture would lose most of its significance.

Mais got undressed in the front bedroom, watching the head-lights of the car through the blind. She took a long time getting into her nightie. She didn't want to cheat herself of the delicious satisfaction of reefing the blankets off the bed and marching out into the lounge, while Vic sat on the edge of the mattress, vul-nerable in underpants and socks. But she was too tired to delay the ritual long. The headlights still burned outside the wire factory fifteen minutes later. She put the milk bottles out with a clatter on the front step, adjusted the sign that said "Pasadena Driving School, 22/- an hour", gazed proudly at the sign that said "California Caterers, Weddings, Parties, Social Functions". They had all been her idea, little lurks on the side, that had grown into respectable business ventures. Vic was organized into the Pasadena Driving School, her mother into California Caterers.

The old woman stuck her head into the hall. "D'you have to make all that racket Mais?" she whined. "I can't get a wink a sleep."

"Ah, shut up," Mais said. "Nothin' bloody well suits you. You've got a roof over your head haven't you? I can slave me fingers to the bone, work me guts out, but no thanks . . . not one bloody word of thanks. You're just like that rotten bludger out there. D'you think I enjoy workin' in the stinkin' mill, do you, do you?"

She thrust her wild, thin face at the old woman, a terrifying figure with her scrawny bosom heaving up and down, two red patches burning on her pale cheeks.

The old woman seemed to shrink into her fat. She was fright-ened of the Frankenstein she'd created, this monster that strode the earth like dung, staring at her out of the vicious wreckage of her own life.

"My stars," the old woman panted. "You're mad, that's what's

109

up with you. They'll come for you in the green cart one of these days me lady and not before time." She slammed the door in Maisie's face. In a storm of tears Maisie rushed into the bathroom, swallowed five Bex tablets and sat huddled on the sofa in the lounge, pressing her knuckles up to her mouth. She sobbed till she was worn out, and exhaustion sent her dragging off to bed, a ghost in a faded cotton nightie. The babies tossed restlessly in their cots, their round cheeks damp with sweat. Her mouth quivered as she adjusted their mosquito nets.

Her body felt bruised all over. It was true. She was goin' off her head. And no one to care, no one to shed a tear.

A Super Constellation roared overhead, shattering the night. The little house shuddered. Maisie clasped her eardrums. She screamed. The long hours in the mill were beginning to take their toll. She screamed and screamed, hardly conscious of the blurred, fat figure of her mother, standing, white-faced, at the bedroom door, the high, frightened voice screeching, "Vic . . . Vic." The babies bawled from their cots. The night rocked with horror.

Vic raced across the road, charged into the bedroom, picked Maisie up by the shoulders and threw her like a rag doll into a corner. She came back at him, yammering with her fists, her mouth open in one long, shuddering shriek. He slapped her hard across the mouth, shaking her up and down till her eyes rolled. Then he gave her one last swipe with his knuckles, felt the blood on his hand, and threw her across the bed.

"Take her," he said dully. "Take her for Christ's sake before I kill the bitch."

Her mother came whimpering out of the hall. He ran cold water in the hand basin but no matter how much he washed, the blood seemed to stay on his finger-tips, staining the cream porcelain, staining his trembling flesh.

When he went back into the bedroom she was lying on the pillow, eyes closed, wiping the blood off her mouth with a grubby handkerchief.

He picked the babies out of their cots, soothing them against his chest with clumsy, masculine tenderness.

"Why doncha do your bloody job?" he growled but she didn't answer. Her skinny hands plucked at the sheet; the grease under her finger-nails and in the pores of her skin gave them a strangely touching quality. Her dark hair fanned out behind her, sooty shadows scooped out the hollows in her cheeks.

Moved by a sudden terrible compassion he sat beside her on

110

the bed. It creaked under his weight, but she didn't open her eyes. He held the babies helplessly on his knee. They were both wet, but they jumped and cooed, delighted with all this attention in the middle of the night. He pressed them against her scraggy bosom, using them as a weapon to try and force some response out of her motionless body.

When she looked up at him it was as if all the weariness in the world was gathered in her eyes.

"Take 'em away," she said. "Take 'em away. They're your kids. You've bought me with them, but you can't make me like it."

"I'll go," he said dully. "That's the best. I'll go away. You can keep the kids."

"That's right," she said, her eyes dilating again. "Desert your kids. Desert your wife. You rotten thing." She thrust her face at him. "If you do I'll bleed you white, yeah that's what I'll do. I'll bleed you white." Her dreadful hands clawed at his sleeve.

Silently he took the children and carried them in to the old woman. She was sitting in a wicker rocker by the window, staring out into the street, plucking nervously at her skirt. "You better take them," he said. "She don't want them." He jerked a derisive thumb across the passage.

"My stars, I wished I'd stayed in me little room behind the meatworks," she said bitterly. "I could only burn a candle in it. The pension never give me enough for the electric light bill. And it was that dark, but it wasn't as dark as this house. An' to think I reared her Vic . . ."

The old woman took the babies in her arms, absently undoing the buttons on their pyjamas, rocking them backwards and forwards on her great, flabby lap.

They were beautiful children, Vic's sons, with round, healthy cheeks and rosy bodies. Their blond curls tumbled on brows as guileless as angels, their eyes were blue and untroubled by all the complexities of life under the sign of the Pasadena Driving School and the California Caterers.

Chapter Eleven

☆

NELL strode home down Belmont Street, through the golden, hazy light of summer. The little girls, their foreheads damp with moisture, spun their skipping ropes dreamily on the pavement . . . slip . . . slap . . . against the baking asphalt.

> "Wash the dishes
> Dry the dishes
> Turn the dishes over"

already rehearsing their future role in the scheme of things.

The housewives were out front in their pinnies, vigorously sweeping the pavements. There was always a jealous rivalry in Alexandria to keep each pavement strip spotless and unsullied. Woe betide the little boys carelessly scattering their orange peel on the way home from school. Woe betide the stray mongs committing nuisances by the telegraph poles.

Belmont Street kept itself respectable. The little semis all had a bit of paint and spit and polish about them. The yards were neatly concreted, the numbers and the door knockers rubbed to a glittering Brasso gold. The front step was always shiny with stove blacking. Little silhouettes of Mexicans, sleeping under palm trees, decorated the front porches.

Farther south, facing the tramlines, was the district of higher class lettings . . . tall semis with carved lintels, and thick, black window ledges where fat cats dozed in the sun. The skinny, arched windows were curtained in flowered brocade and cream lace. The rooftops had come out in a rash of television aerials. Widowed landladies, dressed in decent black, collected the bills out of the letterboxes, or watered the tubs of dusty shrubs with white china ewers, their diamond rings flashing in the sunlight off the tramlines.

Alexandria, particularly the section bordering Belmont Street, prided itself on being a cut above Redfern and Waterloo. The air was a trifle cleaner, the frontages a trifle wider, the rents a trifle higher. The houses were in a far better state of repair. The lame, the halt, the blind, the old, the despairing and the desperate could find no hole to call their own in Belmont Street.

The kids saw Nell's tall, spare figure, long-legged, graceful, radiant with light, coming a long way off. The blue overall was belted tightly round her waist, her sandy hair glistened like a gold cap as she walked.

Nell was vain about her waistline. After thirty-five years and three kids she was still as willowy as an unmarried girl. The kids hurtled towards her, heads down, faces brick red, peddling neck and neck on the old bikes Stan had resurrected off the tip. The dirty white and tan cattle dog, with no collar and bright yellow eyes, yapped frantically at the revolving wheels. Stan had picked him up off the tip too. Only Teddy shrieked in the distance, left miles behind, paddling his little legs along the pavement, propelling his dinky by a method all his own.

"I won," gasped Georgie. "I was jus' comin' round the bend and whoosh. You saw me win didn't you Mummy?"

"You cheated Georgie. I was jus' comin' inter the straight and you cut me orf."

George grinned, lifting guileless blue eyes under a tousle of rough, gold curls.

"Yeah!" he said. "I'm a pretty good dirt track racer."

Joe frowned, and put his head down, shuffling his bare feet on the pavement. He was three years Georgie's senior. It was a disgrace to be second over the finish line.

Teddy's tiny figure loomed on a sky as tenderly blue as a delphinium. He lifted his silk-white thatch, wet, sooty lashes fluttered on his peachy cheeks. He smiled through his tears.

"It's liddle Mummy," he crooned. "Dear liddle Mummy."

Nell squatted down on the pavement, holding out her arms, rocking the moist little body in an agony of love. How sweet it was to be called "dear little Mummy" when you were gaunt, rawboned, and pushing thirty-five. Nell couldn't remember a time when she hadn't longed to be a "little" girl, round and curvy. Only through the blind eyes of Teddy's love had she ever attained that impossible dream. She buried her nose in his neck. "Oh, Teddy-bear you smell lovely," she murmured. "Just like a little scent bottle."

The dog licked her face with a rapturous, drooling tongue, sent her sprawling onto the asphalt. Laughing, she dusted herself down, and they went through the wrought iron gate together, clanging it behind them. The old blue Hudson, badly in need of a new duco, was parked in its usual place in the gutter. The familiar silhouette of a Mexican with a donkey and a big hat moved jauntily across the plaster wall. Stan had refused to let her buy the Mexican asleep under the palm tree. He reckoned it was anti-working-class.

The house was a narrow-fronted brick with a steep, corrugated iron roof. They were buying it on terms. There was a pocket handkerchief of clipped buffalo grass, imprisoned in a low, wrought iron fence. Stan had welded it together in an artistic pattern, from pieces of old scrap.

The front door was open. The smell of stew floated down the narrow hall. Stan was sitting on the back step, barefooted, in an old pair of khaki shorts, his underpants rolled over the top. He was reading the afternoon paper. She kissed him on the cheek. The smell of fresh sweat lingered on his skin.

Darling she thought, but she didn't say anything. A muscle twitched impatiently near his mouth, his eyes were deliberately blank and sardonic.

React, react she thought savagely. It's not that long since you held me in your arms and kissed me with love.

For one dangerous moment she allowed herself the sweet luxury of memory. Their voices echoed and re-echoed down long trembling tides of pain . . . "How do you know you'll always love me. People get used to each other. We might end up like other married couples?"

"I'll always want to kiss you. Round about now I should be wantin' to get out to a football match with the boys, but I can't stop kissing you. I never felt like this about a woman before. I'm even beginnin' to smell like a woman . . ." the puzzled voice, husky with sleep and passion and delight died out of the sunlit garden.

She forced her voice down, deliberately casual.

"Any jobs?" She peered over his shoulder.

"Only in the notorious sweatshops," he said, without looking up.

"Did you get a bit of sleep today?" she said.

"Some. The alarm woke me at two-thirty and I drove up to the kindergarten and picked up Teddy."

"What about this mornin'?"

"Ah, they was hopeless this mornin'. Fair little buggers. I never got inter bed till after nine."

The sunlight glinted on the spikes of his blond hair, the creases in the back of his neck were red with sunburn.

"All right Joe, run the bath," he bawled, over his shoulder.

"Why can't Georgie run it?"

"Didn't you hear me say run the bath?"

"Yes Dad."

"I nutted out a bit of an article for you for that bulletin," he said, with elaborate unconcern.

"Thanks darl. Where is it?"

"On topa the frig. I can't hear that bath runnin' Joe!"

The sound of splashing water filled the little house with a silvery tinkle.

"The branch is goin' to help roneo it tonight," Nell said. "And I gotta finish typin' the stencil yet. I was dead scared I wouldn't get it done. I was stuck on that first article."

"See what you think about it," he said carelessly. But she knew he wasn't careless about it at all. It had taken him long hours of sweated labour, and she could feel him waiting to hear her verdict.

She picked it up off the frig and began to read the familiar, awkward, schoolboyish handwriting, that always tugged at her heart.

"There's a name for a man who lives off women."

The first sentence shocked her and she read on . . .

"W. H. Holler treats his two-year-old racehorses no better than he treats the women who sweat in his Alexandria mill. This week his strappers at Randwick went on strike—they said Holler was running his two-year-olds into the ground. As three-year-olds they were only fit for the scrap heap. It's the same brand of greed that Holler uses in his spinning mills . . . only there it's women, not horses he's using up, in conditions not fit for a horse to work in . . ."

She grinned. "You've sure ripped it into the ol' bastard," she said. "It's terrific Stan. It's got just that punch the girls'll go for."

Her brow wrinkled. "But what about libel? 'There's a name for a man who lives off women!' Can't you get pinched for callin' a man a bludger?"

He chuckled. "Take the risk," he said. "He'd be flat out pinnin' you for it."

"But what about the Party?"

"Bad publicity. Holler'll cop it and shut up. There's a cuppa tea in the pot."

She went into the bedroom, unbuttoning her greasy overall, peeling off the sweaty bra and panties. The lino was cool on

115

her bare feet, slats of pale gold light filtered through the venetians. They were buying them on terms too.

"Mumm-ee I'm stuck," Teddy wailed. She dragged his T-shirt
over his head, and helped him over the side of the bath. The
three kids splashed hilariously, making a lake of the bathroom
floor, their little round heads wet and sleek, their shoulders
glistening like dark satin.

Naked, flat stomached, with small, pendulous breasts and long,
freckled legs, she stepped into the shower recess. The tepid
water washed down over her hips, hung in glittering droplets
on her nipples, and the gilt ends of her eyelashes.

She relaxed, her whole body slumped with relief. The coolness
invaded her brain, washing away much more than the mill dust,
washing away the standover and the rat race, Dick's cunning voice
echoing above the rattle of the rovers: "Ask your delegate. Nell
knows all the answers don't she?" Greenie, the foreman, pussy-
footing down the aisles to catch you glancing at the *Women's
Weekly*; the old, top-off cleaner puttin' the clock on you in the
dunny. Wash it all away . . . down the plughole, out the water
pipes, down the stormwater channel into the Pacific Ocean . . .
all the sneers and snide whispers, all the constant, grinding
struggle to keep on top of it all.

"Why doncha get off that soapbox Nell?"

"Ever tried the Domain Nell?"

"See that ginger-'eaded tart over there. You wanta watch your
step with her. She's a Commo."

"Yeah! Can't you pick the type?"

"Nell, I got diddled outa an hour and a half of me sick pay.
Reckon you could do anythin' about it with the union?"

"Nell, I can't pay me dues this week. Could you square it up
with the books luv and I'll fix you up next time you're collectin'?"

"Nell you been orf your job three times today . . ."

"Nell there's a mob outside the gate clamouring for that job
if you don't feel like pulling your weight."

NO VACANCIES . . . PLEASE DO NOT APPLY . . .

She dried her hair into a rough, gingery halo, pulled a clean
sun dress over her head, wiped a powder puff across her nose, and
went out, barefooted, to have a cuppa with Stan.

"You know, I been thinkin' about that bulletin," she said,
stirring her tea thoughtfully. "It's all wrong. Where's the collective? Where's the political discussion in the branch? I'm pre-
sentin' it to them, cut and dried, and all they have to do is the
hard yakka. I always seem to work the wrong way."

He looked at her quizzically. "That's right," he said.

Her temper flared. If he hadn't agreed so readily she would have criticized herself more deeply. She might even have got somewhere. But now all she felt was a perverse desire to justify herself in his eyes.

"You were in it too," she accused him. "You wrote the article, so you're just as bad. Why don't you criticize yourself occasionally. You call me an individualist . . ."

He laughed at her. "What are you tryin' to do, put words in my mouth agen?"

"We both made the error," she said stubbornly.

"Well, it's no good whippin' the cat about it now," he said. "You'll always work like that till you wake up to yourself. The whole Party works that way."

"Ah, well," she said. "It's better to do something constructive than just sit and sling off at other people's errors . . . armchair Marxists they call them."

"Yet you weren't behind the door in pickin' my brains," he said. "You never are."

She got up to rinse the cups, her hands trembling.

"What's up?" he said, watching the stiff angle of her spine over the sink.

"Nothin'. Why doncha get off me back?"

"I won't be home till half-past eight tomorrer," he said. "Sputnik's demandin' I work the four hours a night overtime."

She looked up sharply. "Who's Sputnik?"

"The foreman . . . because he's always bobbin' round in a circuit." Stan grinned. "But the blokes reckon he's not fit to be Sputnik. He's such an animal he must be Sputnik's dog."

"What's goin' to happen to the kids?" Nell said. "You know I have to leave at ten to seven."

"I can't help that can I? What do you want me to do, do me job cold?"

"Oh, I dunno," she said, putting her hands up to her head. "It's just one damn problem after another."

"That's right. That's capitalism. You got to battle through it, that's all."

"I'm battlin' aren't I?" she snapped.

"No, you're whingin' and puttin' the blame on me, as usual."

"Mumm-ee come an' wipe me botta."

She went inside, turning over several alternatives in her mind at once. I know, she thought, relieved at the solution, I'll ask

Evie to mind them. I'll give her five bob. She'll probably be glad of the bit extra.

Absently she helped the little boys into their pyjamas, doing up buttons, tucking tops into trousers, tying cords round thick, brown bellies.

"Mr. Gunn says today 'What's the biggest animal that ever lived on earth?' and I says a blue whale was. And he says, 'Well, I'm not goin' to argue it out with you Joey.' But it's in me book Mum. I'll look it up for you."

He rummaged through his chest of drawers, his long upper lip puckered, a crease of concentration knitting his brows. She watched him, smiling, thinking how ridiculously like Stan he was, even to the lip, when Stan was nutting out some particularly knotty problem in Marxist theory.

"An' then this kid picks on me so I bleed 'is nose for 'im, and then this other kid comes up an' I bleed 'is nose and then the *third* kid . . ."

"What happened to the third kid?" she said.

"Well, see . . ." Georgie spread out his hands, shrugged his shoulders. "He was bawlin' 'is head orf on the ground . . . with 'is nose blooded too."

"An' Mum the kids at my school . . ."

When she went back into the kitchen Stan had changed into his dungaree trousers, welding burns spotting the wrinkles in the cloth, sweat stiffening the collar of his dark work shirt. He had thickened the stew, and was ladling it onto the plates. They ate early. He had the long drive to St. Mary's in front of him, with a half-past seven start. It was heavy on petrol and oil, but it was the only job he could get after twenty-two years in the boiler trade and twelve years in the Party. He picked up three mates on the way. They were welding Alco diesels at Goodwin's. Compulsory overtime lengthened their shift by four hours every night.

"What do the others think about the overtime?" Nell said, making certain the kids had the right number of spoons, knives and forks, according to age, forestalling a blue by putting the right colour mugs in each place.

"Most of them want it, even though it's killin' them," Stan said. "They got TV sets and houses and hospital bills and Christ knows what else to pay off. One poor bugger fell asleep on the shit'ouse seat last night and slept till mornin'. The day shift foreman found him there and give him the bullet."

"Ah, well," she said. "I dunno. It's a battle. You can't blame them. I had to go to work to fix up the house and help pay the bills. They're only tryin' to grab a little bit of happiness out of life before it's too late."

"They won't grab any that way. All they're makin' sure of is six feet of earth out at Rookwood."

"I don't like this stew. It's erky," Georgie said.

"I don't like it neither. It's erky," Teddy said.

"Gawd struth," Nell exploded. "Doncha know there's no food to waste in this house. Whadda you think your father and me's workin' for . . ."

"We're poor aren't we Mum?" Georgie said, pushing his stew around his plate.

"Yes we are," Nell snapped.

"We're very poor Teddy. Doncha know that?" Georgie's face was serious.

"Gawd struth," said Teddy.

"Christ, look at the time." Stan leapt to his feet, grabbed his kitbag, stowed away his plastic lunch pack, his screw-topped jars of tea and sugar, his little tea billy. It was made out of an empty preserved peaches tin, with a welding rod for a handle.

"Kiss the farver." He bent his head over Teddy's soft, round cheek.

"Ta-ta Dad."

"Ta-ta Daddy."

"Ta-ta Farvie."

The dog leapt against his leg. His work boots crunched on the side path.

Nell followed him out onto the footpath.

"Get home early as you can Stan," she said. "I'll get Ev to watch the kids. She don't start at the grocer's shop till nine."

"That's an idea. Why didn't you say that before instead of tryin' to stack on a blue?"

Her warm lips, smelling of stew, brushed his mouth. Kiss me back she thought fiercely, and for a moment his mouth lingered on hers, as if she'd actually spoken aloud.

Be careful comin' home, don't fall asleep at the wheel, don't drive too fast, she wanted to say, but the words stuck in her neck. She realized the futility of it. Anyway he hated a fuss. Instead she called "Goodbye" and raised her hand in a last salute to courage and love and an aching tenderness, watching the Hudson roll down the slope of the street, and disappear in little spurts of white exhaust in the warm, lilac air. Stan was conserving petrol on the downgrade.

The first lights clicked on along Belmont Street. A thick haze hung over Alexandria. It was the smoke from the Blue Mountains bushfires rolling down over the city, joining forces with the smog that hawked its dirty phlegm through the streets. There was a stink in the air from Lincoln Electric. A little skinny bloke, no shoulders and all legs, an old felt hat crushed down on his narrow, pointy face, strolled by, whistling between his teeth, a couple of greyhounds, with the same narrow, grey, pointy faces, straining at his wrists.

Nell went inside to wash up and type the stencil. The backs of her legs were beginning to ache already, and her head felt as stupid as if she'd been banging it against a brick wall all day.

The clock on Spurway's tower said six-thirty.

Nell switched on the seven o'clock news, listening with half an ear as she typed away at the kitchen table on her old Imperial.

"Today, officials of the Textile Workers' Union gave warning of a huge scale recession in the industry. In an attempt to cushion the effect, the union has consented to a plan, put forward by the employers, for a weekly roster . . ."

Nell's fingers stiffened and slowed on the typewriter keys. She ripped the stencil out of the carriage.

"Each worker is rostered on a two to three day basis . . . no real cause for alarm . . ."

She started to take notes on the margin of the stencil, her fingers trembling, her mind racing ahead of the syrupy voice, seeing the mill, the girls scurrying into its yawning mouth, heads down, shoulders, hips, feet fighting for a foothold in the struggle to live, in that frantic rush to beat the seven o'clock whistle through the gate.

Fear and exultation fought for supremacy in her mind. This is it, she thought. All my life has been a preparation for this moment. And then the fear swamped the exultation. Can I take the responsibility? Will the girls listen to me? Have I the strength and wisdom to lead them anywhere? She sat there, wrestling with her own particular devils of pride and arrogance, searching her mind with cruel, impartial eyes, stripping off the veneers of self-confidence and self-love.

Nell had a brutal, nagging gift for self-analysis. It was her strength and her weakness. She knew that the role of heroine in a working-class struggle appealed to her vanity, her sense of the dramatic. She didn't want to go off half-cocked, and then find herself stranded, way out in front, with the Party discredited, and the girls leaderless and bitter.

It'll happen tomorrer, she thought. Tomorrer's pay day. Old Holler, Spender, the mill manager and the Union officials would have got their heads together, and planned to take action before the next pay period. Whatever they did would be in line with the policy of the textile industry and the Employers' Federation.

They'd send out that slimy little organizer, Creek, to front up for them. She could see them clicking their well-oiled machine into motion, briefing little Creek in the ugly, coffee-coloured room in the Trades Hall. The Trades Hall! Oh! what crimes are committed in thy name behind the anonymity of those drab, coffee-coloured walls.

She tried to think herself into their skulls. What would be the first move? Well, it was simple enough, the radio announcer was telling her quite clearly . . . "a weekly roster on a two to three day basis", and of course it would mean the end of the road for the night shift. She wished she'd made more effort to get some good contacts among the night shift women. They were isolated and could all be picked off without much trouble.

"Two to three days" . . . how the hell could any of the girls manage on that kind of money? Lots of the married women would give it away altogether, and go back to struggling along on the one wage. Others would look for new jobs, but that wouldn't be easy for unskilled women, particularly the older ones who'd been in the textiles all their working life.

They said no lay-offs, but they might decide to sack the married women. She tried to imagine the girls' reaction to a sacking. Would they take it philosophically, with a shrug and a wisecrack? It was always hard to predict what women would do in a pinch. Sometimes they got fighting mad, and then fizzled out, sometimes they just took it and shut up, and sometimes, as she'd seen them do during the war, they stuck out their jaws, and propped, and fought.

Anyway it meant a new approach in the bulletin. It had a tremendous responsibility now. It wasn't enough to have a punchy article with a gimmick beginning. It had to analyse, inform and give the girls a serious lead. But a lead where? Not into a no-man's land of leftist dreams. After all what could they achieve?

"Influx of cheap Japanese textiles . . . tightening up of the overall economy . . . synthetics taking the place of wool" . . . weren't they all legitimate capitalist excuses for cutting down labour, just like mechanization on the wharves, and diesel power to replace coal. There wasn't any short-term answer to these problems. It was all bound up with the muddle and waste of capitalism. To struggle . . . that was all they could achieve, and to struggle meant to suffer and perhaps never to see your reward in a bigger pay packet on Friday. To struggle towards socialism, when all human progress would bring human security. To her it was logical and the mainspring behind the whole of life, but how to explain this to a mob of women who didn't believe in socialism anyway?

Ah well! Her last excuse for a one-woman bulletin had gone, trampled under the feet of history. The branch would just have to put their collective brains together, and help her work this one out. And at the thought of it, the wrangling and the argument, the weary battle against the "old guard" as she privately called them, her spirit failed her. How much easier it would be to tinker around with it herself, after they'd gone.

Savagely she flailed herself with contempt. You're a gutless wonder Nell. A bloody bureaucrat! But her excitement began to trickle away in the face of the long, hard night that lay ahead.

When the comrades came in twos and threes out of the summer dusk, she was just finishing *The Magic Pudding*. The three tousled little heads leaned towards her in the circle of the bed-lamp, the three pairs of sleepy eyes carefully followed every movement of her lips.

> "It's worse than beetles in the soup,
> It's worse than crows to eat,
> It's worse than wearing small sized boots,
> Upon your large sized feet.
>
> It's worse than kerosene to booze,
> It's worse than ginger hair."

"What colour hair have you got Mum?" Georgie grinned.

"Ginger." She made a face at them and they giggled.

"You there Nell?" She heard the flywire door go, and the sound of boots in the kitchen. "Got a cuppa tea for a thirsty man?"

"There's Bill," she said. "I'll be back in a minute."

She stuck her head round the kitchen door. "It's on the stove Bill. Pour yourself a cup."

"I'll have ta shout you a packet a Lipton's one a these days Nell."

He sprawled at the table in the half-dark, legs stretched out showing the open-hearth burns on the knees of his trousers. The blue gas flame reflected on his long, humorous face, the blue light from the open door haloed his long, balding skull. A big, foundry-dark hand cupped his ear against his deafness.

"Have you had any dinner?" she scolded.

"I'm right. I grabbed a Sargent's pie at the pie-ery on the corner."

"I dunno," she said. "Why are Communists so backward about their stomachs?"

His hand shook and he slopped some tea into the saucer. "Don't nag now Nell. That's one reason why I never got married. Women nag at a man. It's nice here, havin' a bit of a siddown, and a cuppa tea in peace, but women've gotta make a man's life over."

His eyes were wistful, gazing round the bright little kitchen, with the kettle singing on the stove, the gum tips on the mantelpiece, and the calendar of Marilyn Monroe, stretched naked and luscious and beautiful as a fairytale.

Nell smiled. "You worry me Bill. You oughta get out of that foundry. It's too hard."

"Leave the ol' sweatshop? Who'd sell the *Tribunes* and collect the finance, and bash their ears if I wasn't there? A new feller got a start today. He says, 'I can tell you're a Commo by the literature hangin' outa your pockets'."

"Well, get a better room then. Somethin'. That dump you're in . . . it isn't good to live alone."

He laughed. "Live alone. You don't know the half of it. Me landlady keeps 'er eye on me. I expect 'er to propose any day now."

She watched him for a moment, her heart aching at the white around his mouth and the sunken shoulders.

Ah Nell! he thought, you're a smart girl but you dunno what a job means to a man. . . . Sure, foundry work's hard. It sweats hell out of a man, it dries him out like a husk, but it burns him down to bedrock. He *knows* who his mates are. They're men and they stick, sweated down to blood and bone. It's part of a man's pride in 'isself. How could I give up and get old and go to work in some pissy peanut factory?"

"Go on Nell," he said gently. "There's the doorbell. Stop takin' the troubles of the world on your shoulders. All this," he waved his hand round the kitchen, "it's too late for me. But I get by alright."

"It's too late for me," he'd said and it was true. In the years when men married and had families, he'd been "on the track", one of an army of jobless men, strung out along the endless, dusty roads of New South Wales, harried from one dole centre to the other, queueing up for your dole tickets and then out again at the crack of dawn, before the demons got on your tail. You couldn't draw the dole twice in the same place.

Love . . . love was a brief, unsatisfactory, amorous episode on a park bench on the edge of a country town.

Nell was thinking about Bill as she scooted down the hall, smoothing her hair, unfastening her pinny and hurling it into the darkened bedroom as she passed.

She sensed there had been compensations in Bill's life. There was mateship, sharing a billy of bitter-black tea, a smoke and a yarn by an ants' nest under the big river gums, jumping the rattler, sharing the dregs of a bottle in the freezing dawn, with the sparks flying back off the rails and stinging your eyes.

And it was the compensations, as well as the hardships, that had gone to make men in the pattern of Bill . . . their whole life a protest, angry and yet compassionate, brutal and yet sentimental.

She opened the door and her heart sank. There was the "old guard" turned out in full force . . . Rae with her mouth already thinned for battle, her neat, immature body implacable as stone; Rita, full-hipped and swarthily handsome, bridling in a new, ruby silk she'd run up that afternoon; old Phyllis with her homemade hat askew, and a blue glass brooch winking on her "best navy", and in the shadows behind them garrulous Mick Shannon, the A.W.U. organizer with his young, red-headed wife as backstop. They spread across her doorstep, immovable and united, spelling doom to all her high-minded ideas of collective discussion and collective decision. She fought down her irritation. They're all good people, she said to herself. It's only because of your own bad work in the past that you're reaping the results now. And she knew that most of her irritation was because they were part of her nagging conscience, each one reminded her of those fatal years when she had come, bursting with self-confidence and enthusiasm into the branch, riding rough-shod over all their cherished conceptions of "Party work", scornful of their achievements, critical of their narrowness.

For years, they had been the Communist Party in the district, battling on whilst others came and went, or just shifted away. It was hard for the branch to get recruits, because they didn't really want them. This was "their Party" and "outsiders" couldn't understand the problems of the area.

"We've lived round Redfern all our lives," they said. "We understand the people." And they did. They understood and loved and suffered and hoped with them, ran the Tenants' Committee, battled for pensions and baby health centres and playgrounds with a fierce, almost maternal jealousy.

"Redfern a slum!" Mick Shannon said indignantly. "I lived here all me life. It's good enough for me. Why, Redfern was the best residential area in Sydney in its day. You insult us when you call it a slum."

Rita was a Waterloo dressmaker. She had been branch secretary for years until Nell came on the scene, running the branch in the same careless, slipshod, generous way she ran her own life. And because she understood the people and had a myriad contacts in the little side streets and alleys of Waterloo, she hadn't made a bad fist of it. She was famous for "bringing in more finance" than anyone else in the South Sydney section.

She "made" for all the factory girls and the Waterloo housewives. Her shabby little lounge room in a smog-blackened semi near Botany Road was perpetually snowed under in an exotic litter of patterns and pieces, and half-cut-out dresses. A dressmaker's dummy, with a bust like Sabrina, lurched under the stairs. Meals were continuously interrupted by the little girl from the back wanting to know, "Could I have me fittin' now luv?" There was nowhere to cut out but the kitchen table. Rita's husband went crook because she never charged enough to cover the cost of her labour.

"Ah! poor things," she said. "They don't get much glamour outa life," and, mouth full of pins, she ran from stove to sitting room, jerking and smoothing, unpicking and running up, bringing a fugitive beauty into the lives of the toiling women of Waterloo.

Nell could hear Snowy and Nick arguing at the tops of their voices all the way up Belmont Street.

"You're just a mad militant Snow. You wouldn't know if you was punched, bored or . . ."

"Now lissen Nick, I said I was startin' at the tomater sauce factory termorrer . . ."

"Yeah! for how long. You'll be orf to bloody Darwin before the week's out."

She heard them plant a couple of bottles in the oleander by the front gate, before she hustled the "old guard" up the hall, watching Rae's implacable little back out of the corner of her eye. Rae had been brought up "a good Methodist" and didn't approve of drinking. She always opposed liquor at branch socials on principle.

The section secretary's motor bike coughed and spluttered in the lane. I hope they get the bloody bottles well planted before he sees them, Nell thought grimly. He'd been a captain in the Salvation Army before he joined the Party.

"Go on through to the kitchen," she said. "I'm just finishin' up. Pour yourselves out a cuppa tea."

Evelyn propped her bike against the back fence. Her high heels clicked on the brick path. She brought the scent of Three Poppies into the kitchen.

"How are y' goin' Bill," she said. "Jeez I must be gettin' old. I borrered the kids' bike and nearly bust me guts peddlin' up the hill."

Nell stuck her head into the kid's bedroom.

> "It's worse than kerosene to booze,
> It's worse than ginger hair.
> It's worse than anythin' to lose,
> A puddin' rich and rare," she recited from memory.

"And that's all for tonight. I got a meetin'."

"Ah! Mummy, tell us about when I was a little baby Mummy."

She stood, framed in the doorway, her thick, auburn hair aureoled with light, her stubborn mouth made tender with love.

"When you was a little baby Joey," she said. "You was enormous, and weighed eleven and a half pounds. They kept the babies behind a glass window in Crown Street, and when the fathers come, they held them up to see.

" 'That's not my kid is it?' says a feller next to Dad, with his eyes nearly poppin' out of his head.

" 'No, it's mine,' Dad says.

" 'Gawd,' says the feller. ' 'E's got a head like a robber's dog.' "

And Stan came in to me, she thought wistfully. It was July and he was carrying a big spray of pale pink blossom, still wet with the rain, and his eyes and his mouth were smiling, and he said, "He's a beautiful baby darl," and I said, "You are a liar Stan," and we both laughed. The woman in the next bed said, "My word your 'usband must be fond a flowers. I like ter see that in a man," and Stan had never carried a bunch of flowers in his life before, and said he felt like a nong-nong.

"See yous later alligators," Nell said. Deaf to their protests she switched off the light, squared her shoulders, and went in to do battle for "Bobbin Up". After all, Stan said, parents have got some rights.

"Well, I don't know Nell," said the section secretary. "I don't like the tone of it much. Doesn't sort of sound . . . dignified to me. 'There's a name for a man who lives off women' . . . doesn't put our Party in a very good light."

Nell's heart sank. She'd been counting on Fred's support. He was a moulder, a man who'd worked hard all his life, and had a bedroom stacked with Marxist classics from floor to ceiling. He was honest and fair-minded, but a bit straight-laced, a hangover from his years in the "Salvoes". Now he pursed his lips, his eyes worried behind his glasses.

"There ought to be more of the Party's policy in the thing." Mick Shannon was laying down the law. "Theres' not a straight-out political article in the whole bulletin. Now when I was get-tin' out a bulletin in the A.W.U. . . ."

"I think you might be hidin' the face of the Party Nell," Fred said gently. "Certainly it's got some very good points, you've linked up with the day-to-day struggles in the mill very well but . . ."

"It doesn't sound nice," Rae said firmly. "I don't think the girls would like it. Nell often exaggerates, and she hasn't got anythin' about peace in the bulletin."

"Have you taken it down to the Centre yet Nell? The Centre oughta see it before it's roneoed."

"It's gotta be out by tomorrer," Nell said stubbornly. "This is a political emergency. Anyway we can't always be wet-nursed by the Centre."

"It'll probably all fizzle out anyway." Rita shrugged her plump shoulders. "When I was in the clothin' trade . . ."

"I suppose I'm old-fashioned Nell but it just don't sound like a Party bulletin to me." Bill cupped his hand against his ear. "And I wish all you comrades would speak up a bit. A man can't chair a meetin' if you're all mumblin'."

"I move we pass onter the political discussion. We haven't had a decent political discussion since I come inter this branch."

Oh! Snowy for Christ's sake shut up, Nell thought, but she only said quietly, "This *is* the political discussion Snow."

"I don't think we're helpin' Nell much. I'll have ta call the branch to order. I agree with Nell that this is a political discussion. Will someone move we carry on . . ." Bill was doing his best to chair the meeting.

"Moved and seconded . . ."

Nell looked desperately around the table, trying to reach through their weary faces, and into their minds. Ev, sitting, half asleep, her broad, powdered face resting on her hand, those broad, useful hands that could turn themselves to anything, and always had, ever since she married a shunter on the railways and had four kids.

"The railways are shiftin' Wally back to Junee. They wanta get him outa the road. He sells too many *Tribs* and he's secretary of the Party branch at Chullora. I been on the Department's doorstep every mornin' for a week. 'Adolescent children needs a father,' I said.

"Some little snot-nose looks at me over 'is glasses. 'Put your complaints in writin' Madam,' he says.

"I'm not complainin', I'm protestin', I says. Workers don't complain."

Mick Shannon with all his years as an organizer behind him, furrows in his face, grey hairs, living out the rest of his life in a furnished room in a residential with a red-haired wife and a canary in the window.

"I'll tell yous how I learned about this word 'slums'. I was talkin' to a mob of unemployed livin' in humpies on the Cook's River bank in 1930. I says, wavin' me arms about a bit, I fancied meself as a bit of a orator in them days. I says, 'Look at these places,' I says. 'It's a disgrace workers livin' in hovels like these in a big, rich country like Australia,' and an ol' woman jumps up, red in the face.

" 'Don't you insult our homes you dirty thing,' she says. 'Comin' down 'ere tellin' us we're livin' in hovels. We're doin' the best we can, and we're as good as you are . . .' poor ol' soul was nearly cryin' . . ."

Phyllis, easing her shoes off, rubbing her bunions together, selling *Tribunes* in the Domain, cheeky, indomitable in her red hat with the red feather on the side.

"That Grouper Short stopped my Frank sellin' 'is *Tribs* outside the Trade Union Club. Why me and Frank's been takin' turns sellin' the Party press in the Ironworkers' Buildin' since Ernie Thornton's time. Frank wanted to flatten 'im, but I says 'No Frank, that's no good. We oughta take it to court.' "

"Comrades," Nell said hesitatingly. "I'd like to tell you what

Stan and me was tryin' to do with this bulletin. Y'see these girls aren't used to politics, they understand they're bein' pushed around by the boss, and tomorrer they'll all be windy about doin' their jobs. We all understand that feelin'. We're all workers. But it's no good givin' them great hunks of straight politics. They'd use it for lavatory paper."

Fred pursed his lips. "Do they use the *Tribune* for lavatory paper?"

"Only about six women in the mill read the *Trib*," Nell said tartly.

"That's a weakness then Nell."

"Six *Tribs* is a start Fred," Bill said kindly.

If you only knew how I battled for them *Tribs*, Nell thought bitterly. A start. My God, it was a bloody revolution.

"This bulletin has got to be simple and it's got to catch their eye. Like that headin'. 'There's a name for a man who lives off women.' They'll read that," Nell struggled on. "But it's got to be brought up to date. After the news t'night they've got to be warned, we've got to tell them about the union sell out. That's their politics . . . politics and life . . ."

She looked at the women despairingly. Why are you makin' me tell you all this, she thought. You know it all as well as I do.

Ev looked up. "They'll read it the way it's written Nell. They wouldn't read a lotta dull political stuff."

"It's alright to talk like that," Rae said slowly. "But it looks different written down."

"Written down, talkin' on the stump, what's the difference?" Phyllis said. "We want somethin' a bit lively, not this ol' dry as dust stuff. Nobody reads it, 'cept a few fellers like Fred 'ere. The wimmen don't want it."

"I know how you could link it up," Rita said thoughtfully. "You could link up about Holler throwin' his three-year-olds on the scrap heap and then say somethin' about he'll play the same trick on his wimmen workers, pension 'em off on a coupla days a week, or throw them out altogether."

"Yeah and then you could say, 'And his right-hand man in these dirty schemes is none other than the union bloke, who's supposed to be protectin' the rights of wimmen workers and, instead, is makin' dirty deals with the bosses,' " said Mick Shannon's red-headed wife, who worked in Berlei's, making brassières.

Mick gazed at her with awe, as if he'd never really seen her before.

The section secretary smiled, a trifle sourly, Nell thought. "Well you seem to have got all the women on side Nell."

Nell was scribbling furiously. "They're beaut suggestions," she said softly. "Thank you comrades." And she smiled, feeling a sense of warmness and oneness with these people she had never really reached before.

The kids trooped in single file through the kitchen and out the back door.

"We wanta go to the dunny Mum."

"Don't take any notice," Nell said. "It's just an act. They do it every time we got anythin' on. They're that frightened of missin' somethin'."

"They're comin' on nice Nell," Phyllis said. "I always wished I'd a had one. You notice it more when you're gettin' on. I lost me one and only, carried it six months. Crook tucker and Frank outa work and all the worry did it. You can't bring kids inter the world easy under capitalism."

Ev winked at the little boys, hitching up their pyjama trousers, strolling very slowly, with elaborate unconcern, back across the kitchen.

"Want me to tuck yous in for the night," she called. They giggled and ran. "I'll just go in for a minute Nell," she said. "It'll settle them down. Aren't they lovely?"

"Have you comrades finished this discussion on the bulletin?" Bill was getting impatient.

"If Nell follows the suggestions made by our women comrades she should have a very successful bulletin," said the section secretary. "But she should try and step up her *Tribune* sales." He bent his grey head to hide the flicker of a smile. His eyes were bland behind his glasses.

Nell grinned. Ah! Fred, she thought affectionately. You're as stubborn as an ol' mule, but I'll win you round yet.

"I move that we congratulate Comrade Nell on her initiative," Bill said. "I think she's got somethin' in this bulletin. Somethin' we could all learn to use."

Georgie marched up and down the hall, singing softly:

> "Dear liddle yeller duck
> Fartin' down the parf.
> Dear liddle yeller duck . . ."

It was his version of a particularly sissy "kinder" song, that offended his rugged masculinity.

130

"That'll do," Nell yelled after him. "If you're not in bed before I count five, by gee! I'll tan your bottom for you."

"Dear liddle yeller duck . . ."

Nell shuffled her shoes on the lino. There was a burst of smothered laughter. "He learns it at school," she said apologetically.

Ev came, smiling, out of the bedroom. "The little devil. He looks such an angel too," she said.

Nell turned to the circle of faces again. "Now if things really do get crackin' tomorrer I'd like some sort of a guide from you comrades . . . say there's a mass sackin' what d'you reckon . . . ?"

Bill and Snowy and Ev stayed behind after the meeting finished, to help roneo the bulletin.

"It's too risky for you to chance plantin' it in the lavatories Nell," said the section secretary. "Better to organize an outside distribution."

Rita volunteered to give it out at the mill gates at seven o'clock. "I haven't got any fittin's till nine luv."

It was nearly eleven before Nell could get down to retyping the stencil. Fred's bike, the sidecar stacked with literature, blurted away towards Botany Road. The footsteps died out of the empty streets.

Bill lugged the Gestetner out of its hiding place in the linen cupboard. Nell had stored it there ever since Menzies' Bill to outlaw the Communist Party. Snowy manipulated levers, stencil, ink and paper with slender, skilful hands.

"I planted a coupla bottles in your oleander bush Nell," he grinned. "They mighta sprouted by now. I'll just nick out and see."

Their fingers smeared with printer's ink, their eyes hanging out of their heads for lack of sleep, they sat, printing and folding the bulletin till well past midnight.

"Get us a pincha carb soda in warm water will you Nell," Bill said. "Me ulcer's playin' up a beauty after Snowy's warm beer."

Ev yawned and crossed the beautiful legs she was so vain about. "My Gawd, I'm glad I got a nine o'clock start in the mornin'," she said. "Well, here's luck."

The first issue of "Bobbin Up" had rolled off the press.

Chapter Twelve

☆

NELL lay awake a long time, alone in the double bed, listening to the sounds from the street.

The cattle dog snuffled and groaned on the mat outside the front door. The night shift whistles blurted and blared through the window. She tossed and turned, naked on top of the sheets, trying to get relief from the heat. Her mind was ticking over and over, wouldn't quieten down. She seemed to be typing, roneoing, folding . . . a million bulletins . . . "Bobbin Up" . . . "Bobbin Up". They came up to meet her, flipping over with a faint rustle in the darkness, but it was only her knees rustling against the bedclothes. "Bobbin Up" . . . "Bobbin Up" . . . there's a name for a man who lives off women.

It seemed to her that this bulletin was the culmination of all her years in the Party, such a small thing, a roneoed foolscap sheet, and yet it marked a kind of political maturity, a lodestar in her long, upward struggle to become a Communist.

Who would have dreamed that ginger-headed Nellie Weber, daughter of a brickyard labourer and a pantry maid in a country pub, could ever have grown up to become a political organizer in her own right.

Who would have dreamed that lanky Nellie Weber, clothing trades apprentice, sewing men's coats for Anthony Hordern's at seven and threepence a week, could ever have helped create a political masterpiece on one roneoed sheet of paper.

And it was the Party that had taught her all this, filled in the gaps in an education that stopped at the Intermediate at Kogarah Girls' High, and lucky to get that far with seven kids to feed and Dad on the dole through most of the thirties.

She had known right from the beginning that there was something in this politics for her, something that answered her gropings and strivings out of the whirring dust of the power machines, the barefooted kids tramping down the Glen, the old, two storeyed house of unlined, yellowed weatherboards, sunk into the Arncliffe rocks, bow-shouldered like her mother.

There must be something else besides this narrow, bitter, cranky life with Mumma squawking up and down the stairs and Dad crawling home from the brickworks, red-eyed, smothered in brick dust. Right from the start, smart little Nellie Weber, with her gawky, freckled legs racing up the hill to catch the train to work, had meant to find it.

She read everything she could lay her hands on, not that there was much in a house where the wages wouldn't stretch round seven kids' skinny little bodies, and seven kids' hungry little mouths. "Nellie get in here and wash these dishes" . . . "Nellie don't talk back when you're spoke to . . ." "Nellie" . . . "Nellie" . . . "NELLIE WEBER . . ."

But her Dad had helped her. He'd always been a bit of a militant. He joined her up in the School of Arts Library and always bought her books for her birthday and at Christmas time.

"Got more brains than the rest of 'em put together, me eldest girl," he used to boast in the Arncliffe pub.

But a fat lot of good her brains did her in Anthony Hordern's workroom. She never finished her time in the clothing trade. She couldn't stomach those five years on a wage that hardly paid her fares.

"Now you're finished," Mumma moaned. "You've lost your trade."

When the war started she was seventeen. She'd put her age up and was working unskilled at Davies Coop for an adult's wage. She learnt a lot in those years, along with all sorts of women, manpowered into industry for the first time. There was a big strike wave in the textiles for ninety per cent of the male rate. The women had marched from the Jumbuck Mills to Bond's, stood outside in the street and called the girls out, and the girls had switched off the rovers and the overheads and the big spindles and the reelers and the spinning machines . . . no mucking about, and a great silence fell over the woollen and cotton mills of Sydney. They'd talked outside Davies Coop and the Coop came out for a few days. There were meetings and picket lines and the scabs that left a dirty taste in your mouth. Scab, it was the dirtiest word an Australian ever used. They could have won that strike, but they went back without a victory. She still had to cop that one sometimes in the mills.

"Commos. Don't talk Commo to me. It was yous Commos lost us the big strikes during the war."

She still felt they'd made a blue going back, even if it was a People's War, and the workers couldn't strike and sabotage its victory. If they'd organized a short, sharp struggle, they'd have won hands down, and got it over with, and got their ninety per cent. Then let the bosses try and take it off them when the war was over. As it was they were still working for a lousy seventy-five per cent in the textile industry. No, she'd thought the Party was wrong then, and even now, understanding all the implications, the moves and counter-moves that had just been a political mystery in those days, she still thought they'd been wrong. They'd gone back to save the international working class, but Nell felt the workers of the world would have understood they had to get their ninety per cent first.

But the strikes had proved one thing to her. They said women wouldn't fight, didn't trust each other, were incapable of uniting, couldn't be organized into trade unions. It was true they didn't have the same attitude to their jobs as men. The married women worked for the jam on the bread of life . . . "till I get me teeth", "pay off the frig", "catch up with the bills", "paint the house". They had a short-term view of work, and most of them were only too glad to give it away and go back home, when "we get on top a things agen". The single ones worked and dreamed towards a tantalizing world, made alluring by all the women's magazines . . . "when I get married and have a baby."

But she'd seen women fight, she'd seen them unite, she'd seen them show a courage and resourcefulness you wouldn't believe existed under all the petty details of their daily lives . . . tea to get, lunches to cut, the shopping on Saturday morning, the ironing on Sunday afternoon. Darning and mending, washing and polishing, and an ache in the kidneys at night . . . women's lives were a constant sacrifice to a mass of little details, but give them a clear issue, and they cut right through to the bone of it, and stood solid as rock.

Those were the days of "Sheepskins for Russia" and mass enrolments in the Party. A little squat Jewish girl at Davies Coop asked her to join.

"I won't join while that woman who works in the weavin' is in it," she said.

The Jewish girl looked disapproving. "We haven't got any time for personal grudges in this thing," she said. "This is a political party."

"This *is* political," Nell said angrily. "That women reckons she's a Communist, and she's in the manager's office half the day, with her legs crossed so you can see everythin' she's got, givin' him all our guts."

But she did join the Party, and went round with the Jewish girl signing up half the mill before the year was out. And the woman who crossed her legs in the manager's office was made forewoman and left the Party.

Nell went to a few cottage lectures and branch meetings, and listened to a schoolteacher who'd come back, give a talk on Russia. They asked her to be branch secretary but she got so scared she never went again. Her brother Warren lent her *The Socialist Sixth of the World* when she was twenty and that was more like it. Warren joined the Party just after the war. He took her to a meeting at Marx House one night and there she met a fair-headed, blue-eyed fellow with a round, Irishy face and muscly shoulders, who'd been in the Air Force with Warren. But Warren was in the ground staff and Stan Mooney was still in his pilot's uniform. He'd been a welder before the war, but he'd run a little guitar club in his spare time and played in a jazz combination.

He put his occupation down as "musician" when he joined the R.A.A.F. He wanted to be a pilot and they didn't like workers in the "gentleman's branch of the service". It didn't do him much good because he never got higher than a warrant officer, even though he had a thousand flying hours up.

They were always taking his stripes off him. "The trouble with you is Mooney you think like a worker," his commanding officer said, more in sorrow than anger.

Nell started going out with Stan. He was a moody, quiet sort of fellow with a terrific line, and it wasn't long before she was spending her nights on the back seat of the old Alvis he used to knock round in. It was winter time and freezing cold but they'd curl up in an old, grey army blanket and forget about the weather and time, and the Party and everything else.

"I made up me mind a long time ago I'd never get married," Stan said. "Marriage isn't for workers, and especially not for Communists. Once you're married the boss has got you tied, hand and foot. You can't fight him, Mum and the kids might starve."

Nell wasn't sure. What she'd seen of marriage hadn't impressed her much. This tingling warmth, this feeling that every time she parted from Stan a piece of her flesh was being torn away, the bleak agony as she rolled over to peer for the time on the luminous dial of his wristwatch, it didn't seem to have much to do with the marriages she had witnessed. But she'd almost run out of excuses and fictitious girl friends to stay with, and Mumma was watching her belly very suspiciously.

When Stan asked her to marry him they cracked a bottle of beer on the back seat of the Alvis and she reminded him of the speech he'd made when they first met.

He grinned. "I haven't got any alternative," he said ruefully. "You're my sort Nell. I never met any sheila I wanted to marry, and there have been plenty of good sorts. There was one in the W.A.A.F.'s. I usta go out and sleep in her bed in Botany, but I never wanted to make it permanent before."

She married Stan in the registry office at Kogarah, with all the family present and Mumma blowing her nose hard in a new lace hanky, relief written all over her face. Nell bought a transparent, black, chiffon nightie that cost her a week's pay. They went away for a weekend, and started back at work on Monday and she'd hardly had the chiffon nightie on her back. But life was one long honeymoon in those days.

"I'll never go back into the factories after the war," Stan had said, but he went back. Not because he had to. He could have bought and sold used cars, been a top insurance salesman, joined a jazz band, bought a profitable little business somewhere with his deferred pay, even stood as the ex-service Liberal candidate for Barton.

But he went back in the factories. His father had been Wobbly secretary of the Leather Workers' Union when he was only twenty-two. Ten years later he was trying to run a big, empty, broken-down residential in Paddington. The right wing had rigged the ballot, thrown him out of office and broken his heart. He was a blackballed leatherworker with a wife and four kids to support. Twelve months later he walked up the stairs, shut the door, plugged up the windows and turned on the gas. He was a happy, good-looking sort of a fellow, with curly hair and a soft mouth. He knew all the latest song hits from Clay's music hall in Newtown. Stan's mother brought the four kids up in Tempe on the widow's pension.

Stan was an enthusiastic Communist. He had a case of Marxist classics stowed under the bed. He educated her so much quicker than the Jewish girl at Davies Coop, he taught her so much more than the cottage lectures or the branch meetings she'd gone to during the war. She joined up again and now she realized that this was what she had been looking for all her life. Everything fell into place like the pieces in a jigsaw puzzle, and the best part of it all was that now she knew she had always been right. There was something more than the narrow, bitter, cranky world she'd been reared in. There was another world to be built, here on earth, based on the kind of brotherhood and selflessness and energy she'd seen displayed long ago in the strike in the textile mills.

It wasn't all plain sailing. She made a lot of mistakes. She made terrible mistakes in her marriage too. She neglected Stan for the Party, her whole life was the Party. It seemed that, after having searched so long for the answer and then having found it, she went a bit crazy. She was out every night in the week, putting leaflets in letterboxes, pasting leaflets on telegraph poles, speaking for the first time one night in a lonely park with the rain falling and a dog listening under a Moreton Bay fig.

Their first baby was only one more exciting incident in a life packed full of interest and adventure and activity. She'd sit Joey up in the old pram, with his bottle and his little tins of baby food and wheel him out to address the wharfies, or give out peace leaflets or round up the women for a special meeting on prices and peace. Stan's mother shifted out of her house in Alexandria, paid two weeks rent in advance, slipped them the key, and went to live with her married daughter.

The house in Belmont Street was always full of Communists, drinking cups of tea, or picking up *Tribunes*, or holding discussions in the lounge room, ignoring Stan, impressed with Nell. Nell was the life and soul of South Sydney section, Stan toiled in Balmain all day, only came home to sleep and eat. But the dinner was never on the table, and there was precious little sleep with fellows coming off shift at three o'clock in the morning and calling in to pick up their *Tribunes*.

Stan tried to make her see reason, but she abused him. Where was his old enthusiasm, his old loyalty to the Party. He was hindering her in her work, a stumbling block on her own individual road to glory. Little Nellie Weber . . . she'd always been smart. "Got more brains than all the rest of 'em put together," Dad had said in the Arncliffe pub.

"I'm only doing it for all the people like you," she cried bitterly, leaving Stan for yet another night to warm up the baby's bottle, while she went out to win the revolution on her own.

"You're a careerist," Stan said. "You've made a career out of the Party. You don't give a bugger about the workers. You're just big-notin' yourself, carving out a slice of your own particular glory, and I'm sick of hangin' around workin' me guts out, helpin' to make you famous Nell."

"Am I careerist?" she asked the district organizer, stung to the quick by the contempt in her husband's voice.

"There's no careers in the Communist Party," he said. "If you want a career join the Libs."

But she knew in her heart he was wrong and Stan was right. It was as if everyone but Stan conspired to put another daub on her feet of clay.

It was only after three kids, a host of blistering rows, and the ruin of her marriage lying pitiful and broken around her, that she learnt her lesson.

You had to live with capitalism and fight it at the same time, but first you had to live. You had to be part of the life of those you tried to lead, not so far out in front they couldn't see you for dust. And it would be very lonely out there without Stan, Stan whom she loved, Stan who had taught her everything she knew, Stan who, somewhere along the years, had changed from a fair-headed, Irishy-faced fellow with warm arms and a kiss that trembled and burnt her lips, to a hollow-cheeked, weary man with a biting tongue and tired, contemptuous eyes.

"Why didn't you tell me?" she cried. "Stan why didn't you tell me?"

"Nobody can tell you anythin'!" he said bitterly. "You know the lot."

And she wondered if she had grown like Mumma, loud-voiced, whinging, intolerant, scurrying humped-back up and down the narrow staircase, making life intolerable in the old yellow house on the Arncliffe rocks.

Mumma and Dad were old now. Only habit and the tugging memories of shared bitterness kept them together. Her mother was still the same. Life had taught her very little. And her father, that valiant little militant, who'd first introduced her to the ideas of the emancipation of the working class, he was a foreman at the brickworks, skinny and shrivel-mouthed, his fair skin flayed scarlet, stringy and dry as the Brickfielder blowing a mouthful of hot brick dust over Sydney from the west.

Nell had lost a lot of ground with her family, while she was so busy being a working-class heroine. They saw through her with brutal ease. Warren had left the Party, and was driving a taxi. He was bow-shouldered like Mumma now and there was a cynical stare in his dark eyes.

WAKE UP LITTLE NELLIE. WEBER, clothing trade apprentice,

daughter of a brickyard labourer and a pantry maid. You've come a long way but you're farther back than when you started. You've got a terrible long, bitter way to go.

As long as she lived, the dominating, selfish, impatient side of Nell's nature would pull her in the direction of the capitalism she fought to banish from the earth forever. She had to learn to be a Communist all over again, and this time a real Communist, who no longer used people up, crawled to those above her, and brushed those below her aside, in the name of the working class. It was painful to look at yourself without the rose-coloured spectacles, to see all the selfish, arrogant, backward residue of capitalism growing like weeds in the mind you'd been so proud of.

It had almost destroyed her marriage, almost destroyed herself and her children, left to breed unchecked it could only end up hamstringing the Party that she loved. She used to think that once you'd joined the Party you'd won the main struggle but she'd discovered it had only just begun. The biggest struggle of all was with yourself. Fighting the boss was a pushover compared to that. No, it wasn't easy to be a Communist, it wasn't easy to love a man and marry and bring up your kids in a world that operated on the principle of bugger you Jack, I'm alright. It wasn't easy but it must be done. She'd seen it done at Davies Coop . . . Davies Coop, Bond's, Vicars, the Jumbuck Mills. She had taken the first big step. She could recognize the enemy now, she knew that it existed. Little Nellie Weber back on the road to the future . . . bobbin up . . . all bobbin up together.

She pulled the sheet up and fell asleep, her arms stretched out to the warm hollow in the bed where Stan should have been lying beside her.

Hours later she woke, cross and swollen-eyed with sleep, to feel him whack her across the bottom.

"What is it? Whassa matter?"

"Wanta see Sputnik? It's due over Sydney at 4.36."

She turned over and groaned. "Go to bed Stan for Chrissake."

"C'mon, put your dressin' gown on. We'll get a good view tonight. There's not a cloud in the sky."

Something was wrong, something she couldn't put her finger on. Then she sat bolt upright in bed. The sheet slipped down and bared her little pendulous breasts.

"What's the time? Why are you home so early?"

"I got the sack. What are you lyin' there in the nuddy for?"

"Why'd they sack you?"

"Reckoned I wasn't efficient so they took me off the weldin' and put me on the grinder, the slowest grinder in the shop."

"Not efficient. After twenty-two years. It's taken them long enough to find out."

He grinned. "For Chrissake cover yourself up. You got tits like razor strops."

"So would you if you'd fed three kids out of them," she said tartly. "Tell me what happened?"

"Ah they never mucked about. Sputnik kept on buttin' in and pickin' on me, sneakin' round timin' me all night. 'How about givin' me a go,' he says, so I turns round and says, 'Yeah, an' how about givin' me a go.' I got the sack for insubordination and malingering."

"After that we need a look at a real Sputnik," she said. She pulled on her cotton housecoat and they tiptoed through the dark house into the tiny back yard, peering up through the starry galaxies of space, so cold, so limitless. It looked so lonely up there that she crept against him for comfort, leaning against his warm shoulder. He was still in his working clothes and she could smell the sweat in his armpits, and that comforted her too.

She remembered when they were kids they used to talk about "where does the world end?" and because they couldn't bear the thought of nothing, nothing but space whirling into infinity they made a game of it.

"What's past the earth?"

"Air."

"What's past air?"

"Nothing." Nothing, nothing, they'd shut their eyes, giddy with nothingness and Warren would burst forth triumphantly: "Yes there is. There's a big brick wall."

It was called "the nothing game".

"Can you see anythin' Stan?" she said. "I'm blind as a bat at a distance."

The three little boys stood huddled together at the flywire door.

"We wanta see Sputnik Dad."

"We wanna see the satillite Daddy."

"What are you doin' out of bed?" she scolded. "You'll never get up for school in the mornin'."

"Alright," said their father. "You can come out if you've got your slippers on."

It was the voice of authority. They charged down the back

steps, three little moonlit figures, craning their necks at the sky, yelling with excitement.

"Where is it Dad. Can you see it?"

"I can't see it, can you Dad?"

"Ssh! Don't shout. You'll wake everybody up." Stan's eyes ached with looking. "I can't see a bloody thing."

Nell thought of the nursery rhyme, and hummed it over softly to herself.

> "Twinkle, twinkle little star,
> How I wonder where you are,
> Up above the world so high . . ."

"There's a Sputnik in the sky," Stan shouted. "There she is. Can you see 'er?"

"You'll wake everybody up Dad," Joe said.

"So they all oughta be awake lookin' at Sputnik, like us," Stan grinned, but he dropped his voice. "Can you see it Nell?"

Faint and far and blurry, moving very slowly, the little star travelled across the sky.

"Yeah, I can see it," Nell whispered. Her voice broke. I must be out on me feet, she thought.

"I can't see it Dad."

"Show me Dad."

"Look, just passin' over that factory chimney. Now it's movin' north."

"Yeah!"

"What a beauty!"

"Look at 'er go!"

The two little boys watched with breathless wonder, the moonlight glistened in their eyes like tears.

"I wanna see the sat-ill-ite," Teddy wept.

Stan swung him up on his shoulder till his little white head seemed to reach the stars. "Now can you see it Ted?"

"I c'n see it . . . I c'n see the sat-ill-ite," Teddy crooned in triumph. "What's a sat-ill-ite Dad?"

"It's a man-made star. The workers put it there," Stan said.

O! little star of Nellie Weber. O little star of Stan Mooney, of Tom Maguire, his brown-eyed wife, and his brown-eyed daughters. O! little star of Shirl and Dawnie, Beth and Alice, Jessie and Lil. O! little star that whirls through space and carries all the dreams of man.

Sputnik grew fainter, glimmered in the distance and disappeared over the rim of the world.

"I'm goin' back to bed," Nell said. "And so are yous kids."

"I wanta come in your bed Mummy."

"Alright but no kickin'. Come to bed Stan. You look done in."

"I got to go to a mass meetin' at nine o'clock," he said. "It don't seem worth while goin' to bed."

There was a smear of grease on his chin, his hair was as pale as Teddy's, and his face very weary in the moonlight.

"Do you reckon the men can get you back?" Nell said.

"They're all solid, even the rightwingers wanted to jack up. But they got the Crimes Act on us out there. If we put an overtime ban on, or have a stopwork meetin', we can be fined five hundred quid per man, per day. They could destroy the union that way."

"But that means you can't fight, you've just gotta sit there and cop the lot," Nell said.

"That's right. Unless we decide to pull it on a course. I says to one little wizened-up Pommy feller, you wouldn't a give two bob for 'im, 'Would you be willin' to go to jail for the right to strike?' and he just says 'Long Bay couldn't be no worse than this.' "

He hesitated, his eyes pleading with her, under the stars.

"If we went out," he said quietly, "it'd be a strike over one man. I'd be askin' them to go out for me, to save me."

"Yes," she said, her voice soft in her throat, groping towards the lonely struggle going on in her mind.

He looked up, across the rooftops, embarrassed at his own nakedness. "That's no good," he said roughly. "If there's gotta be a strike it's gotta be something bigger than that."

"Is that what you're goin' to tell them at the meetin' tomorrer?"

"I dunno. I haven't made up me mind about it yet," he said irritably. He shrugged his shoulders. "I could swing it easy enough, it's not that." His voice, full of bravado, pleaded with her.

"Yeah," she said. "Yeah." She put her hand timidly on his sleeve. They stood, relaxed together, in the moonlight. She felt humble in front of this man who'd come so far and learnt so much. This arrogant, daring man who'd learnt humility out of bitter struggle and argument and failure.

He would never again be the exultant, wild-eyed boy, leaping out of his seat, swaying a mass meeting in the workers' language they understood, taking them out the gate, laughing and chiacking, a bit punchy, because "You gotta have a go, you gotta push the game along." He was forty. Wisdom had come hard and sat uneasily on his shoulders, but it would stay with him now.

She heard the voice of the Redfern organizer: "The trouble with Stan is he'll pull the men out at the drop of a hat, and for what? He's a left wing deviationist, good as a shock worker, but he won't learn tactics."

"Stan Mooney . . . Christ! he's a wild man."

"Stan Mooney, he provokes the boss too much."

"Yeah, but he's a good Party man Stan."

"Ah, he pushes the game too hard."

"I like the ol' Stan. He's always ready to have a go."

"Stan can do a good job in the workshops. But there's no doubt in our minds Nell who's the most developed comrade in the Mooney family."

From such little seeds grows such a monstrous growth of arrogance, such a misery of cross purposes and pride, she thought wonderingly.

For a moment Nell wept for him fiercely, like her own lost youth, the boy in the blue boiler suit standing, yellow-haired and cheeky-eyed in the moonlight, claiming her lips with an impatient mouth. Now that he was gone forever, perversely feminine, she wanted him back—the warm, heroic lover with the tragic laugh who had dared to storm the sky.

"Don't go, don't go," she whispered. "I loved you," but the man in the dark struggling with his own ghost, staring at the stars, never moved or heard her.

There was nothing she could do to help him now. She walked slowly inside, carting a garrulous Teddy off to bed.

"Where's Dad goin' this day Mum?"

"He's goin' to fight the boss Teddy."

"Will they bleed each other?"

Nell smiled. "No, they won't bleed each other."

Silence, only the ticking of the clock in the front bedroom.

"Why, is 'e only a very liddle boss Mummy?"

The dawn streaked over the factories and the picket fences, a breeze rustled the dry coconut palm by the gas tank. The dawn crept into the bedroom, where Nell lay asleep, the freckles standing out on the bony bridge of her nose, Teddy snuggled in the crook of her arm, his lips parted, his legs flung out. She didn't hear Stan take his ukulele out of the case, didn't hear him singing the weariness, the frustration and the bitterness of the long night out of his bones, out of his blood, out of his flesh, but she was conscious that he wasn't beside her, and she mumbled "Stan, Stan," twice in her sleep, but Stan was sitting on the back step in the grey dawn, playing the "Overtime Staggers Rock".

"Sleeptime, worktime, overtime Rock,
Sleeptime, worktime, overtime Rock,
What about playtime? Ain't no play jus'
Sleeptime, worktime, overtime Rock."

He was playing his father climbing the last stair at the top of the residential, the gas light gleaming on his chestnut curls. He was playing the sound of the door shutting, the smell of the gas floated down the stairs in the morning.

"That's what they call me, the Overtime King,
Brain bees abuzzin, ear bells ring.
Went to the boss, I said what's the score,
Wages buys nothin', can't live no more.
He says Ha-huh-ha, you're a lucky free man,
Free to work all the overtime you can.
Well . . . overtime, overtime, overtime Rock,
Yeah! Overtime stagger 'n' Rock."

He was playing the empty bellies rumbling round the kitchen table. He was playing the boy pedalling eight miles to Tulloch's through the lonely rain . . . night shift and the wind cutting through his old guernsey, shrunk up short at the wrists.

" 'If you want to stick to me says me turtle dove,
Days are made for work, yeah, but nights are made for love.
Overtime work makes no one rich,
Your staggers give me the seven year itch.
You stagger about like a broken down crock.
Well I want a man, not a number on the clock.'
Overtime, overtime, overtime Rock . . .
Yeah . . . overtime stagger and Rock."

He was playing the Tempe kids running raggedy-arsed over the mudflats. Skinny Gosnells left school when he was in fourth class and drove past, in his ol' man's bottle-oh cart, standing up, roaring at the top of his voice:

"Ol' Ma Croll
With a pimple in 'er 'ole . . .

Poor ol' Starks,
With an arse full of sparks . . ."

while the kids cheered.

Fonso Brown, the son of a prawn fisherman. He was a sharp lad. He used to slug it out punch for punch with his ol' man, uncouple the trams as they were going along, fall between the couplings, and come out of it with nothing worse than a broken arm and mild electric shock. The last he'd heard of Fonso he was runnin' a book in the Tempe pub.

Cogsie, with the bum hangin' out of his pants. He used to run up and down the river bank in the freezing cold collectin' tennis balls along Cook's River. It was warmer there than the shed he slept in, with a coupla chaff bags for blankets. Cogsie's brother said he lived at Newcastle, and grinned. For all Stan knew he might be livin' in Maitland Jail.

Stan Mooney, dux of Tempe School, but he had to leave when he turned thirteen, " 'Cause his ma only gets the widder's pension." Stan Mooney . . . they reckon he went bad and joined the Commos.

He was playing the men coming, grim-eyed, chiacking each other, out the gates of the B.H.P., the wind off the desert blowing their trousers against their legs. The wind blowing over the shipyard, over Whyalla, blowing the gulls, like bits of white paper, into the gulf.

He was playing Stan Mooney, tight-as-a-spring, jumping out of his skin, his mouth smiling, his voice ringing and echoing back off the steel ribs of the ships . . . sun dazzle glittering in the clear whites of his eyes, sun dazzle searing through his white skin like an arc burn . . . burning, burning and his fingers trembling as he ripped open the telegram from Sydney:

> STRIKE DISASTROUS. CANNOT PULL ON B.H.P. IN THIS PERIOD. MEN MUST GO BACK.

Only the enormous silence and the seagulls crying harshly over the gulf . . . *and the wind blowing* . . .

He was playing the loneliness of it, the defeat and the victory, jobless, catching the train out of Whyalla in the dawn, the shadows slanting across the desert like fingers pointing into his future. Swinging onto the footboard, his coat collar turned up against the wind, his port in his hand . . . two clean shirts, a pair of underpants, undarned socks, a boiler suit and Lenin's *Left-wing Communism, an Infantile Disorder.*

"I've worked so bloody hard Clem I've never even had time to have a woman," he told the Party branch secretary, and the whistle blew lonely across the flat saltbush, he waved his hand, and Whyalla was just a memory of men's voices in bachelor barracks, and heavy, sleepy eyes over study circles on Sharkey's *Trade Unions.*

Back in Sydney with the balls of his feet bouncy on the summer pavements, the air balmy and Nell in the crook of his arm. The little ferries passing and re-passing under the glittering arc of the Bridge across the Harbour.

Sydney here I come . . . the Big Smoke.

Give me Sydney any time.

Jesus! I can lick the world.

AND THE WIND BLOWING . . .

He had pulled his shirt out to get a bit of air on his belly, where the welding arc had burnt a tender, rosy patch on his skin. Welding burns spotted the wrinkles in his work trousers. There were little sun cancers on the backs of his hands. His long, thin fingers plucked at the strings:

"Come home early, staggered thru' the door,
    Kids start screamin', never seen me before.
    Kids run out, dog flies past,
    Takes me for a stranger and bites me on the arse.
    Mumma runs in, what's goin' on here?
    I'm home early love,
    She says, We-el dear
    We'll have some overtime, overtime, overtime Rock,
    Overtime, overtime, overtime Rock.
    Overtime, overtime, o . . . . . o . . . . . overtime,
    Staggerin', staggerin', stag . . . . stag . . . . staggerin',
    Overtime staggers, overtime staggers,
    Overtime stagger 'n' ROCK . . ."

Tomorrow he would file into the meeting hall full of dust and words and smoke, men with worried eyes, no hats, but a laugh to cover their nakedness, carrying their ports, their hopes, their lives into that dusty room.

Men off night shift, men off day shift, frayed collars round a V of sunburnt neck. The chairman thumping on the ink-stained table . . . "How about a bitta shush."

"Well brothers, we're here today . . ."

The union secretary barrel-rolling down the aisle.

"How are y' goin' Hughie?"

"Reckon we can pull on the Act Hughie?"

"How d'ya reckon she'll go Hughie?"

Shrewd, tough-mouthed Hughie, a little five-by-five from the Clyde waterfront, served 'is time on a floggin' hammer.

"Hughie'll give it a go."

146

"Hughie's no arse warmer."

"Hughie'll stand with the men."

AND THE WIND BLOWING . .

"Brother Chair and Brothers . . ."

"Brother Mooney has the floor."

And he'd stand up, the sea of faces would shimmer in the dry sunlight, and the words would stick and burn in his neck, and for the first time in his life he'd say . . .

"No strike. We can't afford to strike on this issue. We can't risk destroying the union. Not for one man. I appreciate your support but it's gotta be a wider issue brothers . . . BROTHERS . . . BROTHERS . . ."

And the roar would be like pain and the sound of the surf tumbling in off the heads and the wind blowing, BLOWING THE DUST OUT OF HIS EYES.

And his eyes would film over and he would know in this moment of defeat, his greatest victory.

Chapter Thirteen

☆

"Overtime luv!" said old Betty, pressing her knee against the starter, and setting the rover in motion. "We've always worked half an hour's overtime every night in the Jumbuck. There's never been no forty hours here. Course we get paid for it and that little bit extra in the pay packet every week is v-e-r-y nice."

"Makes it a terrible long day though don't it . . . seven to four?" Gwennie said.

"You get usta it. And they don't like you to knock it back. Puts you in bad with the boss straightaway. Anyway we just about got the game scunned now luv. It's right on knock-orf time. Jus' nick over and get me enough bobbins for me machine. Mind you get them red ones. None of them useless, half-broken, sawn-orf buggers."

Gwennie joined the press of women round the bobbin boxes, pushing, shoving, clawing to grab the pitifully few decent bobbins. Bad bobbins made the work harder, the machine mucked up all the time, but there were never enough "goodies" to go round. It sickened Gwennie to join in that mad, vicious scramble. She always hung back and was left with an armful of rough-edged, half-broken fawn ones, and so copped a tongue lashing from old Betty.

There was that fat woman with the red face shoving her big bottom half way round the bobbin box, hogging all the room. The cheeky little blonde one pushed her elbow into the fat gut and winked. The pregnant one winced as she leaned too far over the side of the trolly. She put her hand to her stomach while the baby rolled and kicked at the pressure. Gwennie turned her eyes away. How dreadful she looked with the big, swollen belly pushing out her overall. And yet she didn't seem to mind, was always showing the others little bits of knitting she'd done, and laughing and joking about "me condition".

She had a husband too. Perhaps that was why she didn't worry. It was only when you didn't have a husband that pregnancy was something shameful, to be hidden away under a boned corset and a gathered skirt.

Miserably Gwennie hurried back to Betty with her armful of bobbins. Betty picked them over carefully, setting the best of them up on her machine, grumbling and swearing to herself.

"I've told that Dick a million times, they could save a mint a money in this mill if they'd only buy a few more decent bobbins. They'd get twice the doffs. But I dunno. Penny wise and pound foolish, that's the Jumbuck. You're lookin' peaky luv. Sure you feel alright. You should get some a that aspirin mixture from Sister.

"Must be the heat," the little girl mumbled, sick with terror. Last time Gwennie had been to Sister she'd looked her in the eyes and said spitefully: "You're pregnant aren't you dear. I can always tell."

"Sure you're not in the family way luv?" Betty said.

"No, oh! no."

"Must be wind on your stummick. I suffer with it meself. You are married aren't you? You told me you was married." The sharp, little eyes in the round, fat face were exactly like black currants in a bun.

Miserably Gwennie twisted the ring on her finger. She'd bought it at Coles. "Yeah, I'm married."

"Married to a sailor. Wife in every port they reckon." Old Betty shook like a half-set jelly. "Well, there she is, all filled in for the night-shift wimmen, and a doff ready to come orf. I always believe in doin' the right thing by your workmates."

The women were standing by their machines waiting for the first whistle. An air of impatience rippled round the mill. Jeanie was stuffing things into her dilly bag. She always had to race to catch the early bus to Erskineville. Shirl was working like a mad thing, sweat dripping into her eyes, and smearing her mascara. Her big spindles were mucking up on her again.

Behind the long line of rovers the women were packing up tote bags and baskets. Young Ken was busy trying to get sweet with Dawnie, Jessie was rubbing salve on her sore leg, fat Julie was talking to Jeanie's young sister out of the weaving. Beth was working slowly and clumsily trying to fill in before the whistle went. Nell, the delegate, was cleaning her machine with a piece of greasy waste. Alice and Lil, both old hands, were all tidied up, waiting for the signal to switch off.

The long day was beginning to unwind like a skein of wool, twisted to breaking point over your hands.

Only the four New Australians went on working doggedly as if they'd never heard of a knock-off whistle, doffing their spindles, making sure they got the maximum out of their machines before the afternoon shift took over.

"Look at them bloody Balts, all with their heads down and their arses up," old Betty grumbled. "I give the boss a fair go but I don't believe in overdoin' it. No wonder the night wimmen hate their guts. Doffin' every bloomin' machine before they finish up, an' they never even bother to fill in. They'll never be Aussies while they keep that up. They'll work us all outa a job."

"THERE SHE GOES . . ."

The whistle wailed through the long greasy aisles. Backs straightened, wet, weary fingers combed through dusty hair. The roar subsided, silence seeped into the mill, as welcome as a long golden shaft of sunlight.

Betty took her old black handbag down from the hook where she'd hung it every morning for eighteen years.

"You be ready to go on your own machine tomorrer luv," she said. "I told Dick."

"D'you reckon I'm good enough?"

"Nothin' in it. You been with me a fortnight and if I can't train a girl in a fortnight, I'll give up rovin'. Not that they give me anythin' extra for it. You'll be the last one I'll train for a bloody long while. You was lucky gettin' in 'ere Gwennie. You're the last of the Mohicans."

"Me girl friend got me the job."

"Oh yeah, the one they call Dorrie, in the spinnin'." Betty leaned forward, looked carefully over her shoulder, and muttered in Gwennie's ear, "I'm just givin' you a friendly word of advice luv. Tell your girl friend to go easy on the wool. She's makin' it a bit too 'ot."

Gwennie flushed. "Do *they* know?" she said fearfully.

"Jus' tell 'er to go easy, that's all. These greedy ones make it too bloody 'ard for the rest of us. A little bit 'ere and there, that's alright, but when they start windin' it round their bellies and goin' out twice as fat as when they come in, that's lookin' for trouble."

She waddled away towards the washroom, calling a greeting to this one and that one as she passed, grinning at the good-humoured chucking off from the spinners and the reelers.

"How are you goin' Bet?"

"How many did you doff today luv?"

"Get through your fourteen alright Bet?" Eight doffs a day was the norm for each worker.

Betty knew every lurk, every short cut, every bolt and screw and nut on the roving machines. After all she'd been on 'em eighteen years.

Gwennie sidled behind the spinners to put Dorrie wise. "Watch your step," she muttered. "They're onto you. Old Betty give me the office."

Dorrie nodded, shifting the gum to the other side of her cheek. "Thanks kid." She pulled off her overall, took a pile of dusty *True Romances* from the shelf, and strolled nonchalantly across the mill, her big breasts bouncing in a black, skin-tight sweater.

"Jeez, get onto *that*!"

"What a pair a charlies!"

"How'd you like to get your arms round that Curl?"

"I couldn't reach. Jayne Mansfield's got nothin' on 'er."

Dorrie smiled, pulling in her ribs, swaying the cheeks of her bum, as she walked like a movie queen on her way to a gala première.

"Hurry up Gwennie," she called loudly over her shoulder. "What are you draggin' your feet for luv?"

A tall, skinny woman with no bust, a filthy overall, and black holes dug for eyes in her white face, rushed down the aisle, colliding with Dorrie as she came.

"Why doncha look where you're goin'?" she snarled.

"We-el if it ain't bonus-'appy Mais," Dorrie said. She leaned forward, and in a loud voice that carried to every corner of the mill, she said, "Why doncha get a coupla 'cheaters' luv, an' you wouldn't look so much like a man dressed up."

Gwen and Dorrie got off the tram at Foveaux Street. The paper sellers bawled their wares above the clatter of the city.

The old Yugoslav barrowman, his greasy felt hat wrinkled with heat, greeted them as they passed.

"'Allo gurls. Bluddy 'ot." He pushed his hat back and scratched the white rim of his forehead. "You puttin' on weight luv! Y' gets fatter every time I sees y'."

Gwen blushed, turning away from the twinkle in his shrewd little eyes.

"'Alf a dozen oranges, please," she said primly.

He popped two extra in the paper bag. "There y' are. I give y' eight. Don' say I don't do good to y'."

A plump, middle-aged woman in a man's old felt hat and

sandshoes, a man's coat over her cotton dress, picked two oranges off his barrow as she passed.

"Okay Bea, okay," he muttered, spreading his hands out. "That bluddy Bea Miles. She sends me broke yet."

A handsome, toothless man, with soft grey curls, and nothing special to do, lounged against the spiked railing of a dirty old semi. He was the cockatoo for Thomos gambling school.

A Chinese woman in black jacket and trousers padded up the street; two little slant-eyed boys in tight jeans and cowboy hats clicking their pistols at her heels. In the dreamy summer haze the little houses huddled together, all angles and sloping shoulders, climbing up and down the hills. Their slate roofs burned in the sun. A flock of startled sparrows wheeled up, chirping and fluttering their wings on the golden sky. Dorrie and Gwen toiled up the hill towards the flatette they shared in Little Albion Street.

No cicadas sang in Little Albion Street. There were no trees there. Gwennie lay on the narrow bed, her arm thrown across her eyes. The room was filled with a deep blue light drifting up the stairs. A five-pointed star hung trembling at the open window. A light wind stirred the brown hair against her forehead.

"Jeez you got pretty hair Gwennie," Col used to say, combing it back with his fingers.

But I mustn't think about Col.

I gotta get along without Col.

I gotta get over Col.

She sat up. Her head was giddy. Nausea sent her running to the bathroom, but she couldn't be sick. She dry-retched over the toilet, her throat stung with bile, her forehead wet.

"Col, Col," she moaned.

She staggered back into bed. The lumpy mattress bunched under her spine, the sheets were damp and smelly with sweat. She wanted her mother. She wanted the big, round, capable arms and horny hands. She wanted the heavy bosom and the capacious print pinny. She wanted to hear the laborious breath and the loud tread on the steps of the residential in Little Albion Street. She wanted to see the grey, cropped head and homely face bobbing up the stairway onto the landing, the street light glinting on her spectacles.

She wanted someone to brush back her hair and smooth her pillow and wet her temples with eau de Cologne. She drew up her thin legs against her belly where the nausea and the fear knotted in a tight, dreadful ball. For her mother wouldn't come. She was afraid to send for her mother. And Dorrie didn't come either. Perhaps when she was dead they'd be sorry. Self-pity smothered her. And the horror fought with the self-pity and she wept. She could hear footsteps tapping in the street below. The Chinese women called to their children playing underneath her window. The strange, foreign voices made her feel lonelier than ever.

Everyone going about the business of living, only for her there was no place, no place in the whole bright, tingling, clamorous city, the streets blooming with lights and neon signs and footsteps and pubs and espresso coffee bars and picture shows and ferry boats and fun arcades from the Railway to the Quay . . . the city that four months ago had seemed like a great bursting rocket of happiness and noise exploding in the spring sky . . . LUNA PARK . . . JUST FOR FUN. The huge yawning mouth of the hideous, perpetual clown shrieking over the Harbour, the roller coasters, the hooplas, the ghost train, the haunted house, the ferris wheel, the Tunnel of Love and Col's hand in hers, his lips urgent as the blood-red lights kissing above the aerodrome, his voice urgent as the wind on top of the ferris wheel . . . "C'mon darl. It's me last night. C'mon. Doncha love me? I won't get you inter trouble. You want it too doncha Gwennie? Oh! . . . Gwennie . . . darling . . . you want it too."

And the little bed crowded and sagging under their weight, the star hanging like a promise of happiness in the window, the voice of the Chinese woman calling from the street, the murmur of the wireless turned down low . . .

> "Here is my heart,
> More and more.
> Ra de da de da,
> Chanson d'amour."

And now she slept in the same bed, the same star came out over the rooftops of Little Albion Street, the same Chinese children played on the pavement in the dusk, but Col's ship had gone out of the Harbour and Col's letter lay, crumpled with tears, down the front of her dress.

"I am terrible sorry it had to happen like this kid. Marriage is out of the question I'm afraid. I can't afford to get hitched up as yet. Anyway my ship won't be in Sydney for another four to five months. I am sending you a money order to get yourself fixed up. Please let me know when you are okay again . . ."

"Ra de da de da,
Chanson d'amour."

Cooking smells wafted up the stairway, but they only made her stomach buck and shudder. When she swallowed the sour taste hurt her throat.

Perhaps I'm goin' to die now, she thought, and she was almost glad. That would be an easy way out of her trouble. She played around with the idea of going out and throwing herself down the deep blue stairwell, but her body flinched from the impact of flesh and bone shattering on concrete.

She heard the soft-soled shoes run up the stairs, pause on the landing. Somebody turned on the light inside the door. It hurt her head, sent fireworks exploding behind her eyes. She turned her back, whimpering into the mattress, her shoulders hunched against the light.

"For Gawd's sake. You got the place like a morgue," Dorrie said. "No lights, no music, no nothin'. What are you tryin' to do, turn yourself morbid?"

She dumped the groceries down on the little table and switched on the mantel model. Gwennie didn't move.

"You jus' lie there luv and I'll make you a cuppa tea," Dorrie said, copying with every inflection of her voice, every movement of her hands and shoulders, the mother she'd left behind her in the Adelaide City Square. They'd never got on.

"I love you so,
And that is why,
All I have to do

is dream, dream, dream" she sang out of time with the wireless, clattering the cheap white crockery from the cupboard to the table.

"Dream, dream, dream."

She crossed over to the window, twitching the faded pink muslin curtains across, keeping one eye on the thin, rigid back turned to the window. Womanly pity wrung her heart, and Dorrie, for all her tight black pedalpushers and brazen mouth, had plenty of that. She sank down on the narrow stretcher and put her arms round the younger girl. Her big breasts sagged sideways, warm and soft in the white sweatshirt with "Elvis" splashed across the back.

"Lissen luv, you don't want it to get you down like this. No man's worth it. Now if he hadn't sent you the dough you'd really be in strife."

No response. She tried a different tack.

"Gwennie, it don't do no good to cry over spilt milk. What's done's finished with but we can pick up the pieces. I had a talk with the landlady . . . she's a good sport, and she give me an address." She fumbled inside the cleft of her breasts.

Gwennie sat up in bed, red spots burning on her cheeks, her hair tousled and wet against her thin neck.

"Show me." She snatched the paper out of Dorrie's hand. It was an address in Randwick.

"It's an ol' nurse," Dorrie said. "The landlady says she's marvellous. She'll fix you up. So you don't need to worry no more. Just leave it all to Auntie Dorrie."

The little girl on the bed had enormous eyes, ringed with brown shadows, her mouth was moist and unpainted, drooping at the corners. She had tiny breasts, a waist a man could span with his hands, and childish, immature hips and legs.

"I dunno that I want to get rid of it," she said.

"Wh-at!" Dorrie sat back on her haunches, her mouth falling open in incredulous amazement. "You mean you wanta *have* it."

"Why not?"

"Why not?" She flung out her big, suntanned hands. "What would you do with it? Where would you go? How would you keep it?"

"I could put it in a Home."

"Poor little sod. I tell you it'd be better orf never bein' born if that's what you're goin' to do with it. And I know. Me Mum put me in a Home once when me ol' man shot fru' and left her."

"It's wrong to kill something. I don't believe in it," the little girl whispered.

"You gotta think of the future Gwennie. What about your job at the mill? What could you do with a baby? Hide it in the bobbin box?" She laughed a hard, smart little laugh that set Gwennie's teeth on edge. "Anyway we won't talk about it now. Wash your face an' sit up and get some food inter you. It's no good starvin' yourself. That won't stop your belly from growin'."

Gwennie thrust her feet into cheap pink leather slippers with pom-poms on the toes. She splashed cold water on her face and pulled a broken-toothed comb through her tangled hair. She wore it shoulder length, curling round her peaked little face, making it seem smaller and paler and finer-boned than ever.

When she came back Dorrie had laid out the salad and the contents of the paper bags she'd bought at the delicatessen; all sorts of rare and smelly continental delicacies to tempt Gwennie's finicky appetite. Bravely Gwennie swallowed the plainest and simplest of them. Actually when she did eat she felt a lot better. Morning sickness was always minimized by small meals taken often, but there was no one to tell her that, and she was appallingly ignorant. She hadn't even known she was pregnant for two months.

When she did find out and went up to Crown Street Outpatients to confirm the awful suspicion, she fled from the rough and ready handling of the young internes, the inquisitive condescension of the almoner. The old hands took it all in their stride, parrying the almoner's questions with a wise and patient ease, putting the young doctors out of countenance with a mature, earthy wisdom. But at seventeen Gwennie, a trembling, unworldly adolescent from the northern coalfields, had neither the wit nor the maturity to handle anything very much.

She bought herself a boned step-in from a corsetry department and squashed her soft little belly into the required flatness. She wept over her swelling breasts, ate scarcely anything and vomited into public washbasins and toilets regularly and monotonously.

She dared not go back home to Kurri. Her mother had brought her to Sydney, put her in a job behind the lolly counter in Coles, fixed her up with a "respectable" room at the Y.W.C.A. Five hundred and fifty miners had lost their jobs in the north, her father and brother amongst them. Mum had wanted to give her a chance in the city. How could she go back home now? Why she'd written and told them how well she was doing, and how she'd got a better job at the mill, and made nice friends, and was rooming with a South Australian girl she'd met at the "Y" but not to worry as it was very respectable, handy and close to work, and the landlady was like a mother to her and the rent not too bad. How could she go back home now with her belly swollen into a white ball under her gathered cotton skirt?

"You've hardly et a thing," Dorrie complained. "You'll get really sick and then you'll have doctor's bills to pay and miss the time at work. You wanta wake up to yourself kid."

She cleared away in an ominous silence. Gwennie ran the

water into the sink from the little sink heater and began to wash up. It was pleasant to perform even the most monotonous tasks. It took her mind off her worries.

Dorrie lay on the bed, smoking, watching her through a cloud of smoke.

"You better hurry up and make up your mind Gwen," she said brutally. "Because from the look of you it'll soon be too bloody late. How far did you say you was?"

"Three months," Gwen said faintly.

"Three months me eye. You look more like four an' a bit to me. They don't like touchin' you after three you know. Too much risk."

The silence clamoured and wept in the little room. Dorrie got up restlessly, stubbing out her cigarette butt in the top of a jam jar.

"Lissen kid, get your glad rags out and we'll hit the town. It'll take your mind off things. I'm meetin' someone down the corner and I told 'im to bring a friend."

Gwennie set her shoulders stubbornly. "No I don't wanta be in it."

"Well if you're goin' to be pigheaded about it."

"I'd only be sick and that'd spoil everythin'," Gwennie said.

"Ah bum! You won't be sick if you make up your mind not to be. You're too sorry for yerself, that's your trouble. Well suit yerself. I'm not goin' to sit here twiddlin' me thumbs all night like an ol' maid."

"Who are you meetin'?"

"A coupla Yanks. Their ship's in the Harbour. They do things in style. C'mon, don't be a nark. I can't handle two at onct." She peeled off her pedalpushers, standing, big-thighed and magnificent in her cotton briefs. She turned her back and for a moment you could be fooled into thinking it was a strong and beautiful boy who stood preening himself in the mirror. But then she walked across the room, round buttocks shaking and shimmying, and nobody could make any mistake about Dorrie's sex.

"I don't like Yanks," Gwennie said sulkily. "They're too big-mouthed."

"No, but I like what they got in their pockets. Dough-reah-me. And so do all the girls in Sydney. You shoulda seen the performance when the last Yank ship went out. All the little sorts climbin' on the fence and weepin' buckets. There was one little blonde, poor thing, I thought she'd die of a broken heart. 'Paulie.

Come back to me Paulie,' she was moanin' and cryin'. They tried to pull her off the fence but she clung on. She stayed there yellin' till the ship was out the Heads, 'Come back to me Paulie.' It was a great ol' show, better than the pitchers."

She put on her face in the mirror, carefully drawing a full, pouting, sensual mouth on her own thinnish lips, arching her eyebrows with black pencil, smearing green eye shadow on her eyelids, mascara on her thick, stubby eyelashes. She gazed at herself sideways with satisfaction, pulling in her waist and thrusting out her bosom. The points of her breasts were outlined in a purple jersey halter neck. She wore a tight, black, sheath skirt that showed every ripple of her bottom as she walked.

"Yank bait!" She winked at Gwennie. "They reckon the trolls all get down the wharves when the Yanks are due in, with no pants on and sit with their legs wide open. I got a boy friend works at Garden Island. He says the Aussies walk along the wharf havin' a look at everythin' they got, for free. Some of them are only bitsa kids. Jeez, some girls are rough."

She paused a moment at the door. Gwennie stood quite still, staring at the wall, her hands motionless in the soapsuds. Dorrie crossed over to her, put her hand lightly on her shoulder.

"You think real careful about what you're goin' to do love," she said. "And don't bank on your sailor boy comin' home to you. He won't come back. I lost me cherry on the kitchen table to a sailor once. I was fifteen. He never come back neither."

She walked out of the flat. Her stilt heels clicked on the stairs. Gwennie heard the outside door wheeze behind her.

Gwennie undressed and showered in the half light, mechanically hanging up her dress, putting her shoes tidily under the bed. When she had her pyjamas on, she wound up the clock and set the alarm for six o'clock. She lay on the bed, her hands folded across her belly, her thumbnails pressing deep into the rounded flesh, deep, deeper, as if she could exorcise the tiny seed that had grown from a fortnight of shore leave, and a night or two of fumbling, incoherent, tender love.

For to her it had been love, blossoming, unfolding like a beautiful flower in the dark above her little stretcher bed. If she closed her eyes she could still see his face, the straight fair hair flopping into her eyes, high cheekbones piercing his skin, the mouth hard and trembly, the tongue forcing her mouth open. And surely she couldn't have imagined it. Surely it must have been love for him too, else why did his eyes melt when he pulled her down underneath him? Why did his voice break and he cried, "Gwennie, Gwennie, I love you Gwennie," over and over again between his teeth?

So this child she carried was a child of love. How could it be thrown away in a dark house with the blinds drawn, and a woman bending over her with disinfectant on her hands, sharp silver instruments and a sharp voice that said, "Keep still dear. This'll hurt but it'll all be over in a minute."

Her mind shuddered away from the foetus wrenched out of her body, the placenta wrapped up in a piece of old newspaper and flushed down the toilet . . . her baby, Col's baby . . . dead and buried. LUNA PARK . . . JUST FOR FUN!

> "Ra de da de da,
> Chanson d'amour."

Her hands kneaded her soft flesh, her eyes stared up into the dark for a long time. No, the cicadas did not sing in Little Albion Street on Thursday night, but Surry Hills was restless with life and the living.

The old Yugoslav barrowman wheeled his barrow up Foveaux Street, wincing and walking on the sides of his shoes. The cockatoos kept watch outside the dirty house in Reservoir Street, where Thomos two-up school did a roaring, open trade. Shadows slipped in the lighted doorway of a well-kept semi, painted green, where the madam poured the drinks and the girls waited in fresh kimonos upstairs.

An old woman with bruised eyes, in a filthy black dress, lay on the steps of Silknit, struggled to get up, moaned and fell back again. A little, black, rickety-legged kitten purred and rubbed against her legs.

The moon came out over the rooftops, with a face as flat and white and featureless as the faces of the prostitutes in the green semi. The moon shone and dried the tears on Gwennie's face. But no cicadas sang in Little Albion Street. There were no trees there.

In the morning Gwennie woke to the jangle of the alarm. She bathed her swollen eyes in the sink, was sick in the lavatory, pinned her hair, and reddened her mouth.

All the articles for expectant mothers said that morning sickness could be overcome by the expectant mother slowly sipping a cup of weak tea and slowly eating one dry biscuit, before rising. But there was nobody to bring a cup of tea and a biscuit to Gwennie. Dorrie's bed was empty. It had obviously not been slept in.

She picked at a breakfast of grapefruit and coffee, washed up, took her tote bag and hurried out into the street. The kids were already playing hopscotch and marbles, trundling bikes and billycarts up and down the pavements. Workers passed her, bleary-eyed and taciturn, their footsteps echoing hollowly between factories and offices. Somebody carried a bunch of late boronia, its sharp, sweet scent saturating the morning air. A very pale, washed-out summer sky floated across the jumbled roofs of Surry Hills. A Council truck whooshed past, sending a wide sweep of water into the gutters, littered with last night's carousals. Gwennie had to skip to get out of the way. The morning smelt fresh and clean. A steady stream of cars rolled down Elizabeth Street. The plane trees by the railway embankment rustled and glittered with patches of mottled sunlight.

A cripple with a broad white face, fair greenish hair and over-developed shoulders helped the Slav barrowman lay out his fruit in the sun.

"Mornin' miss. By Chri, you're gettin' fat."

A handsome man with tight grey curls and a withered mouth strolled out the front door of Thomos, rolling a cigarette. A middle-aged woman in sandshoes with a man's felt hat on her head, and a man's coat over her cotton dress, wandered past the barrow and carefully selected two of the best oranges. She had a big printed sign pinned on her back. "Shakespeare readings. Any speech on request . . . 2/-."

"Okay, okay Bea," said the barrowman. "By Chris', that bloody Bea Miles she send me broke yet."

Gwennie could see the Alexandria tram labouring up the hill. She ran to catch it. The night was over. The spinning mill waited. The decision could be postponed for another day.

"Who's that?" the stranger said to the barrowman.

The barrowman looked shocked. "Doncha know. That's Bea Miles . . . the most famous woman in Sydney. Everybody knows Bea."

"Is she . . . a mad woman?" the stranger whispered.

The barrowman scratched his head. "I dunno. Some says she got more brains than the politicians. They reckon she wore her brain out at the Uni when she was young. But she seem 'appy enough. She 'ates only two things, coppers an' taxi-drivers, an' she got a lotta mates."

"She ought to be put away," the stranger said. "I'll have a dozen bananas."

"Jus' come up from Melbourne 'ave y'?" said the barrowman, skilfully shortchanging him by threepence.

Over the huddled rooftops, over the crowds pouring into Central Station, over the pigeons strutting amongst the old men, shaking out their newspaper blankets on the park seats, over all the glowing morning of the city, a rich, sonorous voice echoed in Hamlet's immortal soliloquy:

> "To be or not to be
> That is the question:
> Whether 'tis nobler in the mind to suffer
> The slings and arrows of outrageous fortune,
> Or to take arms against a sea of troubles,
> And by opposing end them . . ."

Somebody had slipped Bea Miles two bob.

But Gwennie never heard her. She was rattling towards Alexandria, straphanging in a crowded workers' tram.

Jeez I hope I get there before I'm sick again, she thought.

Chapter Fourteen

☆

Ah! but how the cicadas sang outside the rows of little fibro boxes in Beverly Hills. They drummed and drummed under the sprinklers in the close summer dusk, till even the air throbbed with an unreal excitement.

Julie had been dancing round the kitchen half the night in her nightie.

"What're you lookin' for?" Don grumbled, crackling his paper with a grin. "Lookin' for a bit?"

She flounced off into the bedroom, gazing at him enticingly over one fat shoulder.

"You're awful," she said. She hoped he might put his paper away and follow her, but he never moved, and she felt let down. All the romance drained away out of the night. She stared at herself in the wardrobe mirror. It was an old-fashioned oak suite they'd bought when they were first married, with one of those full-length mirrors on the door. She saw a fat, stubby woman, red-cheeked and black-haired like a plump Dutch doll, a white cotton nightie pulled tight over her breasts. She turned this way and that, seeing the nightie strain tight over her big buttocks and thighs, trying to shift herself into a more attractive angle.

"Pick up the rose and fling it in the corner," she said, reciting over one of her old ballet exercises, but the vision she saw in the mirror was not a thing of grace and beauty but a fat woman with a big bum, making a fool of herself.

It was no use. She sat disconsolately on the edge of the quilt, gazing at her flat, broad feet, weeping inwardly for the youth and the light joy that would never come back again.

There was a wedding photo of herself and Don on the dressing table, a wispy, shy little girl with a straight, black fringe, gazing out from masses of filmy tulle. She had weighed seven and a half stone in those days, and gone in for acrobatics in black tights and ballet slippers. She had taught dancing to groups of giggling little girls in a rickety old hall in Newtown. She could still smell the dust rising off the bare boards, and hear the slap, slap of soft-soled shoes on Saturday mornings.

She heard Don get up and fold his paper away. In half an hour he'd be walking down the roadway in the summer dusk on his way to work. He poked his head in the bedroom door.

"Why doncha get some sleep while the goin's good?" he said.

Julie didn't want him to go. She wanted to pour out all the day's burden into a sympathetic ear, all the little defeats and hurts, the petty bickerings and the triumphs. She wanted to unload them all onto his shoulders, already bowed under a load of their own. It was like a cat and mouse game with them every night. He knew it and was determined to get away, out of the house, before the tirade caught him up and beat him under.

"I offered that Beth and her husband the front room," she said, knowing that talk about increasing their income was about the only thing that would hold him at the door.

There was a flicker of interest in his eyes. "What she say?"

"Jus' palmed me orf with some excuse about gettin' a place of their own in Redfern."

"Well, whadda you keep askin' people for. Blind Freddy could see the way things shaped last Saturdee, when they was here. It's Johnny . . . they couldn't take Johnny. That was it. And when he pulled out his John Thomas and peed into a coke bottle in fronta her, that was the stone finish. I seed it in her eyes."

"Pity about them," Julie snapped. "We gotta take 'im 'aven't we?"

"He's our kid. We got no option."

"Lovely way for a father to talk about 'is own son!"

He ignored that. "I dunno why you keep invitin' people here," he said, "when you know Johnny only embarrasses them. I knew they'd never come back after the first time, even if you didn't. Nobody ever does."

"What are we supposed to be . . . hermits or somethin'?" she said bitterly.

His mouth set. "What's the good of talkin' about it. It's always the same I tell you. People come to see us once. Johnny mucked it up, stutterin' and shriekin' and climbin' all over them. Life's hard enough for everyone without puttin' up with a mad kid inter the bargain. By Christ don't I know it. You feel as if you're orf to Callan Park yourself."

"I dunno," she said wearily. "You try to be friendly with people and they dump you."

"You wanta wake up to yourself," he said brutally. "Nobody wants people with burdens hanging round their neck. Life's hard enough."

"Ah!" she said. "You give me a pain. You're always beat before you start. You wanta make an effort . . ."

"If you're lookin' for a row," he said, "go and have it with yourself. I'm goin' to work."

He turned and went out into the kitchen. She could hear him rattling around, packing his crib tin in his kitbag, getting his plastic mug out of the cupboard.

"That's right," she shrieked after him. "Blame me. You blame me for everythin'. Is it my fault if Johnny . . ."

He stood glaring at her in the doorway. "I dunno if it's your fault or not," he said slowly. "You mighta been muckin' about, playin' up for all I know. You had plenty a opportunity with me outa the place night and day slavin' me guts out before the kid was born. There never were no nong-nongs in my family before."

"You rotten thing," she shrieked, her face twisted with hatred and grief, paying him back for ignoring her half the night. "You're the only man that ever laid a finger on me an' you know it. You rotten thing." She began to cry, her flabby shoulders shaking up and down, her face puckered like a child.

"I don't wanta hear about it," he yelled. "Understand! Pickin' on me all bloody night. Whadda you expect?"

"Oh! I dunno Don," she said sadly. "What's the use of expectin' anything?" Her quietness touched him more than anything else could have done. He sat down on the bed beside her and lent her his handkerchief. He took her hand in his, broad, workworn, the wedding ring cut deep into the swollen flesh. She noticed the deep lines drawn from his nose to his mouth, the way his shoulders stooped as if he carried a load too big for him. He's gettin' old, she thought, soft with compassion.

He was a heavy-built man, well over six foot, broad-chested and lean-hipped. His long, humorous upper lip was freckled and twisted half sardonically. His curly hair was flecked with grey. He wore his trammie's hat pulled well down over his eyes, so that nobody could quite see the hurt and defeat written there. Everything defeated him . . . the long, lonely nights in the tram depot on the switchboard (they'd taken him off driving because of his health, made him into a sort of glorified night watchman)

164

. . . the new fibro house, pathetically bare of furniture (they rented it for £3/15/- a week from the Housing Commission) . . . the muddy, rutty road to the station . . . the three kids to clothe, feed and look after. But especially Johnny, the epileptic, he was always a nagging sore in the back of his mind . . . the way people shied away from them because of Johnny. He could have got above the rest, but Johnny had him beaten into a weary submission. Under his trammie's cap his eyes were always on the ground, hurt and lonely. He looked up at the crucified Christ with the bared bleeding heart, above the double bed, and smiled. That's me, he thought and wasn't even conscious of any blasphemy. He remembered as a small boy being sent off to the priest to confess his childish sins and, at night, kneeling to say his prayers, small grubby hands clasped tight, the lino striking a chill into his knees. Religion offered no solace to him any more. It was alright for the women. Although he was beginning to think it was wearing a bit thin with Julie too.

But for him there was nothing.

"They're collectin' for that Beth for a present for her baby," Julie said bitterly. "I never give nothin'. Why should I? 'Er husband's in work. That Commo woman, she's doin' the collectin'. When I knocked her back she looked at me as though I was lousy."

"Well aren't you," Don said, irritated again, against his better judgment.

"That Commo woman says they know marvellous cures for all sorts of complaints in Russia," she murmured wistfully.

"Might as well be in Timbuctoo for all the good it'll do us."

Julie grinned. "I said to her, if the Commos can cure my Johnny I'll join up tomorrer. D'you hear me Don?"

"What's that?"

"Why can't you listen when I'm talkin'," she cried, snatching her hand away.

"Listen. Jesus Christ! I do nothin' else but listen to your silly chatter night after night . . ."

"A woman likes a bitta companionship," Julie whinged.

"You've had companionship all day in the mill."

"Them!" Julie's voice was loaded with scorn. "They tell orf-colour jokes all day and don't tell none to me, because I never see the point. At least I was brung up a lady."

"Well don't come whinin' to me about it. If you wanta listen to dirty jokes . . ."

"I never said that. . . ."

165

"Ah! shuddup," he roared. "Nag, nag, nag. A man's *gotta* go to work to get a bit a peace."

He left her to it, sitting, trembling with resentment on the edge of the bed, while he flung out into the kitchen, picked up his kitbag, shoved his hat far down on his eyes, and slammed the back door.

She followed him in her mind, tramping down the road, the lights of the little settlement spread out behind him like dozens of cats' eyes in the greenish dusk. He'd walk into the depot, hang his cap on the peg, take over from the fellow on the shift before him. The trammie would say . . .

"Well, how're you goin' Don. Alright?" and he'd say . . .

"I'm not complainin'. No use complainin'. Nobody wants to listen to complaints."

The poor feller, she thought to herself, he don't mean half he says.

She comforted herself with this thought as she tidied up the kitchen, cut Marlene's, young Don's, and her own lunches for tomorrow, ironed a shirt for Don and a dress for Marlene, darned a big hole in Johnny's sock, put out the dirt tin and the milk bottles. She went in and covered the kids up and was worried because young Don was out with that fast little piece in the next street and next thing he'd be getting her into trouble, and they'd be held responsible.

At last she lay, staring into the darkness, the backs of her legs and the small of her back aching with one long, intolerable ache. The pores of her skin seemed choked with grease and wool dust. Everything was very quiet from the kids' room. If only Johnny wouldn't wake up tonight. She rubbed her arm where he'd bruised it in his desperate paroxysm last night. The bruise was just beginning to come out. She must show it to the girls at the mill tomorrow. She took a strange perverted sort of pride in showing off her marks of mortal combat with Johnny. It was as if she cried proudly through all her nights and days, "This is my cross and I will bear it. But everyone will know about my martyrdom to my unhappy child."

Johnny was getting such a big boy now. What was going to happen when he got too big for her to manage? What would become of him? They couldn't afford a private home, it would have to be the asylum, and how could she bear her Johnny in a place like that! She knew it wasn't fair to the other kids. He made their life a misery.

"Watch Johnny. Don't let Johnny do nothin' he shouldn't."

166

"Don't let the other kids torment Johnny."

"Run an' tell me quick if Johnny starts a fit."

MARLENE'S GOT A MAD BROTHER . . . MARLENE'S GOT A MAD BROTHER . . .

They'd bled themselves white for Johnny . . . specialists, clinics, new treatments . . . and the result of it all, the bare boards on the floor, the shabby clothes, her job at the mill, sometimes not quite enough of the right things to eat, the kitchen dresser with a pathetic row of glass cups . . . Johnny had pulled the whole caboodle down on himself one wild evening and broken all her glory-box utility set. Now they had to double up for sweet dishes, and eat off cracked plates. Everything looked poor house and make-do.

"You're lucky to have a house at all Julie," the women at work told her. And it was true enough. At least she and Don could hide their shame inside their own four walls. And it was shame. She had faced that a long time ago, staring dry-eyed into the dark. She felt guilty for having borne such a child, Don felt guilty for having fathered him. The doctor said it was an injury at birth. She remembered how the child's head was all pushed out of shape with a big dint in the forehead like a celluloid doll. Yet Johnny had been a pretty baby. He was still an attractive boy, till you looked closer and noticed the wildly vacant blue eyes, that seemed to stare inwards at nothing.

There had been the hospitals and the Church, in that order. To them both she had gone, seeking salvation, and never found it. "It's God's will my dear," said Father but she couldn't accept it.

"Whenever he sees grass Doctor, he seems sorta drawn to it. He falls down with his face in it." Johnny was four years old then. She had stood in the hospital consulting room before a famous specialist, giving his services condescendingly to the public hospital.

He looked at her, without humanity, leaning back in his chair, his long, paper-thin hands tapping with a fountain pen impatiently on his desk.

"Your child's a hopeless case Madam. Nothing can be done for him. Much better to put him in a Home among those of his own mental level. Hopelessly retarded! You don't seem to grasp that at all."

She could hear Johnny crying outside. The students were examining him. When she came out, with the hot tears pricking at the back of her throat, the crowd of young men, white-coated, self-satisfied and impersonal, were gathered round the little frantic figure. The little boy was in despair. She gathered him up in her arms with a burning tenderness.

"You're s'posed to be so intelligent," she cried scornfully. "Tormentin' a poor little feller that's not all there."

Johnny had another fit that night, arching his tiny back in convulsion after convulsion.

"Oh God let him die," she prayed, holding him against her body. "If I'm wicked punish me, only let him die."

But he never died. And she never quite gave up hope, trailing the weary round of doctors and hospitals, specialists' consulting rooms, burning candles, confessing her sins . . . always tireder, always poorer as the years wore her hopes as thin as her dresses.

She had two other children. Young Don, her eldest boy, had always dreamed of being a jockey. They had apprenticed him to a stable at fourteen. The stable belonged to W. H. Holler, the owner of the Jumbuck Mill. It was Dick, the foreman, who'd said a word in the right places and helped to get young Don in. Dick wasn't a bad sort and they belonged to the same church. Donny was wildly excited, but when he came home in the weekends Julie was worried. Always undersized, he looked half starved, eyes and freckles huge in a pinched, dough-white face. His spindly arms and legs stuck out like sticks from a cheap, ill-made suit. She wondered if the kid was being used up. But she didn't have to worry about Donny's racing future for very long. At fourteen and a half he started to grow. He grew like a giant, nothing could stop him. He lay in bed at night, curling up his legs in an agony of terror, trying to stop this nightmare growth that meant finish to all his glamorous dreams. By his fifteenth year he was almost as tall as his father, with a big, rangy bony body and huge hands and feet. In that year he started as a bobbin boy at the mill, trailing the bobbin cart up and down between the rows of machines. His offsider was a half-witted, skinny boy with a twitching eye and a bulging white adam's apple. Dick had got young Donny into the mill. He wasn't a bad sort and they were in the same church.

Their youngest child was a girl. Don and she had been delighted with Marlene. She was such a completely ordinary little girl. All the time Julie was carrying her she had been afraid even to look into the eyes of her husband, afraid that one of them might blurt out their terrible fear . . . "Will this one be alright. Will this one be normal?"

Marlene was a fat, roly-poly little girl with her mother's straight black hair and pink cheeks. She was spoilt and pugnacious, always getting into mischief and answering back. Julie had dreamed of a dainty little girl in a ballerina's tu-tu, with golden Shirley Temple curls, but she was grateful. She never worried about Marlene. She would be okay. But young Donny—sometimes, watching him, her heart twisted. Already he had the cheated, suffering look of his father engraved on his unformed, freckled face.

She had wanted so much for her children, all the things she had never achieved, but already she felt that she and Don had failed them. The only bit of excitement there had ever been in her life was her dancing teacher days and her courtship with Don. Life had taken on a new shining depth in those months. She felt she was really living. All experience seemed heightened and deepened. Even the most ordinary, everyday things were bathed in a golden glow, and life smelt exactly like the wet purple violets in the little flower stalls along Martin Place.

She remembered with a blush and a giggle, the first time Don had ever taken her out.

"Where d'you wanta go?" he'd asked, gazing down at her.

"Fairy Bower," she said shyly, with a little bubbly laugh. "That's where I'd love to go. I've always wanted to see it."

He gave her an odd look. "What d'you wanta go there for?" he mumbled.

"It's such a pretty name," she said dreamily.

They had met by the entrance to Manly ferry in the half dusk. The Harbour was bathed in a milky glow, where sea and sky merged together on the horizon. The first lights shimmered twice-over like huge, shivering, golden flowers, their reflections dangling up and down, down and up in the clear water.

So they had gone to Fairy Bower, stepping around and over the couples lying clasped in each other's arms, her eyes averted, her face getting hotter and hotter, pinker and pinker.

"Didn't you know what goes on here?" he said, almost sorry for her.

"No," she whispered.

"I didn't think there was any girls as dumb as you any more," he grinned. "I thought you must be invitin' me to have a do."

She stumbled on, her heels sticking in the bright green grass. "Let's get outa here," she said piteously.

I'm not that dumb now though she thought, and when Don gets home in the mornin' he'll haveta have a good long talk to young Donny. We don't want no shot gun weddin's in our family.

The furniture loomed up in dark, hideous shapes around the room. The cicadas sang their heads off outside the little fibro boxes, but Julie never heard them. She was dead asleep, her legs sprawled out, her mouth half open, dreaming of herself floating mistily in a mass of tulle, her ballet slippers rosy with light, her pounds shed away. Seven and a half stone she danced and piroutted, swirled and smiled to the music of the cicadas drumming in the oleander bush on the front lawn.

The locusts were still singing when she woke next morning. Already the sky was pale and smoky with the promise of "another stinker". But at least she'd got one good night's sleep in, the first for weeks.

The kids were still lying tumbled across their beds, their lips parted, their hair soft and sweaty on their foreheads. The tabby cat had crept in the open window during the night and lay purring on Johnny's stomach. His little crooked fingers were clenched in its warm fur. He looked so comforted and at peace with the world for once, that she couldn't bear to send the cat flying into the yard. She woke young Donny with a gentle shake, and they swallowed a plate of "Weeties" together at the kitchen table.

He had dark shadows under his eyes and he didn't look up from his plate.

"I know you was out till midnight with that little sort down the street," Julie said. "No good sittin' there lookin' like a Sundee School teacher."

"We went to the pitchers," he mumbled.

"What's she like?"

"She's orright."

He got up, anxious to put an end to the inquisition. "I'll walk on slow Mum. You c'n catch me up. You always take too long."

She smiled at him. "Alright," she said. "When you're as old as me it'll slow you up a bit too."

She felt better tempered than she had for a long time, so good tempered in fact that when she raced down the front steps and brushed against Don at the gate, she grinned at him sideways, and gave him a shove with her bottom as she passed.

"Cheeky bitch," he muttered, but he smiled, and she knew that he was mollified.

"Ta-ta luv," she called and waved to him from the corner of the street. He raised his hand, standing tall and stooped shouldered and weary in his crumpled uniform, outlined against the smoky sky.

The locusts drummed like nerves behind her hurrying footsteps. Already a dark semi-circle of sweat stained and spread in the armpits of her cotton dress.

She saw young Donny, lanky and round shouldered, beckoning her from the railway embankment, his freckled face concerned. "C'mon Mum," he yelled. "She's almost in."

Puffing and panting she climbed towards him, already hearing the sound of the electric train clicking over the rails, seeing the workers surging forward to the edge of the platform. They swung through the doors just as the flag went down, and she started.

"Made it," gasped Julie and they smiled at each other, with the comradeship of the shared morning scramble, the shared triumph of another train caught, another day begun.

It took a full hour to travel from Beverly Hills to the Jumbuck, but Julie and Donny were always early. Donny always left his mother at the tram stop. It was *infra dig.* to be seen trailing into the mill tied to her apron strings. Julie understood how he felt and let him go, his long legs shambling through the sunlight, his big, knobbly wrists banging helplessly against his trouser legs.

She strolled along slowly, taking everything in with her bright, inquisitive eyes, dawdling at the doors of the factories, peering into the half-dark interiors, getting a hot gust of oily air from the machine shops, trying to gauge whether it would be better there than the Jumbuck. It was a game she played with herself every morning.

On the corner of Belmont Street she saw Nina, the New Australian girl, kneeling on the pavement, with a crowd of wailing cats round her ankles. She was pouring a bottle of milk very carefully into a plastic bowl. The cats climbed against her thin knees, black, tabby, tortoiseshell, marmalade and grey, hollow ribbed, bony headed, the insistent clamour of their miaowing echoed down the streets, and lanes of Alexandria.

The sunlight filtered past the factory buildings onto Nina's pale, tarnished hair. She was like a pitiful half-starved cat herself, shabbily dressed, high, almost transparent cheekbones, and oblique hazel eyes . . . too washed out to be pretty.

Julie waddled past, her heart melting at the sight of Nina, haloed among the stray cats in the concrete jungle of Alexandria. Poor soul she thought. There must be some good in 'er.

Nina played Saint Francis every morning on the corner of Belmont Street. The bleak loneliness in her eyes was something Julie half comprehended. She paused, compelled by an urge to sympathize, to communicate her understanding.

"They like it," she said, nodding her head at the cats.

Nina didn't look up. She wore a frayed white blouse, not particularly clean, thrust into an old skirt, heavy shoes chapped her thin ankles. A golden cross dangled over her breasts. Julie smiled at the cross. This was something she understood. She pulled her own cross out of her big bosom, and the sunbeams sent it swaying and dangling like a tangible thread between the two women in the ugly asphalt world.

Julie pointed to the cross. "Like yours," she said and grinned. A small watery smile crept into Nina's suspicious eyes. Julie was encouraged.

"You feed them every mornin'?" she said slowly and distinctly, exactly as she talked to Johnny in his more stubborn moments.

Nina nodded her head.

"Like Saint Francis?" Julie said.

"Yes, yes. Like Saint Francis," Nina was grinning now. She stood up. "Here," she said, "in this country, plenty of milk." Her face grew sullen. "In my country nothing, no milk, nothing." She spread her small bony hands against her skirt. The cats lapped greedily at her feet.

"Where d'you come from?" Julie said.

"Ukraine . . . a Ukrainian . . . not my country any more now." The pale head shook like a faded flower on a broken stalk.

Julie patted her arm sympathetically. She paused, giving the girl a chance to move off with her, but Nina stood quite still, her face rapt over her kittens, her eyes hooded with distrust. "Better hurry," Julie said. "The whistle'll blow soon," but Nina didn't answer.

Julie waddled on. Poor kid, she murmured to herself. Poor kid, looks as if she needs the milk 'erself.

When she looked back Nina was still standing in a shaft of sunlight, the cats a moving mass, twining and rubbing in and out of her legs. Julie shivered. She couldn't put her finger on it but it gave her the creeps.

A plump, handsome woman with big, liquid brown eyes stopped her at the gate.

"Somethin' to read in your tea break luv," she said, thrusting a leaflet into Julie's unwilling hand.

Julie wandered towards the doorway, unfolding the leaflet as she went. All around her footsteps hurried past, strolled past, in a constant stream, snatches of conversation, silent, absorbed faces, work-scarred hands, and each hand clasped an identical leaflet, each pair of eyes scanned it with a vague and contemptuous disinterest.

Julie unhooked her disc off the board, put her big, flat foot over the doorstep of the mill. She always felt this reluctance every morning, this panic just as she stepped across the threshold. She saw the inside of the mill, dark, dark as the hobs of hell, waiting to enfold her with its heat and its sweat and its clamour. She would take one last, drowning look at the world outside, twitch one fat shoulder resignedly, take a deep breath and plunge into the darkness, splintered with light from the tiny holes in the corrugated iron walls.

The cranky old gatekeeper came snooping out, his head poking out of his shoulders like a sly, inquisitive lizard. "I wouldn't take that inside if I was you," he said sourly. "It's Commo stuff."

Julie looked at him haughtily. "Tellin' us what to read now are you Cec," she said and with a twitch of her skirts, she swept into the mill.

She dodged behind her machine, unhooking her overall from a rusty nail. In the privacy behind the rover she unfolded the leaflet. There was a far, faint rustle on the still air as everybody else did the same.

"BOBBIN UP" she read in big, bold letters across the top. "This is a Communist Party leaflet, written for and about the Jumbuck Mills for the Jumbuck workers . . ."

Dick stuck his head over the top of the rover.

"Busy," he said. Julie screwed the leaflet into a little ball in her fist and dropped it carelessly underneath her machine, pushing it back into the shadows with her toe.

"I didn't hear the whistle," she said pointedly.

Dick laughed. "Get off your high horse," he said. "Terrible touchy all you girls are this lovely mornin'."

Julie waited until she saw his broad back and baldy head disappear between the rover aisles. Then she bent down and picked up the crumpled ball of paper, carefully smoothing it out on the bench.

"THERE'S A NAME FOR A MAN WHO LIVES OFF WOMEN," she read. She was still reading when the starting whistle went at seven o'clock.

At seven-fifteen Dick hopefully sent old Plonko Charlie, the sweeper up, to clean up any spare paper lying round the mill.

But there was no spare paper. Any spare paper in the Jumbuck was carefully stowed amongst snowhite breasts, or in the pockets of worn blue overalls, to be carefully assimilated over a "cuppa" in the tea break.

"THERE'S A NAME FOR A MAN WHO LIVES OFF WOMEN . . ."

"Bobbin Up" was definitely a best seller, outselling even *True Romance*, Marc Brody and Carter Brown. Old Plonko Charlie gave up looking and went behind the bobbin boxes, where he kept his bottle of bombo permanently planted.

Chapter Fifteen

☆

Jeanie was two minutes late. By the time she got the kids from Fivedock to Erskineville and then caught the bus to Alexandria, it was always the same. Five minutes late and docked a quarter of an hour.

Well, it was no good rushing now. She strolled in the gate, giving the doorman a grin as she passed. A handsome woman with liquid eyes pressed a leaflet into her hand. "S'pose it's another of them red-hot bargain rorts," she thought gloomily, and didn't unfold it.

She paused a minute in the mill doorway. Outside there was bright sunlight. She felt it warm and clean on her face and hair. Inside it was dark and hot as hell. The steam hissed out of the pipes, giving the atmosphere that wet, muggy heat they said was essential for working the wool.

Clanking machinery, the smell of wool and grease, the over-alled women wiping sweaty hands over their hair, hit her hard, as it always did when she came in out of the morning sunlight.

Today was Friday thank God, pay day. But it had started badly. Two old cats up the street had told her nextdoor neighbour they'd report her to the Welfare for taking her kids on the tram every morning at half-past five. She had to take them that early to get to Mum's and then out to the mill for a seven o'clock start.

They thought it was criminal to have children out at that hour. Wonder do they think it's criminal to have little children living in a leaky, ill-ventilated house? All she wanted was to work till she and Alec saved up enough to get the deposit on their house . . . that beautiful dream house on the little block of land out in Blacktown, that one with the pink and black bathroom, real tiles and the kitchen with the stainless steel sink, and the new baby in the frilled bassinet on the front porch.

Dreaming of her house, she even smiled at the leading hand. He was only the pannikin boss, always putting you in to the foreman and nice as pie to your face. Anything to keep his lousy job, standing over a mob of women. She dragged her overall on, over her dress. No time to change now.

"What machine will I go on Dick?" she said.

"You're late agen."

"That's right. You try gettin' from Fivedock with two kids every mornin'."

"Better go on the big spindles agen."

"Not them bloody things. I had them yesterday, muckin' up on me all day," she snapped.

"Well someone's gotta work them."

Oh! sure, sure and that someone's gotta be me, weak heart and all, luggin' the great things in and out all day, sweating and lugging and then it breaks down and the wool knots in a thick hard skein. Cut it off and start again, and it breaks down, over and over. Pity they didn't put a bit of new machinery in the place instead of making us work with this old rubbish.

She threaded up the spindles and started her machine.

Next to her Shirl grinned over her shoulder. "Glad you come to take over the damn things Jeanie. I was stuck with the two machines."

"Been muckin' up much?"

"Ever since the whistle went."

They shrugged their shoulders resignedly. It was funny how, when you first went to work in the mill, you couldn't hear a thing. Your voice got hoarse from shouting all the time. Then, after a while, your ears must get extra sensitive or something, because you just talked ordinary and could hear every word.

Someone had taken her old box, the one she sat on when the spindles were going reasonably well. Ah! well, if they was going to break down all morning, she wouldn't have much use for the box. Wonder what Dick and that greasy foreman are muttering about over there behind the bobbin bins. Looks as if they're cooking up something.

Shirl was singing . . . must be feeling happy today.

> "Everybody goin' out and havin' fun,
> I'm just a fool for stayin' in and havin' none.
> I can't get over how he set me free,
> O lonesome me."

"What've you got to sing about?" said Jean.

"Jack and me's gettin' married today. Brought me new blue silk dress in. Mum give her consent. You know why." She

176

winked. "We're goin' to the registry office after work. We got Mum to come good last night. Worked on her for hours. So the baby'll have a father after all." She grinned, trying to sound hardboiled. But she didn't fool Jean. Shirl's had a tough life she thought. I'm glad things is working out for her okay.

"You wanta be careful liftin' them heavy spindles, or there won't be no baby to have a father," Jean said.

"I won't be doin' it after today. I could kiss the buggers today. Long time no see." Shirl laughed. "I'll be dressed up in one of them maternity smocks next month, and when the baby's born it'll have nylon frocks, all the works."

"Yeah, that's what I thought once and look at me now. Two kids and still here," Jeanie sighed.

"But you'll get your house. Then you'll be alright. Did you see this?" Shirl dived into the bosom of her overall, pulled out a carefully folded leaflet. "It's hot stuff. Rips it inter the ol' Jumbuck. These Commos have got some good ideas."

Jeanie took it out of her hand. " 'Bobbin Up' . . . what is it?"

"It's all about the mill. Didn't you get one?"

Jeanie fumbled in her handbag. "Yeah but I thought it was just a ad. Here it is."

Together they bent over the bulletin, dark head and tawny head, eyes swivelling back and forwards from spindles to paper.

"Look out, here they come."

They both bent their heads, tying off the ends, doffing their spindles in a sudden burst of activity, as the foreman and the pannikin boss, young Ken trailing at their heels, moved down the aisle. Dick darted over to the machines.

"Look as if you're workin' hard even if you're not," he grunted. "The big boss is comin' through with visitors."

There was a stir down the end of the mill and in they came. Three ladies dressed to kill, stepping daintily through the grease, their foreheads wrinkling at the noise, their nostrils faintly lifted.

Jean thought, My forehead's wrinkling too, been wrinkling for years but I'm only twenty-eight.

They passed with the tall, cold boss, talking in high, affected voices. The women by their machines looked after them with distaste. Nothing illustrated so well the great gulf that lay between two classes. Here they were, dirty, sweaty, chained to a cantankerous machine, gazed at as if they were creatures from another planet. Then, when the whistle blew, they'd rush to the washroom, try and scrub off the grease with cold water in the cracked hand basins, comb their hair, put their lipstick on, and rush home to children and husbands, tea to be cooked, kids to be bathed. And, at the end of the week, enough money in two pay envelopes to pay the instalment on the frig or the house or the second-hand car, or buy some more cups, because we've only got three and one's a glass one. Never quite out of debt, never quite catching up.

"How would we get on if you got pregnant?"

"Gawd knows."

"Other people manage."

"Do they? How about Gladys Smith! They ate mince all last week. Got three kids and she's expectin' another."

"I don't go much on mince do you?"

"Maybe if I work hard on the overtime till next Christmas we'll catch up."

Maybe . . . ?

"Listen," said Dick. "Yous had better all shake it up. I've got me job to keep same as yous women. I don't like to put the wood on yous but the boss has got it on me. Says there's not enough work comin' outa this section. So shake it up, all of yous."

The spindles whir, the bobbin cart trundles down the aisles, short women, tall women, old and ugly, young and pretty, varicose veins and shapely thighs.

"Hey Curly. Take a look at that one. I wouldn't mind givin' 'er a tumble. Get a load a that, when she bends over!"

"I'm goin' over to the lav for a smoke," said Shirl. "Keep an eye on me machine will you Jeanie. S'pose we'll haveta keep it goin' now Dick's doin' his lolly. The only place you can read in peace in this joint is on the dunny seat, and I'm goin' to finish that 'Bobbin Up'."

"Better look out for that old bitch in the washroom. She reckons she's goin' to bust into the dunnies, see what we're usin' them for."

"If she busts in on me she'll get a shock," Shirl laughed.

"Hurry up then luv and I'll nick over next."

So now Jeanie had two machines to watch. Filling this one, doffing that one, joining the ends when they snapped off.

"Hey Tony come over here and putta bitta grease on this thing will you? Might make a difference. Gee! You got an easy job. Wished I could get around with an oilcan. We do twice the work of yous men and get half the dough."

"Should be 'ome havin' babies."

"What would we do for money?"

"Plenty a money. Australia, she's a real good country."

"Ah! sure. For the heads it is. You'll find out."

Tony went on his way chuckling. Nothing could spoil his imperturbable good humour.

"Hallo Jeanie. Here I am again."

It's the union delegate, not a bad sort. Tries to do the right thing but she can't do much with this lousy union. Has a meeting twice a year, and if you're seen there, the union boss tells the mill manager and you get the bullet.

"Hallo Skin. How much do I owe you?"

"A fortnight, that's all. What're you workin' two machines for Jeanie?"

"Shirl's gone to the dunny and Dick's right on our hammer. Been naggin' at us all mornin'. You know how he is?"

"Turn it off. I always do. You gotta go to the lav," Nell said.

"Yeah but then Shirl'll get inter trouble. You know what they're like."

Yeah . . . we know what they're like!

Shirl came back through the row of machines, a cupid's bow carefully drawn on her upper lip. "That ol' bitch was in there. I was smokin' in the lav and she starts tryin' the door, screamin' about reportin' me at the office. I told her to go ahead, I wasn't shiftin' for any boss's crawler. She did her block and started yellin'. Fat ol' bitch. Won't worry me. Won't be here after tonight."

Nell grinned at her, watching for Dick over her shoulder. "How about your dues Shirl?"

"You again. Can't you ever give a girl any peace. What I wanta know is what's this lousy union ever done for me?"

"It never will do anythin' while you don't go to the meetin's," Nell said.

"I know, I know an' get picked for a Commo or somethin'."

"Why don't we all go together. Then no one can get picked?"

"You know how it is. I got a date and Jean has to cook tea and put the kids to bed."

"Yeah!" Nell said sorrowfully. "That's just what they count on. That's why we're workin' for low wages in this rotten dump. No showers, no decent lunchroom . . . and the union makin' deals with the boss behind our backs."

"Okay, okay Nell. Jump off your soapbox and save it for the Domain. You read the Commos' leaflet?"

Nell smiled. "Yeah, I read it. Whadda you think of it?"

"Pretty good," Jeanie said, looking thoughtfully at Nell's quiet, freckled face, her bland blue eyes. "I wonder who told them all that about the Jumbuck Skin?"

Shirl nudged Nell in the ribs. "Here comes Dick. You'll be in strife, collectin' in the boss's time."

"What's goin' on here. Why aren't you back to your machine Nell?"

"Because I'm collectin' for the union. When are you goin' to join Dick?"

"Haven't been financial for two years Nell. Don't intend to be neither. I work too hard for me wages to hand it over to those bludgers. Why don't yous all wake up to yourselves?"

"Yeah an' all get to be pannikin bosses overnight. We know," said Jeanie. "You better go and see poor ol' Lil, Nell. She got diddled outa her sick pay when she was off last week. See if the bloody union can do somethin' useful for a change. I'm goin' to make me tea. Must be nearly time!"

Jeanie took out her old enamel teapot, cracked at the spout, hidden behind a row of machines. The women went over to the water boiler, laughing and joking, with teapots and billies, little twists of tea, plastic mugs. The whistle sounded its long, mournful note over the mill.

Miraculously the terrible noise stopped, everyone relaxed, sweaty hands wiped on grease-stained overalls, tired legs twined round old butter boxes. Gee! what would we do without that cuppa?

Only four machines, conspicuous in the silence, clattered on. The four New Australians were finishing their run through on the overheads.

"Watch this," said Jeanie. "I'm goin' to have a go at that Maria. She's the besta the bunch."

She strolled across the mill. "Switch 'er off Maria," she yelled. "The whistle's gorn."

Maria kept her head down, the sweat pouring off her muscly body. She was a broad-faced, brown-skinned Hungarian, broad hands scarred with work, her hair pushed away under a black kerchief. Up and down, up and down went her thick, brown arms among the yellow-white strands of wool.

Jeanie pushed her shoulder. "Switch 'er orf Maria," she said quietly. "You make it bad for all your mates."

Maria looked up. She searched Jeanie's face, seeing there only a deep, honest sympathy, but a firm sympathy that would stand no mucking about. She glanced around the mill, took in the silent groups of women huddled round their tea billies, their eyes on her flying hands.

She shrugged her shoulders and switched off her machine. Then she strode across and spoke to the other New Australians. The mill was all quiet at last. Jeanie smiled.

"Atta girl Maria," she said. "You catch on quick."

The women unfolded the leaflets, read them through carefully as they sipped their cups of scalding tea.

" 'Bobbin Up' . . . that's a good name!"

"You gotta hand it to the Commos. There's not a word of a lie in it."

"D'ya reckon they really will put us on short time?"

"They will when it suits 'em."

"There's a name for a man who lives orf wimmen. Callin' old Holler a bludger. It's pretty close to the truth though. I put a bet on one of 'is horses once . . ."

"I'm goin' to the lav."

"What! In your own time. Whassa matter with you?"

"So me old man and me aren't speakin' today. He come home off night shift, just as I left. That goes on all the week. By the weekend we're that pleased to see each other it'll all have blown over."

"I'm workin' till I can get me false teeth. Look awful without any."

"I reckon they'll end up killin' us all with these bombs. The Yanks let off five in eight days. Get the heads out there to fight the wars. Then there wouldn't be none."

"We'll be in our new house by autumn. Then Gawd knows how we'll pay it off. We'll haveta sit on butter boxes."

"Pinch a few from here. At least you're usta sittin' on them."

Jean sat and dreamed about her new house. Maybe she'd have to work for a while after they moved in. They didn't have much. Jimmy was too big for his cot. He'd have to have a new bed. She'd love to get the kids two of them divans, the polished ones with drawers underneath. And a carpet in the bedroom. Even feltex would do.

"There's a new Depression comin' alright," said Nell. "You can see it in the papers all the time. Course the heads try to hush it up."

"Mum says we're mad to try and own our own home," said Jean. "Reckons we'll lose it same as she and Dad did in the last one. I can remember the rent man usta come and Mum usta send me to the door. Once I got a helluva hidin'. 'Me mother's in the bedroom and she says to tell you she's not home,' I told him. Kids!"

"If you can get the loan over enough years you'll be right," Nell said, "but if the payments are too big you'll never make it."

"I want to own me own home, and get on. Alec's got it in him. He's a hard worker. I don't take no notice of Mum. She's got Commo ideas like Dad. He's on the wharves and she gets them off him. Reckons the system's goin' to collapse." Jeanie gave the smug, superior smile that drove Peggy Maguire wild.

"It's goin' to collapse alright," said Shirl. "But as long as I'm married and the kid's got a name, I'm not worried. I've seen everythin' now."

"Anyone'd think you was ninety instead of nineteen."

Jean was thinking about the Depression. She saw a little girl with big eyes and straggly rat tails of hair, cramping her feet into shoes a size too small. Mum used to get them from the Welfare. That must be why I've got such rotten feet now she thought. She surveyed them, wide and calloused . . . thrust into dirty, pink, felt slippers, slopped over on one side.

The whistle blew. The short, luxurious quiet was over. The banging, clanking and belting in your head was on again. The women folded the bulletins, back they went in the clefts of the breasts, the shabby handbags, the overall pockets.

The heat grew intense towards midday. The women's shoulders and hair were white with fine, accumulated wool fluff. So were their lungs.

"Drink milk," the bosses said. "It helps prevent lung disease, helps to combat catarrh, asthma and TB."

There was a clause in the award that said bosses had to supply free milk but it wasn't done at the Jumbuck. Plenty of the women bought and drank a couple of cartons or more a day, most had catarrh, some had asthma, some probably had TB. The sun beat down on the corrugated iron roofs, pressed its way through the chinks in the walls like millions of tiny, fiery eyes in the gloom, the steam grew hotter, the sweat poured down the tired faces.

Old Charlie, perspiring plonk from every pore, whooshed buckets of water between the rovers. The women slopped about, grease sticking like an extra sole on their wet slippers.

"Turn it up Charl. We'll be swimmin' for it soon."

"You gotta do it," Charlie whined. "You gotta do it to make the wool run proper."

A girl got her long blonde hair caught in a reeling machine and was freed by a fellow worker before she was scalped.

"For Gawd's sake tie the bloody stuff up in a hankie or somethin'," yelled the pannikin boss. Tempers were getting frayed.

Jessie who had bad legs ever since she'd slipped on the greasy, wool-strewn floor, went to Sister in first aid, was told to stop loafing and get back to work.

In the last Depression she'd worked over a machine till she was eight months pregnant, her belly getting in the way of the whirring cogs. Then they sacked her. Might fall in the machine and muck it up, she thought bitterly.

Al, who was thin and anaemic and suffered from asthma, fainted just as she was showing Gwennie, the new girl, how to tie a weaver's knot. Beth, who was six months pregnant, worked slowly and clumsily, the sweat pouring off her heavy body. Gwennie wore a track to the toilet, dry retching over the stinking bowl.

No one was sorry when the whistle went. Maria switched her machine off a second before time. The New Australians looked surprised but they followed suit.

Jeanie grinned, nudging Shirl. "Look at that. Maria's wakin' up to herself. She's alright."

It was heaven to get the weight off your legs. Some of the girls sank down on their old boxes by the greasy machines and ate just as they were, too tired to care much. Others went outside by the factory wall, and a thin, withered grass strip. It was blazing hot but at least there was a whiff of fresh air in between the smog. Alexandria on a summer's day was no paradise, a horizon of factory chimneys belching out their smoke on the brassy sky of summer. The girls slumped against the hot brick wall, eating their dry sandwiches and pies listlessly, taking great gulps of tea.

"They reckon they're puttin' off the married women in some of the mills," Al said.

"They'd have to put off three-quarters of the Jumbuck then."

"I heard on the wireless the other day that women make up twenty-eight per cent of the workers in Australia," said Nell. "You'd think they'd start payin' women decent wages when there's so many of them workin'. We're keepin' the country rich."

"What makes you think it's rich. Bloody old Menzies is sendin' us downhill every day." Jessie rubbed salve tenderly into her swollen leg. The smell of Zambuk mixed with Sargent's pies and salad sandwiches.

"Did you hear about the union agreein' to short time at Bond's?" said Al. "Fancy havin' to live on two days' work a week. You wouldn't be in the race."

"Well, I don't reckon women should get the same wages as men. Men have got more responsibilities. They haveta keep a family." Julie looked self-righteous.

"I haveta keep mine since me old man ditched us, but no one puts the extra in *my* pay envelope."

"Married women shouldn't work anyway," Julie said.

"What are you workin' for then?"

"So we can pay off the frig and pay the doctor's bill for young Marlene's tonsils . . ."

"That's what we're all workin' for luv."

Julie changed her tack. She knew when she was beaten. But she didn't like it.

"That Balt girl reckons they got no milk in Russia Nell," she said. "She's out feedin' all the stray cats in Alexandria every mornin'."

Nell's temper flashed. "How the hell would she know? She's been in D.P. camps all over Europe ever since the war. The Nazis took her outa the Ukraine when she was twelve years old, and filled her up with so much rubbish, she wasn't game to go back."

Julie's mouth gaped. "How do you know?" she said truculently.

"Because I asted her," Nell snapped.

"I wonder what happened between Dawnie and young Ken," Julie said. "He's treatin' her like she's got the mange or somethin' . . ."

Jean was wanted down the front office. She went, full of fears. Young Jimmy had caught polio, Joanie had got run over on the way to school. Perhaps Alec was hurt at work. When she got out the front there was Alec, no smile on his face, just a grim look that meant something serious was up.

"What's wrong luv? Why aren't you at work?"

"Took a sickie. Thought I'd check up with the War Service about our land. Found out plenty too."

"Why, what's wrong then?" It was a cry from her heart. For one dreadful instant she saw her beloved house, the baby on the porch, the pink and black bathroom slipping into the dark abyss of loss. She heard her mother's words, saw that wide-hipped, toil worn figure in the shabby weatherboard become herself, saw the futile waste of all that rising before dawn, working the spindles all day, stumbling home at night with two weary grizzling kids.

"What's happened Alec? What's wrong?" she said.

"They sold us a pup the bastards. The War Service won't go

on with it. The Council's not puttin' the water through yet, not for years maybe. So they won't build."

"But all the other people, the family next to us. Their house was started . . ."

"We're all in the same boat darl. The agent never bothered to tell us about this little technicality . . . no water. There was another bloke there. He was ropable. His family's all out at Hargrave Park and his wife's expectin' their fifth kid. They sunk all their dough in their block a land. Reckons he's goin' to get a petition up and we'll all go on a deputation to the Council. I said we'd go."

"Now look Alec. Maybe you got it all wrong. Maybe if we just go and see the Council quietly on our own. We don't wanta go gettin' mixed up in no Commo stunts. It never got Dad no-where. He's still battlin' away on the wharves at sixty and Mum in that rotten little dump in Erskineville. We'll wait and see. Maybe it's not as bad as it looks. Remember that nice feller we saw who sold us the block, the one in the spotted bow tie. We'll go and see him . . ." She was babbling on desperately, holding onto his arm.

Alec smiled gently. "You're havin' yourself on Jeanie. Still, maybe we better wait and see. No use goin' off half cocked. The bloke mighta been a trouble maker for all I know. I'll go and have a talk to those estate agents now. P'raps we can find a way round it. Anyway don't worry."

He patted her hand absently, a little thin fitter, with a prematurely aged face and bright, intelligent eyes.

They kissed and he watched her walk from the sunlight into the mill, watching how her body was thickening out like her mother, her overall pulled tight, buttons straining over her hips and heavy thighs. Yet her long, dark, swinging hair and velvety brown eyes were those of a young girl.

She waved to him bravely before she disappeared and he heard the whistle blow for back to work.

Inside as Jeanie started up the spindles, her brain was whirling. She couldn't adjust herself to the loss of the dream that made all her life worth while. Often when the going got really tough, when the big spindles were mucking up, Dick throwing his weight about, and her head felt it would burst with the blood pounding up from her unsteady heart, she clicked off to that little house with the bright garden, shining from kitchen to bedrooms with its compact newness. And now that her dream was about to be snatched from her, she couldn't believe that

that was to be all her life . . . the stinking mill, the rotting little house in Fivedock, the struggle to pay the inflated rent, until she was too old and heartsick to care.

Alec and she mustn't get mixed up in anything Commo. Sure, the Commos had some good ideas. She agreed with a lot of what they said. But you had to look out for yourself. You couldn't afford to get branded red. Look at her father, been in and out of work for years, just because he couldn't keep his big mouth shut. Maybe that's why she and Alec had been wiped by the War Service, and the Council and the estate agents, or whoever had wiped them. Maybe they'd heard about Tom Maguire being a red. But still all the people with land out there couldn't be reds.

But they'd better be careful . . . real careful.

Chapter Sixteen

☆

THE mill was paid on Friday afternoon, round about three o'clock. The bosses didn't get much work out of them after that. Everyone went mad, singing and shouting, just like a lot of kids let out of school.

The mill workers walked up in single file to a little, pimply faced clerk with glasses, who gave them their pay envelopes as if he could hardly bear the contact with their greasy, sweaty fingers. There was a lot of chiacking and pushing in the queue. Big fat Julie who used to be an acrobatic dancer, did the splits the whole way up the aisle between the roving machines, and said it would take her a week to get over it.

The girls got their pay first, the handful of men followed. The first one to open her pay packet was Lil. She took out the little slip. She was sacked.

She stood quite still in the centre of the mill, her little, quick hands clasped together, a vacant bewilderment in her eyes. A shaft of sunlight streamed onto her grey head, her skinny body shrank and trembled, as if the rover she'd worked for so many years had risen up and dealt her a murderous kick in the solar plexus. NO VACANCIES, PLEASE DO NOT APPLY . . .

Then came Julie, Nell, Jessie, Beth, Gwennie and Bet, all married or growing old, all a week's pay in lieu. The women stood in little groups, gazing at the tiny slip of green paper with stricken eyes. For each one it meant the end of a dream, for many it meant more than that, it meant a bitter struggle for survival.

The single girls and young widows were the only ones kept on. Business was slack. The mill might have to close down altogether. Even those left would have to go on short time, perhaps averaging two or three days a week, if they were lucky. The rumours flew from mouth to mouth. There would be more retrenchments if things didn't look up. The frightening shadow

187

of depression huddled the little groups closer together round the silent machines.

If only I hadn't told them I was married, Gwennie thought piteously. I might've kept me job. If only I hadn't lied about it. Old Betty sat on her box beside the rover, twisting a piece of wool waste over and over between her calloused fingers. After eighteen years, after eighteen years of "giving the boss a fair go", after all the new girls she'd trained, the cranky machines she'd nursed through her broad, blotched hands, the doffs she'd taken off, to be chucked in a corner like a broken old bobbin.

Nell was the first to recover. "Well I'm damned if I'm takin' this lyin' down," she cried. "How about it girls? Whaddabout a trip to the boss?"

"Don't do nothin' silly Nell. You don't wanta get yourself in bad," Dick said.

Nell whirled round, her whole body accusing, her ginger hair frayed around her cheeks in little points of fire.

"Get meself blackballed you mean you animal. I've worked round these lousy mills too many years not to know the score. Why was this all kept so dark? Scared of a bit of trouble? Scared we might all jib if it got around?"

"Ah get off your high horse Nell, we all knows you're a Commo."

"And not ashamed of it neither," snapped Nell. "Okay girls, we're callin' a meetin', official, convened by the delegate. We'll have it right here and now. Everyone in favour?"

"You can't call no meetin'. You're sacked," said Dick grimly.

The foreman pussy-footed up, the girls caught the gleam of his bifocals as he peered round a drawing machine.

"As for you Mr. Green, why doncha come and show yourself like a man, instead of leavin' Dick to do all your dirty work?" Nell said.

He crept out, bow-shouldered in his grey dust jacket, his voice humble and yet sneering in the same breath.

"Now Nell. We all know you're quick tempered. Redheads always are." He smiled placatingly. "Good at your work too. But the old firm has to make retrenchments. We all regret it very much, but you know yourself there's a recession in the textiles. When this bit of a slump is over perhaps . . ."

"When it's over," cried Nell. "Why you old fool. How can it be over? It's only just begun and it'll get worse. And if we stand here and cop it we're the ones who'll carry it on our backs like we did the last one. Isn't that right Jessie?" She appealed to the woman with the swollen legs whose bitter history was written on her face. "Isn't that right Lil?" She appealed to Lil, the Redfernite. Her skinny, wiry body and peanut-brown skin told the whole tragedy of "battling".

They nodded their heads. They were afraid to fight, afraid and old, yet they knew there was no alternative.

"Nell's right," said Lil. "I'm no Commo but I know she's right. And it's the same for the younguns as us old women and the married women. What they're doin' to us now they'll do to yous all as soon as they're ready. Cut your wages down to the bone." She paused for breath. It was the longest speech Lil had ever made in her life.

"I'm with yous all," said Dawnie. "It's true what Lil says. They'll sack us or put us on short time next week or the week after. I reckon they might've warned us. It's a rotten trick." She glared across at Dick and Greenie, keeping out of the way behind the overheads, glared at young Ken, shilly-shallying first on one foot, then the other, between Dick and the angry women. Where was he to go? Desperately he shuffled in the no-man's land, somewhere in the centre aisle.

Nell looked around. She saw doubt and distrust written on the women's faces. Were they being sold another pup, they'd been sold so many. They searched their minds, their experience. Julie thought of the holy picture above the big double bed. She thought of the Church and what Father would say. She thought of the Housing Commission home with the bare floors and the scanty furniture, she saw the three kids looking at her with their soft, honest eyes, she saw Don coming off night shift, dead beat, to mind the kids while she went off to work.

Jeanie saw herself, a little girl, trying to pinch her feet into the Welfare shoes. All her dreams had tumbled about her ears so fast in one short day, she could hardly get her breath. Anger was building up in her, a blinding, bitter anger, her mother's anger, her father's anger, the anger of her children, of her hard-working husband. We work hard, we do the right thing, and what do we get out of it . . . cheated and sacked and pushed around.

Shirl thought of her life, in and out of Welfare Homes, once in the Girls' Home at Parramatta, her sick mother with a mob of kids and no hope of bringing them up decent. She thought of Jack who would be waiting outside to marry her tonight, the only decent bloke she'd ever latched onto. She thought of the baby growing gently, exploringly inside her.

189

But all Al could remember was Dadda's voice, thin and worn like an old, grooved record . . . "Yeah! It's a free country, we're all free to starve in it. I been a battler all me life Al . . ."

"C'mon girls," said Nell. "We gotta fight. No one can do it for us."

The women surged forward.

"Remember what happened last meetin'. That skinny bloke, that Commo called it. He got the sack and you all lost time." Dick was shouting, his voice out of control, his desperate eyes on the foreman.

Greenie put his hand wearily on Dick's sleeve. "Let 'em go Dick. It won't do 'em no good." But he and Dick were swept out of the way like greasy wool waste littering the floor. The women had made up their minds. They gathered round Nell, talking, discussing, the young ones supplied the energy, the old battlers supplied the ideas, the caution and the tactics.

"C'mon yous men, are you with us or against us?" Nell called.

The men held a hurried conference. "No one's callin' me a bloody scab," said young Curly.

"This is woman's business," whined old Plonko Charlie.

"It's everybody's business," said big Clem, still sweating from his long, hellish hours in the dyeing room.

Dawnie's eyes challenged Ken across the quiet mill. "Comin' Ken?" she said.

The sunbeams played in the pale silk of her hair. She had a smudge of grease on one soft cheek, her little breasts rose and fell with the quick beating of her heart.

Ken's face worked, his legs were like jelly, he almost sobbed aloud in the awful silence.

"Comin' Ken?" said Dick, so close in his ear he jumped guiltily.

"Yeah, sure Dick," he said. He didn't look back, but he heard Dawnie's voice as clearly as if she'd stood on tiptoe and spat in his face.

"You scabby bastard," she said and there were tears in her voice.

"You stick with me luv," Julie said, grabbing the raw, bony-knuckled hand of her eldest son.

Ken stood alone outside the mill. He mooched down the footpath, hands shoved in his pockets, eyes surly. The coconut palms rattled at his back. He licked his lips in a dry wind off the pavements.

"C'mon Ken. How about a noggin' kid?"

He looked up hopefully but it was only Dick, beckoning him

from the street, as he beckoned him day after day in the mill. Automatically his feet turned to obey that cheerful, bullying voice. "Hurry up Ken. Get your finger out," . . . away from the barbed wire fence, the turreted bricks . . . Jumbuck Mills . . . Worsted Spinners and Weavers . . . Enquiries, Office, Dispatch, Receiving . . . NO VACANCIES.

He followed Dick into the dim coolness of the nearest bar, and swallowed the schooner he paid for. The sour taste of the beer smarted his throat.

He was crying soundlessly, tearlessly, with Dick's round, damp face grinning beside him, and Dick's voice saying, "Well, you got a good job for life now son," and Dick's hand patting him genially on the back. And Dawnie's soft blond hair blew against his crying mouth.

The men and women held their meeting in the shadow of the silent machines, while the foreman pussy-footed off to tell the mill manager.

"I move we have a deputation to ol' Spender. He's the only one can tell us where we stand." Jessie was in her element. She used to be active in the Labour Party when she was young. Her face was flushed, her breath laboured in her chest as if she'd struggled up the hill to catch her tram.

"Election by show of hands," Nell said. "I nominate Bet. She's been here longer than any of us."

"No, no . . . not me Nell. I can't talk, I can't say nothin'." Old Betty mumbled and fiddled with her dress, uselessly tying and untying her perfect weaver's knot.

Nell looked around the silent, expectant faces. Who, she thought, who? We want people who won't do their block or be stood over neither. Dignified people.

"I nominate Nell."

"I nominate Lil."

Four on the deputation. Nell, Jeanie, Jessie and Lil. They moved off down the long greasy aisles, their footsteps sounding hollowly on the cement floor, the mill workers parting silently to let them through. Past the offices, with the girl on the switchboard watching owl-eyed. Knees shaking a bit, the clerks whispering and shoving, congregated in the doorways, the enormous silence. Jeanie dug Nell in the ribs. "You do the talkin' Skin. I always said you oughta be on the Domain."

Spender kept them cooling their heels in his outer office just long enough to sap their self-confidence. His secretary kept on typing, one cool nylon shoulder twitching nervously under their gaze.

"Mr. Spender'll see you now," she said, jumping up and spilling her files onto the floor. Nell bent to help her pick them up. She looked at Nell with bright, innocent eyes. "Thank you," she said. Timidly she plucked at the sleeve of Nell's overall. "Good luck," she said. "I wish I had the guts to tell him off."

Nell sailed into the office, head held high, heart thumping like the big spindles. Don't you muck up on me now she thought fiercely.

Spender sat stiffly, pretending to be absorbed in his papers, ignoring the press of bodies by the door, the movement of feet on the carpet. When he looked up his mouth was stiff with dislike, his long fingers tapped impatiently on the desk.

He saw a red-headed woman with an insolent, freckled face, two old hands who ought to have had more sense, and a girl with deep, velvety, angry eyes watching him steadily from the doorway.

"Come in, come in," he said impatiently. "No use wasting my time and yours." And he had the strangest feeling that he was the fly struggling in a sticky web of his own making, pinpointed by four pairs of pitiless eyes.

He was prepared for them, prepared with high sounding words and vague promises of better days to come. "After all you can hardly hold me responsible for the economy of the country, can you girls?"

"I been in this mill a long time Mr. Spender." Old Lil's voice was trembling. She put her knotted hands flat against his desk top to control them. "I c'n remember when you come here . . ."

"Yes, yes, I know Lil. A long time. And don't think the firm doesn't appreciate long service," he said hastily, wiping away fastidiously at the polished mahogany.

"It don't really seem as if it does Mr. Spender." Jessie was watching him out of those shrewd, bright blue eyes.

"Y'see we really need the work Mr. Spender," Jeanie said earnestly.

She leaned towards him, till he could see the beginning of her soft breasts under the greasy overall, and turned his eyes away. "Jessie keeps her husband and I'm savin' for me house . . ."

"It all boils down that pie in the sky isn't what we've come for," Nell said quietly. "We want to know exactly where we stand."

"As far as I'm concerned you stand outside the mill gates,"

he snapped. He always turned nasty under pressure. Old Will Holler had often considered replacing him because of this flaw in his managerial ability.

"The trouble with Spender is, he's a pommy. He doesn't understand the psychology of the Australian worker. But he knows his job backwards. He's honest, conscientious and intelligent. I can't sack a man because he comes from the old country."

But many a time old Will, called away from his billiards, or his stud farm at Windsor by a frantic call from Harvey Spender, "doing his nut" as old Will put it, had occasion to curse this flaw in the character of his otherwise "impeccable servant".

There had been the memorable occasion when he closed the mill gates on Christmas Eve and refused to let the workers go home at three o'clock after they'd been paid. Lovely cold bottles of beer had been smuggled into the Jumbuck all day, everyone was a bit merry and "ready for a blue". Harvey nearly had a riot on his hands. The telephone rang and rang in the big house overlooking the Harbour.

"Open the gates you bloody fool," old Will roared, purple in the face from his long run up from the tennis courts. He was over eighty but he believed in keeping himself fit. So Harvey had to open the gates. But it rankled. His authority had been questioned. He hated Australian workers, and this carroty-headed woman, defying him in the sanctity of his office, was one of the worst examples he'd ever dealt with.

"We'll have a conference with the union Miss Weber . . . or is it Mrs. Mooney," he said nastily, putting his hand on the phone. It was a crack at Nell. All the women worked under their single names. It saved on their husband's taxation. The management knew about it, but it had suited them to close their eyes in the past.

"Sure, ring the union," Nell said. "I've no doubt you know the number well enough Mr. Spender. Get them to send out the organizer, but tell them we've made up our minds. We want reinstatement. Every last one of us. Then we can battle it out from there."

"Are you dictating terms to me, Mrs. Mooney?"

"We are."

"Then I'll treat you as you're treating me, with absolute contempt. I'll deal with you as a mob of troublemakers set on destroying my mill." His long cold face seemed to freeze on the words. "And not only my mill, but the textile industry as a whole."

They knew what he meant. He had only to put his hand on the phone and he could have them tabbed in every mill in Australia. The icy chill of fear gripped them. This was their bread and butter and he knew it. But they didn't waver. The interview was over.

After they'd gone he stood for a long time gazing out the window onto the ragged factory skyline of Alexandria. The sunlight glittered in his eyes as it had glittered on that woman's bold red head. He heard her harsh, unyielding voice, saw again her whip-thin body outlined in sunbeams in the middle of his carpet. She had destroyed the peace and the sanctity of his office, a fanatic, a born rabble rouser.

He picked the crumpled leaflet out of the "in" basket on his desk, and smoothed it with trembling fingers. That red-headed bitch had written this leaflet. Every nerve in his body told him he was correct. He dialled a number and the phone started ringing and ringing in the big house overlooking Sydney Harbour.

The deputation reported back to the silent workers crowding round the machines.

"Whadda we do now?" Jeanie said.

"I've got an idea," said Nell. She was excited but she was keeping her head. She knew she was weighted with terrific authority. On her head rested the responsibility of all these men and women, their right to live and work and be treated as human beings. "We'll stay put, here where we are, where we get our bread and butter. We'll bloody well refuse to be sacked. We'll battle it out right here in the mill."

"That's what they did at Glen Davis," Gwennie said. "My brother was in that. But it's different for the miners. They've got their union. And the wives brought the men food to the pit top."

"What about our kids?" said Julie. "Who's goin' to get the tea, and all that? My husband's gotta leave. He's on night work."

"But I'm gettin' married tonight," wailed Shirl. "Right after work. We got it booked at the registry office."

Nell wiped her hand wearily across her sandy hair. It was a big, capable, freckled hand, worn with mill work and housework. "We'll haveta figure this one out," she said gently. "We've all got problems. I've got three kids of me own and Stan on night shift." She turned to Betty, still sitting motionless on her box by the roving machine. "What d'you reckon Bet?"

She held her breath. If old Betty supported the idea the whole mill would swing in behind it. She held tremendous sway in the

Jumbuck, but for years she'd been a real "trusty" . . . "one of the royals" as Dawnie put it . . . an old and faithful employee of the firm, a most vociferous supporter of all the union's most right wing policies, a thorn in Nell's side ever since she'd tried getting some action around conditions on the job. Old Betty had always resented Nell. The Jumbuck belonged to her and she'd say what the Jumbuck workers wanted, not some blow-in Commo with a lotta jumped-up, red-ragger ideas.

Old Betty looked up. Her shrewd, currant-black eyes were full of tears.

"Fight the bastards," she said. "Fight 'em Nell. Break 'em. They sacked me after eighteen years. I trained 'alf their bloody workers for 'em, I doffed twice as much as I 'ad to, I looked after that machine like me own baby." She began to cry, her big bosom heaving up and down, the tears running down her flabby cheeks, and collecting in the wrinkles of fat around her neck.

"We'll fight 'em Bet," said Nell, her hand on Betty's greasy old shoulder. "We'll fight 'em luv," and Nell's voice shook with sobs too, till she had to fight to control it.

She looked up. The New Australians were standing bewildered beside their overheads, their eyes roaming like nervous, hunted creatures from one determined face to the other.

"My Gawd," said Nell. "I forgot all about the New Australians. Jeanie, Jule, will you help me explain it to the New Australians."

"We'll talk to Maria," Jeanie said in her brisk, matter-of-fact voice. "She's got a bit of gumption."

"There's the afternoon shift too. We gotta get them on side. Otherwise the whole thing's a flop." I wonder have we bitten off more than we can chew, Nell thought. Panic ran around her head for a couple of minutes but she forced it away. Jeanie and Julie were talking to Maria. She seemed to be giving them a pretty good hearing. They're better than I am, Nell thought humbly. I'm real sectarian about them New Australians.

The knock-off whistle wailed and wept and shuddered over the mill, weeping in the heart of old Betty, her hand caressing the oily surface of her rover, her face blotchy with tears; weeping in the heart of old Lil, her last great illusion shattered like a broken spindle, her mind wool gathering, reeling out through the long rows of machines, aching, and breaking and burning with the burden of her thoughts.

A little snub-nosed girl with a thick body and eyes like brown pansies came singing and swinging to herself through the aisles of roving machines.

"Dream, dream, dream,
Dream, dream, dream,
Whenever I want you all I have to do is
Dre-ee-ee-m, dream, dream, dream.
Only trouble is, Gee whiz,
I'm dreamin' me life away."

She stopped, gazing openmouthed at the silent mill. Where was the noise, where was the clatter, where were the hurrying figures, stowing their goods and chattels into their dilly bags, where was all the rush and bustle of the mill, packing up on Friday night for the glory of the brief weekend?

Jeanie came to meet her. "I won't be goin' home tonight Patty," she said. There was an air of importance, an air of exciting maturity about Jeanie that Patty had certainly never noticed before.

"What gives?" Patty said, her brown eyes big as saucers.

"We're on strike," said Jeanie.

"Whaffor?"

"A lot of us got the sack, so we all decided to strike."

"Then whadda you doin' here. Havin' a meetin'?" It was the knowledgeable voice of Tom Maguire's daughter speaking.

"It's a stayput strike," Jeanie said haughtily. "You know, like the miners."

"Jesus!" Patty's lips parted in admiration. "Jesus, I never thought you had it in you. Why, they kept this real dark in the spinning section. We never knew a word about it."

"They would," said Jeanie bitterly. "We're only the poor old unskilled mugs. The bunnies!"

"Lissen," Patty leaned forward, her small face earnest, her lips puckered into a firm, grave line. "D'you reckon they'd let me be in it? On a sorta sympathetic basis, you know? I never been in a strike in me life."

"C'mon," Jeanie said. "We'll ask Nell and the others. I don't see why they'd buck about it do you?"

Together they moved into the circle of quiet faces, watching the afternoon shift coming through the door.

They were a string of weary looking women who came on at four o'clock and worked through till nine, then all day Saturday and still didn't make a week's wage. They left housework and children, some worked two jobs, but not many. *They* were regarded as cranks, or worse, by their workmates.

"Tried to stop us comin' in t'night," said big, rawboned Dais.

"Reckoned there was a dispute or somethin'. That right? I says if there's a blue I wanta know about it."

Nell explained what had happened. "You'll be gettin' the bullet too Dais. You're married."

"Every woman on this shift is," Dais said thoughtfully.

"They'll be cuttin' our shift altogether. That'll be the next move," a thin, worried-looking woman from the spinning section broke in.

The afternoon shift clustered round the day shift women. The second whistle went, but nobody budged.

"Well girls an' boys, whadda you say? Do we stick it out or not?" said Nell. "I think when they see we mean business they might start talkin' sense, but I can't guarantee nothin'."

Shirl thought. "Gee, that's buggered it. Now maybe Jack'll never marry me. If we leave Mum stew long enough she'll withdraw her consent and start stackin' on an act. Anyway what's to say Jack won't change his mind, just like Roy, if I don't grab him quick. Then what'll become a me and the baby? It'll be like Davie all over again."

She thought of the new blue dress on the hanger behind the washroom door, with the wind from the half-open window gently lifting the skirt. She had a mental picture of Jack, broad-shouldered in his best navy suit, shoes shined, hair slicked up, waiting for her to show, waiting for the bride that never came. She felt bloody savage. She couldn't desert her mates but . . . ah! well it was all the lucka the game and she'd never had any luck. She was like Ma with her lottery tickets.

Julie thought of the kids and Don waiting for her as the night came down. Maybe Don could take a sickie tomorrow. He'd ring the mill and they'd tell him she was still inside. He'd think she'd gone mad. Perhaps she had. But if it was him, wouldn't he do the same in her place?

Jean thought: After all I said to Alec about keeping out of trouble and here I am on strike. Mum'll keep the kids tonight. She'll find out what's happened soon enough. She'll back me up anyway and so will Dad. There's some things you just can't cop. Alec would know it too. Taking her house off her and then her job, all in the one day. That was a bit too thick.

Gawd knows how long we'll be here, Gwennie thought. And that means I can't make up me mind about the baby till we get out again, and she was glad and sorry for Dorrie because she'd spent the night with her Yank and missed her pay and missed all the fun. Won't Dorrie be wild, she thought, and giggled.

And Al . . . all Al could think about was her father's face, but she kept mixing it up with the face of the wharfie who'd spoken to her on the stairs. Steve . . . Steve Waters, that was his name. Steve Waters would think all this was right on. She smiled.

Nell thought: I hope I'm telling them right. I hope this way we can win. She thought of the kids home from school and Stan cursing her because of his eight o'clock start. They'd really be in strife now, both out of a job and the venetians to pay off and owing all that on the house. But Stan'd back her all the way when he found out. Oh! Stan am I doin' it right, she thought wearily. I wish you was here to give me all your experience, all the things you're learnt in a lifetime of struggle.

O! little Nellie Weber, are you doing it right this time?

"The only one we'll have trouble with'll be that Maisie," the women on afternoon shift reckoned. "She works two jobs in two mills and she's hungry. Got twin babies, leaves them with her old woman. They don't even know they got a mother. She lives on Bex and is she cranky! Wouldn't like to be her ol' man. Bet she rules the roost. Works through the tea break and all. She's real bonus-happy."

Maisie was the fly in the ointment. She came in, dressed in a filthy old overall, looking as if she hadn't had a wash or a sleep in a month.

"Not me," said Mais. "I won't be in that. I'm not goin' to be branded in every mill in Sydney. I got me livin' to make."

"So have we all Maisie," said Nell quietly. "You're married. You'll get the sack tonight, same as the rest of us."

"Not so sure about that," said Mais. "I'm a good worker. Might make an exception for me. Anyway there's other mills. I'm sweet at Vicars."

"Sure," said Jeanie. "But if they're laying them off here it'll be the same story everywhere else. The Jumbuck's the biggest mill in Sydney."

"I'll worry about that when the time comes." Mais hitched her overall across her skinny bosom. "Right now I'm startin' up me machine or me bonus won't be worth takin' home."

Hundreds of eyes followed her as she walked to the reeling machine. Hundreds of eyes watched her put down her bag, put her hand on the lever. The women moved forward and as they moved Maisie backed down the aisle.

"What's up with yous all?" she cried shrilly. "Can't a woman earn 'er own livin' without . . ."

"Are you with us or against us Mais?" said Jessie. "Because if you're against us you better get . . . an' quick."

"You've all gone mad," Maisie screamed. "You're a buncha no-'opers."

"Start runnin'," said Lil. "Start runnin' back home to them twins of yours."

Nell put out her hand. She felt wiser, older, better than she'd ever felt in her life before. "Sit over there and think about it very careful," she said gently. "You wouldn't wanta be labelled a *scab*!"

Maisie turned away, she shrugged her shoulders. There was a sneer in every line of her tall, skinny body. She reached over with a toss of her head and turned on the machine. No one moved, no one spoke. She sat quite alone, her hands going about their accustomed tasks automatically, the sound of the reeling thunderously loud in the silent mill. For ten minutes or so she went on working. Then she put out one dirty, skinny hand and switched off. Her head dropped on her chest, her shoulders began to shake. The sound of her harsh, dry sobbing echoed through the long, greasy aisles, rising and falling, falling and rising, like a long, floating thread, lost in the silent aisles, where the wool dust collected and the sunlight filtered across the spindles.

"Here comes the union organizer," said Nell, with a grin.

He came, stepping daintily over the wool waste, his briefcase in his hand, a little, fat, round-faced rightwinger full of words and wind.

"Well girls," he said with false cheerfulness. "What cooks? Mr. Spender phoned me. He's very worried. Can't we iron this thing out between us?"

"We can, Mr. Creek, if we get our jobs back," said Nell.

"Well Nell, I don't see how it can be done. Mr. Spender doesn't see how it can be done. There's retrenchments all through the textiles. It's happening everywhere."

"Maybe we'd better take over the factory and run it ourselves if the bosses can't do it Mr. Creek."

"Now Nell, that's silly talk, dangerous talk. Things will look up. You and I are too old in the head not to know that."

"We're all too old in the head to be taken in by a lotta natter," grunted Julie. "Are you goin' to fight this thing out with us or not Mr. Creek. Words are cheap."

"I think you're all acting in a pretty silly way. After all Mr. Spender can't provide jobs for you all. It's not his fault. This is a business firm not a charitable organization."

199

"We want our jobs *back* Mr. Creek. If things are that bad, you'd think old Holler would've had to sell up his nice big mansion in Vaucluse. I haven't seen nothin' about him goin' bankrupt in the papers. We want you to help us, but if you won't, well, we'll go it alone," Nell said.

"As union organizer I can only advise you all to pack up and go home, and I'm afraid the ringleaders in this affair will find it very difficult to get employment in the textiles at all."

"Is that a threat Mr. Creek?"

"Take it how you like Nell," he snapped. The gilt was wearing off the gingerbread.

"These are our instructions to you as organizer Mr. Creek. We want full reinstatement, no victimization and then we'll pack up and go home."

"Take that to the boss you dirty crawler," snapped Lil, losing patience. "You helped him diddle me outa me sick pay. Go an' do a job for the workers for a change."

"I'm not taking that kind of talk from anyone, let alone a bunch of Commos," the little man whinged. He shuffled his small, shiny shoes on the concrete. "Now girls, let's be calm about this thing . . ."

"Get goin' Mr. Creek and don't come back without an answer," said Nell.

"Yeah, do your job."

"Get us our jobs back."

"Let's see some results, you bludger."

The women were crowding closer. It was getting dark in the mill. The workers became part of the huge, gloomy shadows of the machinery. To Creek the whole atmosphere was menacing and foreign to his shiny office, where he took his orders, not from the textile workers, but the bosses of the big textile industry.

"All right girls. Right . . . I'll see Mr. Spender. We'll work out something, you can depend on that . . . something between us." He was backing down the aisle, his face gleaming white and sweaty in the shadows, his small, dapper figure lost behind the big spindles.

"Bastard," said old Betty. "Never even said he was sorry . . . after eighteen years."

She spat into the corner, and wiped her mouth on the back of her rough old hand. "Leaves a real rotten taste in your mouth don't 'e," she said.

Jeanie tugged at Nell's sleeve. "Shirl's bawlin' all over her new blue dress in the washroom," she whispered.

Nell felt ashamed. Jeez, I'm a hard bitch, she thought guiltily. I been so wrapped up in runnin' everythin' I never even give a thought to that poor kid, eatin' her heart out over her weddin' dress. How would I've felt if someone had told me I couldn't marry Stan that day at Kogarah. I woulda torn them in two.

"Let's have a talk to the others," she said.

"Shirl's breakin' her heart in the washroom," she told them. "She was all set to get married tonight. Her boy friend's waitin' in town for her."

"It's not fair," Jeanie said. "After all," she grinned sympathetically, "none of us is gettin' married t'night, are we?"

"No but I got kids ter look after."

"And my ol' man'll be ropable. . . ."

Nell listened with a sinking heart. It was the opening all the waverers had been looking for. And what would happen when the women saw Shirl, with her eyes shining, racing out the gate in her new blue dress. Why half the mill would follow her.

"You don't get married every day of the week," Jessie said. "I reckon we better tell 'er she's free ter go."

The women were restless. Nell felt their indecision, their longing to escape. The novelty had worn off, and now the darkness and the isolation were beginning to get on everyone's nerves.

"Well, what d'you say?" she said nervously. "We can't all go, but what about young Shirl?"

"Let 'er go," said old Bet. "Poor kid. She might never be asted twice . . . like me." She chuckled sardonically.

Nell pushed open the door of the washroom. It was getting dark, only a faint light filtered through the dirty, barred window high up near the ceiling. At first she couldn't see her. "Hey Shirl," she said softly. Nell had always liked Shirl. There was something in that hard, rebellious spirit that reached out to her like a cry for help. And yet she knew that Shirl's courage was like granite, and no whimper or whinge would ever pass that tawdry cupid's bow.

She saw the glow of a cigarette and a shadow hunched, knees up, against the concrete wall, facing the row of lavatories. "Thank Christ you can have a smoke in peace at last Nell," Shirl said, and Nell could feel her grinning at her own pain, setting her teeth there in the darkness, covering her nakedness with a wisecrack.

She slid down beside her, glad of the moment's respite, the quietness, almost the loneliness, sitting beside Shirl, each wrapped in her own thoughts. Shirl never pried into your privacy, and she expected the same courtesy from you.

"Here Skin," she said. "Have a fag. Gawd knows when we'll get any more, and I'm nearly out."

"You better go and meet your boy friend," Nell said abruptly.

Shirl stiffened beside her. "Whadda you mean?"

"What I said. He'll still be waitin' for you won't he?"

"I guess so." She blew angry smoke rings into the corridor. "Since when have you been tellin' me what to do Nell?"

"Ah, come off it," Nell said wearily. "We all reckon you're mad if you don't go. D'you think your bein' here is goin' to make that much difference one way or another?"

Ah, Shirl, she thought, don't fight me, or I'll beg you to stay. I need you, I need your youth and your courage and your hardheadedness. And most of all I need you standing solid, not going out that door with your blue dress on and freedom in your eyes, for all these restless women to follow.

"You're a bloody liar Nell," Shirl said. "What are you spinnin' me this fairytale about meetin' Jack for?"

"It's no fairytale," Nell said savagely. "I'm tellin' you, you're free to go. There's the door. You can get married tonight if you get a move on. What was that you was sayin' to me this mornin': 'As long as I'm married and the kid's okay I don't care what happens.'"

Shirl stood up, carefully brushing down her skirt. She dropped a slim, grimy hand on Nell's shoulder.

"You're a good sort Nell," she said stiffly. "But you're not leadin' yours truly up the garden. You oughta know the ol' Shirl better than that. She don't run out on 'er mates, ever."

She stood, leaning against the door jamb, her eyes gentle, her body outlined in the faint grey light, the high, delicate cheekbones, the firm, cleft jaw and burnished hair.

"C'mon Skin," she said. "Buck up or I won't invite you to the weddin'." Tenderly she touched the skirt of the blue silk dress, hanging like a little ghost of love behind the door. "It'll keep," she said.

Nell looked up at her, her throat tight, her mouth quizzical. "One a these days Shirl," she said. "I'm goin' to recruit you to the Communist Party. After the weddin'."

They went back into the mill together. Nell walked over and switched on the lights.

"How about a cuppa tea girls," she said.

Silently they got out their billies and their chipped teapots.

202

Those on afternoon shift shared out their sandwiches with the day shift workers. Sitting there by the silent machines they swapped yarns, talked quietly together. Over in the corner, by the overheads, Maria still muttered earnestly to the New Australians, explaining, arguing, gesticulating, her broad, brown hands magnified a hundred times in the shadows on the wall.

Patty began to sing:

> "He's got the whole world in his hands.
> He's got the whole world in his hands,
> He's got the whole world in his hands,
> He's got the big wide world in his hands."

Julie nudged her ribs. "Wasn't it Friday you was goin' on Rumpus Room?" she whispered.

Patty grinned. "Yeah," she said. "But Rumpus Room was never like this."

> "He's got the wind-and the rain in his hands,
> He's got the wind and the rain in his hands,
> He's got the wind and the rain in his hands,
> He's got the whole world in his hands."

Jeanie took a long, hot gulp of her cuppa. Maybe they'd win or maybe they'd lose, but whatever happened they'd shown they was people. They'd have learned somethin', how to stick together, how to stand up for themselves. Maybe Dad and Mum was right . . . about a lot of things. She didn't know yet but she was findin' out for herself. And she'd tell Alec when she got home . . . they'd go on that deputation about the land.

> "He's got the itty bitty babies in his hands,
> He's got the itty bitty babies in his hands . . ."

sang Patty Maguire, and then suddenly she had a brainwave:

> "We've got the whole world in our hands,
> We've got the whole world in our hands . . ."

The sweet, true voice rose up over the shadowy mill, over the rooftops and factory chimneys of Alexandria, over Stan Mooney playing his ukulele to his three sons on the back step in Belmont Street, over Tom Maguire carrying his kitbag through the hustling city, over Len lying on the bed waiting for Beth in Moller Street, over Don dishing up tea and swearing at the kids in Beverly Hills, over young Jack, riding down High Street, smarting with rage and disappointment, over Linnie, standing at the front gate looking anxiously down the hill towards Tempe Station. Over the rivers and streets, the neon signs and the hamburger joints, the electric trains and the hurrying footsteps, Patty sang and the mill workers joined in.

"We've got the whole world in our hands."

O! Shirl and Dawnie, Beth and Al, you've got the whole wide world in your hands.

O! Lil and Jessie, Gwennie and Julie, you've got the whole wide world in your hands.

O! Patty and Jeanie, Betty and Maria, even Mais, lying asleep over the reelers, your tears wetting the wool dust, you've got the whole wide world in your hands.

O! little Nellie Weber, with your red head on the sky, shake the brick dust out of your eyes, you've got the whole world in your hands.

"We've got you and me brother in our hands,
We've got you and me sister in our hands,
We've got everybody here in our hands,
We've got the whole ... wide ... world ... in our hands."

Lil spread a bag on a butter box for the pregnant Beth. "Rest your legs luv," she said. "It's likely to be a long wait."

The first Virago Modern Classic was published in London in 1978, launching a list dedicated to the celebration of women writers and to the rediscovery and reprinting of their works. While the series is called "Modern Classics" it is not true that these works of fiction are universally and equally considered "great," although that is often the case. Published with new critical and biographical introductions, books appear in the series for different reasons: sometimes for their importance in literary history; sometimes because they illuminate particular aspects of women's lives, both personal and public. They may be classics of comedy or storytelling; their interest can be historical, feminist, political, or literary. In any case, in their variety and richness they promise to confuse forever the question of what women's fiction is about, while at the same time affirming a true female tradition in literature.

Initially, the Virago Modern Classics concentrated on English novels and short stories published in the early decades of the century. As the series has grown, it has broadened to include works of fiction from different centuries and from different countries, cultures, and literary traditions; there are books written by black women, by Catholic and Jewish women, by women of almost every English-speaking country, and there are several relevant novels by men.

Nearly 200 Virago Modern Classics will have been published in England by the end of 1985. During that same year, Penguin Books began to publish Virago Modern Classics in the United States, with the expectation of having some 40 titles from the series available by the end of 1986. Some of the earlier books in the series were published in the United States by The Dial Press.